# WOLVES' HOLLOW MURDERS

DONALD F. AVERILL

Inquiries and Book Orders should be addressed to:

Great Writers Media
Email: info@greatwritersmedia.com
Phone: (302) 918-5570

ISBN: 978-1-956517-48-4 (sc)
ISBN: 978-1-956517-49-1 (ebk)

Rev 10/07/2021

To my brother, Rich, who
didn't have enough time to find gold,
but made many friends while on the quest.
We miss you.

# CONTENTS

# ACKNOWLEDGMENTS

Thanks to Jill Nicklos, Sandra Reeves, Barbara Schroeder, and Efren Sifuentes for reading and helping to edit my stories. Special thanks to Miles Athey, who mentored my start to writing. Information about the Oregon Trail was obtained primarily from Wikipedia and Rand McNally state roadmaps.

# PART 1

# CHAPTER 1

# THE BEGINNINGS

Levi was tired of war, tired of sitting his horse, and had been in the same worn-out, smelly clothes for over a month. He hadn't bathed or shaved in over a week, but expected to get a haircut from his mother, and his father would let him borrow a straight razor. As he rode the final quarter-mile to his home, he began thinking of what to say to greet his mother, father, and sister. The horrors of killing had been the normal for so long he wasn't sure how to react to his family. He had to avoid telling them of the carnage he had seen.

"Whoa, Bravo." Captain Levi Collins had arrived at his parents' farm outside Pittsburgh, Pennsylvania from Virginia. It had been just two months since the Civil War had ended, but Levi had been gone for almost three years. Levi gave the familiar farm buildings a once-over and dismounted in front of his two-story home. He slapped his hat on his pants, knocking off some of the road dust, tied the reins to a column, and walked across the porch to the farmhouse door he had known since a child. But something was not the same, or was it that he had been gone for so long he had just forgotten things? It was late afternoon—was it the sun's rich yellow light? He didn't notice anything very different, except the flowers in the porch planters were red and yellow. His mother had always put blue and white flowers in the planters. Hat in hand, he knocked, expecting to see his mom or sister, Helen, at the door to greet him.

The door swung open, and a stranger was standing in front of him. "Can I help a you?" he said with a strong accent. Levi was taken by surprise. *Who is this guy?*

"I'm Levi Collins. My parents and my sister live here."

"No more. We bought from Miss Helen. Your sister maybe?"

"When did you buy the property?"

"Almost year ago. Miss Helen move to city. She get married. I give you address." The man said something unintelligible to some-one behind him, turned back to Levi and handed him a piece of paper with an address written on it. Levi looked closely and recognized Helen's writing.

Levi thanked the man, climbed back on Bravo, and rode down the lane toward the city. He had expected things to have changed while he was away, but losing the farm had never been in his thoughts. Levi thought it was a little peculiar that the man hadn't mentioned one word about his parents, only Helen.

The address had been easy to find; he had ridden through that part of Pittsburgh with his father years ago. His father wanted Levi to see what money could buy, and the young man had been impressed with the upscale residential neighborhood. Levi wondered who Helen had married. Whoever the man was, Levi was sure they had never met. He tied his horse to a metal ring on a stone column and made his way to the door. The door opened after the first knock. Helen threw her arms around her brother and said, "Levi! It's so good to see you! I didn't know if you were coming back. We lost track of you about the time Mom and Dad passed away."

"It's good to see you, Helen. You look great! Did you say Mom and Dad are gone?"

"Yes, a year ago last December. They're buried at Quiet Meadows Cemetery. Dad got sick first and then Mom. They didn't make it through the winter. It was so cold that winter; they couldn't keep up the farm. After they were buried, I hired a man to help, but I couldn't run the farm. I don't know how Mom and Dad did it all those years. Frank asked me to marry him, so I had him sell the farm in your name and moved into town. Frank bought this house when I told him I would marry him. You'll like Frank; he's about your age. He's a banker and real smart—like you," she smiled.

"Did you get a good amount for the farm?"

"Not really. It was hard to sell a farm during the war. People were afraid to spend much money, not knowing what the outcome of the war would be. I had Frank put half the money in an account under your name at Frank's bank. It's at Three Rivers Bank on Franklin and First, downtown. Oh, I'm so glad you're alive and back. I saw you dismount—I couldn't get the door open fast enough! You'll stay with us for a while, won't you?"

"I—I guess so—for a while. I'll look for a job and help with costs. I'm not sure what I will be doing, but I've been thinking about going out west, maybe farming. There's some rich farmland out in Oregon. Say, what is your name now?"

"Wisdom. Frank's dad is a big-wig in business—Boston and New York, Frank Wisdom, Senior."

"My God, Helen! He's a powerful man—knows people in Washington. I've seen his name in the newspapers in Virginia and New York."

"Well, my Frank wants to do things his way; he doesn't want his dad butting in."

Levi was pleased Helen was happy with her marriage, and she had become prettier than ever. Her auburn hair was in curls, and she wore a beautiful dress instead of a shirt and work pants. Her life would be simpler now; she would be part of the social world of a big city. She wouldn't be worn to a frazzle by carrying out farm chores.

Thirty-year-old Levi stayed with Helen and her husband from June through the winter of 1865. Levi worked for a blacksmith, as a carpenter building sheds and outbuildings, and as a surveyor, but the jobs were only temporary. The activities of war had fueled Levi's desire to do something more exciting. Levi didn't fear the unknown; he relished confronting and conquering new challenges.

Frank Wisdom was two years younger than Levi but had all the answers. He was egotistical and grated on Levi's sense of calm and thoughtfulness. Frank had never been in the military, but he knew all about it. The two men didn't get along very well, and Levi recognized that his days with the Wisdoms were numbered. Levi spent few evenings at the Wisdom residence, partly to avoid arguments and partly because he was looking for reliable men possessing similar itches to move on to less regimented surroundings. However, playing cards and drinking were not getting him any closer to what he desired. The men he met had grand aspirations but little desire to leave the East. They talked big but were afraid to leave the status quo. Their network of friends facilitated a sense of entitlement and fostered shady business practices. Being scalped by Indians was not a pleasant thought, but boasters couldn't have it both ways. The true western travelers had to take some risks to obtain rewards.

Newspaper stories of the developments in the West had captured Levi's interest, and in January, 1866, he began planning to ride to western Missouri, join a wagon train, and settle in the far west, ending his journey in either Oregon or California. Helen and Levi had a tearful goodbye the first week of February. Levi disliked saying goodbyes and had a lump in his throat, making it difficult to talk. Helen had shed a substantial number of tears. After missing the counsel of her brother for three years, Helen was afraid she might never see Levi again, but was seven-months pregnant, and emotional.

"I'll write you about the baby. We haven't picked any names yet. I'll send the letter to general delivery, St. Louis."

"Okay, Sis. Take care of yourself; get lots of rest and good food. I'll write and let you know where I'm going—if I know. By the way, you did a good thing when you sold the farm."

Levi swung his five-eleven muscular frame into the saddle on Bravo, waved his black Stetson to Helen and Frank, and led his pack animal, a strong second riding mount, down the cobblestone street toward the cloudy western sky. Captain Levi Collins had calculated the trip from Pittsburgh to Independence would take about two months, covering 14 to 15 miles per day in the foul winter weather.

After a boring week of careful riding across the snowy landscape, Levi stopped in Breton, a small town in Ohio. He lived and worked in a livery stable for a week before moving on. Two days of blizzard conditions had forced him to stay longer than he had originally planned. As Levi rode farther west over rough torn-up trails, he encountered a few emigrants, sometimes families in oxen-drawn wagons and others on horseback. The travelers moving west realized the requirements of travel beyond Missouri and wanted to make the journey through Nebraska and Wyoming during warm weather. The known trails followed the streams and rivers to provide water and grass for the animals.

As winter turned to spring, the warmer weather made traveling easier for men, their horses, and draft animals. Grasses seemed to be escaping from the melting snow, and the trails began to dry out making them easier to traverse. By the end of March, Captain Collins had passed through Ohio and Indiana and had stopped, mid-afternoon, in a small town in Illinois called Periwinkle. He had covered slightly over 500 miles since leaving Pittsburgh. He tied his horses to a post outside the town barber shop, which was across the street from the local saloon. Levi watched closely as three men dismounted and entered the watering hole. *I wonder if those men are who I think they are. I'll see after I get cleaned up.*

Levi went in the barber shop and asked the barber, "How much for a shave, haircut, and a bath?"

The bespectacled, balding barber didn't look up from the man he was shaving. "Four bits. Take a load off. It'll be ten minutes before I kin git the bath water heatened up. Sit 'n read the local paper, if ya kin read."

Levi sat down, picked up *The Periwinkle Ledger*, a weekly, and began to read about Indian attacks in the Montana and Wyoming Territories. The attacks had occurred the year before in September.

The story was written as if the raids had happened in the last few weeks. He began to think he should join a wagon train or at least ride with some men he could depend on in tight situations. The men he thought he recognized earlier just might fit the bill. Following the scrub and razor, Levi headed across the street. The three riders' horses were still tied up outside the What Ales Saloon. Levi stepped inside and closed the door quietly, looking for the three men. They were standing at the bar with their backs to Levi. He moved to the side and worked around a couple of tables of card players so he could see the faces of the three horsemen. Sure enough, the three men were the Jeffers brothers from Ohio.

Levi pulled the brim of his hat down and edged next to the closest and smallest of the trio. "You gray-bellies lookin' for a fight?"

Tom Jeffers turned slowly toward the voice and said, "Who the hell are you calling us gray-bellies." James and Ron Jeffers stepped back from the bar, dropped their hands to their side arms, and looked at Levi. Tom recognized Levi first and winked. "We'd better go outside, mister. Don't want no bystanders to get hurt."

Levi took off his Stetson, smiled, and looked at each man. Tom said, "Captain! How the hell are ya? You fooled me for a bit, but I recognized that scar on your cheek hiding under your hat."

"Good to see you boys." Levi shook hands with each of the brothers. "God! You've grown since I last saw you, James. It's been only nine months."

"Yes, sir. Two inch and 'bout 20 pounds."

"Ron, you about the same?"

"Yes, Captain. Don't want to burden my horse any," he grinned.

Each of the brothers was slightly taller than Captain Collins in stair-step fashion. Tom, the eldest, was an inch taller than Levi. Ron was an inch taller than Tom and James was the tallest and youngest of the three brothers.

Tom said, "We're headin' west, Captain. Got an itch to see some action and maybe strike it rich. Thought we'd go to Colorado—maybe on to California. Got any plans?"

"Same as you boys; home is too tame for my likes. You know, there's more safety in numbers—could I join up with you? I was reading in the barber shop about some Indian skirmishes. Indians choose their prey when they have distinct advantages of numbers. We should probably ride with some wagons—a lot more firepower."

Ron spoke up, "That's about what we were thinkin', Captain. Should find a group ready to head across Nebraska 'bout the time we git to Independence. We thought about goin' by rail, but it's too costly for the three of us and nine horses—besides, the railroad don't go all the way."

Tom added, "We'd be proud to have you join us, Captain. We're heading out in the mornin'—'bout six o'clock. You have two pack horses? That's what they say we need."

"I'll pick up another horse or a mule on the trail—haven't needed another pack animal yet. See you boys in the mornin'. I need to get some eats and sleep." Levi took his horses to the livery and went to a rooming house next door, had a steak dinner and went to bed. He got up at 5:00 a.m. After some bacon, flapjacks, and coffee, Levi went to the livery. The Jeffers were saddling their mounts and settling up with the liveryman when Levi arrived. Five minutes later the four men were riding toward St. Louis.

# CHAPTER 2

# TUCKER

Four days later, Collins and the Jeffers boys rode into St. Louis. While the Jeffers relaxed at the Flour Barrel Saloon, Levi found the post office.

He had to stand in line about five minutes in front of the general delivery cage to see if Helen had written. The clerk searched through a small stack of letters and handed Levi an envelope. Levi tore the envelope open and read that Helen had a son named Frank Levi Wisdom. The baby was healthy, as was Helen. She made no mention of her husband. She hoped Levi was not sick or injured and wanted to hear from him directly before he was on the trail and no postal service was available. Helen had written a post script that a friend of hers, Harriet Blodget, had remarked that her uncle had found gold about a hundred miles northeast of Fort Boise. Only a few people knew of the discovery, so Levi was to keep it under wraps.

Levi sat down at a writing table and wrote to Helen, telling her of his trip, meeting the Jeffers, and thanking her for the news about a place near Fort Boise. Levi said he would write again when the opportunity presented itself. He addressed the envelope, attached a three-cent stamp, and dropped his letter in the outgoing mail slot. Levi folded Helen's letter and stuck it in his pocket.

The next day, the four men began the trip to Independence. Levi had estimated it would take them about two weeks to cross Missouri. They camped along streams and rivers, occasionally with other travelers moving west. Many people they met had wagons pulled by oxen and, at most, traversed 15 to 20 miles per day. Eight days into the trip, the men stopped at a small town, Elbow Bend, to replenish their supplies. As they passed a corral, Levi noticed a gelding with similar markings as Bravo, but at least a hand taller. The Jeffers went on to a general store while Levi examined the horse that had caught his eye. Levi bought the horse, a blanket, and a used saddle.

After the men had restocked their supplies, they rode slowly to the western edge of the settlement, forded the Bends River and set a pace to make up for the time lost in town. Toward evening, they stopped near a stream where there were trees for shelter and good grass for the animals. Levi set out on foot to gather some wood for a fire when he heard some whimpering from behind some shrubs and small trees. He drew his gun, crouched, and slowly worked his way around the thicket and peered over the foliage where it was thinnest. At first, he thought it was a wolf, perhaps caught in a trap, but as he stepped over some of the shrubs to get a closer look, Levi saw that it was a dog, covered with mud and dirt. Apparently, the animal had been struck and thought to be dead, and was accidently buried alive. The dog had crawled from its shallow grave. Whoever buried the animal probably couldn't dig very deeply in the semi-frozen earth. There was no telling how long the dog had been in the undergrowth. Levi estimated a couple of weeks, maybe longer; the dog's ribs showed through his matted fur. The animal was extremely weak, but Levi recognized bravery and gumption when he saw it.

"Stay here, boy. I'll be back."

Levi holstered his gun, picked up the pile of firewood he had collected, and returned to the camp site. He started a campfire, grabbed the blanket from behind his saddle, his canteen, a tin cup, and told the Jeffers he would be back shortly. They should go ahead with supper without him. Levi kicked a path through the shrubs and underbrush to the dog. The dog mustered the strength to lift his head and look at Levi as he knelt next to the animal. After filling his cup with water, he offered the dog a drink, but the animal was having difficulty lapping the water. Levi picked the animal up after wrapping it with his blanket. The dog was able to drink about half the water. Levi filled the cup to the brim a second time and the dog continued lapping up the liquid. Levi realized, under all the matted fur and dried mud, the animal was an Irish setter, a good bird dog.

Levi washed the dog's head and paws with the last of the water in his canteen. When the water was exhausted, Levi picked the animal up in his blanket and carried it back to camp, about 50 yards away.

Tom said, "Whatcha got there, Captain? Somethin' to eat?"

"Hardly...it's a dog, a bird dog. Somebody left it, thinking it was dead."

Tom went over and looked at the dog. "Pretty bad shape. Maybe you should shoot it—put it out of its misery. It might be the best thing to do."

"I'll shoot whoever shoots this dog." Levi looked at each of the Jeffers and they understood Levi wasn't fooling. "You boys tired of buffalo? Well, it won't be long and we'll have some quail and prairie chicken, soon as the dog has healed." Levi prepared a place to sleep and laid the dog on the ground next to his saddle. As the men ate, Levi cut some buffalo meat into small pieces for the dog. The dog hardly chewed the meat, just swallowed the pieces, drank some more water, and went to sleep.

Ron said, "Captain, what ya gunna call the dog?"

Levi thought for a minute, smiled, and answered, "Tucker. I figure the dog's all tuckered out." The Jeffers laughed.

As the sun dropped behind the hills, Levi gathered more wood and built up the fire so he could see more clearly. He took a coil of rope and began making a carrier that he could hang on one side of his pack horse. He planned to put Tucker in the blanket and let his horse carry the dog and some of his supplies. The rest of his supplies would go on the gelding.

When the men woke up, they noticed Tucker had crawled next to Levi during the night. As they ate, Tucker got up on all fours for a minute, but was pretty shaky, so he lay back down on the blanket. Levi gave Tucker part of a biscuit, some water, and a piece of buffalo meat. The men were eating bacon and James gave Tucker a small piece, but the men didn't want to overdo the feeding and cause the dog to vomit. The Jeffers cleaned up the campsite and got ready to move out while Levi adjusted the load on his pack horse so Tucker could be carried on one side in the sling-like carrier he had fashioned from the rope and blanket. Before the dog was placed on the back of the horse, Levi took Tucker, wrapped in a blanket, and had the pack horse get accustomed to the dog's smell. The pack horse accepted the dog riding on its back without incident.

After four hours on the trail, the men stopped to make coffee and munch on some biscuits Tom had made the night before. Levi untied the carrier and lowered Tucker to the ground. The dog surprised the men, especially Levi, by walking around the fire sniffing each of the men. The food and rest had energized Tucker, but the dog was still a bit shaky. The men watched the dog go to the stream and drink, then return to Levi. Levi gave Tucker some dried buffalo, a piece of biscuit and watched as Tucker relieved himself on a small tree.

Ron commented, "Looks like the plumbing works, Captain."

Levi answered, "Yep. Say, you men can call me Levi. I'm not the leader of this group; we should all have equal say. Besides, somebody might get the wrong idea and think we are deserters or something. So, no more Captain. All right?"

The Jeffers nodded. James smiled and said, "But if we git 'n a fight, you're Captain Collins."

Levi laughed. "Well, in that case, all right. Shall we get out of here?"

Two days later, the four men, twelve horses, and a dog, arrived in Independence, Missouri, a bustling town catering to people getting ready to cross the Missouri River into Kansas and start west across Nebraska. Most all the business was centered on outfitting wagon trains for the trip through the plains. The four men split up and walked around the business district. Tom was to get some maps, and Levi checked the corral area on the western edge of town, while James and Ron got cleaned up and found a boarding house to stay overnight. They all wanted to relax and get a good night's sleep.

Levi discovered a wagon train was leaving the next day and would be ferried across the river from three locations. He talked with the wagon master and made arrangements to join the wagons on the other side of the Missouri in a couple of days.

The four men got back together at the Buffalo Hide Saloon for dinner. Following a big dinner and several drinks, they went to their rooms to get some sleep. Levi carried Tucker into the boarding house in a blanket to conceal how dirty the dog was. Levi had wanted to wash the dog in a stream along the way, but thought the water was too cold for the weakened dog. When Maude, the lady that ran the boarding house, saw the dog, she stopped Levi just as he was about to go upstairs to his room.

"Hey mister, what have you got there?"

"My dog, ma'am. He got hurt on the trail—needs a warm bath if I can get some water and soap."

"I don't want that dirty animal in one of my rooms unless you pay double. I'll have extra cleanup tomorrow."

"Have a bathtub here? I'll pay extra. If you don't have a bath, I'll get a refund for the room and find a livery to stay at. The dog has to stay with me."

"The bath ain't for animals, but if you clean up, I'll charge you four bits. I'll get you some water from the fire in the kitchen. The tub's down the hall—last door on the right. It ain't locked."

"Thank you ma'am. You'll never know the dog was there. I promise."

Levi carried Tucker into the bathing room and noticed a valve to open to run water into the large wooden tub. He let some water trickle out of the pipe on his hand to see how cold it was. Levi was assuming the water was from rain collected on the roof. He would have to wait for Maude to bring some hot water to warm up the rainwater. There was a tap on the door and Maude entered carrying two wooden buckets of steaming water. Levi took one of the buckets and poured it into the tub. Maude opened the valve on the water pipe and added several gallons of rain water with what Levi had put in the tub. Maude tested the temperature of the water and poured half of the other bucket of hot water in the tub.

"That otta do it mister. How'd the dog get so filthy?"

"He was buried alive."

"My oh my! Who would do such a thing? They should be shot."

"That's my thinking, too. Well, thank you for the water. Here's four bits." Levi held out his hand with a 50-cent-piece for Maude.

Maude waved her hand at Levi and said, "It's on the house. The bath is a present for that poor critter. What's his name?"

"Tucker, ma'am. That's very kind of you."

"Yer welcome. I want to see what the dog looks like when he's all cleaned up. I like surprises." Maude smiled and shuffled down the hall to the lobby talking to herself.

Levi put Tucker in the water and expected the dog to try to get out of the tub, but Tucker sat down in the water and looked at Levi.

"So you like the water. Okay, I'm going to get you all wet now, and then I'll add some soap and scrub you good. I bet you won't like the soap."

Levi used the empty bucket and poured bath water over Tucker, tossed a bar of soap in the water and started scrubbing the filth from the dog. Tucker seemed to enjoy the bath, liking all the attention and the warm water. Levi could see the reddish-brown coat of the Irish setter as the mud was washed away. Levi drained the dirty water from the tub and rinsed Tucker in some lukewarm water. As the rinse water drained away, Tucker started to shake his body, but Levi covered the dog with the blanket just in time to keep from getting sprayed. After drying Tucker with the blanket, Levi used a scrub brush to comb Tucker's coat, amazed at the transformation that had taken place. After taking Tucker to his room, Levi returned to the bath and tidied up. He had followed through with his promise to Maude.

# CHAPTER 3

# A PLACE TO BED DOWN

Twenty-eight wagons had assembled to begin the trek across Nebraska. There were about ninety people, including a few children, but mostly adults looking for a new start in Oregon or California. Few of the travelers exhibited any lust for gold, but most of the men probably had the thought secreted behind farming as their chief reason for emigrating west. Less than 20 of the pioneers were women, and nearly all were married. The leader of the wagon train was Major Joseph Langley, a swarthy man of about 50 years. He sported a thick gray-black mustache, was over six feet tall, and about thirty pounds overweight. He possessed a booming raspy voice. When he spoke, everyone listened.

The major rode up to three of the wagons, said something to the drivers, and started riding slowly to the west. The three wagons fell in behind Langley, single file, and the journey began. The remaining wagons and riders on horseback followed the leaders. Levi and the Jeffers sat watching the spectacle unfold, the covered wagons stretched out in single file for a quarter of a mile.

"What're you thinkin', Levi?" asked Tom.

"Better give me a few days. This is just the beginning. Let's watch and learn. Be observant for what we think are mistakes, but we're new at this, so talk it over before we go to the old man. There might be a reason for what they're doing. I'm going to ride along with some of the wagons and get to know the people—see who we can depend on in a pinch."

"Good idea. We'll do the same."

The four men split up and rode to different parts of the string of wagons. Each man settled in beside a wagon and rode along in silence. Tom was focused on a woman driving one of the wagons. She was a nice looking blond and glanced over at Tom and smiled. Tom returned the smile, but when the man beside her looked suspiciously at Tom, Tom's smile quickly faded. In all probability, the man and woman were husband and wife.

Tom tipped his hat and said, "Tom Jeffers."

The man replied, "Nathan and Annabel Cabot. We're headed to Oregon, got some fruit trees to plant—cherries and peaches. We think they'll grow nicely along the Columbia, near the mountains."

"Don't know much 'bout growin', just diggin' wells and mines," Tom replied. "Hope you and your wife are successful." Tom kneed his horse and moved ahead to the next wagon.

Levi had started meeting people in the same manner as Tom, but now Levi was riding at a greater distance from the wagons and the noise level would have made conversation impossible. Levi was observing the wagon train as if he were an architect investigating a large building for strengths and weaknesses, intending to remodel it. He was portraying the enemy, sizing up the opposing army, deciding where to attack. He made mental notes for nearly an hour, riding slowly from the front of the procession to the rear, and then slowly rode toward the lead wagon where Tom was riding with James.

Tom and James were discussing the women they had met as they investigated the qualities of the pioneers in the wagons.

"Any good lookers?" asked James.

Tom answered immediately, "The Cabot woman, 'bout halfway back—first name's Annabel—married to Nathan. Some men are just lucky, I reckon. You see any?"

"Just one, and get this, she's not hitched. I wouldn't mind chasing her 'round a wagon a few times—name's Priscilla Bolton. She's with her brother and an uncle. I forget their names—was concentratin' on the woman. They're nearly at the end of the line—kind of dusty back there. They might have to move up closer to the lead wagons. I was thinkin' maybe the wagons ought to be movin' side by side—those followin' would eat less dust. Maybe the Major has already thought of that."

Levi commented, "Sounds like you two are looking to get married."

Tom replied, "Not directly. Got to have somethin' of value to provide for a woman and family."

"Yah, like gold," James grinned.

Tom stated, "Well, maybe some land—a good farm or ranch for wheat and livestock."

Levi had been thinking about the letter Helen had sent. There was that provocative comment about gold not far from Fort Boise. *Maybe the Jeffers would be trustworthy. I think I'll share Helen's letter with them.* "Where's Ron?"

"Don't know, bet he's talkin' to a woman somewhere," Tom replied.

Levi said, "I need to share something with you men. I've been saving it—thinking about it some."

James put two fingers in his mouth and made the loudest whistle Levi had ever heard. Bravo reared back, reacting to the unexpected loud noise.

"Whoa! Easy Bravo. Jesus, James, where the hell did that come from?"

"Just callin' Ron, Levi. He'll show up directly. When bullets are flyin' and everybody's yellin', a loud whistle is the only way to get somebody's attention," James smiled.

As the three men continued riding, Levi checked his pocket to be sure he still had Helen's letter. It was there waiting to be displayed and read to the Jeffers. In a few minutes, Ron rode up and slowed to the pace of the other men. His pack animals weren't with him.

"You need me for somethin'?" Ron asked. "I thought I heared James whistle."

"You did—about broke our ears," acknowledged Levi. "I've got something to tell you. My sister sent me a letter, picked it up in St. Louis. Been waiting to tell you about it, but first you got to know it's a secret. Can't tell anybody or we might lose out. Where're your other horses?"

"I left 'em tied to a wagon, the Wellsandt's—they're farmers. They've got two youngsters—boy and a girl. Kids're excited 'bout travelin', everythin's new to 'em."

The Jeffers and Levi rode about thirty yards away from the wagons and stopped. As Levi unfolded Helen's letter, Tom pulled his horse up next to Levi. Levi read what Helen had written about the gold discovery northeast of Fort Boise.

"Dang, Levi. How long were ya gunna keep that a secret?"

"I had almost forgotten about it until you men were talking about gold—having something to offer a woman. But we've got to keep it quiet. We don't want a bunch of Yahoos following us around. We can only tell a couple more people we can trust—like a cook or a blacksmith—someone that has something to offer for a share of what we find. So, promise to keep your yap shut."

Each of the Jeffers nodded affirmatively.

As the shadows began to make it difficult to see gopher holes and ruts in the trail, Major Langley halted the wagons' forward progress and formed two concentric circles with the wagons. When the animals were unhitched and allowed to graze and drink, tended by the young people and some of the men, Langley gathered the rest of the adults for a meeting.

"We had an easy day today, no storms, no breakdowns, and no Injuns. I have a question to ask. How many scouts do we have?"

There was no immediate answer, but several travelers looked at each other to see if anyone would answer. Tom and Levi spoke up in unison, "Five."

"That's correct. Who are you men?"

Levi stepped forward with Tucker by his side and said, "Levi Collins."

Tom answered, "Tom Jeffers."

The Major quizzed, "Any military experience?"

Tom took the lead and said, "Yes Sir, three years in the Union Army with my brothers, Ron and James, and our friend, Levi, here. We're ridin' together."

Langley said, "Any other military men?"

"Yes Sir. We're Bill and Wade Dendricks." Two men, one slightly taller and thinner than the other, and slightly above average height, stood and faced Major Langley. The shorter man, Bill, said, "We were on the losin' side." A murmur went through the crowd. The Dendricks turned toward Levi and the Jeffers, looked them in the eyes, and extended their hands.

Levi stepped forward and extended his hand. "Glad to have you men with us. If we have a fight with Indians, we know who we can count on."

The Jeffers followed Levi's example and shook hands with the former Confederates.

The major asked another question, "What arms do you gentlemen have? I mean, in addition to your side arms."

James answered, "56-50 Spencer carbines, Major, and some shotguns."

The Dendricks gave the same answer, to which the major said, "I noticed most of the guns in the wagons are muzzle-loading muskets. You must stay undercover when you reload, unless you want an arrow. Arrow wounds cause infection and commonly, death. I'd like you men with Spencers to spread around so we have firepower on all sides. Everyone make sure your water buckets and barrels are full when we hit the trail in the morning. Are there any questions?"

One of the women called out, "Has anyone seen any Indians?"

Major Langley replied, "Not yet. We probably don't need to worry until we are past Fort Kearny, but keep your eyes open. Be alert. We should reach Fort Kearny in about 20 days. You will be able to buy goods there to replace things you are out of. Well, better get some sleep, we'll be off again at dawn. If the weather holds, we'll make another 20 miles. Good night."

The meeting over, travelers drifted back to their wagons and began to gather the livestock, bringing the animals inside the circle of wagons. In half an hour the sun would go down. Dark clouds could be seen on the western horizon. Flashes of light from above the black cloud layer betrayed the lightning. Levi estimated the stormy weather was 50 miles away. The wagon train had nothing to worry about; there was very little wind and a nearly full moon was in the eastern sky.

As Levi was walking back to his horses, a young woman approached him and said, "Mr. Collins?" Levi stopped and looked at the pretty woman, who he suspected to be Annabel Cabot or Priscilla Bolton, from what he had overheard the Jeffers talking about.

"Yes ma'am. Can I help you?"

"I'm Annabel Cabot. I'd like to invite you and your friends to rest under our wagon tonight. I would feel much safer knowing you men and your guns were close by—unless you have other plans, of course."

Levi stared at the golden-haired woman in front of him with the moon over her right shoulder. He didn't quite know what to say, Annabel spoke confidently and was much prettier than his sister. Levi hadn't had many opportunities to associate with beautiful women. It was time he said something; his silence might be misinterpreted. He didn't want to act like a dunce.

"Afraid your husband can't take care of you?" questioned Levi.

"Husband? Oh, you mean my brother, Nathan. Truthfully, you are correct. Nathan's not much of a fighter, but I suppose he could learn. Maybe you could give him some instruction. He and I are both teachers, but we want to start some apple orchards. We have seedlings in our wagon. Our uncle will be at Fort Boise, waiting for us."

"Fort Boise? That's sure a coincidence. The Jeffers and I are going to Fort Boise. I'll take you up on your offer, Miss Cabot. Which wagon is yours?"

Annabel turned around, scanned past several wagons, and pointed. "It's over there, the one with the blue sideboard."

"All right. I'll get my gear and tell the Jeffers about your offer. I'll see you in a few minutes. Thank you. Tucker, go with the lady." Levi motioned for Tucker to follow Annabel.

# CHAPTER 4

# BIRDS, DUST, AND A STORM

Levi fetched his horses and informed the Jeffers about Annabel Cabot's offer to have them sleep under the wagon. Tom decided to join Levi, but Ron and James were going to join the Dendricks for a night under the stars. The younger Jeffers wanted to get to know the Dendricks, to determine what kind of men the former Southern soldiers were. Levi didn't tell Tom that Annabel and Nathan were brother and sister; he figured Tom would have to find that out for himself. It might provide some laughs.

Levi was having difficulty detecting the blue sideboard in the failing light, but he saw Tucker sitting beside the back of a wagon, no doubt the Cabots'. Levi removed the packs from his horses, piling his things against the front left wheel of the wagon. Tom dropped his gear beside Levi's. Annabel and Nathan joined the two men, and they talked for about fifteen minutes before Annabel excused herself and climbed in the wagon. Tom crawled under the wagon and prepared a spot to sleep while Nathan and Levi said a few more words.

"Nathan, how would you like to hunt some birds in the morning?"

"Uh—all right, but all I have is a musket. That won't work, will it?"

"Not unless you are one hell of a shot. I've got a shotgun and Tucker will help us. I'll rouse you at dawn. We'll ride out a ways so not to disturb anyone. Maybe we can get a couple of prairie chickens. I'm getting tired of buffalo for every meal."

"All right. See you in the morning."

By the time Levi laid out his bed, Tom was fast asleep, breathing heavily, but not snoring. Levi rested his head against his saddle and looked up at the bottom of the wagon. His eyes closed and he was dead to the world. Tucker circled beside Levi, dropped to the ground, and curled up next to his savior.

Morning came too soon. Levi heard the song of some mourning doves and opened his eyes. The sun wasn't up yet, but the sky in the east was beginning to lighten. He looked at Tucker, who was watching his master. Tucker seemed to know he was going hunting today. It was still chilly; in fact, it was cold. Levi could see his breath as he slipped into his heavy shirt and jacket. Sleeping beside his dog had its rewards; he hadn't felt the cold during the night, but perhaps it was a result of being extremely tired.

Levi parted the wagon cover and looked in to see Nathan sitting up and yawning. He whispered, "I'll be right with you, Levi. I've got to pull on my pants and get my coat." Annabel was still asleep, her head covered by a thick quilt, but a few blonde curls stuck out.

While waiting for Nathan, Levi opened one of his packs and pulled out a double-barreled sawed-off shotgun. He took a half-dozen powder loads and some paper-wrapped shot from a small bag and stuck them in his pocket with his shortened ramrod. The men saddled horses and rode away from the wagon train about a quarter-mile to some grassy areas away from the well-traveled trail. Levi wasn't sure of Tucker's stamina, so he rode with the dog in his lap. Fortunately, they weren't going far, because Tucker, eating like a growing puppy, had gotten heavier in the last week. Tucker's ribs were becoming hard to see and his reddish coat was silky smooth. Levi was getting uncomfortable when they reached a hunting area. Nathan and Levi tied their horses to a dead tree sticking up out of the dry semi-barren soil and walked to one of the grassy spots.

Tucker's instincts took over, and he began searching through the grass. Levi loaded both barrels of his gun, hoping to return to camp with some plump game birds. Tucker suddenly stopped, frozen in place. Levi walked quietly to Tucker and let out a yell. Two birds flew up from the grass and Levi used both barrels to bring the birds down. Tucker ran to the closest bird, a prairie chicken, and stood beside it. Nathan picked up the dead bird and Tucker ran to the second one. Levi collected the second prairie chicken and said, "Good boy, Tucker," and gave the dog a pat on his back and scratched his neck. They rode back to camp with fresh meat. Tucker was steady on his feet, and made the return trip on his own.

When the prairie chicken hunters got back to the wagon, Annabel and Tom were preparing breakfast. Tom had made some of his famous biscuits—at least that's what he called them, and Annabel had made coffee and cooked some bacon.

Nathan handed the two birds to Annabel and said, "Look what I shot, Sis." Nathan looked at Levi and grinned. Tom heard what Nathan said and questioned, "She's your sister?"

Levi started laughing, amused at Nathan's sense of humor about having shot the birds, and Tom's realization that Annabel and Nathan weren't husband and wife, but brother and sister.

Annabel frowned, and then smiled, when she realized what had just occurred. She looked at Nathan and commented, "Which end of the gun did you point at the birds, or did you throw it at them?"

"Oh, all right. Levi shot the birds but he had help. Tucker located them for us. All Levi had to do was pull the triggers."

Levi replied, "Next time, Nathan, you do the shooting. I'll watch and poke fun afterwards."

Tom walked over to Levi and jabbed him with his elbow. "Why didn't you tell me they weren't married?"

Levi smiled and said, "You were asleep. I didn't want to wake you for such a trivial thing."

Tom got a little excited. "Trivial? That's not trivial!"

Annabel pretended to ignore the conversation between Levi and Tom, but she was entertained with their banter. It was only the second day of the three-month journey to Fort Boise, and two young, fairly handsome men were interested in her. *This could be a very interesting trip.*

The next five days were dusty and exhausting, even though the wagon train's advance across the plains was still in its infancy. The humidity added to the dirt made everyone uncomfortable. The major knew most complaints would gradually diminish as the days passed into weeks and the weeks into months. After several complaints about dust being kicked up by the leading wagons, Major Langley had the wagons travel abreast when possible, so there were no following wagons to be eating the leader's dust. When the terrain did not allow traveling abreast, different wagons were chosen as leaders so the same people were not always eating dust. The order of the wagons was chosen with a deck of cards. The emigrants accepted the alternatives with little grumbling since everyone was being treated equally.

Neither Tom nor Levi could resist riding in the vicinity of the Cabots' wagon, but they didn't want to be pests, so they limited their social visits with Annabel to a few minutes both mornings and afternoons. Sometimes they used a visit with Nathan as an excuse to see Annabel. She enjoyed the attention from the two men since their visits interrupted the monotony of the daily travel. She was amused by the dirty faces of the two men, each day's dusty riding resulting in mud spots around their nostrils, eyes, and mouths.

It was during the late afternoon of the twelfth day when Levi noticed a darkening in the southwestern sky. The normal afternoon breeze had died and the animals were becoming skittish, the horses more so than the oxen. Tucker began traveling under the

Cabots' wagon, occasionally leaving to run beside Levi's horse, and then returning to the wagon.

Tom rode up to Levi and asked, "What's goin' on, Levi? The animals are actin' a mite peculiar."

Levi pointed ahead to a rider approaching rapidly. "Here comes the major. We'll know in a minute—might be those yellow-brown clouds to the southwest. They look bigger than a few minutes ago."

"Yeah—noticed that too—kind of strange lookin', specially the color."

Major Langley rode in fast and pulled up in front of Tom and Levi. He yelled, "Get the wagons in two concentric circles and rope them together. Leave the oxen hitched. Get the livestock in the center and tie them down to stakes. It's goin' to be a big blow—dirt, rain, hail—you name it. Get the word out now! We don't have long."

James and Ron rode up and listened as Tom relayed the information. The lead wagons had started pairing up and circling with the major leading the formation. As the circles formed, the drivers and passengers got to the ground and started roping the wagons together and gathering their livestock.

Levi, the Jeffers, and the Dendricks helped with anything they could to hasten the readiness for the storm. Levi recognized that dust was going to be a problem, so he warned everyone to cover their faces with wet cloths and keep their eyes shut as much as possible. Most of all stay in, or preferably under, their wagons.

It wasn't more than ten minutes after all had received instructions that the wind gusts hit, and the sky darkened to yellow-brown. Almost simultaneously with the dust came lightning, sounding to the military men like hundreds of firearms going off in all directions. Tom, Levi, the Cabots, and Tucker huddled together under the Cabots' wagon.

"How long will this last?" Annabel inquired seriously. "The noise is frightening." Tucker and Annabel were huddled together with Nathan. Tom and Levi were leaning against the wheels chewing on pieces of straw.

Tom answered, "Don't rightly know—maybe when the Lord runs out of ammunition, but I'm guessing the wind will let up before long."

"How can you be so calm?" Annabel asked as she first looked at Levi and then Tom.

Levi replied, "It just appears that way. I'm concerned, but there's nothing I can do about it, so I try to relax and enjoy the sounds of nature. It will pass; we will dust off, and continue on our journey. Everything that's important to me is right here, and we'll have something to talk about in the future." Levi felt like he had said too much, but Annabel's expression of concern relaxed to a gentle smile. He had apparently said the right words. Tucker came over to Levi and laid his head on Levi's outstretched legs. Levi gave Tucker a scratch behind his ears and said, "Good dog, Tucker."

# CHAPTER 5

# FORT KEARNY

The wind blew for most of three hours, letting up when the sun was nearing the skyline. As the sun touched the horizon, the brilliant red-orange disk changed the bonnets of the covered wagons from white to salmon. The moon was yellow-orange against the darkening eastern sky. As the emigrants emerged from under their wagons, Major Langley was making his rounds checking to see if everyone was all right, and to find out if there had been any damage.

The major asked, leaning down from his horse, "Everyone all right here?"

Nathan answered, "Yes Sir. We're just dirty."

"Good. The dirt will wash off easy enough. We'll stay here tonight and get a good start in the morning. You might clean the sand from the grease on your wheels, and remember to clean the nostrils of the oxen." With that, he rode to the next wagon.

Annabel had moistened some clean rags and handed them to Tom, Levi, and Nathan. Tom and Nathan wiped their faces and returned the rags to Annabel. Tom said, "Thank you, ma'am," and smiled. Nathan took back his rag, went to the Cabots' oxen, and wiped their nostrils free of the accumulated dust.

Annabel moved to Levi, and before he had a chance to hand her the cloth and thank her, she said, "You missed a spot." She put one hand on his chest, took the cloth from him and wiped his forehead. She touched the scar on his cheek carefully and asked, "How did this happen, was it a bullet?"

Annabel's touch was gentle but thrilling, almost making his heart skip a beat. Levi looked into her light-blue eyes and said, "No ma'am. I was struck by a tree limb when chasing a Reb. I fell off my horse and the Reb got away. I never got shot in all the fights I was in. Tom did though, twice I think. Isn't that right, Tom?"

"That's the truth, once in the arm, and once in the leg. The doctor said they were superficial—didn't have to dig the bullets out. I didn't miss a fight. I can show you the scars."

Annabel had stepped back from Levi and looked at Tom's face. "You look respectable."

"Right handsome, huh?" Tom commented and smiled.

"Well, you got all the dirt off your face by yourself," she grinned at Tom and Levi.

Levi returned the cloth to Annabel and said, "Thank you, ma'am."

"Please call me Anna. Annabel, Miss Cabot, and ma'am are a bit formal for good friends, and we'll be traveling almost like family for another two months. I'll miss you both when we separate at Fort Boise, but I hope we can keep in touch with letters," Anna smiled.

Tom said, "I ain't much for writin' letters, but Levi can tell you about me."

"That reminds me, I've got to send a letter to Helen when we get to Fort Kearny. I think the mail goes to St. Louis from there."

Anna's smile faded and she said, "Is Helen waiting for you?"

"Helen's my sister in Pittsburgh. She had a baby boy about two months back. She wants me to write whenever I have a chance. Her name is Wisdom now."

A smile returned to Anna's face and then her expression changed to surprise. "Oh my gosh! *The Wisdoms?* I've heard of that family, they're important people."

"Well, her husband Frank is a horse's ass. He's too big for his britches."

Anna started laughing and Levi, surprised at his language, said, "Excuse me," then chuckled.

Three days later, one of the forward scouts contacted the leading wagons and told them Fort Kearny was only a day away. The news spread rapidly through the wagons. Everyone was anticipating the sight of some buildings after nearly three weeks of boredom moving slowly across the monotonous landscape of dirt, rocks, and clumps of grass occasionally decorated with a few wildflowers. The safety of the fort would offer a chance to see new faces, get caught up on news from the east, and restore dwindling supplies to the level they had when beginning the trek across the plains after crossing the Missouri.

Upon arrival at Fort Kearny, the wagons were parked in predetermined locations devised by Major Langley. He advised the pioneers to have at least one person stay with each wagon at all times to prevent stealing by Indians or whites trying to take advantage of the situation.

Nathan decided to stay with the wagon while Anna went into the fort to get supplies.

"Would you accompany me to the fort, Levi?" Anna asked.

Levi answered, "It would be my pleasure," and tipped his hat. Levi didn't need much, but he wanted to send a letter to Helen. Anna also wanted to send a letter to a friend in Philadelphia, Anna's hometown. They found the post office, wrote their letters, and handed them to the clerk. The clerk checked to see if the proper postage was used and remarked when he noticed Levi's return address, "Mr. Collins, there's a package for you. We handle the mail as well as things shipped by rail and stagecoach. The package arrived from Pittsburgh about a week ago."

The clerk reached under the counter and retrieved a wooden box about three feet long.

"What is it, Levi?" quizzed Anna.

"I don't know, but it must have come from Helen."

"You're right, look what's on the box," Anna commented. She pointed at the printing. *From Helen Wisdom* was printed on the box. "Open it!" Anna said excitedly. "Is it your birthday?"

"No. My birthday isn't 'til November. We need a hammer, the box is nailed shut. We'd better wait until we get back to the wagon."

Levi estimated the weight of the box to be about eight to ten pounds. What would Helen have sent him? As he followed Anna to the general store, his curiosity kept increasing. Levi didn't realize Anna wanted to know the contents of the box more than he did.

Anna went directly to the tools, picked up a hammer, and handed it to Levi.

"Open the box—please! I can't stand it."

Levi laughed, took the hammer, and broke the end of the box open. He pried one side of the box off with his hands and lifted out an object wrapped in several layers of paper. He knew what it was immediately, but he let Anna remove the paper.

"Oh! It's a big gun. Look at the fancy engraving! You were a Captain?"

The fancy shotgun was engraved with *Captain Levi Collins* and there was a piece of paper wrapped around the stock and tied with a string. Anna handed the paper to Levi.

"Yes, I was a Captain in the Union Army."

"I'm impressed. I thought you and the Jeffers were all privates."

Levi thanked Anna for the paper, which he unfolded and read. Helen said Frank saw the gun in the window of a gun shop and, since it was a new innovation, he wanted Levi to have it for hunting and fighting Indians. The gun was a breech-loading, double-barrel shotgun that used the new brass shells. Frank had included one hundred shells with the gun. When Levi opened the shipping crate, he had seen shells packed in the end of the box, so he knew what it was before Anna had removed the paper.

Anna handed the gun to Levi and said, "That is a beautiful gun! Do you still think Frank is a horse's ass?" She grinned, wondering what Levi would say.

"Yep. Just not as big as my original estimate," he smiled. "I'll give my old gun to Nathan. He needs a shotgun."

Levi repacked the box to make carrying the gun and shells easier, and returned the borrowed hammer to the tool area. Anna had gathered the items she wanted, paid the bill, and they started back to the wagon.

"How long were you a captain?"

"About two years. I was a Lieutenant for about a year and got promoted when our captain was killed. I might have become a major if the war had lasted longer, but I'm glad it's over now. I wonder how long Langley has been a major."

"He's not a real major, Levi. The Wellsandts told me Langley was never in the military. He just uses major as a title for being in charge of the wagon train, for respect and authority, I guess."

"I'm glad you told me that. The Jeffers and I will be more help than I formerly figured if it comes to a fight."

Major Langley decided to hold the wagons at Fort Kearny another day before continuing toward Fort Laramie. A few of the pioneers disagreed with his decision, but most of the travelers enjoyed the rest after they realized they had come about 300 miles, and Fort Laramie was an even greater distance away, as much as 350 miles. It would take the wagons about three weeks to reach Fort Laramie following the North Platte River much of the way. What they didn't realize at the time was that Fort Laramie was at a higher elevation, not far from passes crossing the Rocky Mountains. The wagons would be traveling up a gentle slope along the southern bank of the shallow Platte River. Major Langley reminded the pioneers to boil the light-yellow water taken from the slow-moving river.

The major gathered the travelers in the morning and said, "I've changed my mind. We will cross the river and follow the northern side to Fort Laramie. There is better grass for the animals on the other side of the river. When you are crossing the water, don't stop. Your wheels will sink in and you'll get stuck. It will slow us all down. All right, let's move out."

The wagon train stayed on the south bank until almost reaching the mouth of the South Platte. The crossing to the northern bank went smoothly with only one wagon being temporarily stopped in the river. Ron and James Jeffers assisted the family by pulling the wagon with ropes tied to their saddles.

# CHAPTER 6

# INDIANS!

The wagons had left Fort Kearny and had been moving steadily on the trail for a week. The fort was now about 100 miles behind them. The sandy haired Olson boys, Seth and Joseph, had ridden north a half mile from the wagons to exercise two of their horses. They were supposed to ride out, turn around, and return to the wagons, but Joseph, the fourteen-year-old, wanted to watch a large flock of migratory birds that had landed nearby. Seth, who was sixteen, about six-feet tall, agreed to stop, and the boys dismounted, led their horses to a clump of tall grass, and peered around the growth, which was over five-feet tall.

"Look at those birds, Seth! There must be thousands of 'em. I wonder if they're good eatin'."

Seth stood tip-toed and looked over the grass, but he didn't see the birds; his eyes were riveted on a mounted Indian carrying a rifle about 20 yards away. The Indian wasn't paying attention to the birds or the boys; he was looking straight ahead and occasionally scanning to the north, riding slowly in the same direction as the wagons. Seth put one hand over Joseph's mouth and put his index finger up to his lips to indicate Joseph should be quiet.

Seth whispered to his brother, "An Indian! Let's git outta here!" The boys mounted their horses and rode as fast as they could back to the wagons. As they rode, Seth yelled at Joseph,

"Head for Cabots' wagon. We gotta tell Mr. Collins about the Indian."

Levi was riding beside the Cabots' wagon talking to Anna about her plans for the orchards she and Nathan wanted to help their uncle develop along the Columbia River. They looked away from the wagons when they heard yelling and two galloping horses and riders approaching rapidly. As the horsemen got closer, Anna said, "Those are the Olson boys. I wonder what they're screaming about."

Seth arrived slightly ahead of Joseph, slowing to match the speed of the wagons. Out of breath, Seth gulped some air and yelled, "We saw an Indian, Mr. Collins." Seth pointed out to the north. "Should we warn the others?"

"Hold up a minute, son. What did the Indian look like?"

"He had a gun across his saddle, a big knife at his waist, a buckskin shirt, and blue pants."

Joseph, out of breath, said, "That's what I seen, too."

Levi asked, "What color was his hair?"

The boys answered in unison, "Yellow, sir."

"Well, boys, you just described one of our scouts, riding on the north side of the wagons. Indians don't have yellow hair."

"But he looked like an Indian!" Seth insisted.

"Have you ever seen a real Indian, son?" quizzed Levi.

"N—No, just pictures."

"I'll tell you what. We'll ride out there and I'll introduce you to that man. He's called Yeats Bernard. He's been guiding wagon trains for over ten years. Right now, you'd better take care of your horses. We'll ride out there later. Okay?"

"Okay," Seth answered, a little embarrassed, "But we sure thought he was an Indian."

"Boys, one last thing. I think you should ride closer to the wagons. If that had been an Indian, you probably wouldn't be here talking to me."

Joseph and Seth looked at each other, then at Levi. Seth said, a little sheepishly, "Yes sir." The boys rode slowly back to their wagon discussing what to tell their parents.

Levi noticed Anna's expressionless look. "Do you think I was too hard on those boys?"

"No, Levi. I think you did a good job. What you suggested might keep them alive for the rest of the trip."

"Thank you, ma'am. You sometimes surprise me with your comments, but it's nice to see that we think alike on important things—like staying alive during the journey."

During the next week the wagons passed several landmarks including Ash Hollow, Jail Rock, and Courthouse Rock. It wouldn't be long before the spire of Chimney Rock would be visible in the distance. It was about mid-day, two days west of Courthouse Rock. The spire of Chimney Rock could be seen jutting up from the horizon, as well as a thin trail of smoke. At first Levi thought the smoke was part of the landscape, but by the time he pointed it out to the Jeffers, Levi noticed some movement in the thin gray column and then some irregularities. It had to be smoke and it couldn't be very far away.

One of the forward scouts rode up to the front of Cabots' wagon and asked, "Where can I find Levi Collins?" Levi was about 20 yards off to the side of the wagon and watched Nathan point toward him. Levi turned Bravo toward the wagon and stopped. The scout, Lenox Ewing, introduced himself to Levi and the Jeffers and said, "The Major would like a couple of you boys to join me to look into that smoke column over yonder." Ewing pointed toward the smoke Levi had indicated to the Jeffers. The source of the smoke appeared to be a little south of the southern, well-travelled side of the Platte, about three miles ahead of the wagons.

"Tom, stay with the Cabots. Ron, James, and I will go with Lenox to take a look."

"Yes sir," Tom replied looking over at Cabots' wagon. "Better take your shotgun, Levi."

"Right." Levi tied his pack horses to the back of Cabots' wagon and pulled the new shotgun from storage on his bigger pack horse. He had been carrying a dozen of the new shells in his saddle bags since they had passed Courthouse Rock. Ron rode up and said, "Ready Captain?"

"Yeah, let's go."

Levi, Ron, and James joined Lenox. They rode fairly hard for a couple of miles and Lenox signaled them to stop. It appeared the smoke was coming from just over a small hill in front of the riders. Lenox dismounted, as did the others, and while crouched, made his way to the top of the hill. Lenox was a wiry man of about forty, and stood about five-foot seven. His face was misshapen; the right side longer than the left, and his medium-length black hair was parted in the middle. His scruffy beard had been trimmed to partly conceal his distorted features.

Levi was impressed with Lenox's movement, which was with purpose and yet graceful. Levi wondered if the man had ever been a sniper. The men crawled on their bellies until they could see the source of the smoke. A stagecoach was on its side with smoke drifting up from the bottom of the passenger compartment. Several bodies could be seen on the ground near the coach, but there was no movement. A horse was down, but not dead, trying vainly to get up.

Lenox said, "Cover me." and stayed low to the ground, running the forty yards to the smoldering coach. Levi watched as the scout peered into the coach, then moved to the nearest soldier's body and checked for a pulse. Lenox stood up and motioned for Levi and the Jeffers to join him. As the men approached the badly damaged stagecoach, they checked the rest of the bodies for life. There were twelve bodies—eight soldiers, a male and female passenger, the driver, and the shotgun rider. Levi pulled a small notebook from the soldier nearest the coach and turned through the pages. A Lieutenant, Ned Anderson, had been in charge of the soldiers, escorting the Reverend Lester Nolan, his wife Eloise, and daughter Clarissa to Fort Laramie.

The four men gathered on a sandstone knoll a few yards from the smoldering coach.

Levi looked at Lenox and asked, "What's the count?"

"Twelve dead. They were stripped of weapons and ammunition. Four soldiers were scalped. Horses were taken except for that one—leg's broke. I'll shoot it."

Levi replied, "There's a girl missing—daughter of the dead couple in the coach—don't know how old she is, but she must have been taken. Hope she's a little one. James, you and Ron get the Reverend and wife out of the coach, Lenox and I'll gather the soldiers." He looked for a spot where graves could be dug and pointed, "Over there—area looks like it's mostly soil."

James climbed on top of the coach and dropped through the open door to the inside, landing on an empty canteen. He kicked it aside, took out his skinning knife, and started cutting and breaking off the arrows protruding from the bodies. Ron had climbed on top of the sideways coach to pull the bodies out as James raised them from the bottom of the wreckage. As James began to lift the woman's body, he was surprised by a cry, "Don't hurt me!" At first, Ron thought the woman he was lifting had cried out, but she was dead, and the voice didn't fit; it was the voice of a child. As Ron hoisted the woman's body, a little dark-haired girl, about 4 or 5 years old, was cowering in the corner, clutching a small rag doll. She had been hiding under her dead mother's clothing.

James smiled and said, "Well now, missy, what's your name?" James knelt beside the youngster and could see the fear in the little girl's eyes. She was looking at his knife, so he sheathed the big blade.

The little one stuttered, "Cla—Clarissa."

"I'm happy to make your acquaintance, Clarissa. My name is James. Can I hand you up to my brother? He's up there." James pointed through the open coach door toward the sky.

Clarissa looked up through the opening to the blue sky and said, "In heaven?"

James smiled and said, "No, he's up on top of the coach."

Clarissa nodded and struggled to her feet. James placed his hands around Clarissa's waist and lifted her through the open coach door to Ron.

"Ron, this is Clarissa. I think she needs to talk with Levi."

Ron held the child so Levi could see her. "Levi, I have some-one you need to talk to. Her name's Clarissa."

Levi answered, "I was going to get a shovel from the wagons. I guess I can make a delivery to Annabel. She'll know what to do." Levi rode up next to the coach and Ron handed Clarissa to him. Using his knees, Levi guided his horse away from the coach and bodies. With Clarissa cradled in his arms, Levi started back to the wagons. He had ridden about two-hundred yards when he heard the muffled report of a gun from behind. Lenox had taken care of the severely injured horse.

"So your name is Clarissa. What is your dolly's name?"

Clarissa held her doll tightly against her chest and replied, "Amy."

"My name is Levi. I'm going to take you to our wagon train and have you meet a very nice lady named Annabel. I think you'll like her. She will take care of you for a while. How old are you, Clarissa?"

Clarissa opened her right fist, held up four fingers, and said, "Four. Where is my mama?" Clarissa twisted her body to look behind Levi, so Levi adjusted her position. He placed her arms around his neck and her feet on his thighs so she could look behind him. He held her tightly with one hand on her back.

"Your mama is in heaven now, Clarissa. Your mama and papa both went to heaven so they could be together forever. They left you here so you can do special things. You know, I have a dog named Tucker, and he needs to be combed and petted. Tucker has a beautiful reddish-brown coat. Do you think you could help me take care of Tucker?"

"Is Tucker big?"

"He's pretty big, but he's real friendly. I think he'll like you. You can play games with him, and he will protect you."

"I can brush him?"

"That's right."

As Levi and Clarissa approached Cabots' wagon, Tucker ran out to greet them with a couple of barks and a wagging tail. Levi rode up next to Anna and Nathan. "This is Clarissa. Her mama and papa went to heaven. I told her she can stay with us for a while and help with Tucker. What do you think, Cabots?"

Anna looked at Nathan and then at Levi, and nodded. "Hello Clarissa. I'm Annabel and this is my brother Nathan. Would you like to stay with us?"

Levi watched Clarissa nod her head and reach toward Anna's outstretched arms. Levi assisted Clarissa's transfer to Anna and said, "I need to borrow some shovels; we have twelve graves to dig."

Nathan stopped the oxen and untied two shovels from the outside of the wagon. When he handed them to Levi, he said, "Reverend Hastings is in the fourth wagon ahead of us. He could conduct a service."

"Thanks Nathan. I'll keep that in mind, but we don't know how risky it is to be out there. I think we'll just bury the dead and get back to the wagons. Our guns might be needed here. If we hear any gunfire, we'll come a runnin'. We'll catch up to the wagons in an hour, maybe two. If you see the Major, tell him what we're doing."

# CHAPTER 7

# BURIALS AND MORE DEATH

Nathan secured the shovels to one of Levi's pack horses and handed Levi the rope lead. Levi urged Bravo away from the wagons and began the return trip to the burial site. When he had gone about 50 yards, he heard a whistle from the wagons and turned to see Nathan and Anna waving, and pointing toward the ground behind him. Tucker had jumped down from Cabots' wagon and was chasing after Levi. Levi slowed the horses and was about to tell Tucker to go back, but he changed his mind. When Tucker got closer, Levi said, "Okay, Tucker, come on. You need some more exercise and time with me. Your digging won't help much though, but your nose might come in useful," he smiled. Tucker went ahead of Levi and went right to the burial site.

Lenox, Ron and James had taken wood from the coach and spokes from a broken coach wheel to make grave markers. Lenox and James had scratched numbers into the wood with their knives, not able to identify the bodies except for the Lieutenant, Reverend Nolan and his wife. As Levi dismounted and removed the shovels from his pack horse, Tucker circled the damaged stagecoach several times, and then sat on a limestone hillock, about 15 yards from the bodies, sniffing the air.

"James, you and Ron dig while Lenox and I watch for trouble. We'll take your places when you've got half of them buried." Levi picked up three small boards and carved the names for the known bodies.

As the brothers buried the dead, Levi scanned the limestone hills and outcroppings looking for anything out of the ordinary. Lenox walked the perimeter of the area, occasionally stopping to shield his eyes from the sun, searching for movement away from the site. Levi watched Lenox approach and listened to him comment, "I can't see nothing strange, but I been watchin' yer dog. He smells somethin'. Them Indians stink worse than we do, that's fer damn sure."

"I think you're right. Someone's watching us from that rise over there." Levi motioned with his rifle barrel, indicating the hill to the southwest about 200 yards away. "Tucker has been pointed that way and sniffing the air since he sat on that little rise."

Back at Cabots' wagon, Clarissa looked at Nathan, and then shifted her eyes to Annabel. "Are you and him going to be my mama and papa?"

Annabel Cabot hadn't expected that question and didn't know what to say. "We'll see, Clarissa. I think we have to become good friends first. I'll be able to answer all your questions by the time we get to Fort Boise, but the fort is a long distance from here, so try to be patient." Anna watched Clarissa's eyes at first stare ahead at the wagon in front of them, and then her eyelids gradually closed. The bumping and rocking of the wagon had helped Clarissa fall asleep in Anna's arms. Anna put Clarissa behind the wagon seat on some pillows and watched the little girl. Clarissa was dreaming, her face was contorted, and her hands were moving as if she were shielding herself from an attacker. Anna reached back, patted Clarissa, and said, "You are safe with us, sweetie." Tears flowed down Anna's cheeks as she watched the orphan's fitful motions.

Nathan reached over and put his arm around his sister. "Annie, everything will work out. You handled Clarissa's question very nicely. What are you thinking?"

"I don't want to raise a child without a husband, and who would want me if I have a four-year-old child that isn't even mine?"

"I can think of two men on the train that would marry you—Tom and Levi. I don't believe Clarissa would have anything to do with it. I have a feeling Levi would marry you no matter what, but I'm not sure about Tom."

"So you think Levi likes me?"

"I've seen the way he looks at you, but Tom is a bit more obvious about it. It might be that Levi is scared to get involved. He lost his parents and their farm, and his sister married into a wealthy family in the last two years, so he probably wants to be sure about anyone he starts a relationship with. He doesn't want to lose someone else. Levi might not know how you feel about him."

"Well, I like Levi a lot more than Tom. Levi is more reserved, more capable, and smarter than Tom, although Tom is a nice man."

"Tom usually rides by to see you by this time of day, but I haven't seen him today."

"Levi comes by, too, but we know where he is. I hope they don't have any trouble out there away from the wagons. I don't think we could hear gunfire because of all the noise from the animals, wagons, and people yelling."

"Don't worry about Levi, Annie, he'll be fine. Remember, he survived three years of war."

"Well, I hope they don't have any problems. Burying people that are strangers is a bad enough experience."

Nathan added, "You know, if you decide to mother Clarissa, I will be her uncle; Uncle Nathan. I kind of like the sound of that—Uncle Nathan." Nathan looked at Anna and smiled, Anna smiled back.

Levi and Lenox were covering the last grave with heavy stones they were able to break away from some of the limestone hillocks nearby. Tucker was getting restless, repeatedly pacing and then stopping, giving a whine, and looking toward the hill he had been facing when he first arrived with Levi. Ron and James were lashing the shovels to Levi's packhorse and mounting their horses, glad to be finished with the burial duty.

Levi said, "I think we'd better get back to the wagons. Tucker seems to be aware of some activity nearby. Let's ride out of here. We've probably overstayed our welcome."

"I'll report to the major and spell the man that took my place," Lenox commented. "I'll tell the major about yer dog, Levi. He might wanta double the guard."

It was about four in the afternoon when the burial detail returned to the wagons. Lenox rode to the front of the wagons to talk with the major, James and Ron went back to Boltons' wagon where their horses and gear were located. Levi rode to the Cabots' wagon.

When Levi approached the wagon, Anna said, "I'm so glad you're back. Did you have any trouble?"

"Not much. The digging was a little difficult in places, but we were able to dig deeply enough and cover the graves with stones to keep the critters away. We didn't see any Indians but Tucker smelled them. We're sure they were watching us. How are you and Nathan—and Clarissa? Where is she?"

"She's here in the wagon sleeping." Anna pointed over her shoulder.

Levi noticed a little hand from inside the wagon poke Anna in the back. Anna turned and leaned back so she could talk to Clarissa. Then, Anna turned back to Levi and said, "My mistake, Clarissa isn't sleeping. She asked me if you were the man with the dog. She thought she remembered your voice."

"I'm the one, Clarissa. Tucker is pretty tired; maybe he can ride in the wagon for a spell. I'll let you brush him for me." Levi, raising his eyebrows, looked at Anna for consent. Anna smiled and nodded, granting permission. Levi dismounted and helped Tucker scramble into the wagon, extracted a brush from his saddlebag, and handed it to Anna. Levi said, "I'll be back in a few minutes. I have to talk with the major." He mounted Bravo, waved, and rode toward the front of the wagon train about a hundred yards away.

Lenox was riding with the major thirty yards in front of the lead wagon. As Levi approached the two men, he watched Lenox give the major a weak salute and ride ahead to reclaim his scouting position.

"Howdy, Levi. Lenox was just telling me about your dog. Lenox thinks the dog got a good whiff of some Indian activity. I think we'll double the guard tonight. Will you and the Jeffers help out?"

"I can't speak for the Jeffers, but I'll help. I was going to tell you about my dog's excitement, but Lenox has already taken care of that. The little girl from the stagecoach is with the Cabots—name's Clarissa Nolan. Her father was a minister—headed to Fort Laramie."

The major thought a moment, and replied, "I'll contact the authorities when we arrive at the Fort. The Army will notify the church and send out a detachment. They'll give those men a proper burial at the Fort. I don't know what the church will want to do about the Nolans."

Two riders suddenly appeared over the rise in front of the lead wagon, the men crouched low in their saddles, their horses galloping. It was Lenox and Tom Jeffers, who had been temporarily riding point while Lenox was on burial detail. The men pulled up in front of the Major and Levi. Lenox yelled, "Indians—thirty or more ridin' hard behind us—better git ready—looks like a fight!"

Levi yelled at Tom, "Warn your brothers! I'm heading for the Cabots' wagon. Get the Dendricks boys and spread out along the wagons. They might come at us from the trailing wagons, maybe on foot—use your scatterguns up close. Try to knock 'em down at distance if you can."

Tom whistled loudly, three times, to warn James and Ron that there was trouble, and rode toward the end wagon, pulling his rifle from his saddle scabbard. Some of the wagons had moved side-by-side which shortened the length of the strung out wagons. As Levi rode past several wagons he yelled for the people to take cover under the wagons, and get their guns ready. As Levi reached the Cabots' wagon, he could hear gunfire from the front of the wagon train. He recognized the sounds, the shots were from 56-50 Spencer carbines.

Levi thought, *"Must be from the scouts and Dendricks,"* but there were too many shots to be coming from only half a dozen guns. He suddenly realized the guns taken from the soldiers by the Indians were being used in the attack on the wagons. He yelled at Nathan, "Get Anna and the girl some protection, quick!"

Nathan vaulted into the wagon, opened a large tool box, pulled the tools out and pushed Anna and Clarissa into the nearly empty heavy wooden box. He handed the sawed-off shotgun to Anna, said, "Be careful, it's loaded and ready to fire—just pull the triggers." Nathan closed the lid, dropped to the ground, and joined Levi under the wagon. Levi handed Nathan a dozen shells and his new double-barrel shotgun. Levi crouched under the back end of the wagon and waited with his Spencer carbine.

A half-dozen screaming Indians on horses, just emerging over a small hill on the north side of the wagon, appeared to be headed directly for the Cabots' wagon. Levi waited until they were within 50 yards and blew the two leading warriors, carrying rifles, off their horses. At thirty yards two more attackers, launching arrows, were shot by Levi. They fell from their horses, in all probability, dead. Their horses ran wild, away from the wagons. An Indian had gotten within 20 yards of the Cabots' wagon and had thrown a lance. The lance fell short and stuck in the earth next to the wagon. Nathan was tracking the Indian with Levi's new shotgun and fired both barrels. The warrior's body fell from his horse and rolled within ten feet of the wagon, blood dripping from the corpse to the dry earth.

The two men had just begun to relax when they heard Anna scream from above them. Levi started to roll from under the wagon, but hadn't made it to his feet when he heard a shotgun blast. An Indian tumbled to the ground from the back of the wagon. Most of the man's head was missing. Levi dragged the body and placed it behind some boulders away from the wagon. Nathan tied a rope around the legs of the Indian he had shot and pulled the body about thirty yards from the wagon. The men didn't want Clarissa or Anna to see the dead bodies up close. It was calm after the noise of gunfire, yelling, and pounding horses' hooves let up.

The quiet was occasionally interrupted by a pistol shot. Victory yells from some of the emigrants were heard and a few riderless horses could be seen galloping away from the wagons. Lenox, his pistol drawn, rode up to Levi and asked, "Any live ones around?"

"Maybe—you'll have to check farther out—50 yards or so." Levi motioned with his rifle. "Might be some carbines to pick up—probably taken from the soldiers we buried. Ask the major about giving them to the people in the wagons."

Levi climbed into the wagon, a little fearful of what he might find. He said a quiet prayer as he moved to the tool box and tapped on the lid. "Anna, are you and Clarissa all right? You can open the box, there's no more danger. The Indians are gone, or dead."

The top of the box opened and Levi could see Anna shaking, but still holding onto the shotgun. He took the gun from Anna for self-preservation, helped her up, and she clung to him, teeth chattering. Levi encircled her with his arms and held her tightly. Anna was able to squeak out, "I was so scared. He had a knife."

"Everything's all right now. You did fine."

Levi looked into the box and saw Clarissa trying to sit up, squinting. She raised her hands, shielding her eyes from the bright light after being sheltered in complete darkness. Levi lifted her from the toolbox with his left arm, and Clarissa reached out to Anna. Anna had stopped shaking, but still had her arms around Levi. She looked up at Levi as she took Clarissa in her arms and said, "Are you and Nathan all right?"

"We're fine. We heard you yell, and then a shotgun blast. We were worried you and Clarissa might have been hurt, but an Indian fell to the ground from the wagon so we figured you were all right."

"So, I did shoot somebody? I wasn't sure I aimed correctly. I just pulled the trigger like you said."

"You surely did. We moved the body away to get it out of sight. You and Clarissa don't need to see dead bodies—even if they're Indians. We'll clean the blood off the wagon cover when we get to Fort Laramie. We'll be there in a few days.

# CHAPTER 8

# ON GUARD DUTY

**A**s Levi and Nathan helped Clarissa and Anna down from the wagon, the major rode up, took off his hat, wiped his forehead with his wrist, and asked, "Everyone all right?"

"Yes Sir," answered Nathan.

"How many heathens did you get?"

Levi replied, "Four with a rifle and two with shotguns. We dragged the closest ones over behind those rocks." Levi pointed with his shotgun.

"The count is nineteen, then. We lost our northern scout, Niles Bristen. He was killed before the attack—couldn't make it back to the wagons. Mr. Wellsandt got clipped by an arrow, not serious, and one of the Wellsandts' chickens got killed. I'm guessing they'll have chicken dinner tonight." The major smiled. "Do you think one of the Jeffers will ride scout until we reach Fort Laramie? I'll hire on a new man there. I'll need another guard for the wagons tonight. Can you help, Levi?"

"Sure. You'll have to ask the Jeffers, Major. If two of them work together, they might do it."

"Nathan, hand me that lance so I can git a closer look."

Nathan pulled the wooden shaft from the ground and tossed it to the major. He looked closely at the markings and said, "Thought so, it's Sioux. They're a pretty tough bunch, great horsemen and good tacticians. We had the upper hand 'cause of superior weapons, and men that knew better how to use 'em. They'll remember this fight though." The major handed the lance to Nathan and said, "Bust this lance in two and leave it on the ground. Don't put the pieces with the bodies though; we don't want to disrespect the Sioux." The major tipped his hat to Anna, and rode toward the end of the wagons to check if there were any other injuries.

Nathan leaned the lance against the wagon, and stomped hard on it, breaking the shaft in two, making it useless as a weapon. He kicked the fragments away from the wagon, climbed into the back, and replaced the tools in the box. There was one item on the floor of the wagon that didn't belong, a steel knife. Nathan leaned out from the wagon and handed the knife to Levi.

"That's Army issue—must have been taken from the stagecoach detail." He gave it back to Nathan and said, "Better keep it—I'll give you some tips on how to use it, for both hunting and fighting."

Levi hadn't seen Tucker since before the attack. Levi looked around the nearby wagons, but Tucker had vanished. A whistle and a call for the dog produced results. In less than a minute, Tucker appeared and sat by the front of the wagon waiting for an assist. Levi helped Tucker in the wagon with Clarissa and Annabel. Clarissa hugged Tucker and Tucker licked Clarissa's face, making her laugh and turn her head away from the wet tongue. No one could recall seeing Tucker during the fighting.

A few minutes later, the Major and Tom Jeffers rode by on the way to the lead wagons. In another ten minutes the wagons in front of the Cabots' pulled ahead. As the shadows were lengthening, the emigrants passed Chimney Rock. The wagons were circled and campfires sprang up beside each of the wagons. There was plenty of conversation during dinner that evening.

The sun had gone down before the travelers began eating. Those saying grace thanked God for their meal, and for protecting them from injury. In addition, they asked the Almighty to accept the souls of those killed into heaven. Most of the campfire gatherings were rather somber, but the Army veterans were telling jokes and laughing. That was part of the way they coped with bloodshed. Some of the emigrants, especially those of a more pious nature, thought that jokes, being told after the killing earlier in the day, were distasteful. The major was making the rounds and set the pioneers straight about the demeanor of the former soldiers. Major Langley informed Levi that two of the Jeffers would be joining him as forward scouts. The men they relieved would patrol the north flank of the wagons, the most susceptible to attack. The river to the south hindered attacks because the bottom of the Platte was like quicksand. Levi was to begin a three-hour stretch as a night guard starting at eleven o'clock. Levi would be on foot patrolling five wagons.

After eating, Annabel put Clarissa to bed and rejoined the adults at the campfire. She sat on the ground beside Levi and said, "I'll make some more coffee. You'll need to stay awake until two in the morning. I'll leave the coffee on the fire so you can get more while you're on watch."

Levi could see the fire light dancing in Anna's eyes. He felt like kissing her, but said, "Thank you. That would be very nice." Perhaps it was too soon for kissing, and it would have to wait for a more private setting. He certainly didn't want to force himself on her. "How is little Clarissa doing?"

"She seems to be all right. She misses her mama, but we're getting along fine. She asked me if you were going to be her papa." Anna looked at Levi for several seconds, smiled, and then said, "I told her I didn't know the answer to that."

Levi didn't comment. He didn't know what to say. Everything he could think of saying would make him sound like an idiot. He reached into his pocket, pulled out his father's old watch, checked the time, and wound it. The time was 10:21. Anna reached over to Levi's wrist and turned it so she could see the hands. When she touched his arm, that same tingling sensation came over him again. Levi thought of telling Anna that he loved her, but the time wasn't right, they had to get to know each other better. He had to be sure his feelings weren't just physical, but mental as well, and the journey was only half over. Perhaps his feelings for her would diminish, or change completely before they reached Fort Boise.

Besides, after Fort Boise, they might not see each other again. There were too many uncertainties.

"I'd better get some things from my packhorse. It's going to be cold tonight, the sky is clear, and there's a halo around the moon."

By ten-thirty, all but a few of the campfires had been extinguished. Most of the travelers had gone to bed, except for the eight men scheduled for night watch. Nathan, Anna, and Levi talked for another quarter-hour about the future. The Cabots' plans for orchards were detailed for the next five years. Levi was purposefully vague about his plans. He still didn't want to reveal the gold discovery he and the Jeffers were going to investigate in Idaho. He wanted to tell Anna, but he wasn't sure about Nathan.

Anna stared into the glowing embers as Levi evaded mentioning what he intended to do in the mountains of Idaho. She stood up and said, "I'll make that coffee, Levi. Why don't you stir up the fire and add a little more wood. You'll have some hot coffee to begin your watch. I've got to go to bed. What about you, Nathan? Tomorrow will be another long day, no time for naps."

"Yeah, Sis. I'd better turn in too. See you in the morning, Levi."

"Good night Cabots. See you tomorrow."

Levi tended the fire, and then knelt beside his saddle under the wagon and slipped into his wool coat. He checked his handgun and hunting knife, turned around expecting to see Anna at the fire, but only saw the coffee pot. Anna had gone to bed. Another opportunity had slipped away. He sat beside the fire and looked up at the night sky, recalling the summer constellations. He found Cassiopeia, the big W shape, the mother of Andromeda. The stars reminded him of Anna, how the campfire flickered in her eyes. The minute hand of his timepiece was approaching twelve, so he filled his metal cup with hot coffee and began his night watch. Besides the Cabots' wagon, Levi was responsible for the two wagons ahead of theirs, and the two wagons behind.

He didn't check his watch, but it must have been about one o'clock when Tucker appeared. Levi was standing next to the Cabots' wagon looking across the moonlit countryside. At first,

Levi thought some varmint was rubbing against his boot, but it was Tucker sitting beside him.

"Can't sleep, eh?" Levi looked closely at his watch, the moon providing enough light for him to check the time. "One more hour and we can go to bed."

Tucker got up and then sat back down, looking up at Levi. Levi began walking again with Tucker at his side. Tucker would occasionally stop and peer into the moon-lit landscape, attracted by the sounds or scent of prowling nocturnal creatures. After circling the five wagons twice, Levi returned to the coffee pot and poured another half-cup. The fire had gone out but the coffee was still hot. The pot had been moved against the rocks around the fire to keep it hot for a longer time. Levi didn't know who had done it, but he suspected it had been Anna; she seemed to always be looking out for others. Perhaps she couldn't sleep after her harrowing day. Levi was sorry he had missed her, if it had been only to exchange a few words.

Levi warmed his hands over the rocks next to the coffee pot, preparing to patrol the wagons again. As he rose to his feet, Tucker ran to the front of the Cabots' wagon and sat down, looking up at a figure covered with a blanket, backing down from the driver's seat. It was Anna. Levi rushed over and grabbed her hand, helping her to the ground.

"Thank you," she whispered. "I can't fall asleep. I keep thinking about killing that Indian, and you being out here by yourself."

"I'm not alone, Tucker is with me," he smiled. "Thank you for fixing the coffee and keeping it warm by the rocks."

"You're welcome." Anna wrapped her blanket tighter and said, "I have something to ask you.

When we were talking earlier, you didn't seem to have much in mind for your future. Is that really true?"

Levi should have expected that question. Anna was smart, very observant, and had listened closely to what Levi had said. She wouldn't have much interest in a man that wasn't thinking ahead, but he decided to change the subject for a moment.

"See that big W of stars?" He pointed into the sky. "That's Cassiopeia, the mother of Andromeda and the wife of Cepheus."

"Oh yes—I remember that story. My father gave Nathan and me a book of mythology for Christmas when I was eleven years old. There were star maps with the stories. Nathan and I used to lie on the grass in our backyard, look up at the stars, and trace the constellations."

Levi continued, "I was thinking, you would be Cassiopeia, and Clarissa would be Andromeda. I don't know who Cepheus would be though—maybe someone on the wagon train or someone back home."

Anna suddenly realized Levi wasn't sure she was interested in him. She smiled slightly and said, "Hmm, I'll have to think about that."

Levi rubbed his hands together to increase the circulation and said, "It's really cold tonight—no cloud cover. Aren't you chilly with just that blanket and no coat?"

"A little. I thought if I talked to you for a few minutes, I would feel more secure, and then I could climb back in bed, curl up, get warm, and fall asleep, but I hadn't planned on shivering. So, what have you in mind for your future?"

"My answer could take a few minutes." Levi made a suggestion, "I'll share my coat, you share your blanket, and we'll both warm up a bit as I explain." He smiled as he began to unbutton his heavy coat. He slipped his right arm out of his woolen jacket and held it open so Anna could move closer to him. She hesitated for a second, but dropped the blanket off her shoulders, and let Levi put his coat and arm around her. Levi grabbed her blanket, and with Anna's help, they pulled the blanket over the coat.

Anna looked up at Levi, smiled, and said, "Good idea, this is much better."

Levi smiled and responded, "I agree. A warm body can make a big difference on a cold night."

"Levi, you still haven't answered my question about your future. You must have something in mind. Is it a secret? Don't you trust me?"

"It's not really a secret. I just want to limit the knowledge of where I'm going to a select group of people." Levi smiled and continued, "In your case, it will require a deposit."

Anna looked a little puzzled. "A deposit?"

"Yes, but just a little one. Kiss me on the cheek." Levi put his right index finger on his cheek.

Anna's frown turned to a smile, and she turned to kiss Levi's cheek, but he turned his face quickly and they kissed on the lips. "You tricked me!" But Anna didn't pull away. She said, "I think that was a pretty good deposit."

Levi couldn't take his eyes from Anna. He grinned and said, "Yes, that was more than adequate. Now I can tell you my plans, but right now I have to get back to patrolling the wagons. I've been depending on Tucker too much. Do you think you will be able to sleep now?"

Anna sighed, smiled, and lightheartedly said, "I'll sleep like a baby. Good night, Levi."

Levi tipped his hat, grinned, and whispered, "Good night Annabel. I'll tell you my plans tomorrow, no more deposits will be necessary. Come on, Tucker."

# CHAPTER 9

## DISCUSSION AND PROMISE

At 2:00 a.m., Tom Jeffers relieved Levi. Levi crawled under the Cabots' wagon, covered himself with a wool blanket and fell asleep. Tucker curled up next to Levi, and, using his teeth, pulled the edge of the blanket over his hind end. It was 5:30 and the eastern sky was beginning to lighten before Levi heard anything. Levi hadn't heard Tom return from his early morning patrol, but Tom's deep breathing indicated he was sleeping soundly. Levi could just make out Anna's humming as she arranged some twigs and buffalo chips for a fire. Levi watched Tucker get up, stretch, and sit beside Anna as she lit the kindling.

"Good morning, Tucker. Did you have a good night's sleep? How is Levi today?"

Tucker looked up at Anna, gave a little whine, and stood up wagging his tail.

"I'll bet you're hungry, big boy."

Levi responded, "Me too, but wake me up tomorrow."

Anna laughed. "It's already tomorrow. You'll have to take a nap this afternoon with Clarissa. You youngsters need your rest."

"There's not enough room in your wagon for me to lie down. I don't know how you, Nathan, and Clarissa find room for sleeping."

"Don't worry—I'll tie you to your horse, very tightly. You're correct about the lack of space. Tonight, Nathan will be joining you under the wagon. Besides," she grinned, "I'm tired of his farts."

Levi crawled from under the wagon, chuckling over Anna's comment. While on his knees, he packed his belongings for traveling. Levi left his things leaning against the closest wagon wheel, went over to Anna, who had started coffee, and gave her a peck on the cheek. Anna was putting bacon in the skillet, smiled, and said, "Thank you for the nice early morning engagement. I'll have some bacon and eggs in a few minutes."

Levi and Anna hadn't seen Tom watching them from the back corner of the wagon. He had just gotten up, relieved himself, and was returning to get some breakfast. He had heard Anna say the word *engagement*. He cleared his throat and moved toward the fire.

Levi said, "Morning."

Anna followed with "Good morning, Tom. Is everything all right?"

"Yeah, after an hour's sleep. Nothing happened during my patrol. So you and Levi are engaged?"

Levi reacted quickly and said, "You must have heard the word *engagement*. Anna didn't mean we were engaged to be married, she meant the talk we had last night was an engagement—like a meeting, or a fight."

Tom felt a little anxious and responded with, "Have our plans changed—have you made a better deal?"

"No. Anna doesn't know anything about our plans. I was going to tell her today."

Anna was frowning and said, "Are those the plans you are going to tell me about today?"

Levi glanced at Anna, noticed her questioning look, said "Uh-huh," fished Helen's letter from his pocket, and handed it to her. "Please read this, Anna, and you will have an idea of what the Jeffers and me are going to do."

In the dim light, Anna held the note near the fire and read it, refolded the paper, and gave it back to Levi. Clarissa called to Anna, so Anna turned toward the wagon, and as she walked away from the fire, said, "We'll talk later. I want to know all about your plans, if you'll confide in me."

Tom frowned and looked at Levi. "What does that mean?"

"I think we have to tell her everything we know—which isn't much, but we can tell her what we would like to do. I told her we only want a few people to know where we intend to go."

Nathan joined Tom and Levi and said, "What are you gentlemen discussing? Does it involve Anna? Her mood has certainly changed from earlier when she got up."

Levi said, "We've got to eat and get on the trail. It won't be long before we'll have to cross the river to get to Fort Laramie. Maybe the major will fill us in today about the crossing. We have to be on the lookout for Indians, too. We'll talk about Tom's and my discussion tonight during supper."

★　★　★

The wagon train passed Scott's Bluff around noon and didn't stop until 6:30 that evening. The scouts reported seeing a few Indians, but the Native American observers kept at a distance from the wagons.

The wagons were circled, unloaded, and the men were taking care of the animals. The women and children busied themselves building fires and cooking. The sun was nearing the horizon when the travelers began their evening meal. The fading sunlight and light from the campfires provided enough illumination for the travelers to see what they were consuming. The day of moving west had been longer than normal. Usually, most everyone had gone to bed at sunset.

Clarissa had eaten first, and Anna had put her to bed. Tom, Nathan, Levi, and Anna were gathered around the fire. Tucker had been fed and was sitting near the fire, not for warmth, but to eat any food which fell to the ground, or any scraps offered to him.

Anna was sitting beside Nathan and asked, "Levi, tell me what you and Tom have planned."

Levi thought for a few seconds, and then replied, "Well, our original intention was to find some rich farmland in Oregon and start a ranch—grow wheat and raise cattle, but after I got that note from Helen, the Jeffers and I decided to try our luck looking for gold—not to get rich, but to get some money to start a bigger ranch, and have some security for our future wives and children."

Anna was very serious. She looked at Levi and said, "So, what is going to happen when we get to Fort Boise? Will we just go in separate directions? Will we ever see each other again?"

Levi looked into Anna's eyes and replied, "I've been thinking about that all day. I want to see if I can get some gold to finance a farm, but I would like to help you and Nathan start your orchard, which I am willing to do—after I try to find some gold. So, to compromise, I will look for gold for a maximum of six months and then join you, Nathan, and Clarissa. Would you be willing to do that?"

Anna said, "Let me think for a minute." She went over to the wagon, checked on Clarissa, and returned to the campfire. "Okay— except for one thing. I want you to come see us at Christmas if the six months isn't up yet."

Levi answered immediately, "It's a deal. Let's shake on it— Tom and Nathan are witnesses."

Anna stood up, walked over to Levi, smiled, and said, "Better yet, kiss me."

Levi put his hands around Anna's waist and started to kiss her, but Anna grabbed Levi's neck with both hands and kissed him for what seemed a long time. After the prolonged kiss, Anna stepped back, smiled, and said, "I just wanted you to realize what you'll be missing if you break your promise."

Levi grinned and said, "I would never break a promise to a smart, beautiful woman. We'll have to figure out a way to communicate though. I won't know where to deliver the gold Christmas ornaments."

"I've thought about that. I'll send you a letter with my address in November, General Delivery, Fort Boise. You can bring the Jeffers with you, if they want to come."

Levi looked at Tom. Tom grinned and said, "Sounds good to me. We'll be tired of our own cookin' by then. Maybe we can bring some fresh deer meat or salmon."

Nathan said, "Why not bring some Indians, too—kind of like Thanksgiving? We can have a big dance and all get drunk, have some arguments and fights, maybe a knifing or a shooting. Then we can have a burial with flowers and singing."

Levi was surprised by Nathan's sarcastic comments; normally Nathan kept his thoughts to himself. Apparently he had wanted to enjoy a quiet family celebration of Christmas, but Anna had invited Levi *and* the Jeffers. Anna had made a nice gesture to Tom since he had been standing with them during the conversation.

"Nathan, I'm surprised at you. Those comments were unnecessary," Anna scolded.

Nathan responded, "Don't criticize me, Anna. You're my sister, not my mother."

Levi saw the shocked look on Anna's face. He could feel her frustration and decided to separate brother and sister before things got worse. Levi grasped Nathan's left arm above the elbow and led the younger man away from the campfire to the other side of the wagon. Nathan tried to twist away from Levi, but found that he was no match for Levi's strength, so he cooperated.

Levi recognized Nathan's behavior. After hard-fought battles, some of his young soldiers had lashed out against their friends. It was a type of mental stress that only rest and time would remedy. Levi said, "Nathan, I think you're overtired. Let's take turns driving the wagon tomorrow. We both need to get some rest. I slept about three hours last night. While you drive, I'll sleep, and after a few hours, we'll exchange places. Let's fix the wagon so we can lie down comfortably. What do you think?"

"Maybe you're right. I'm awfully tired of looking at oxen asses all day long, and the constant heat is depressing. Sometimes I fall asleep holding the reins. Anna has kept me from falling off the wagon more than once. I didn't think this trip was going to be so monotonous, and I didn't think I'd ever kill anyone. I just want to start an orchard; I don't want to kill Indians. Anna didn't even ask me if I wanted you to help us develop an orchard."

"Well, I like you and Anna, and I grew up on a farm, so I might be helpful. If I find some gold, I could keep things going until the crops are productive. If I don't find gold, I'll find something else to keep the orchard progressing. But I don't want to interfere with you, Anna, and your uncle, either."

"I guess it's all right with me. I know you like Anna and Clarissa. Will you and Anna get married some day?"

"That's a ways off. If we get married too soon, we might discover that we aren't compatible. We have nearly two more months to get to know each other better. We might find out we don't see eye-to-eye on things that are important. Maybe she will like Tom better than me. You know, a woman is always correct."

Nathan grinned and said, "You got that right."

Nathan and Levi returned to the fire to find Tom petting Tucker. Anna had said goodnight to Tom and gone to bed. The men talked for a few minutes, extinguished the fire, and crawled into bed under the wagon.

The next morning, Levi and Nathan got up first, started a fire, and made coffee. Levi looked around the camp expecting to see Anna, but she hadn't gotten down from the wagon. He asked Nathan, "Where's Anna? Is she all right?"

"She's in the wagon with Clarissa. A couple of days ago she said she was tired of getting up every morning to make breakfast. I guess today is her day to rebel and she's probably still mad at me for what I said."

"Well, let's have breakfast and get ready to travel. Better think about what you said to Anna."

Nathan hung his head sheepishly. "Yeah, I guess I should apologize."

Levi gave a little whistle to Tucker and said, "Are you hungry?" Tucker barked and moved closer to Levi. Levi yelled at Tom, who was still under the wagon, "Tom, get some bacon from Anna if you have nerve enough to get her up."

The men could hear Anna in the wagon say, "I'll get it. You men will probably drop it in the dirt. Then Tucker will be the only one to eat it. We'll be there in a minute." Levi watched Tom lean-ing against the wagon yawning, arms folded on his chest, waiting for the ladies. Levi poured coffee into two tin cups and walked over to Tom.

"Here's something for you while you wait," Levi grinned and gave a cup to Tom. Tom said, "Thanks," took a sip and said, "Who made the coffee?"

"I confess," answered Levi.

The bonnet opened and Anna stuck her head out and said, "Levi, when you make coffee, put a pinch of salt in it. It'll take out the bitterness." Tom and Levi stepped over to help Anna get down from the wagon, but she lowered Clarissa to their waiting arms first. Levi carried Clarissa on his shoulders to the campfire, reached up and gently lowered her to the ground. Tom helped Anna climb down from the wagon and they joined the others at the fire.

Anna asked, "How are you gentlemen this morning?"

Levi didn't give the others a chance to answer and said, "Tired. Nathan and I are going to spell each other at the reins today. While one of us drives, the other will sleep. Is there enough room in the wagon for one of us and Clarissa to lie down?"

Anna smiled and answered, "Sure. If we have to, we'll make bunk beds. Here's the bacon." She gave a package of bacon to Tom.

Nathan put an arm around Anna's shoulder, looked down at her, and said, "I'm sorry for what I said, Sis."

Anna grinned and replied, "Don't worry, Nathan, we'll prob-ably have a few more words before this journey is over. Traveling like this is not easy on any of us. You men should eat, we've got to pack up and get the wagon rolling."

Clarissa was holding onto Anna's skirt with one hand and rubbing her eyes with her little fist. Everyone had oatmeal, bacon and eggs, and coffee, except Clarissa. Mrs. Wellsandt had given Anna some fresh goat's milk for the four-year old. As they readied the wagon and oxen, Tom announced, "I'll be bedding with the Wellsandts for a time. Wellsandt has one arm in a sling, and his wife can't drive the team. They'll need help until after we cross to the south side of the river. I'll stay with them until we get to Fort

Laramie." After the men shook hands, Tom mounted his horse, tipped his hat to Anna, looked down at Clarissa, said, "See you, little lady," and led his packhorses away from the Cabots' wagon.

Clarissa waved to Tom, ran over to the wagon, and started climbing the front wheel spokes. Levi lifted her into the prairie schooner, secured his horses to the wagon, and climbed in the back. He would sleep while Nathan handled the oxen for a few hours. Anna poured some river water on the fire, stirred the ashes, added more water until the embers were out, and climbed up beside Nathan. They were about two days from Fort Laramie.

# CHAPTER 10

# WAGONS AND A GUN

The sun was overhead when Levi woke up in a sweat, his clothes stuck to his body. Clarissa was looking at him as if she had done something wrong. Levi blinked a couple of times, combed his hair with his fingers, wiped his wet hands on his shirt, and looked at Anna. She was smiling.

"What?" quizzed Levi.

"Oh, nothing. I had Clarissa poke you. You looked as if you were dreaming." She laughed. "I thought it would be safer if Clarissa did it. I didn't want you to be mad at me. It's time to take over. Nathan is falling asleep."

Levi moved behind Anna. Nathan passed the reins to Levi and crawled into the back of the wagon. Levi stepped over the seat and sat beside Anna, his clothes drying quickly in the warm air.

"I was having a dream," Levi announced, grinning.

"What was it about?"

"I was driving a buckboard seated beside a beautiful, curly-haired, blonde woman. We were all dressed up, headed for a church."

"I don't believe you," Anna frowned.

"Well, the woman was wearing a hat made of fruit. Pears, apples, peaches, and cherries were arranged on the hat. It was quite nice." Levi looked at Anna and then laughed. Anna slapped Levi's arm and said, "I didn't know you could be so funny."

"It happens right after I wake up. After I'm awake for a while, I get serious," Levi smiled.

Levi looked back into the wagon. Nathan and Clarissa were both sleeping soundly even though they were being jostled about, the wagon seeming to hit every rut and bump in the trail.

"Those seedlings are really growing. In another month you won't have enough room in the wagon for all your things. Something will have to be thrown out. Have you things you can part with?"

Anna thought for a few seconds and replied, "No. We have few personal possessions. Can we move some items to the outside of the wagon, or maybe get a bigger wagon at Fort Laramie?"

Levi thought for a minute. Anna was looking at him, waiting for a reply. Levi's eyes were apparently scanning, but he wasn't looking at anything. He was constructing something in his mind.

He finally answered, "I have an idea. You can help me when we get to the fort. We're going to build a two-wheeled wagon to pull behind us. As soon as we get to Fort Laramie, we'll find an old wagon that we can rebuild as a cart. Is there a saw in your toolbox?"

"Yes, we have a saw, a hammer, nails, and a can of screws. I'll show you tonight. If we have to, we can purchase some more things at the Fort. I like your idea." Anna smiled, grabbed Levi's arm, and squeezed it.

Nearly two days of traveling over barren countryside with the only water coming from the yellowish Platte made longing for the mountains a prominent thought of nearly everyone on the wagon train. Some of the scouts and Major Langley were the only travelers that knew of the upcoming difficulty of the mountain terrain. The majority of the emigrants had never seen the western mountains, but had heard stories, some unbelievable. They looked forward to trees, shade, and fresh water from mountain streams, but were more concerned with Indians than the mountains. The wagons crossed the Platte in the morning, a half-day before reaching Fort Laramie in the late afternoon.

As the dusty wagons approached the Fort, two uniformed riders came out to meet the emigrants. They talked with the major for about a minute, gesturing to a flat area north of the fort. The major, James and Ron Jeffers, and Lenox showed the drivers where to locate their wagons. A large grassy area for feeding horses, oxen, and the Wellsandts' goat, was nearby, as well as a gently flowing creek that skirted the west side of the fort, emptying into the Platte. The fort had no fortified walls, but was composed of a number of buildings nestled in a fairly flat area surrounded by several irregularly shaped mounds of earth. The fort was not very picturesque; there were few good sized trees, little grass, but lots of dirt, some scrubby trees and bushes, and Clarissa's favorites, some brightly colored wildflowers that added some optimism to the various shades of the brown surroundings.

Anna, Clarissa, and Levi left Nathan and Tucker in charge of the wagon while they entered the Fort to buy items to restock some dwindling supplies. In addition to foodstuffs, Anna purchased several yards of material for Clarissa's new clothes. Clarissa had been wearing the same clothing since the Indians had massacred her parents. While the ladies were shopping, Levi met with the Fort commander, Major William Haliday. Levi climbed a flight of stairs to a balcony and was greeted by a Sergeant.

"Yes Sir?"

"I'm Levi Collins. May I see the major?"

The sergeant turned smartly and knocked once. Levi heard, "Yes?" come from behind the door. The sergeant opened the door and ushered Levi into a smoky room. The major was sitting at a desk in a small office lit by two kerosene lanterns. A small cannonball was atop the desk, apparently being used as a paper weight. He put down his pen and stood when Levi stepped toward his desk, the floor squeaking. The sergeant introduced the two men, they shook hands, and the six-two, gray-haired, somewhat gaunt major motioned for Levi to take a seat. There were two old muskets leaning in the corner behind the desk, and an American flag was tacked to the wall behind the officer.

Major Haliday began the conversation. "Major Langley told me you had a significant role in warding off the Indian attack. You were a Captain in the Union Army?"

"Yes Sir, but that's behind me now."

"I don't believe your wagons will have any more Indian trouble."

"Sir?"

"Word is that the wagon train with the sky wagon should be left alone, attacking it is bad medicine—too many guns."

"The sky wagon, sir?"

The major grinned, "Apparently you have a wagon painted blue."

Levi laughed, "The Cabots' wagon has a blue sideboard. I've been riding with them."

"Well, one of our Indian scouts told us twelve braves attacked the sky wagon to steal the yellow-haired woman for their chief, but all twelve braves were killed. That was good work, Captain."

"The Indians have exaggerated, Major. There were a half-dozen braves, I shot four, and the Cabots got two more with shotguns." Levi laughed. "That must be how tall tales get started."

The major added, "Whatever. The word is out—the Indian express has probably carried the news 300 miles to Fort Hall by now. That's why I don't think you'll have any more trouble. You should have safe passage through the mountains."

"That's good to know, sir. Say, can you tell me where I can find a broken wagon? I'd like to make it into a two-wheeled cart."

"You need to talk with Silas Roebling, but he drives hard bargains. You'll have to watch out for him; he's a pretty shrewd businessman."

"Does he have any weaknesses?"

The major replied immediately, "Guns, and like most men, pretty women."

Levi thought to himself. *I've got both, but only one is negotiable.* "Where can I find Mr. Roebling, sir?"

"He has an office above the livery, four doors down on the right. The sergeant will indicate where to proceed. If you'll excuse me, I have some paperwork to process—reports to Washington."

"Oh, before I go, I need to tell you about a stagecoach massacre. Reverend Nolan and his wife, eight soldiers, and two coachmen were killed. We have the Nolans' little girl, Clarissa, with us. I've drawn a map so you can locate the graves." Levi laid a folded piece of paper on the Major's desk.

"Well, Captain, we have no facilities for a little girl here. She needs a woman to take care of her. I believe it would be better for her to stay with the wagons. If I find out anything about her relatives, I will send a message ahead to Fort Hall or Fort Boise. A telegraph line is being put in to connect forts. Maybe it will be completed before long. I might send a telegram."

Levi stood, thanked the major, and stepped onto the balcony. The sergeant snapped his left hand up from his side and pointed his index finger toward Roebling's office.

Levi looked into the sergeant's eyes and said, "Thank you."

The sergeant responded, "Sir," and saluted. Levi almost returned the salute.

As Levi traversed the balcony, he saw Anna and Clarissa walking across the fort parade ground. Levi whistled to get Anna's attention, did an about-face, walked past the major's office, and descended the stairs to ground level. Clarissa, hugging some green yard goods, and Anna met Levi at the bottom of the stairs.

"Did you find everything you needed at the store?" Levi asked.

"Not everything. We have to get a few more things. Did you have any luck?"

"I'm on my way to see a man, Mr. Roebling, about the wagons. His office is up there." Levi pointed to the balcony. "I'm not sure how long it will take. Can you ladies get back to the wagon without an escort?"

Anna looked at Clarissa and said, "Sure. We're a powerful team, aren't we Clarissa?" Clarissa smiled and nodded.

"Okay. I'll see you back at the wagon."

Levi walked to the far end of the balcony, climbed the stairs, and found Roebling's office. Levi knocked once and heard, "Come in." Roebling stood about five-eight, was about half-bald, wore glasses, and had a gray, well-cropped beard. His office was sparsely furnished with a small table, four chairs—one padded, which he occupied, a bookcase about one-third full with ledgers and a sloppy, dusty, stack of papers, and a kerosene lamp hanging from the ceiling directly over the table. He was standing, playing solitaire.

"Mr. Roebling?"

Roebling looked up between his glasses and his eyebrows. "What can I do for you?"

"Name's Levi Collins. I'm looking to buy a severely damaged covered wagon and a yoke of oxen. Major Haliday said you might help me."

Roebling laughed, dropping his cards on the table. "That's a good one! You want a perfectly good team to drag a broken wagon? You some kind of tenderfoot?"

"No sir. I want to rebuild the wagon into a two-wheeled cart and attach it to a regular wagon. The oxen are needed to pull the extra weight. If you have something I can use, what would it cost?"

Roebling scratched his chin and said, "A hundert-thirty-five bucks."

"That's a little steep, isn't it? A new wagon and a yoke of oxen should be about $160."

"Maybe in St. Louis, but not out here. I get spare parts off damaged wagons left on the trail. Costs me good money to haul them pieces to the fort. I have to make money, you know, I ain't here for my health."

Levi had about ninety dollars left to get him to Fort Boise, and he couldn't ask Cabots for money. They would need every cent they had to get them to their destination. The only other bargaining chips Levi had were a fancy shotgun and his labor, but he needed to see how much damage there was to Roebling's old wagons before he could haggle. Roebling and Levi walked outside the fort to the west where a half-dozen wagons were sheltered under a sloping roof attached to the two-story barracks. Three other broken wagons rested on piles of oxen yokes and damaged wheels.

Levi evaluated the three broken-down wagons while Roebling watched. It only took a minute and Levi made an offer. "I can make a functioning wagon from what you have and I'll throw in a special gun, if you'll let me make a cart from the other two wagons, and include a yoke of oxen. A good wagon and a fancy gun are worth more than a hundred thirty-five bucks. What do you say?"

Roebling frowned and said, "You must have one special firearm, Collins. I'll have to see it before I make a deal like that."

"I'll fetch the gun. I think you'll be surprised. I doubt if there's another like it west of the Missouri. I'll be back in your office in ten minutes."

Levi returned to Roebling's office with the shotgun concealed in a blanket. He didn't want Anna to figure out what he was doing. She would object to him trading his fancy gun for a cart and two oxen in order to haul plants across the western territories. Levi had originally planned to have the gun altered so the barrel would be shorter, but he wanted a first-class gunsmith to do the work. The long-barreled gun was too awkward for fighting, making it only good for hunting. He needed a gun that could be used for both, similar to the gun he had given Nathan. Levi had made up his mind to part with the gun.

Levi laid the wrapped gun on Roebling's table. Roebling began exposing the gun, and as he revealed the stock and finely engraved details on the breech, trigger guard, and barrel, he took a deep breath.

"Holy Christ!" Roebling exclaimed. "This is one beautiful firearm." Roebling picked up the gun as if it were a piece of fine china, not wanting to drop it. "Has it ever been fired?"

"Once, each barrel—killed an Indian, but it's got my name on it. You'll want to take it to St. Louis, Chicago, or San Francisco and get your name put on it."

"No, I like it the way it is. No need to make any changes, it looks more authentic. You've got a deal—any shells to go with it?" Roebling shook hands with Levi and picked up the gun again.

"I've got 98 shells left. I'll deliver them tomorrow, but I need to get busy with those wagons today. Would you agree to that?"

"I'll agree to that. I have a man that can help you, his name is Asa Adams. I'll donate his time."

"Thanks Mr. Roebling, you are a generous man."

Levi was pleased with the results of his trade. He could buy a cheap sawed off shotgun that would be more useful to him than that fancy gun from his brother-in-law. When he had received the gun, Levi felt that Frank was trying to buy his friendship, or trying to prove to Helen that he liked Levi, or both. Levi was sure Frank possessed an ulterior motive. Now that the gun was gone, Levi could at least be grateful to Frank for a gift that he could use to make someone he was fond of happy. Of course, Frank would probably never know the gift had done more than he intended, helping to expand a young industry in Oregon.

# CHAPTER 10

## TOO MUCH SUN

It was about seven o'clock the next morning. The normal chill to the air had already vanished. Following breakfast, everyone was getting ready to carry out their obligations. As the Cabots' wagon crew began dispersing, Levi poured himself another cup of coffee. He shielded his eyes and looked toward the sun. It seemed unseasonably warm and was probably going to be a hot day. He leaned against the wagon and made a mental list of the tools he needed. Levi was to meet Roebling and Asa Adams on the west side of the fort after gathering the tools from the Cabots' wagon. Anna and Clarissa were going to do some more shopping while Levi worked on the cart. Levi went to check the horses, and returned, looking for Anna and Clarissa, but they had apparently gone to the fort.

"Hey Nathan, have you seen the ladies?"

"Yeah, they went to talk to Mrs. Wellsandt about goat's milk."

Levi was about to tell Nathan where he would be for the day, when he saw Anna and Clarissa walking toward the wagon. Levi was holding a blanket he was going to use to carry tools.

"What's the blanket for?" asked Anna.

"I was going to put it on the ground so I would have something to cushion my knees as I work on the cart, but first I'll use it to carry tools."

Anna commented, "I hope you don't have to work too hard today. It's going to be a hot one."

"Well, first I have to fix a wagon for Mr. Roebling. I need to borrow some tools and go to the west side of the fort where the broken wagons are, but I'll have a helper, courtesy of Mr. Roebling. His name is Asa Adams. I haven't met him yet. You can stay here so you won't get dirty."

"Would it be all right for Clarissa and me to visit you—bring you lunch?"

"Sure," Levi answered. "Hey! We'll have a picnic. Bring enough for Mr. Adams, too. I'll have this blanket so we can sit on the ground near the stream."

Anna's face lit up with a big smile. "What a good idea! That should be fun. Clarissa and Tucker can play in the water if it's not too deep." Anna grabbed Clarissa's hand and said, "We're going on a picnic. Won't that be fun? We'll take Tucker and sit by the stream. You can help me make some sandwiches. We'll take some dried fruit, and some pickles, too"

Clarissa's eyes opened wide with excitement. She had heard about picnics, but had never been to one. Her parents had never had time for such foolishness. She didn't know what to say, but she twirled around, clapping her hands, almost falling down.

Levi watched Nathan check over the wagon, making sure the wheels were greased and all the hardware on the tongue and wagon bed was tight. Levi was impressed with Nathan's attention to detail, keeping the wagon in tiptop shape.

"Nathan, can I borrow your hammer, nails and screws, and a saw?"

"Sure, Levi—need some help?"

"Thanks for the offer, but someone has to stay with the wagon. Roebling has loaned me a man for the day. I think we'll be okay. You can inspect the cart for any flaws in construction when I get it finished. You seem to have a keen eye for detail."

Levi gathered the implements he needed from the tool box and placed them on his blanket. After folding the corners of the blanket together, he climbed down from the wagon, and swung his blanket-bag with tools over his shoulder. He smiled at Anna and said, "See you later," and began the walk back to the fort. He hadn't gone more than a few steps when he stopped, gave a short whistle, and Tucker darted out from beneath the wagon to join him. Anna was smiling and waving.

"Did I wake you up?" Levi quizzed Tucker, leaned down to give him a pat, and headed toward the broken wagons. As Levi approached the wagons, he saw a large Negro pulling the damaged wagons away from the barracks' wall. Levi looked at Tucker and said, "That must be Mr. Adams."

Levi dropped the blanket of tools on the ground and stepped over to the big Negro, extending his hand. When Levi saw the Negro's hand, he wondered how much pain the handshake would cause. Levi was relieved when the big hand didn't crush his fingers. The larger man had a gentle, but firm, grip.

"I'm Levi Collins."

"Yessa. Mr. Roebling said he busy. He say you not very big, so I should help. I's Asa, Asa Adams." He smiled, his conspicuous white teeth seeming to divulge cleanliness and reliability.

Levi replied with a serious note, looking Asa in the eyes. "Not very big? I'm bigger than most men, present company excluded."

"Just joshing, Cap'n." Asa laughed. "Want to see you react."

"Tricky, Asa. It's nice to meet you. I'm going to need your help building a wagon and a cart. How'd you know I was a captain?"

"Mr. Roebling tell me. I can help with wagons. Tell me what to do."

In nearly two hours, Levi and Asa had assembled a complete Conestoga wagon except for the bonnet. Levi was standing in the hot sun, admiring the wagon, and said, "Good job, Asa." There was no answer. Levi turned around, but Asa had disappeared. Levi leaned against the barracks' wall in the shade of the eaves for a couple of minutes to take a breather and wipe the sweat from his hat band, when Asa reappeared, carrying a big bundle of white cloth under his left arm. He extended the bundle toward Levi as he approached.

"Bonnet from Mr. Roebling. He got extra. He say he got 'nother, but torn—maybe we can use it on cart."

"Very good. We'll need one about half size for the cart. I think Roebling is a better man than his reputation would lead one to believe."

"He always fair, but businessman," Asa replied with a grin.

"Well, let's get to work on the cart. We'll have to saw one of those broken down wagons in half. Have any good ideas?"

"What this cart look like?"

Levi pulled a piece of paper from his pocket, unfolded it, and smoothed it against the wall.

Asa looked at the crude drawing for a moment, turned, and dragged a wagon bed further away from the wall. Levi was impressed when Asa dragged the wagon effortlessly; the wagon bed weighed several hundred pounds. While Asa began removing the bows on the wagon, Levi picked up a straight piece of lumber and, using a nail, made a scratch in the wood for the length of the cart. Asa held out his hand and Levi gave him the board. Levi watched Asa mark the old wagon, making scratches with a nail where the cuts should be made. Asa put the wagon bows in a neat pile for later reuse.

Levi picked up the saw and began to cut the bottom wagon boards. The oak was extremely hard and Levi's arm was beginning to tire before he had cut across the bottom of the wagon. Just as he was going to rest his arm, he heard Tucker bark. Looking up, Levi saw Clarissa and Anna walking toward the work area. Levi laid the saw on the overturned wagon, checked his watch, and greeted the two ladies. The time was eleven o'clock. Anna was wearing a blue dress with white trim and a wide-brimmed blue hat. She looked as if she were going to church or a Sunday afternoon get together. Clarissa wore a similar dress made from green material. Anna carried a basket, which Tucker was sniffing, his tail wagging.

"Is it time for the picnic?"

Anna replied, smiling, "If you have the time, we have the food."

Asa had picked up the saw and was continuing the cut Levi had started. Levi raised his voice so Asa could hear over the noise from the saw. "Come on Asa, we've got something to eat. We're going to sit beside the stream."

Asa stopped sawing and replied, "You go. I finish cutting wagon first, will be hungry after." His big smile exposed his bright white teeth.

"Okay. Join us as soon as you're finished."

"Yessa."

Anna, Clarissa, Levi, and Tucker made their way about thirty yards to a grassy area beneath a large cottonwood on the stream bank. Levi laid out the blanket in the shade under the isolated tree after kicking some stones out of the way. Levi had to tell Tucker to lie down on the blanket, the setter wanted more stones to be kicked so he could chase after them.

Anna opened the basket and handed out sandwiches. She looked back at the barracks and could see a large Negro walking toward them. When Asa arrived at the blanket, Anna stood up and said, "I'm Annabel Cabot, Levi's friend. This is Clarissa. She was rescued from an Indian attack on a stagecoach. Please sit down and have something to eat. I made some sandwiches, and I brought some dried fruit and pickles. Help yourself to anything you like."

"Miss Cabot, Clarissa, happy to meet you ladies."

Clarissa had never seen a Negro before, and she was staring at the big man. Asa noticed her intent look and said, "Bad sunburn, Miss Clarissa, pickin' cotton," and smiled, showing his rack of white teeth. Clarissa accepted what Asa said as a matter of fact, took another bite of her sandwich, and asked Anna, "Can I have a pickle?"

Anna corrected her, "May I have a pickle?"

Clarissa nodded and said, "Yes."

Anna laughed, gave Clarissa a pickle, and asked, "Where are you from, Mr. Adams?"

"Asa, ma'am. Cotton Bend, Alabam. You?"

"Fisherton, Ohio, Asa. It's a small town near Columbus. Levi is from Pittsburgh, Pennsylvania. He grew up on a farm." Anna looked at Levi and then back at Asa. "I don't know if he told you that."

"Same as me, but on plantation. Picked lots of cotton 'til ran away—New York. Miss Musgrave taught me to cook. I cook most anything, real good," he beamed.

Levi was holding the sandwich Anna had handed him, but hadn't taken a bite. He felt a bit peculiar, as if his mind had left his body and was looking down at the picnic area from above the tree.

Anna was watching Levi, wondering what he was thinking about. His eyes looked dull and he appeared to be staring ahead, but at nothing in particular.

"Levi?"

There was no response, so Anna touched Levi's shoulder and said, "Levi, are you all right?"

Levi looked at Anna with a blank stare, but didn't say anything. "I think something is wrong, Asa. Levi is never like this."

"I know what's wrong."

Asa got up and ran to the wagon area, grabbed a canteen, and returned to the picnic blanket. He pulled the cork from the canteen and gave it to Anna.

"He needs water. Too much sun."

Anna held the canteen to Levi's lips and poured water into Levi's mouth. Levi swallowed several times, and then choked, spraying water all over Anna's dress and his shirt. She kept pouring water into Levi, more slowly this time, and Levi kept swallowing. Anna felt Levi's forehead, it was hot and dry. Asa had been right, Levi was suffering from sunstroke. He needed some salt, too.

"Clarissa, get me a pickle for Levi."

Asa opened the container for Clarissa, and she extracted a large dripping pickle which she handed to Anna and wiped her wet fingers on her dress. Anna held the pickle to Levi's mouth and said, "Take a bite, chew it, and swallow. You need some salt and more water. Asa, please hand me the pickle container. Anna held the jar to Levi's mouth, tilted it, and poured some of the juice into Levi's mouth. Levi made a face, but swallowed and coughed, then reached for the canteen for a drink of water.

Levi looked at Anna and said, "What's going on?" He looked at his shirt, which was wet from water and pickle juice, and noticed Anna's dress was wet. "How did we get wet? Did Clarissa fall in the stream?"

"No Levi, you had too much sun. Asa and I have been giving you water and salt, in the form of pickle juice. We spilled some on you, and you coughed some water on me. I think you'll be all right now. You have to stay out of the sun and rest for a while. Give me your shirt. I'll wash it in the stream, the water is pretty clear. You can put it on wet, and it will help you cool down."

Anna helped Levi remove his shirt, exposing his muscular, somewhat hairy chest. Anna tried not to stare, but she admired his physique, much more developed than Nathan's. She took his shirt to the water and returned in a few minutes, the shirt dripping wet.

Levi put his shirt back on, but didn't button it. He picked up the sandwich from the blanket and took a bite, and then said to Anna, "I'm sorry I didn't introduce you to Asa. Things weren't right in my head, but I think I'm okay now. I was having a dream, seeing things from up in the sky. I hope that doesn't happen again, it was very strange. I'll have to drink more water on hot days like today...must remember to carry my canteen."

# CHAPTER 11

## CART AND SOUL

The picnickers spent another half-hour talking, eating, and drinking water. Anna was nearly force- feeding Levi with pickles and water. When Anna tried to get Levi to eat a fourth pickle, he refused, saying if he ate another one, he would throw up, but he thanked her for her concern. Clarissa and Tucker were playing fetch along the bank of the stream. When Clarissa threw pieces of dried branches into the water, Tucker would jump into the stream and return with the sticks, shaking his body, spraying water everywhere. Clarissa would run away from Tucker, laughing, trying to avoid the showers. After tiring of the fetch game, Clarissa picked a few wildflowers and presented them to Anna. Anna put a few of the flowers in Clarissa's hair and placed the others in the picnic basket.

The ladies walked back to the damaged wagons with the men and said goodbye. Levi sent Tucker with them for protection on their return trip to the encampment.

Asa had done a first-rate job of cutting the wagon in two, and the two men put a back end on the cart. Levi decided to remove the front axle and replace it with a rear axle with larger wheels, but only one wheel was available. The other wheels available were too small or broken, beyond repair.

"We've got to find another wheel, Asa. Are there any more broken wagons around?"

"Not in the fort, but some a little ride away."

Levi considered their options. They would need a wagon to tote a wheel. It would be too awkward to carry one on a horse, the load would be too difficult to balance, but Bravo and one of the pack horses could pull the wagon they had repaired.

"Okay. I'll get two horses and we'll take the wagon we fixed. How far will we have to go?"

"Not sure, Cap'n. Three places not very far, but we need to measure the wheel."

"I'll get some string, too. Take a load off in the shade. I'll be back in about ten minutes."

Levi disappeared around the berms outside the fort, and returned with a full canteen, two horses, Tucker, and a ball of string. Asa was singing an old song he'd learned as a young man on the plantation when picking cotton. Asa hitched up the horses, and Levi used the string to measure the wheel, knotting the string to indicate the wheel's circumference. The two men climbed in the driver's seat, Tucker jumped into the wagon, and they were off with Asa at the reins.

"What were you singing, Asa?"

"Old pickin' song mama taught us in the fields."

"Where are your parents?"

"They dead."

"Sorry to hear that. How'd they die?"

"Daddy got hung for somethin' he done, and mama got shot trying to help. I wasn't very old—'bout six or seven, but I was good size. I didn't know. They just never got home one night. Mama's friend, Miss Kindle, raise me. She raise five children."

"So how old are you?"

"Can't rightly say, 27 or so, I think. Celebrate at Christmas. Jesus and me have same birthday." Asa smiled and yelled, "Giddy up!" The horses picked up the pace, and after riding south a couple of minutes out of sight of the fort, they followed some deep ruts and spotted two wrecked wagons about 20 yards apart. There were only three wheels, and two of them were severely damaged. For some reason, the third wheel looked too small, but Levi measured it anyway. He had Asa hold the string on the rim and the knot was about half an inch short of completing the circle.

"Close enough, Asa. This one will work. We'll have to remove the broken piece of axle back at the fort. Let's load up." Levi grabbed one edge of the wheel, expecting Asa to grab the opposite edge, but Asa said, "Let me." Levi was a little reluctant to release his grip, but did. Asa picked up the wheel, and swung it into the wagon in one easy motion. Levi saw firsthand how powerful a man Asa was. A normal man of better than average strength would have had trouble getting the wheel in the wagon by himself.

Levi said, "I don't know what you've been eating, but I could sure use some of it." He grinned at Asa, and Asa grinned back, showing his white teeth. "Let's get back to the fort. We'll get this wheel mounted, attach the tongue, and we'll have the cart completed." Levi climbed into the wagon with Asa, grabbed the reins, and began following the wagon tracks back to the fort. They had gone about a quarter mile when two riders appeared, moving slowly toward the wagon along the tracks from the fort. As they got closer, Asa said, "Strangers," but Levi recognized the men.

Levi stopped the wagon and waited for Billy and Wade Dendricks to get close enough to converse. Levi asked, "You boys out for a ride?"

Wade spoke up, "No. We come out to get that there wheel. It's ours. We're sellin' it to Mr. Roebling."

Levi replied, "I don't think so. Asa and I have the right of possession. There aren't any markings on it to indicate it's yours. I doubt you even knew it was out here."

Billy and Wade had their rifles across their saddles, ready to swing into action. Wade said, after patting his gun, "These make that wheel belong to us. You give us the wheel, and the wagon, or you're both dead. We'll leave you out here to rot. Where'd you find that Negra, under a rock? We'll shoot him first, he ain't worth a damn. Ain't that right, Billy?"

"Damn right," Billy grinned.

Levi parted his lips, and with his teeth clenched, whispered to Asa, "I've got a knife in my belt behind my back, when I yell for the horses to go, grab the knife, and dive from the wagon. I hope you can use the knife."

Levi commented, "Look fellas, if you're so intent on having this wheel, you can have it and the wagon. We'll walk back to the fort."

Wade said, "No siree, Captain, you're a dead man and that thing sittin' beside you is dead too."

Billy impatiently said, "Come on, Wade, let's get this over with. The Negra's probly a runaway, the Yankee ain't worth a buffalo chip, and let's kill that damn dog."

Wade started to lift his rifle, but glanced at Billy, grinning. Levi noticed the chance and yelled, "Giddy up!" As the wagon jerked and rolled forward between the horsemen, Levi leaped off the wagon on the right side, and Asa tumbled off on the left. Wade got off a shot at Levi, but Levi hit the ground and rolled, drawing his handgun as he turned over on the ground. Levi fired once and knocked Wade off his horse, and shot again at the body on the ground to make sure Wade didn't shoot again. Asa had avoided a shot from Billy, and had thrown Levi's knife accurately, the sharp blade slicing through Billy's neck. The brothers were both sprawled on the ground, gasping, dying. Levi whistled twice and the wagon slowed to a stop about 50 yards away. Tucker jumped from the wagon and came back to sniff the bodies.

Levi limped over to Wade, picked up the rifle, and then Billy's gun saying, "Damn, Wade got me in the leg, Asa. Tear off Billy's shirt and wrap my leg, he got me good." Levi looked at his right leg and could see blood oozing from his pants, running down toward his boot. Levi watched Asa pull the knife from Billy's throat, cut off the dead man's shirt, and fold it into a bandage. Asa tied the bandage around Levi's thigh, and lifted the smaller man into the wagon.

"Better tie those horses to the wagon, and throw the bodies in here with me. Let's get back to the fort before I bleed to death. Take me to the Army surgeon, he'll patch me up. Damn, three years of war and nothing but a scratch, now I catch a bullet while hauling a wheel."

In about two minutes the wagon was rolling as fast as possible, considering the rough terrain. Levi felt every bump of the fast moving wagon, and was drinking from his canteen all the way to the fort.

Asa stopped the wagon in front of the Army hospital, called for an orderly, and dumped the dead men on the ground. When the orderly exited the hospital door, he stopped and looked at the bodies. Asa yelled, "They's dead, this man needs help." Asa was already carrying Levi from the wagon and the orderly helped get them through the door into the operating area.

Captain Jervais, the Army surgeon, said, "What have we got here?" He looked at Levi's bandaged thigh and said, "Cut this man's pants off, get me some alcohol, clean rags, boiling water, and some sutures." The orderly was moving too slowly, so Asa pushed him out of the way, and used Levi's knife to cut away Levi's right pants leg. The blood soaking into the fabric had made the wound appear much worse than it really was. There was an entrance wound on the inside of Levi's right thigh and an exit wound in the back of his thigh near his right buttock, but the bullet had missed an artery and just nicked his hamstring. Fortunately, the doctor wouldn't have to probe for the bullet. The doctor cleansed the area and spoke to Levi, "This is going to hurt like hell, so drink some whiskey, and bite down on this piece of leather. When I put alcohol on the wound, it will sting and burn. I'm going to have your friend hold you down when I use the needle."

Levi took a couple of swallows from the bottle and said, "Okay." Levi was already in pain, so he didn't care what the doctor did, he figured the pain couldn't get much worse, but he was wrong. When the alcohol hit the torn flesh, Levi tried to move his leg away, but Asa held him fast. There were times during the next few minutes Levi nearly passed out, but he could still hear the soulful sounds of Asa's singing. He closed his eyes and bit down hard on the leather.

"There! It's all over," commented the doctor. "You were damn lucky, son. You almost lost your family jewels. We need to get you a clean pair of pants—and you won't be riding a horse for at least a week, maybe longer. You need to change those bandages twice a day until the seepage stops. Clean the area with whiskey a couple of times a day, at least when you change the dressings. I hope you have someone to help you."

Levi was thinking that Anna would help him, but he realized the wound was in a position that would make treatment from Anna a little embarrassing for both of them. However, Nathan could help him change the dressings.

Asa commented, "I can do it. Mind I join the train, Mr. Levi?"

"I don't mind, if you want to leave your job here at the fort. You can take over Dendricks' gear, they can't use anything where they've gone, it's too hot."

"Good. I get back pay from Mr. Roebling. Now I take you to Cabots' wagon and finish the cart."

Levi smiled, and then grimaced from the pain when he tried to move. "I'd appreciate your help. I've been meaning to ask you, where'd you learn to handle a knife like that?"

"New York. Lived in bad part of city, lots of fights. Man tried to stab me, so I killed him instead. After, I run off to go west."

"You always hit what you aim at with the knife?"

Asa smiled, "No. I aim at his heart." He pointed at the center of his chest and grinned.

"Well, Asa, you missed good."

# CHAPTER 12

# LEVI IS FORCED TO REST

Asa carried Levi to the wagon and drove slowly to the encampment. Levi pointed to the Cabots' wagon where Anna and Nathan were busily adjusting the contents, trying to provide more room for sleeping. The cart was going to provide needed space for plants and supplies. Tucker sat watching Clarissa's every motion as she watered some of the plants that had been moved from the wagon to the ground. Anna waved as Asa pulled the horse-driven wagon alongside the Cabots' Conestoga. Levi struggled to his feet holding onto the driver's seat. Anna couldn't help noticing his bare leg and the large white bandage.

"Levi! You're hurt! What in God's name happened? Did you have an accident while working on the cart?"

"No accident, Anna, I was shot."

"What happened? Who shot you?"

"Wade Dendricks. He's dead, and so is his good-for-nothing brother. They were going to kill Asa, Tucker, and me. We had no choice. Do you mind if Asa travels with us? He'll be a big help, The Army doctor told me not to ride for at least a week, maybe longer. Hey Nathan, can you help me off the wagon so Asa can continue working on the cart?"

Nathan and Asa carried Levi to the campfire area, and Asa drove off with the wheel to complete construction of the cart. Anna retrieved some pillows and a blanket from the wagon and fashioned a resting spot. When Levi was comfortable, he explained what had happened.

Anna listened intently and then remarked, "I don't mind having Asa with us. He is a very nice, hardworking young man. So the Dendricks were going to shoot you over a wheel? I thought they were nice when you met. They turned out to be sore losers."

Levi said, "I think they were ignorant opportunists with a chip on their shoulders. Do you know where the Dendricks were bedding down? Asa needs to recover their belongings. He can put their equipment and food to good use, but their clothes will be too small. I doubt Asa has enough money to buy his own outfit. We'll have six more horses, so maybe he can sell three of them to Roebling or the Army. Roebling might want some of their guns, too. Then Asa will have enough money to buy some things."

"I'll ask around. I'll check with Mrs. Wellsandt; she knows more people than I do. The Major will know for sure. I'll tell him what happened to the Dendricks."

"All right, but if you go very far, take Tucker with you, or wait until Asa returns with the cart so he can accompany you. That might be awhile, though. Ah—I need another pair of pants. Could you please bring me my big sack from under the wagon?"

Anna retrieved the bag containing Levi's clothing and pulled out a pair of pants. "Will these be all right?" She held up a pair of wrinkled dark brown trousers.

"Sure, those will do. Thank you."

She handed the pants to Levi and he sat there looking at her.

"Can I help you?" she asked.

"Got another blanket so I can have some privacy?"

"Oh! Sure." Anna walked over to the wagon, reached in and came back with another blanket. "Did the bullet strike anything important?"

Levi knew what Anna had in mind, but he decided to tease. "It did, it went into my leg and came out by my rear end."

"But I mean *really* important."

"My leg's really important to me."

"Levi! Don't you know what I mean?"

Levi frowned and continued the dumb act. "I guess I don't know what you're talking about."

Anna was becoming more frustrated and blurted out, "I mean your privates!"

Levi couldn't hold back any longer and broke out laughing. "I knew what you meant. My privates are just fine. I was teasing. Don't you think it's funny?"

Anna pouted for a second and then broke out laughing. "I think you're just a little crazy, teasing me like that. For a minute, I thought you were just dumb." She sat down on the blanket covering his legs so he couldn't change his pants. Levi reached over to Anna and tried unsuccessfully to pinch her. She escaped, laughing. She stood over Levi, watching him struggle removing his old pants, saying several times, "Need any help?" Each time, she laughed. After Levi had pulled on his clean pants and buttoned them, Anna pulled the blanket away, folded it, and put it back in the wagon. She returned to Levi, sat down beside him and kissed his cheek. "Does it hurt?"

Levi smiled, "Does what hurt?"

Anna laughed, "Not again!"

Levi smiled. "Yeah, it hurts, but not as much as putting whiskey on it. It should feel better tomorrow. Oh, you can burn those old pants, unless you know a one-legged man."

Anna said, "I'm going to talk to Mrs. Wellsandt. I'll be right back. Don't run off." She stuck out her tongue and laughed. She snapped her fingers, said, "Come," and Tucker followed her as she hurried off between the wagons. Nathan and Clarissa had finished watering the plants and were wrapping them to help retain moisture.

Levi heard horses approaching and looked away from the wagon to see his horses pulling the cart with Asa walking alongside. Asa hadn't gotten the bonnet on the wagon, but had made a temporary harness from ropes so the horses could pull the cart the short distance from the assembly area to the encampment. Asa had reasoned Nathan and Anna could help him with the wagon cover. Anna could sew up part of the torn bonnet better than he could, after it was adjusted to fit the cart.

Asa untied the horses from the cart and returned them to the pasture area where the oxen and Bravo were munching on grass. He returned to Cabots' wagon and knelt beside Levi.

"Cart works good. Wheels roll straight. We need a hitch for the wagon to pull cart. I 'll get oxen tomorrow from Mr. Roebling."

"Good job, Asa. I have an idea for a hitch. Perhaps you can make it tomorrow. Anna said you can travel with us."

"What did Mr. Nathan say?"

Levi grinned, "He has no choice, but I don't think he'll mind. We'll have one more person to help with the chores."

"You like Anna. You like Clarissa. They like you. Would make a good family."

"You're a smart man, Asa. Don't say anything, but I hope at Christmas we'll make some plans for the future, but there are too many variables right now."

Asa smiled. "I can keep a secret."

Levi sketched what he was envisioning as a hitch for the cart to attach to the pulling wagon. Asa watched and asked questions as Levi drew the apparatus. As the two men discussed building the hitch, Anna returned, walking alongside Major Langley, who was leading his horse. Tucker found Clarissa and they began to play.

The major was introduced to Asa and he sat down beside Levi. "Sorry to hear you got shot, Levi. Anna told me what happened. The Dendricks surprised me, although Wade had an argument with Mr. Jackson about a week ago. I was notified by Major Haliday's office clerk about the two bodies at the Army Hospital. He wanted to know what to do with the corpses. I told him to bury them without any fanfare. I've been telling Anna the standard procedure for distribution of possessions of the deceased. Since we have a man joining the wagon train, and he will need some things, he will be allowed to have three horses. Asa will be allocated half of the Dendricks' food and other supplies. The remaining things will be equally distributed throughout the wagons. Their other three horses will be sold and the money will be distributed equally, probably only a few dollars for each wagon, but every bit helps. Their possessions are being gathered at the Jacksons' wagon. Anna knows where it is—Mrs. Wellsandt gave Anna directions. You should go there in the morning and retrieve the things you're entitled to. That's about it. Any questions?"

Levi asked, "What about their guns? Asa could use some weapons."

"Major Haliday has their rifles. Asa can have one of them. We'll have to check their gear to see if they had side arms and knives. Asa can have one of each."

"Okay. That sounds fair. Thank you, Major."

# CHAPTER 13

# BACK ON THE TRAIL

Anna, Nathan, and Asa hitched horses to the cart, went to the Jacksons' wagon, and loaded what the major had said they could have from the Dendricks' belongings. Nathan went to the store at the fort and bought a pint of whiskey for Levi before returning to camp. Anna and Asa had returned after about an hour and emptied the cart so Asa could get a hitch fashioned by the blacksmith at the fort. Asa took the cart into the fort and showed Levi's drawing to the smithy. While the metal coupling for the cart tongue was being fashioned, Asa got the yoke of oxen and his back pay from Roebling. Asa paid the blacksmith and drove the cart to the west side of the fort and reattached the bows, which had been removed when the wagon was cut in half. Then, Asa returned to the camp to reinforce the rear floor of the wagon so a U-shaped bolt could be installed to complete the hitch mechanism.

Earlier, after the other adults had left camp, Levi sat with Clarissa and told her a story about a baby bear and an owl, lost for a time in the forest, but the two animals were saved from danger by a small pioneer girl. The story had unforeseen consequences—Clarissa asked so many questions, Levi's imagination was becoming exhausted. Anna's return to camp rescued Levi, and allowed him to get more rest. Clarissa and Anna removed the remaining supplies from the wagon so Asa could install the bolt in the floor. After the work on the wagon was completed, the wagon and cart were coupled and packed for travelling. Now, there was plenty of room for sleeping in the wagon, only a small quantity of supplies had to be removed at night, to be repacked the next morning.

After the old bonnet was stretched over the bows, Asa cut off the extra loose material and gave it to Anna for use as patches. Anna hadn't had time to work on the bonnet, so Asa had done the best he could. He was a good cook, but readily admitted he couldn't sew worth a darn. Levi lounged on the blanket all day, sleeping most of the time with Tucker beside him. Levi would occasionally awaken, watch the activities around the camp, and drift off to sleep again. Late in the afternoon, Anna sat beside Levi watching him sleep. Clarissa and Tucker had been playing near the wagon and they joined Anna.

Anna looked at Clarissa, put her finger to her lips and whispered, "Be real quiet, we don't want to wake Levi; he needs to sleep so he will get better."

"I heard that!" Levi opened his eyes, sat up, and pushed his hat back on his head. Clarissa stepped back, surprised.

Anna said, "I thought you were asleep."

"How could I sleep with you breathing so heavily," he grinned. "I'll bet you snore loudly, too."

Anna replied, laughing, "You'll never know. Do you want something to eat? We all had sandwiches a couple of hours ago. I was thinking we'd have an early dinner and go to bed. We have to get up early tomorrow to get back on the trail."

"I can wait for dinner, but thank you for asking. Say, I hear chickens. Did our neighbors let their hens loose? I've been looking around, but I don't see any chickens."

"Those are our chickens. Asa got them. We have a chicken coop on the other side of the cart. We'll have some fresh eggs, and Asa needed eggs for cookies and other recipes. We can't always get eggs from Mrs. Wellsandt."

Levi smiled and replied, "I'm sure glad I hired him."

Anna shook her head, smiled, and replied, "You're impossible!"

Nathan came over to Levi and asked, "Want to change those bandages? We can do it under the wagon. We'll drape some blankets over the wheels so nobody will see your naked butt."

"Sounds good, but you'll have to help me up. I've been on the ground all day—could have a hard time standing—balance might be off, and my leg is stiff and sore."

Nathan helped Levi to his feet and over to the wagon. Levi gingerly got to the ground, crawled between the back wheels which were draped with blankets, and Nathan applied new bandages after cleaning the wounds with warm soapy water and whiskey. After the bandage was applied and Levi had pulled up his pants, Nathan held out the whiskey bottle and said, "Want a sip?"

Levi responded, "Sure, as long as it's medicinal. I'm not much of a drinker. I like to have a clear head."

"Same here, but after seeing those wounds, I think I'll take a sip, too. Remind me to never get shot," Nathan chuckled, "especially not in the butt."

Levi took a little drink and handed the bottle to Nathan. Nathan took more than a sip, coughed, replaced the cork, and crawled out from under the wagon. With Nathan's assistance, Levi limped back to the campfire. Gaining his equilibrium, he folded his blankets, carried them to the wagon, and laid them on the driver's seat. Although he was slightly dizzy, he felt his activity around the campsite had contributed to his well-being. He tossed the old, blood-stained bandages on the fire and watched them burn. Levi wondered how many times this procedure would reoccur before he could ride again. However, there was a benefit from being shot; he would be riding in the wagon with Anna when she wasn't walking.

The morning activity in the fort signaled the emigrants to rise and get trail-ready. Anna looked at the little clock hanging from one of the wagon bows near her face. There was just enough light to see it was a few minutes after five o'clock. She put on a jacket, got down to the ground, and kicked a boot sticking out from under the wagon, assuming it was Nathan's.

"Hey, time to get up, Nathan."

Nathan groaned and said, "All right, I'm awake."

Anna turned around and saw Asa lighting the kindling for the campfire. She walked over to where Levi had been sleeping and said, "Good morning, gentlemen."

Levi and Nathan both said, "Good morning." Asa had gotten the fire going and followed with, "I'll take over today, Miss Anna."

"Oh, thank you, Asa. I'll get Clarissa up so we can repack the wagon. No one will have to wait for us today. As soon as you're up, Levi, bring me the pillows and extra blankets."

"Okay. I'll walk off some of the stiffness and be right there."

Everyone heard a trumpet at 7:00 a.m. signaling the wagons to get moving. The hustle and bustle of the wagons moving out were pleasing sounds, the string of wagons was going westward again. More new experiences, including climbing mountains, were in everyone's thoughts. It took nearly a half-hour for all the wagons to get back on the trail. The Cabots' wagon was near the middle of the train, the six oxen having no difficulty pulling the wagon and trailing cart. Asa walked alongside the cart watching the hitch to make sure it was working properly. Tucker seemed to be enjoying the movement of the wagons, animals, and humanity. He would dart in and out from under the wagon and cart, occasionally running ahead for a few minutes and then returning, tail wagging. Tucker had apparently stored up considerable energy while inactive at the encampment.

By eight-thirty, the wagons were crossing the Platte to the north side. The wagons travelled northwest for the remainder of the day, never straying far from the river. According to the major, the pioneers had travelled a little more than 20 miles when they stopped and set up camp for the night. Levi had slept during the day, but he was awakened repeatedly from the noise and bumping of the wagon and cart. Conversation was difficult because of the noise. He had a question to ask Anna and Nathan, but it would have to wait until evening. Asa walked most of the day, but in the middle of the afternoon, climbed on one of his horses and rode up and down the length of the string of wagons. Late that afternoon, Nathan and Asa checked and fed the oxen, horses, chickens, and Tucker. Anna and Clarissa started a fire for cooking dinner after collecting enough buffalo chips to fill a large burlap bag. Asa and Anna combined talents to prepare the evening meal. After dinner, beds were prepared, Clarissa fell asleep quickly, and the adults sat around the fire discussing the day's activities.

The snap and crackle of the fire were the only noises besides the human voices and the occasional moos of cattle. When there was a lull in the conversation, Levi finally asked his question.

"Anna, tell us about your parents. Are they still alive?"

"Our mother, Susan, died of cholera somewhere between Fort Kearney and Fort Laramie and was buried along the trail. When we came on this journey, I wanted to watch for her grave, but we have been on the north side of the river. She was buried on the south side. Our father, Leland, sent us a letter from Fort Hall notifying us of her death. He was continuing on to Oregon to start an orchard, but we never heard if he ever reached Oregon. We don't know if he is alive."

"When did your mother pass?"

"That was eighteen years ago, when Nathan and I were five and eleven years old. They had gone west and were going to have us come out to Oregon when we were old enough to make the trip, but it never happened until now. We were raised by our aunt and uncle, Jennifer and George Cabot. After Nathan and I both had jobs, our aunt and uncle went to Oregon and started farming. Uncle George is going to meet us in Boise and take us to the farm in Oregon where we can start an orchard. Aunt Jennifer had to go to Connecticut to care for her mother."

"Well, from what I have seen of graves along the trail, you probably wouldn't have found your mother's resting place. Most of the grave markers have been lost to the elements, or theft to make markers for other, more recent deaths, and some were probably used for campfires. So, don't feel bad about not being able to find your mother's marker."

Anna replied, "I hadn't thought about all that. Thank you for telling us that."

"Say, how old would your father be now?"

"He was thirty-three when they left for Oregon, so he would be 50 now—if he's alive. Maybe we can ask around when we get to Fort Boise. Maybe someone knows something about him, but I don't think the chances would be very great."

"We can always try, and hope for the best. Think of how it would be for your father to see you both now, all grown up."

Anna responded, "Yes," with tears in her eyes. "It would be wonderful to see him again after all these years. I don't think we would recognize him, but he has a reddish birthmark on his left ear."

Levi commented, "I'm sure he wouldn't recognize either of you."

"Oh! I just remembered something. Mother had a little locket with our pictures in it. Maybe father took it when she died."

# CHAPTER 14

## SNAKES

For two full days, the wagon train moved slowly northwest and then turned directly west, having skirted the northernmost waters of the North Platte. Levi had been bored to death being confined to the wagon, except for resting stops, meals, and of course sleeping on the ground at night. Two more days of traveling directly west through somewhat hilly country hadn't been quite as bad as the previous two days. Anna had unpacked and given Levi a copy of *The Farmer's Almanac*, which he read when he wasn't telling Clarissa stories, or answering her seemingly never ending questions. It wasn't that her questions were annoying; they made him realize how much he didn't know. However, in some cases, Levi had found the answers in the almanac.

Levi had been mulling things over while riding in the wagon. He decided he had been too cavalier with Anna, and perhaps he should apologize, but deep down he thought he hadn't gone too far. He wished he had known about the loss of her mother and father sooner, but it was his fault; he could have asked about her parents long ago. She had not volunteered the information, so perhaps she had been sensitive for nearly two decades about their vanishing. Nathan and Anna knew their mother was dead, but they still had hopes of finding their father alive. Levi had seen the tears in Anna's eyes when she talked of him. When Anna was eleven, she must have had a strong relationship with her father. He must have been a take-charge type of man, much like himself. Maybe that explained Anna's interest. It might not be romantic, but Anna had kissed him, suggesting she wanted him to show up for Christmas. Whatever the case, Levi decided to temper the teasing and be more serious with Anna.

The next day, the wagons passed through Emigrant Gap after making a gradual climb to the southwest. As they passed through the gap, the major informed everyone there was to be a meeting that evening. The wagons stopped and camp was established in the late afternoon. The animals were fed before anything else was done. The oxen deserved a rest after the climb through the gap and winding through the hills. Only about twelve miles had been covered instead of the usual 20 or so. When the relatively early meal was completed, the travelers gathered in the center of the wagons.

Major Langley made an announcement. "South Pass is two weeks away, maybe longer if we have rain. We will be seeing higher mountains around us, and we will be moving along the Sweetwater River. The river winds around and if we follow the river closely, we will have to travel much farther than necessary, so we will cross the river several times before we reach South Pass. There shouldn't be any problems, the crossings are straight forward. Be cautious, but don't be afraid. In some places, your wagons might float, don't be alarmed—just keep moving forward. Men on horseback will assist you if you lose control. We will be passing through rattlesnake country in the next few days before we get to the Sweetwater River. We'll pass Devil's Gate when we near the river."

A murmur ran through the settlers when the major mentioned rattlesnakes; they hadn't been a problem, but they hadn't seen many. Major Langley waited for the talking to cease and continued on. "I will need a rider on a sure-footed horse to patrol one side of the wagons to watch for snakes. The wagons might disturb some of the snakes and they will try to get out of the way. In case they get mad, they might strike anyone walking, so be on the lookout for snakes. Levi, can you ride yet?"

"Not without a big pillow, Major." Everyone gave a hearty laugh and the major smiled. "I'll be riding again about the time we reach the Sweetwater. I've been limbering up my leg some, but I don't want to start leaking where I'm not supposed to." The crowd laughed again.

The major continued, "Well, I need a rider that's a good shot with a hand gun to take care of any troublesome rattlers."

Asa volunteered, "I'll do it."

"Who said that?"

"Me, Asa Adams." Asa stepped out from beside Anna and Nathan.

The major explained, "Folks, this here's Asa Adams. He's with the Cabots and Captain Collins. He's a good man. We can depend on him. Okay, Asa. Tomorrow you'll ride on the left side of the wagons. Make sure you shoot away from the wagons so no one catches a ricochet. It's best not to kill our friends, just the snakes." Everyone laughed again. "One of my men will patrol the right side. Any questions?"

There was no response, so the major said, "Okay, that's all I have to say. Have a good evening. See you in the morning."

After breakfast the next morning, Asa saddled one of his pack horses named Grits, checked his sidearm, swung into his saddle, and rode to the wagon that was going to lead the train. As the wagons pulled out, Asa rode beside the front wagon for a few minutes and then drifted back about five wagons, swung out about ten yards and rode slowly back to the first wagon, and then rode ahead to talk with the major.

"Major, where best to ride?"

"The first few wagons will stir up the snakes, and they'll try to get out of the way. Start back about wagon four or five and keep a watch out. Drift back and forth a few wagons. If they're coiled up, they're ready to strike, but if they're moving away, let them go. Shoot the ones coiled up."

"Yessa. I can do that."

Asa turned and rode back to the fourth wagon, turned around, and began an intense watch for snakes. He hadn't noticed the next wagon back was Cabots'. He slowed his horse and let two or three wagons pass and then gradually returned to his original position. As he passed the Cabots' wagon, Clarissa yelled, "Hello Mr. Asa!" Asa looked to see where the voice had come from, saw Nathan and Anna and a small hand sticking up from below the seat. He waved his hat briefly but refocused his eyes on the ground and saw Tucker stopped and barking. Then he saw it, the biggest snake he had ever seen in his life, coiled and ready to strike, its rattle pointing up from the ground. Asa didn't have time to think—drawing his gun was automatic. He fired two bullets, the first missed, but the second hit the snake in the head. It rolled over and over, writhing on the ground with Tucker still barking at it. Asa dismounted, pulled out his knife and cut off the snake's head, throwing it as far away from the wagons as he could. Tucker started to chase the head, but Asa whistled and said, "No!" Tucker ran back to the Cabots' wagon and disappeared underneath. Asa picked up the snake, placed it in a small burlap sack, and stuffed the sack in one of his saddlebags.

Fortunately, when Asa was placing the snake's body in his saddlebag, the Cabots' wagon had passed him, so Clarissa, Anna, and Nathan hadn't seen what he had done, but he wasn't worried about what Levi would have thought. Asa suspected Levi had tasted snake meat before. Asa had watched the wagon to make sure his actions hadn't generated any questions. He wondered if the others were as tired of buffalo meat as he was. That big snake contained a significant amount of meat, but how was he going to cook it? Maybe he would make a stew. Miss Musgrave had never mentioned how to cook a snake. Asa was going to have to try out some methods. He and Tucker would taste and adjust. Asa saw several other snakes that day, but they were too far away to cause trouble.

The wagons were gradually moving to higher elevations as they progressed toward the Sweetwater, taking a sinuous path around hills to avoid climbing and descending. Asa had attempted cooking the snake meat three times in two days, but without much success. Asa found the meat tough and Tucker would only sniff at it and walk away. Asa would have to get some input from other cooks before he killed another snake to use the meat for human consumption. Since he hadn't been able to make the snake meat agreeable as to odor or taste, he had kept his trials to himself. In the next three days before reaching the Sweetwater, Asa had killed three more snakes, but after trying to cook the first two, he gave up on the third and just kicked it out of the way of the wagons.

# CHAPTER 15

# THE RIVER AND THE READER

Ten full days had passed since Levi had been shot. He had been limbering up his legs by walking along the wagons for the last day and a half. The day before, he discovered how stiff his sore leg still was, even though he had tried to do a little exercise each day following passage through Emigrant Gap. He hadn't counted on his left leg being weak also. He had tried to walk for a quarter of an hour, but he failed to keep up with the wagons. Asa brought Bravo to him so he could ride back to the Cabots' wagon.

It was the morning of the eleventh day. Levi had good intentions, thinking he could surely walk well enough to keep up with the slowly moving wagons. He saddled Bravo, and when the wagons began moving, Levi walked beside the wagons with Bravo until he began to lose ground, and then he climbed into the saddle and rode for about an hour. He had been riding alongside the Cabots' wagon, dismounted, and was able to make significant progress, doubling the previous time afoot before mounting Bravo the second time. As Levi rode to the front of the wagon train, he encountered an old wooden sign written with charcoal that said Devil's Gate was an hour away. That meant the Sweetwater was a little over an hour—maybe two, away.

The travelers stopped for food and rest after rolling past Devil's Gate. It seemed the animals could smell the nearby water; the cattle mooed loudly, and were munching on patches of grass. A warm, humid, southern wind was blowing, carrying the cottony masses from cottonwood trees growing on the banks of the Sweetwater. The blue western sky was gradually being concealed by billowing white clouds. As the women prepared food, the men were watching the rising cumulus clouds, debating whether to tether the animals. Nearly everyone was expecting a storm; they hadn't had significant rain in nearly sixty days, but the sudden buildup of enormous thunder clouds was something few of the travelers had seen, and they didn't know what to expect. This was very different from the dust storm they had endured days earlier.

The horses were dancing aimlessly, nostrils flaring sporadically, their agitation made more evident by excessive whinnies. Asa and Levi almost simultaneously stated that there was a storm coming and the stock had better be tethered. Just as they spoke a rumble could be heard in the distance, the noise apparently shaking the ground, almost as if they were experiencing an earthquake.

The sound had alarmed Clarissa, who was playing with Tucker. She ran to Anna for protection.

Asa had just taken care of the horses and returned to see Clarissa looking up at Anna for reassurance.

Asa smiled and said, "You know that noise, Clarissa? A farmer just dumped a big sack of potatoes on the ground."

Clarissa looked up at Anna and frowned, wondering if Asa was teasing. Anna whispered something to Clarissa, who looked up at Asa and said, "That was thunder, not potatoes."

Asa responded, "I think you're right. Those potatoes would be real big to make that noise. Do you think we should get under the wagon or in it?"

Anna answered, "I think Clarissa and I will get in the wagon. You men can get under it."

"Where will Tucker go?" asked Clarissa.

"Do you want Tucker with us?" quizzed Anna.

"Yes. He might get scared under the wagon and run away."

Nathan and Levi returned from talking with the major and informed the others about the weather. Nathan said, "Major Langley thinks we're going to have a real downpour, with strong winds, and maybe some hail. He's seen hail from that type of cloud formation before, some of it more than an inch in diameter. It might spook the livestock. Hail that big can knock a man out—just like rocks."

Levi added, "I think we should all get under the wagons and put blankets against the wheels to keep hail from bouncing under the wagon. The major said the ground might get covered enough to look like snow, and it might get cold, so let's put on coats."

Another atmospheric rumble was heard, louder than before. Anna and Clarissa hurried, hand in hand, to get their coats and blankets, and taking Levi's advice, crawled under the wagon. Asa and Nathan wove some blankets through the wheel spokes and Levi grabbed the almanac from the back of the wagon. Just as everyone had gotten settled beneath the wagon, rain drops began to fall, and then the wind increased in intensity. The temperature was dropping and they heard a sound they had never experienced before. The animals were making more noises, and then a few hail stones could be seen bouncing on the ground as if someone were throwing biscuits. The noise from the large hail stones striking the ground and bouncing off the wagon sides and bonnets made a racket too loud to talk over. Everyone watched and waited for nature's primitive music to end.

Levi held up the almanac, grinned, and said, "This storm was not predicted!" Anna and Nathan laughed, but Asa just stared at the book. Clarissa, sucking on her thumb, was curled up in a blanket next to Anna      .

Asa inquired, "What's in that book, Levi?"

Levi held out the book and said, "All kinds of things. Here, you can look."

Asa looked a little nervous. "No, that's all right; just tell me."

Anna sensed Asa's discomfort and had to ask. "Asa, can you read? Don't be ashamed. Lots of people don't know how to read. I can teach you, if you like."

"No ma'am. I know the letters, but I don't know how to put them together, or figure the sounds that they make. I don't think I can learn, I'm too old."

"Well, I'm sure you can learn. I think you are a very smart man, and you are not too old. How would you like me to show you after dinner each night? By the time we get to Ft. Boise, you'll be able to read."

"I'd like that, Miss Anna."

Levi said, "That sounds like a contract to me. Nathan and I are witnesses. Did you ever go to school, Asa?"

"I did once, but Miss Kindle said I was big enough to work, so I never went to school again...was long time ago. I wished I had. I never read a book. I always wondered what those pages said; maybe tells how to cook a snake," he grinned.

Anna frowned, "Cook a snake?"

"Somethin' to try. I get tired of buffalo."

Levi remarked, "We'll probably have some venison when we get in the mountains, but I'm curious to taste snake meat; might be an interesting change."

The large hail stones had stopped pelting the campsite and had changed to much smaller particles, which fell for about ten minutes, making the countryside look like it was snow covered.

The sun appeared and the air began to warm again. The earth looked like it was steaming as water vapor, illuminated by the sun, rose from the ground. Clarissa had been watching the giant hail stones bouncing across the ground. She had to have one of those white rocks. She looked at Anna and asked, "Can I get one of those white things?"

Anna stuck her head out from under the wagon and checked the sky. It appeared the storm clouds had moved off to the northeast, and blue sky was reclaiming the western atmosphere. The winds had calmed and the animals were eating grass sticking up through the thin layer of hail stones.

"Sure, Clarissa, bring some of them to us so we can see them up close."

Clarissa crawled on her hands and knees until she was clear of the wagon and cautiously approached the nearest large hail stone. She wasn't sure how to touch it, so she squatted down and looked at it closely, then reached out and picked it up. She looked back under the wagon at Anna and said, "Cold!"

Anna smiled and said, "Bring it to me, Clarissa."

Everyone was emerging from the protection of their wagons, marveling at the large hail stones, the suddenness of the storm, and its rapid passage. There seemed to be a competition to find the largest hailstone. Some enterprising men and women were gathering the large chunks of ice in buckets and sacks to be used as a refrigerant.

The Cabots, Asa, and Levi watched the helter-skelter motions of other travelers as Clarissa crawled back under the wagon. She gave the large hailstone to Anna who picked up a rock and smashed the piece of ice. Peering at the pieces, Anna remarked, "Look Clarissa, it's made of small ice balls, all frozen together. How could something so heavy come out of the sky? Isn't Mother Nature interesting?"

Campfires were restarted, meals were prepared and eaten, and the wagons were on the move again. In less than an hour, the Sweetwater River was crossed the first time. The water was deeper and clearer than in the Platte, but slowly moving, and no one encountered any problems. The animals were allowed to drink freely before moving on. Three hours later, the wagons stopped to make camp for the night. After supper, Anna sat between Asa and Levi, who were sipping coffee and talking about the somewhat freakish storm.

Anna held up a small book and said, "Are you ready, Asa?"

"Yes, Miss Anna."

"This is a book called a reader. We will start with the alphabet and then a few short words. I'll give you the book, and you can look at it when you have time, and tomorrow we'll do more. It will take some time to get a good start, but after a couple of weeks, you will be able to go faster. Be patient, I'm a little out of practice myself. We'll both make mistakes." Anna grinned. "All right, let's get started."

# CHAPTER 16

# RIVER CROSSINGS

The second Sweetwater crossing occurred just before noon the following day. After the last wagon had cleared the river, the emigrants stopped for lunch plus an additional hour's rest. A few minutes after 5:00 p.m., another river crossing was completed, and the travelers set up camp for the night. Nearly everyone was complaining of being very tired, not just because of climbing hills, but the movement to higher elevations was causing lightheadedness, especially during hill climbing.

Asa and Anna prepared supper while Levi and Nathan tended the animals. Tucker and Clarissa looked for firewood and saw some rabbits not far from the wagons. When Clarissa returned to the wagon with Tucker and a few small, dead branches, she said, "We saw some rabbits and a chair."

Asa replied, "Rabbits are good for eating, Clarissa. Where'd you see them?"

"No! You can't eat them—they're my friends."

Asa smiled, "Okay, we'll leave the rabbits alone. Where's the chair? We can use it for our fire. There isn't much to burn around here."

"I don't know. I can show you."

Levi remarked, "Let's go for a ride, Clarissa. You can show me where the chair is. Tucker will come with us."

Levi made eye contact with Anna and she nodded her head.
"Can I go with Levi, Mommy?"

"Sure, Levi will take good care of you."

"Come on, Clarissa, let's get Bravo."

Levi swung Clarissa up into the saddle and he sat behind her on his saddlebags. His right leg was still a bit tender, so Levi decided he'd better get more padding. They rode 20 yards to the Cabots' wagon and Levi called to Anna, "Could you please hand me a blanket? I need to cushion my behind."

"Okay. I don't want you to suffer," Anna laughed as she handed Levi a blanket from near the campfire.

With the folded blanket under his rear end, Levi and Clarissa began slowly riding toward the Sweetwater River. Tucker was running ahead of them, seeming to know exactly where they were going.

Clarissa looked at Levi, raised her right arm, pointed, and said, "Follow Tucker."

Levi had to chuckle, he had never been under the command of a little girl and a dog. When they were within about 50 yards of the river, Clarissa pointed downstream and said, "Over there, Levi. It's next to the water."

Sure enough, Levi could see an old chair with one leg broken off, lying on some rocks about ten feet from the water's edge. Levi dismounted and led Bravo toward the chair. Clarissa was laughing at Tucker, who was swimming across the river. When he reached the other bank and shook his body, Clarissa clapped her hands together and said, "Good dog, Tucker." Levi continued walking Bravo downstream until he saw an object half in the water. As they got closer, he could see it was a small wooden dressing cabinet, probably discarded to lighten the weight in a wagon. He dropped the reins, pulled the cabinet out of the water, slid open the top drawer, and found it was stuffed full of clothing. The other two drawers were also full and the contents were wet. Levi tied his rope around the dresser, climbed on Bravo and lifted the small cabinet off the ground. After securing the rope around the saddle horn, they returned to the broken chair, which he tied to the other side of the saddle.

"Well, Clarissa, let's go back to the wagon, we're loaded."

Clarissa looked around and said, "Where's Tucker?"

"Oh! I'd better call him." Levi whistled and a few seconds later, they heard a bark and saw Tucker running toward the opposite river bank. He didn't even stop, dived into the water, and began swimming toward Levi and Clarissa. They watched Tucker swim across the river and come out of the water, stop, and shake his body. Clarissa laughed when she saw the water spraying in all directions.

Levi yelled, "Come on, Tucker, it's time for supper. Let's get back to camp."

Supper was ready when the furniture gatherers arrived at the wagon. Asa helped Clarissa down from Bravo as Levi undid the knots in the rope, letting the chair and cabinet fall to the ground. Clarissa ran over to Anna talking excitedly about Tucker swimming in the river. Nathan picked up the cabinet and carried it to the campfire. Asa broke the chair into small pieces and fed the fire, the dried pine lumber burned quickly and brightly before he had to add more buffalo chips to maintain the campfire.

As they were eating, Anna asked Nathan, "What's in that little cabinet?"

He smiled, "I don't know, but I'm guessing underwear."

Anna tried again, "Levi, what's in the cabinet?"

"Clothing, but I didn't look closely, most of it is wet. The cabinet was half submerged in the water. Somebody must have thrown it out to lighten their load, so it must not be very important."

Nathan said, "Underwear—got to be. I bet it's brown, they threw it out so they wouldn't have to wash it."

"Nathan!" Anna gave Nathan a dirty look.

Asa laughed and said, "Let's take a look."

The top drawer was full of small shirts and stockings, perhaps to fit a small boy. A small blanket was packed into the second drawer. The third drawer held a small pair of shoes and two pairs of pants, about the right size for Clarissa. As Asa pulled things from the dresser, he gave them to Anna, who folded them nicely.

Anna observed, "I think these things belonged to a small boy who must have perished earlier on the trip, and his parents realized it was time to leave the things behind. I feel sad for them, but we can thank them for giving us some more clothes for Clarissa."

Everyone was quiet, thinking of how difficult it must have been for someone to leave the boy's things beside the river. Levi was wondering what his name was.

"Let me put these things in the wagon and we'll get to your lesson, Asa. We need to practice some words before the sun goes down." Anna yawned as she reached down to pick up the items on the blanket.

"Yes Ma'am. I'll get the dishes washed and put away."

Levi broke up the cabinet and piled the wood next to the campfire, retrieved the almanac from his saddlebags, and sat down to read about planting corn. Nathan was already nodding off and would retire early.

Another river crossing occurred at noon on the third day of travel along the Sweetwater. During the next two days, crossings took place in mid-afternoon. Major Langley called for another meeting the morning of the sixth day along the river. He instructed the travelers to stock up on water and discard any unnecessary possessions not made of wood; they needed to lighten their loads. The wagons would be away from the river until they returned to the river on the eighth day for the last crossings.

The ruts from previous wagons were easy to follow through the scrubland. As the wagons moved along the dusty trail, grasshoppers flew up from the grayish-brown, stunted shrubs, and clung to the wagons and travelers as they walked alongside the wagons. Nathan was no longer driving the team, having relinquished the reins to Anna to lighten the wagon's load. The progressively steeper slopes and higher altitudes were causing the oxen to labor under the load of the wagon plus the cart. As they moved across the arid country, they encountered many discarded items, including a pot-bellied stove and numerous broken rifles. The guns had been intentionally destroyed so no one else could use them, especially Indians.

The emigrant's water reserves had been depleted signifi-
cantly during the two days away from the river, but no one was
burdened with the thought of not having water, they knew they
were returning to the river before long. Two more crossings of
the Sweetwater took place on the eighth day after passing Devil's
Gate. The crossings were only a half-hour apart, just enough time
for everyone's clothes to dry out before getting wet again. No one
seemed to mind after being away from the river for the previous
two days. There was one more river crossing, and then they would
face a new obstacle, an extremely rocky path up a relatively steep
incline several hundred feet in height.

Nathan was walking beside Levi and said, "I'm glad we're
through crossing that river. It seemed like we weren't going anywhere, having to cross that river so many times."

Levi responded, "I'm tired of getting wet, too. The maps show
that after we get over this hill, we'll be near South Pass, the halfway
point between the Pacific Ocean and Independence, Missouri."

"Have you ever seen the Pacific Ocean, Levi?"

"No. I was never west of Pennsylvania before I started this
journey. Like most everyone on the train, everything we see is new
to me. Those mountains in the distance dwarf anything in the
East. I wonder what it would be like to climb to the top of them."

Snow topped mountain peaks could be seen in the distance,
but they were several tens of miles away. The travelers were staying
to the valley floors and only infrequently had to scale steep slopes.
The high, semiarid desert regions were monotonous, occasionally
invaded by rivers and streams with grass and trees near the water.
It was the second week of June and after a day and a half of expo-
sure travelling in a southwesterly direction, they swung directly
west and made camp. During the next week the wagons would
move at night, with animals and humans resting, avoiding the sun
during the heat of the day.

The next river crossing was on the Big Sandy during the
middle of the night. Fortunately, a full moon greatly assisted their
safe passage. Extra time was spent at the crossing to fill vessels
with water, and provide food and drink for the animals. Following

three more days of desert travel, the wagons arrived at the Green River, which was a dangerous waterway to cross with loaded wagons, without many helpers on horseback. Major Langley had sent a rider ahead the day before the wagons arrived at the river, and a rope ferry, owned and run by Mormons, was ready to transport the wagons. Langley had made a deal with the Mormons to carry all the wagons and livestock for $160, which was a little more than five dollars per wagon. The emigrants gladly paid the fee after they had heard a number of stories of lives lost in attempting to cross the rapidly flowing Green River. It took half a day to get the wagons and livestock across the river, but no accidents occurred, partly due to low water levels. The high water from spring runoffs was no longer present.

# CHAPTER 17

# MOUNTAINS AND NEAR DISASTER

The emigrants had encountered difficult terrain for wagons to traverse and several stops to fix wheels were necessary. They skirted mountains, but made use of wood from nearby forests for fires and wagon repairs. Trees were becoming more common as they neared the Hams River. After crossing the Hams, the wagons went northwest, staying slightly north of Bear River. Descending the hills had become a problem, some emigrants nearly losing control of their wagons and their heavy cargo. The foot breaks were judged to be inadequate in a couple of instances. Major Langley gathered the emigrants together and set up a procedure that allowed the wagons to descend steep slopes to valleys below without major risks. In some cases, the backs of the wagons were roped to several riders on horseback who were able to prevent the wagons from becoming runaways, or causing the oxen to be driven into the ground by the wagon tongues. The taut ropes strained the horses and riders, but each pair of riders worked every third wagon.

The Jeffers, Asa, Levi, and the scouts were instrumental in preventing accidents. The Cabots' wagon plus cart offered a problem because of the added weight and lack of brakes on the cart. Asa and Levi unhooked the cart, took the wagon down the steep inclines, and then used two oxen to guide the cart downhill. The entire procedure was cumbersome, requiring most of a day to accomplish, but was successful. When the last wagon reached the valley floor, everyone was tired, but in a celebratory mood, camp was set up, and all had a good night's rest.

Montpelier was the next settlement on the route where the emigrants were able to get some assistance. Unfortunately the small town was only two years old, and limited aid was available. They were able to buy some feed for their horses, do some minor wagon repairs, and purchase a few varieties of food they had missed while travelling, especially pork and fresh vegetables. A few of the men bought some whiskey.

After a few hours, the wagons moved on and the emigrants camped for the night about a day away from Soda Springs. The next morning, Major Langley asked for a vote on a small change in plans.

He wanted to know if the travelers would like to take a short-cut over a well-forested small range of hills.

There were no rivers to cross, but the trail had a few narrow spots. It would cut a half day off their travel time and they would be able to enjoy some shade and wildlife. The yeas outnumbered the nays two to one so the wagons turned directly north and began ascending a low hill.

The trail curved around a second, larger hill and then dropped slowly to a narrow valley before ascending another rocky hill, nearly devoid of trees except at the very top. In a ravine below to the left, a small stream snaked its way around boulders, and disappeared into the ground. The remnants of a wagon, apparently having gone over the edge of the narrow trail, could be seen amongst the rocks below.

Nathan was driving the Cabots' wagon around a sharp right turn. He was well aware of the danger, having seen the remains of the wagon at the bottom of the ravine, so he stayed as close as possible to the rocky wall at the right of the trail. Unfortunately the cart, trailing behind the wagon, began to climb the rock wall, and before he could stop the oxen, the cart tipped over, blocking the trail.

Anna, Clarissa, and Asa were walking behind the cart, and when Asa saw what was happening, he had grabbed Anna around the waist with one arm, and Clarissa with the other, and carried them out of danger from the overturned cart. Levi was about a wagon back on the trail and he rode up quickly to see what had happened when he heard a crash and saw a cloud of dust rise up.

Asa put Anna and Clarissa down and looked up at Levi, saying, "Looks like we have a problem."

"Yeah, we're blocking the trail. We'd better think of something fast. Anna, you'd better check the plants to see if they're damaged."

Levi dismounted and walked to the overturned cart. Nathan was standing on the ground behind his wagon. He pushed his hat back, looking at the mess, and said, "Damn it!"

"It's not your fault, Nathan. The wagon and cart were too long to make such a tight turn. Let's see what we can do before Major Langley arrives."

Asa and Levi began looking up the rocky wall and then over the edge of the trail to the ravine below. The two men looked at each other and smiled, having gotten the same idea.

Asa stated, "I'll get my ropes."

Levi yelled at Nathan, "Get your ropes, Nathan, we've got some work to do. Anna, can you remove the plants and set them on the trail next to the rocks? We need to empty the cart so we can push it over the edge."

Anna protested, "No Levi! We'll have to throw things away, there's not enough space in our wagon for everything."

"Don't worry, Anna, we're not going to let the cart crash. We're going to secure it to some trees, and after the other wagons have passed, we'll pull it up and fix it. It looks like the axle is broken."

Nathan, Anna, and Clarissa had finished removing the contents of the cart just in time for Levi and Asa to begin the tie-off. It took the two men about ten minutes to lower the cart over the edge of the trail and secure it to two large trees about 20 to 30 feet down the steep slope. While Levi and Asa were carrying out their plan, Major Langley arrived and saw what had happened. He didn't say a word, just turned his horse around and rode off.

When the last of the wagons had passed by, Levi instructed Anna, "Please take Clarissa and Bravo and find Nathan. He's stopped in a wide spot on the trail, maybe a mile or two from here. Have him bring back two oxen. Our horses don't have the strength to pull the cart up the steep slope. Asa is already looking for a tree so we can fashion a new axle."

"All right, but you'll have to help get Clarissa on Bravo with me."

Anna mounted Bravo and Levi set Clarissa behind Anna on the blanket roll. It would be uncomfortable for the little girl, but the short ride would take only a few minutes. She would probably enjoy riding a big horse with Anna.

Levi waved to the ladies and directed his attention to the ravine. His eyes scanned the cart and the four ropes pulled taut, preventing the cart from plunging to the rocks below. Levi expected to see Asa below, cutting down a small tree, but he couldn't detect anyone or any motion amongst the rocks. He could see a rope extending toward the bottom of the ravine from a small tree about 20 feet below the location of the cart. Levi gave a loud whistle, and waited, but there was no response. He looked around and saw Asa's horse, Granite, standing quietly beside the trail, so Asa hadn't ridden off. *Where the hell did he go?*

Levi sat down in the dirt at the edge of the trail where he could see into the ravine. He watched for a couple of minutes and then whistled again. This time, Levi heard a responding whistle from a distance off to the left. Asa was walking up the trail toward Levi, about 50 yards away, waving his arms and whistling again. As Asa got closer, Levi noticed the big man was sweating and breathing hard.

"Found something way down there," Asa pointed to the rocks below. "That wreck has a good axle. We can pull it up after we get the cart back on the trail. We'll need the ropes that are holding the cart. The rope I had to get down there wasn't long enough so I climbed a ways without it, but I couldn't get back up to the rope. I had to move down the ravine to crawl back up to the trail. I found something else, Levi."

"What's that, Asa?"

Asa pulled his shirt from his pants and a book dropped to the ground. As Asa picked up the book, he said, "I don't know all the words, just three; Jonathan, Swift, and Travels. The other word starts with the letter *G*."

"It's Gulliver's, Asa. That's a man's name. It's a fictional story, but one you should read. You'll have to show that to Anna. Good for you, Asa, you're learning to read pretty well."

"Fictional story?"

"Yes, make believe."

"Oh. So if I told you there was a new wagon down in that ravine, it would be fictional?"

"Not really."

Asa frowned.

Levi smiled and said, "That would be a lie."

Asa smiled and then laughed. "I guess it's all in the way you look at it."

Nathan could see Levi and Asa talking on the trail where the cart had been pushed off into the ravine. He was riding Bravo guiding the oxen that had been the lead pair pulling the wagon and cart. Levi waved to Nathan and he acknowledged with a less than adequate military salute. He stopped the oxen about ten yards short of Levi and said, "I got a quick start. Major Langley told me to bring the oxen to help pull the cart up from the slope, and I brought some more rope. Tom is staying with the ladies."

"How'd Tom get involved?" quizzed Levi.

"Langley mentioned our problem and Tom volunteered to help out."

"Tom had better mind his manners, or there will be a dead body at the bottom of the ravine."

Nathan grinned and commented, "Don't worry, Levi, Anna can handle a shotgun."

"Well, let's quit jawin' and get that cart up here so we can fix the axle. Asa found an old axle in the ravine. Let's get a couple of ropes on the oxen and I'll go down and release the cart from the trees. I'll toss another rope up here from the cart so we'll have three tow ropes. That should carry the weight."

A half-hour later, the cart was on the trail. The broken axle was removed using tools from Asa's saddlebags while Asa retrieved the axle from the ravine with Nathan's help. The replacement axle and wheels were attached, the cart was reloaded, the tongue was attached to the oxen, and the three men began the short trip to meet with Anna, Clarissa, Tucker, and Tom. Levi figured it would take about three hours to catch up with the other wagons, provided they were stopped. In the back of his mind, he worried some about Indian attacks. *Had the tale of the sky wagon reached this far west?* The wagon train would probably have reached Soda Springs and the emigrants would be settled in camp for the night outside Soda Springs. The major had commented that Soda Springs had a population of about one hundred souls.

# CHAPTER 18

## SHOSHONES AND SODA SPRINGS

Nathan had pulled the sky wagon off the trail about a mile from the wreck so the other wagons could pass. Tom had ridden up to the Cabots' wagon about the same time Anna and Clarissa had appeared on Bravo. As soon as Tom understood he was to protect Anna and Clarissa, Nathan had taken two oxen and returned to retrieve the cart from the hillside.

It took about 20 minutes to reach the Cabots' wagon from the repair site. Asa was mounted and rode a little ahead of Nathan and the repaired cart. Levi walked alongside the cart leading Bravo. As they approached the wagon, Asa pulled up about thirty yards away and signaled Nathan to stop. Asa couldn't see any activity around the wagon. Anna, Clarissa, Tom, and Tucker were out of sight, perhaps in the wagon.

"Wait here, Levi. Cover me!"

Asa dismounted, withdrew his rifle from the scabbard, levered a bullet into the breech, and moved Granite closer to the Cabots' wagon. A threatening arrow was sticking into the blue sideboard of the wagon. Levi, pistol drawn, crouched to present a smaller target as he cautiously approached the wagon.

Levi called out, "Tom? Anna?" There was nothing but silence. Levi climbed into the wagon and lifted the lid of the tool chest, hoping to find Anna and Clarissa, but he only saw tools. As Levi climbed down from the wagon he said, "Nobody's here." He motioned for Nathan to bring the cart closer, gave a concerned look to Asa, and whistled twice. A barely audible bark could be heard from a stand of trees about 50 yards away, and then Tucker appeared, running toward Levi. A piercing whistle was heard from the trees, it had to be from Tom, he was the only person Levi knew that could whistle loud enough to break an eardrum. Levi whistled back, and Tucker ran even faster.

Tucker arrived panting. "Good boy, Tucker. Are Anna and Clarissa safe?" Tucker wagged his tail and barked twice as he put his paws on Levi's chest. Levi knelt and stroked Tucker's back when the dog dropped to the ground.

"There they are!" exclaimed Nathan, standing in the cart, pointing toward the trees where Tucker had emerged running after Levi whistled.

Levi climbed on the spokes of a front wagon wheel and looked toward the trees. Sure enough, Tom was leading his horse plus the four pack horses, and had his rifle on his shoulder as if he were a soldier on patrol. Clarissa was marching beside Tom with a long stick on her shoulder as if she were holding a rifle. Anna was on the other side of Tom carrying Nathan's shotgun with both hands, trying to avoid tripping over rocks and weeds. Levi mounted Bravo, rode to them, and took the pack horses' reins from Tom.

He leaned down to Anna and said, "I'm glad you are all okay. When I saw that arrow, I thought you had been carried off by Indians."

"We're so glad to see you, Levi. You three showed up just in time. When the arrow hit, we grabbed our guns and ran for those trees. There were three of them on horseback, two with guns. They were just starting to climb into the wagon when they heard you coming and rode off."

"Thanks for getting the ladies out of danger, Tom. You did the right thing."

"When the arrow hit the wagon, I had Anna take the shotgun and head toward the trees with Clarissa and Tucker. I grabbed the pack horses and followed, thinking the horses would shield us from bullets and arrows. They would have taken the horses, but they wouldn't have risked wounding them. We watched the Indians for a few minutes and then they left. Like Anna said, I think they heard the cart coming. They mounted and rode away, but I'm guessing they're probably watching us."

"Well, if there are only three of them, we have enough firepower to handle any problems. Let's attach the cart to the wagon and get out of here."

Asa was already attaching the cart to the back of the wagon as Tom and Levi were talking. Nathan was moving the oxen to the front of the wagon and hitching them to the other two teams. Ten minutes later, they were on the trail heading toward Soda Springs. Nathan, Anna, and Clarissa were riding in the wagon and the three men, all expecting trouble, were on horseback with their rifles ready.

Asa and Tom were riding about ten yards in front of the oxen and Levi was trailing about 25 yards behind the cart with Tucker roving about, first on one side of the wagon and then the other. As Asa and Tom rounded a small hill, veering to the left, they suddenly stopped. There were three Indians on pinto ponies blocking their path. Two of the braves held rifles and the third had a bow with an arrow notched, probably waiting to react to a threatening gun being raised. The brave in the center moved his horse forward and said something Anna and Tom couldn't understand. Asa, however, did react and called, "They're Shoshone from the Fort Hall area. Levi, they want to see the big gun in the cart."

Levi stepped out from behind the Cabots' wagon with his rifle pointed at the Shoshone that had spoken. "Tell him to send the man with the bow to take a look in the cart. If they try anything, the man speaking will be the first to catch a bullet."

Asa moved forward and spoke, and signed with his hands to give the Indians instructions. The archer dismounted, left his bow on the ground, and walked to the cart, giving Levi a contemptuous look as he passed by. Levi understood: this was the land of the Shoshone. The Indian vaulted into the cart, rummaged around, then reappeared, and dropped to the ground. He walked past Levi without even glancing at him and returned to talk to the Indian that had spoken to Asa. They exchanged several words, after which the leader told Asa they were mistaken. They had been lied to by a trader from Fort Laramie who had said the sky wagon had big guns. The three Indians turned their mounts and rode slowly from the trail and dropped out of sight behind the trees.

Clarissa started crying and buried her face in Anna's dress. "It's okay now Clarissa. The Indians are gone and no one was hurt. Levi, Nathan, Tom and Asa are okay. Look and see." Clarissa wiped her eyes and looked at the four men to make sure everyone was all right as Anna had said. Clarissa looked toward the trees where the Shoshones had disappeared and said, "If they come back, I will hit them with my stick." Anna hugged Clarissa and said, "Let's let the men do the fighting. They are trained to do that. We will help only if we have to. Okay?" Clarissa smiled and nodded.

Levi looked up toward the sun, already past the zenith, and commented, "Let's get going, we've lost another half hour. At this rate, we won't catch up with Major Langley until supper time. We can eat something as we travel, but we'll still have to take a break to rest the animals."

Soda Springs wasn't much of a town; people drifted in and out, some to get a few supplies and some to visit the springs, having been told of their healing qualities. A sign said population 113, the previous enumeration, 97, having been crossed out with charcoal. There was no telling when the counts had been taken. The dirt streets were not laid out with any semblance of order, but within a few years, the town would probably grow and have a nice grid pattern of streets and avenues. The hot springs were numerous in the area, so Levi thought it might be difficult for a surveyor to establish any regularity to the town's layout. Houses had been built to avoid large rocky areas and spring water.

As they drove the wagon and cart into the little town, Levi's initial concept of Soda Springs changed. There actually was a main street where several businesses were located. There were two apothecary/saloons, a livery, a general store, and a small hotel/restaurant. Behind the general store was a small lumberyard, and about a hundred yards farther east, toward the mountains, were five tepees. Another small building sat by itself 50 yards to the north. Anna found out it was a school house, and on Sundays, it doubled as a church.

Nathan stopped the wagon next to the general store, and Asa, Anna, and Clarissa went in to shop. Tom and Levi took their horses to a watering trough as they talked about the encounter with the three Shoshone braves. Nathan jumped down from the wagon and began checking the oxen and remembered he was going to buy some more feed for the chickens.

The proprietors of the general store, Mr. and Mrs. Hadley, were discussing reordering merchandise for their shelves when Asa entered the establishment with Anna and Clarissa. They grew silent as they watched Asa investigating saddles and rope. The Hadleys appeared to be in their forties, were both slightly over-weight, and wore spectacles. They both had black hair, although some gray strands were creeping into Mr. Hadley's thinning hair and moustache. Mr. Hadley stood about five-nine and his wife was two inches shorter; both wore aprons.

Asa was admiring one of the saddles in the store window dis-play. Asa's saddle had belonged to one of the Dendricks and was not very comfortable. The price tag said $40.00, but he could afford it; he had only spent a few dollars since he joined the wagon train. He had been thinking of leaving the wagons at Fort Boise, riding to the Oregon coast, and then south to California. He wanted to see the Pacific Ocean and try mining for gold in California, but he wanted a more comfortable saddle.

Anna was talking to the Hadleys at the counter, having gath-ered several items, including a few pieces of candy. Clarissa was watching the candy like a hawk, ready to pop a morsel into her mouth. Anna encouraged her. "Go ahead, Clarissa, you can have a piece of candy, but just one." Clarissa smiled and picked a red lump from the counter top and placed it in her mouth, but she expected it to be chewable, and extracted it from between her lips. She held it out for Anna to take, but Anna recognized the difficulty and said, "It's hard candy, dear, you have to suck on it, not bite it." Clarissa tried again, smiled, and held up two sticky red fingers.

Asa stepped toward the counter and bent down beside Clarissa holding a red bandanna.

He smiled and said, "Here you go, Missy, wipe your fingers on this, the color won't even show."

Mrs. Hadley looked at Anna and commented, "Do you know this...ah...person?"

"Yes, Mrs. Hadley. My friend, Asa, is travelling with us. He is a wonderful cook. He was trained in New York at a fine restaurant. He is a man of exceptional talents."

"Well, if you say so. Are you, your husband, and daughter going to Oregon?"

"Oh, I'm not married. My brother and I are traveling together to Oregon and we are taking the little girl to Fort Boise. She's an orphan."

Asa was counting out money for the saddle and said, "I'd like to buy the saddle in the window. The tag on the more expensive one says forty dollars, is that correct?" Mrs. Hadley looked at her husband, who stepped up to the counter and said officiously, "That's an old price, it should be eighty dollars." Asa looked at Hadley in disbelief, put his money back in his pocket, and walked out of Hadleys' store. He almost said something to Mr. Hadley that might have created a scene, and he didn't want to expose Anna and Clarissa to any loud voices and bad language.

Anna recognized what had happened immediately, grabbed Clarissa's sticky hand, and said, "I really don't need these things. I'll get them later elsewhere. Here is a penny for the candy." Anna tossed a penny on the counter, walked from the store, and slammed the door. Anna and Clarissa met Levi outside where Anna told

Levi what the Hadleys had done to Asa. Levi was irritated and said, "I think I'll tell the Hadleys a little story."

Levi entered the store, walked around looking at a few things, and then concentrated on the saddles. The forty dollar saddle looked to be a pretty good buy, so he asked, "Is that the correct price for the better saddle?"

Mr. Hadley stepped over beside Levi and said, "Yes sir. That is a very good saddle, made from some of the finest leather. I doubt if you'll find another of that quality within a hundred miles."

"You are a lucky man, Mr. Hadley."

"How so?" replied Hadley.

"See that man across the street with the dog? His name is Asa. He told me you wanted eighty dollars for the saddle, but he couldn't afford it. He thought you were prejudiced against people with dark skin. Without a doubt, if his dog had been with him, the animal would have attacked you. The dog is very sensitive to a person's tone of voice. Back in Periwinkle, Illinois, a merchant treated Asa badly. The shop owner was trying to cheat Asa, but the dog sensed the tension in the man's voice, attacked, and bit off two of the man's fingers on his right hand. The town sheriff told Asa to take the dog, get out of town, and never come back."

"You know that's true?"

"Yes, Mr. Hadley, just as true as I'm standing here talking to you. I was in Periwinkle the day it happened. So, if you go outside in the vicinity of that dog, you'd better be careful. Maybe you should keep your hands in your pockets. I don't think the dog will bite your legs, but I'm not sure."

Hadley thought for a moment, and then asked, "Do you want to buy the saddle?"

"No, Mr. Hadley. After the way you treated Asa, I wouldn't buy anything in this store. Good day." Levi tipped his hat to Mrs. Hadley, exited the store, and walked across the street to talk to Asa.

After Levi explained to Asa what he had told Hadley, Asa smiled and said, "So you told him a fictional story."

Levi grinned, "Yup. We know it's fictional, he doesn't, and therefore, it was a lie. Hadley might be watching us, so why don't you pet your dog."

Asa smiled, gave a whistle, and called, "Tucker, come see your daddy."

# CHAPTER 19

# FT. HALL, THE SNAKE, AND ROCK CREEK

Twenty-five minutes later, the Cabots' wagon was parked with the rest of the wagon train about a mile from Soda Springs. Most of the women and several men were busy washing clothes and drinking from the bubbling water, abundant in the area. Tucker took one taste of the water, turned away, and lay down beneath the wagon. Asa and Anna prepared supper and everyone went to bed after a few moments rehashing the day's activities. Asa had to tell the story Levi had related to Mr. Hadley about Asa's vicious dog.

After two days of travel, the wagon train was in the vicinity of Fort Hall, but Major Langley informed everyone the fort was no longer manned by troops, so the emigrants moved into the Snake River Valley and continued west on the south side of the river. The valley was green, fish and birds were plentiful, in stark contrast to the plateau above, which was nearly barren except for occasional scrubby trees, weeds, a few wild flowers, and snakes.

Every chance she had, Clarissa roamed with Tucker collecting wild flowers and presenting little bunches to everyone she saw. She had become the little flower girl to the emigrants and everyone watched over her. Before her afternoon nap, she would give a blue flower to Levi, a white one to Anna, purple to Asa, and yellow to Nathan. She couldn't explain why she had chosen those colors; it was like a law of nature. Whenever she couldn't find the proper colors, she would promise to get two the next time. However, in several instances, Clarissa talked Asa into taking her for a ride to find the flowers she needed.

It had been six days since passing the Fort Hall area when the wagons stopped in the early afternoon at Rock Creek, a stage-coach and freight stop on the trail from Salt Lake to Fort Boise and towns along the Columbia River. There was a small store where passengers, drivers, and Army escorts could purchase needed items. While Anna and Clarissa were in the store, a coach arrived, accompanied by a dozen soldiers. When Clarissa saw the soldiers, she buried her face in Anna's dress and began to cry.

"What's wrong, Clarissa?" Anna held Clarissa's head in her hands, the tears streaming down the four-year-old's cheeks.

She sobbed, "I don't want you to go to heaven! I want you to be with me."

Anna knelt in front of Clarissa, put her arms around the lit-tle girl and held her tightly. "I'm not going to heaven, Clarissa. I believe we are going to be together for a long time. Nathan, you, and I are going to meet with my uncle in Fort Boise and go to a farm by a big river."

Clarissa whimpered, a tear dripping from her nose, "I want you to be my mama. Promise you won't leave me."

"I promise." Anna stood up and pulled a handkerchief from her pocket. "Now let's wipe those tears away and see if we can find some candy. Okay?" Anna truly hoped she could keep her promise, but it would rest on whether Major Haliday had found Clarissa's relatives.

A nice-looking, well-dressed, young woman, carrying a very young child, had entered the store and was watching Anna and Clarissa with some concern. She spoke to Anna, "Is your daughter all right?"

"Yes. I think she was scared by the stagecoach and the mili-tary men. Her mother and father were killed by Indians not long ago. The stage and escort riders reminded her of the massacre."

The woman stepped closer to Anna and said, "The poor thing. That is so sad."

Anna extended her hand toward the woman and said, "I'm Annabel Cabot."

The young woman was wearing gloves, but reached out and shook hands with Anna. "I'm Helen Wisdom. Actually, Helen Collins now. Please excuse the gloves."

Anna couldn't believe her ears. "My God! You're Levi's sister, Helen?"

"Why yes. You know Levi?"

"I sure do. He's travelling with my brother and me."

"You mean he's here in Rock Creek?"

"Yes. Just a minute, I'll get him. He will be so surprised!" Anna took one step toward the door, but suddenly stopped and stepped back in front of Helen, who had her back to the door. "Don't turn around; Levi just came in the store." Anna smiled at Levi and waved to him. "Levi, there's someone you should meet. Come here."

Levi walked over and stood beside his sister, but was looking at Clarissa. He could see she had been crying. He squatted beside Clarissa and said, "Are you all right, sweetie?"

Clarissa answered, "Yes, Levi. I...I'm all right now."

Levi stood up and turned toward the woman with the baby just as Anna said, smiling, "Levi, I think you know this lady."

Levi still hadn't looked at the woman; he was glancing at the baby in her arms. He shifted his eyes to her face and was shocked. "Helen! How did you get here? Where's Frank?" He wrapped both arms around Helen and hugged her, mostly on one side to avoid squeezing the baby.

"It's so good to see you, Levi. I didn't know when, or if, I would ever see you again. Frank is history. I divorced him, took all my money and the baby, rode the train as far west as I could, and then took stagecoaches to Salt Lake City. I was able to get on this stage to Fort Boise. It's a Wells Fargo coach carrying an Army payroll to Boise and Walla Walla. Frank Junior and I are the only passengers and the men have been really nice. I'm traveling as Mrs. Wisdom. I told them about you."

"Mrs. Wisdom, it's time to go. Can I help you with anything?" It was Lieutenant Ashton, about Levi's age and build, but not as handsome. Ashton was in charge of the cavalry detail protecting the coach from Salt Lake to Fort Boise.

"Oh, my gosh! I'd better go. I believe it would be better for me to go to Fort Boise with the baby and wait for you to arrive. Don't you think?"

Anna answered, "Oh yes. You'll get there days ahead of us. If you like, you can try to find my uncle, George Cabot. He's a big man with a large belly, a wonderful laugh, and very kind. Maybe you can stay with him until we get to Fort Boise. If I know my uncle, he will be near a place where they serve good food."

"Levi, when you get to Fort Boise, I'll explain everything. It was nice meeting you, Anna, and you too, Clarissa. Clarissa, you can tell me all about your trip, and you can help me with my little boy, okay?" Clarissa smiled and nodded. "Bye, Levi. Stay out of trouble!"

"Okay, Sis. You still have to meet Asa, Nathan, the three Jeffers, and Tucker. We'll all see you in Fort Boise in about a week. Have a good trip."

"It was wonderful to see you and meet some of your friends. Could you please buy me some dried apricots and bring them to the coach? I don't want to slow down the stagecoach by making them wait for me."

Levi bought a pound of the fruit and ran after Helen, catching up with her as she was getting into the coach with Frank Junior. The last thing he said before the door closed was, "Need any money?"

Helen answered back as the coach started moving, "No, but thanks for asking. Bye."

Levi had a lump in his throat, but choked out, "Bye Sis. Take care." He waved as the coach pulled away, the six horses and wheels kicking up small clouds of dust. The soldiers waited until the stage was moving at full speed, mounted their horses, and followed by twos about a hundred yards back. Levi went back to the store and joined Anna and Clarissa.

Anna spoke first, "I wonder what happened in Pittsburgh? Did Helen say anything more?"

"Nope. I guess we'll have to wait a week to find out. Should be an interesting story. Frank must have done something really stupid, but that wouldn't surprise me. God! I still can't believe Helen is here."

Anna smiled, "So Frank is back to being a full-size horse's ass?"

"Yep."

# CHAPTER 20

## FORT BOISE

It took the wagon train three and a half days to reach Three Island Crossing on the Snake River. Helen had been the topic of conversation for most of two days. The Cabots' wagon crew had all made guesses why Helen had left Frank Wisdom and everyone had been relying on Levi for some clues. All Levi could do was to repeat what he had said earlier—Frank must have done something really stupid. By stupid, Levi included hitting Helen. Levi knew she wouldn't stand for that, no matter what the cause, but Levi couldn't imagine his even-tempered sister doing anything to deserve being struck.

Three Island Crossing was not without difficulty. The three parallel islands in the river misrepresented the danger present in the four waterways. The water in the first channel was fairly shallow, but the second and third channels were deeper and the water ran more swiftly, which caused the wagons to be pushed sideways. Fortunately, the watertight wagons could be kept from drifting downstream by riders with ropes. The first wagon attempting to cross ran into problems, almost overturning. Asa and Ron Jeffers were close by and were able to get ropes to the wagon and prevent the contents and Mr. Cardozo from being washed away. Subsequent crossings were made without incident.

Once the wagons were on the north side of the Snake, they ascended to the top of the plateau above the river valley and headed northwest. Stagecoaches from Salt Lake had overtaken the wagons every two or three days since they had left Rock Creek. The coaches were a little upsetting to Clarissa, but less severely than the Rock Creek incident. The lack of soldiers accompanying subsequent stagecoaches seemed to lessen the effect on the four-year-old. However, Clarissa quit playing with Tucker and quit collecting wildflowers, even though they were plentiful, especially blue and white ones that dotted the plateau. Anna noticed the changes in Clarissa and mentioned them to Levi the day after crossing the river.

"Levi, Clarissa isn't having fun anymore. Something is really bothering her. I'm wondering if she thinks we are all going to leave her when we get to Fort Boise. Remember, I told her long ago, I would make a decision about being her mother when we arrived at the fort. What can I tell her? If a relative wants her, what can I do?"

"If a family member claims her, you will have no choice but to let her go, unless, of course, the relative doesn't want to accept her. You can tell her you will visit whenever possible and that you love her. I don't know what else you can say."

"Maybe I should tell her if I ever have a girl child, I'd want her to be just like Clarissa, but no one will ever replace her."

"Well, maybe we shouldn't worry. Let's see what happens when we arrive at Fort Boise. Major Haliday was going to send us a message if he found anything about Clarissa's relatives. Perhaps he didn't find out anything."

Anna reflected for a moment, smiled, and said, "I hope he didn't find anyone."

In forty-eight hours, the dusty, nearly worn-out wagons rolled into the Fort Boise area. The emigrants set up camp next to the Boise River, had supper, relaxed, and planned activities for a couple of days at the Fort. They would be restocking supplies, repairing wagons, and cleaning off trail dust.

The next morning, following breakfast, Levi started toward the fort. Anna was staying with Clarissa at the wagon while Levi went to the telegraph office to see if there was a message from Major Haliday. Tucker sat, watching Levi walk away from the wagon, looked at Anna and whined.

"Go Tucker, go with Lev!" At the first sound of the word *go* from Anna, Tucker ran to join Levi.

As Levi walked into the Fort, he was trying to decide whether to go directly to the telegraph office or look for Helen. A moment of thought removed the indecision; first, he would get the telegram, if one existed. Helen would still be asleep or caring for the baby and the Army telegraph office would have someone on duty 24 hours a day. Levi asked the first soldier he saw for directions to the telegraph office. Levi had to laugh when the man didn't utter a word, but pointed; the office was clearly marked ten-yards in front of him.

A message was coming in when Levi entered the small office. The telegrapher was leaning over the key, writing. The line grew quiet, the message was put in an envelope and the soldier looked at Levi.

"May I help you, Sir?"

"My name is Levi Collins. Is there a message from Major Haliday at Fort Laramie?"

The young man sifted through a small stack of messages, pulled out an envelope, and said, "Here's a message from Fort Laramie for Captain Collins and/or Annabel Cabot. It arrived just after the line was fixed. Damn Indians keep cutting the wires. Last time the line went down was three weeks ago."

Levi ripped off the end of the envelope, pulled out a piece of paper folded in the middle and began to read, REGRET TO INFORM YOU NO RELATIVES FOUND IN U.S. EUROPEAN FAMILY CANNOT ACCEPT CHILD. HOPE YOU FIND NICE ADOPTIVE FAMILY. SINCERELY-HALIDAY. Levi smiled as he folded the paper and inserted it into the envelope.

As Levi turned toward the door, he yelled, "Thank you!" Tucker was waiting outside the door and got to his feet and ran after Levi, who had begun to run back to the wagons with only one thought. He had to tell Anna and Clarissa the good news. When

Levi was ten yards from the wagon, he yelled, "Anna! Anna! We got a telegram!" He was out of breath and couldn't think of what to say when he saw Anna and Clarissa, all he could do was hand the envelope to Anna.

Anna pulled the note from the envelope, read the message, and picked up Clarissa, swung her around almost hitting Levi. "I can be your mama, Clarissa!" Anna hugged Clarissa and reached out one arm to Levi, who moved toward them, and threw his arms around his girls. Tears of joy were running down Anna's cheeks and Clarissa started to cry in happiness. Anna looked at Levi and kissed him.

When Levi saw Anna's face, tears began to well up in his eyes, but he considered the outward display of feelings to be unmanly and he looked away. It struck him how important being Clarissa's mother meant to Anna and he couldn't speak. He looked back at Anna and Clarissa as he held them in his arms, and when Anna looked up at Levi, tears began to run down his cheeks. Levi didn't try to stem the flow, if Anna loved him as much as he loved her, she would understand the tears.

"I love you so much, Levi."

Levi swallowed with some difficulty, but was able to choke out, "I love you too, Anna, and I love you, Clarissa."

Clarissa responded, "Will you be my papa?"

Levi wasn't sure how to answer, so he said, "If you want me to be your papa, and Anna wants me to be your papa, then I will be your papa." Levi glanced at Anna and she nodded. Levi bent down, kissed Anna, and then lifted Clarissa and kissed her forehead.

Clarissa squirmed and said, "Can you put me down? I have to find some blue and white flowers."

Levi put Clarissa down and she yelled, "Come, Tucker, we have to make a bouquet."

Anna and Levi stood arm-in-arm watching the four-year-old scamper off, darting like a bee from flower to flower, occasionally picking a wildflower that was just the right color. Tucker followed close behind, waiting for Clarissa to add each flower to the gathering in her hand and move on.

Levi was reminiscing, smiled, and commented, "I think Clarissa must have heard from my mother; she had white and blue flowers in the planters on our front porch."

As Nathan and Asa joined the happy couple, Nathan said, "You must have gotten good news. I was watching, but I couldn't hear what was said. Am I an uncle?"

Anna smiled and replied, "Yes, both of you are uncles now. Major Haliday said we are free to adopt Clarissa. Isn't that great? Let's find Helen and Uncle George and tell them the good news."

"I've got to hear what Helen is going to tell us about leaving Frank. I hope he's worrying about me coming after him with that fancy shotgun. I'll ask the neighbors to watch our wagon while we're in the fort. I want all of us to go together. Let's find Clarissa." Levi whistled and could hear a nearby bark. Mrs. Machesic, the neighbor from an adjacent wagon, was holding Clarissa's right hand, leading her around the rear of the Cabots' wagon. Clarissa's left hand held a cluster of little blue and white flowers.

Mrs. Machesic was about the same height as Anna, about ten years older, had a pleasant oval face, and wore her black hair in a bun. She had on gray pants and a too-large brown work shirt, probably her husband's. Wet spots on her clothing indicated she had just finished doing some laundry. "Clarissa tells me she has a new mama and papa. The flowers are to celebrate."

Anna replied, "We are adopting Clarissa. She will live with us in Oregon on an orchard. Could I impose on you and ask if you could watch our possessions while we are in the fort?"

"No problem, dear. My husband and I are going into the fort later this afternoon. We'll be here until about three o'clock."

"Oh, thank you. We should be back in about an hour."

Levi had noticed The Boise River Lodge when he had visited the fort earlier. It was the largest non-military structure in the fort. It appeared to have an eating area on the ground floor and rooms for rent on the second floor. Helen, the baby, and George Cabot were probably staying there. Adjoining the lodge was the Wells Fargo Office, making stay-overs convenient. The Cabot wagon group headed for the lodge.

Anna and Clarissa entered through the open double doors first with Nathan, and the others following. Tom Jeffers had joined the group in the courtyard, having come to the fort with his brothers to buy some ammunition. Levi had called to him, wanting Tom to meet Helen. Ron and James went into a gun shop on the opposite side of the fort.

Anna's eyes took a few seconds to adjust after being in the bright sunlight and entering into the lodge. She noticed Helen first, sitting with a large man at a table for four. Helen saw Anna and Clarissa and directed George's attention to the group entering the lodge.

George stood and caught Anna as she rushed over to give her uncle a hug.

"Whoa there, girl! You'll knock me over—I'm an old man!" He held her at arm's length and commented, "My God, you have become a beautiful woman! How did my brother have such a pretty daughter?"

"Thank you. It must have been mother," Anna laughed. "It's so nice to see you again, Uncle George. How have you been?"

"I've been fine." He patted his big stomach. "Who are all these people? I think I see Nathan."

Nathan was the first to step forward and shake hands. Anna introduced Levi, Asa, and Tom as Clarissa stood quietly beside Levi with Tucker. Anna picked up Clarissa and said, "This is Clarissa, my daughter."

George was a bit startled, but didn't comment. He dropped to one knee and said, "I'm George, Clarissa, your grand-uncle. Can I pick you up?"

Clarissa nodded and George stood up holding Clarissa, saying, "Well, another pretty girl in the family, I hope we get to be good friends." Clarissa was entranced with George's wavy, silver hair and asked, "Can I touch your hair?"

"You sure can, but don't pull on it," George grinned, and everyone laughed.

Levi took over the introductions and presented Nathan, Asa, and Tom to Helen. Helen was seated holding Frank Jr. and Tucker came over, sniffed the baby, turned away, and sat down next to Levi.

# CHAPTER 21

# HELEN'S STORY AND
# PARTING COMPANY

Levi couldn't hold back his curiosity any longer and had to ask, "Helen, what happened to make you leave Frank?" Levi noticed Helen seemed a little unsettled hearing the question. He realized she had just met these people and might not want to share her personal life with his friends, but after pausing for a few seconds, she began to relate what had occurred in Pittsburgh.

"It was about two months ago. Frank came home from the bank late; there had been something wrong with the accounts. The bookkeeper couldn't balance the books and Frank had to help him. Frank found the problem; it was a simple error caused by reversing the order of two numbers. The bookkeeper made some excuse for not finding the mistake, something about forgetting the rule of nines, whatever that is. Frank got mad, telling him to do a better job or he would be fired. They argued. Frank left the bank and came home, still fuming.

I had kept his dinner warm, but he said it wasn't good and threw it on the floor, breaking the dinner plate. The loud noise caused Frank Jr. to start crying, so I picked him up. Frank got mad at me and yelled that I should leave the baby alone and get his dinner. I put the baby down, but he kept crying, and Frank kept yelling at me to keep the baby quiet. What was I to do? I picked up the baby and Frank grabbed him from me and nearly threw him in his crib. I yelled at Frank to be careful, he would hurt little Frank. Then, Frank picked up a pillow, put it over the baby's face, and glared at me. I yelled at Frank to stop, but he pushed me away. I yelled at him that he was going to smother Frank Jr., but he wouldn't listen; it was as if he had gone mad. I picked up the poker from the fireplace and swung it as hard as I could at Frank's arm, the one holding the pillow. I really wanted to hit him in the head, but I didn't want to kill him, I would probably end up in prison, and then, who would take care of little Frank?"

Helen paused, looked around at all the concerned faces, took a deep breath, and continued, "Frank grabbed his arm and yelled that I broke it. He stepped away from Frank Jr. and I took the pillow. The baby was okay but still crying. I started to pick him up and Frank hit me with his fist, knocking me to the floor, so I grabbed the baby and ran out of the house next door to the Jacobs'. Mr. Jacobs is a lawyer and his wife, Pamela, and I are good friends. I told them what happened and Mr. Jacobs said I could claim cruel and inhuman treatment. He said he would help me get a divorce; he never liked Frank. In the meantime I could stay with them. I got some of my clothes, all my money, and as soon as possible, we left on a train. When I couldn't go any further west by train, I took stagecoaches until I got here. I was lucky to happen upon you at Rock Creek. I knew then that everything was going to be all right."

Levi responded, "I'm glad you and the baby are all right. If I'd been there, I'd have broken his other arm and his nose. He's nothing but sh..." He looked at Clarissa and said, "crap."

Anna sat beside Helen and put her arm on Helen's shoulder. "Can I hold the baby?" Helen placed little Frank in Anna's arms and the women began talking quietly. Levi motioned for the men to move to another table. After they were all seated, Levi asked George, "Have you another wagon and someone to ride with?" Before George could answer, Levi added, "I don't think it would be a good idea for you and Nathan to travel through the Blue Mountains with two wagons, two women and a baby."

"Good point, Levi. I've got three men with me, they're staying over at the Army barracks, and I brought a wagon for the plants. I imagine Anna and Nathan are pretty sick of dealing with those little trees in their wagon."

"Actually, they haven't had to worry about the plants. Those seedlings have been growing in a cart behind the wagon. Asa and I made a cart from an old wagon at Fort Laramie. Asa did most of the work, and we added a yoke of oxen to pull the extra weight. We had only one mishap, but we recovered. What are your plans?"

"We'll transfer the plants to my wagon, and in the morning, if everyone is ready, we'll be off to Cascade Fruit and Vegetables; that's the name of my farm in Oregon. I figure it will take us about three weeks. I assume Helen and the baby will be coming with us, is that correct?"

"Yes sir. Tom, his two brothers, Asa, if he wants to join us, and I are going into the mountains northeast of here and do some gold mining. Helen and the baby shouldn't make the trip. It would be too dangerous for them. What do you think, Asa, do you want to come with us?"

"I'd be proud to, Levi. I was going to look for gold in California, but if I can do it here, that's even better. Here I'll be with people I trust and if I went to California, I would be by myself. I could get killed for my gold." Asa stood up smiling and shook hands with Levi. Asa added, chuckling, "And, if I went to California, I wouldn't have my dog."

Levi explained the joke to George, who laughed and slapped Asa on the back saying, "You are a funny man, Asa. Anna tells me you are a good cook. When you are through hunting for gold, you have a job at our farm to cook and help with the crops."

Asa replied, "Thank you." He smiled and added, "If I find enough gold, I'll buy a farm and be in competition with you."

"Aha! You not only have a good sense of humor, but you're also smart. I'd better be careful."

The remainder of the day was used to ready the wagons for two different journeys, one to the northeast into the mountains, and the other further west along the Columbia River. The Jeffers and Levi bought mining equipment and loaded the cart after removing the small trees, and Asa readied the harness for the oxen. Tucker kept getting underfoot and had to be tied to a post to keep the men from tripping over him. Tucker knew something different was happening—Anna and Clarissa weren't with the men as before.

The two groups of travelers assembled for supper in the lodge. The three men working for George Cabot, as well as James and Ron Jeffers were included, making eleven adults. As everyone was getting seated, Anna posed a question to the others, "Do you know what day this is?"

George Cabot answered, "I saw some red, white, and blue banners being put up, so my guess is July 4, Independence Day, or maybe the day before."

"That's right, Uncle George. Today is Independence Day. There will be fireworks tonight outside the fort. I think Clarissa will like it, unless it is too loud. The big noises might scare her and the baby."

After a big meal, while the adults talked about the upcoming trips, Clarissa roamed around the lodge, curious about everything she saw. When she noticed a mounted bear's head high on the wall over the bar, she walked over to Levi, pulled on his shirt, pointed at the mounted animal head, and said, "What's that?"

Levi glanced where Clarissa was pointing and answered, "That is the head of a bear." Levi thought that was the end of it, but unexpectedly, Clarissa asked, "Where's the rest?" "Well, the fur was made into a rug or clothing and the meat was made into steaks."

"Did the bear go to heaven?"

"Is a bear one of God's creatures?" Levi asked.

"Yes, but if the bear was a bad bear, would it go to heaven?"

Levi was going to tell Clarissa to ask her mama, but he decided to attempt an answer with, "I think all creatures go to heaven and

God decides which ones can stay." Clarissa seemed happy with the answers and scampered off to play with Tucker. Levi was relieved with the end of the questions. In his remotest thoughts, he hadn't considered how difficult being a little girl's papa was going to be.

Levi watched Anna stand and come over to him. She bent down and said, "What was that all about?"

"She wanted to know about that bear," Levi answered as he pointed up to the mounted head.

He smiled and continued, "I *barely* knew what to say."

Anna laughed and replied, "I thought you only joked in the morning."

Levi replied, "There are a few exceptions." He grinned and stood up. "Let's go see the fireworks."

At 5:30 a.m., everyone was up and eating breakfast, talking about last minute preparations for their journeys. The Cabots were going to stay with the wagon train all the way to The Dalles, on the Columbia River, and turn off to go about a mile to the Cabots' farm. They had to wait for the wagon train to move out so had a chance to say goodbyes to Levi's crew.

Ron and James Jeffers and Asa hitched up the oxen and were ready to move out as soon as everyone had their horses ready. Since Asa was going to drive the cart, he sold one of his pack horses at the fort. The cart was packed to nearly overflowing with mining tools and food for five men. Levi was talking to Anna and Clarissa, and Tom was talking to Helen as the other men waited, impatient to get started toward the mountains and begin their search for gold.

Tom had taken a liking to Helen when he first laid eyes on her and the baby. He was commenting to Helen about visiting the Cabots for Christmas with Levi, his brothers, and Asa.

"It was very nice meeting you and the baby. I guess I'll be seeing you at Christmas. Anna is going to send a message to Fort Boise in November giving us directions to the farm."

"It was nice meeting you and your brothers, Tom. I'm wondering if you gentlemen will be able to get to The Dalles by Christmas. Mr. Cabot says it will take us about three weeks to get there."

"Well, horses can travel much faster than wagons, ma'am. I believe it should only take us about a week, especially since we have people waiting to see us. I hope to get to know you much better when we arrive for the holiday. Take care of yourself and the baby."

Helen smiled, "I will. Good luck in the mountains. Be careful and watch out for Levi for me. Good bye."

Tom smiled, tipped his hat, and said, "Good bye, Helen." He motioned to Levi that he was joining the others, and walked away. He took about ten steps, stopped, did a relaxed about-face, and looked back at Helen. She had watched Tom walk away, and when Tom turned around, she waved to him. Tom removed his hat and waved back at Helen. Now he had something to look forward to when they rode to The Dalles for Christmas, he wouldn't have to moon over Anna, who was his friend's girl. Tom wondered what Levi would think of his interest in Helen.

"I'm not going to say goodbye, Levi. It sounds too final and it will be just a few months before

we start planning for the Christmas season and the New Year. If I tell you goodbye, I know I'll start to cry, and that will make you and Clarissa feel sad, too. So good luck with your search for gold and take care of yourself. I'll send a letter to you at Fort Boise at Thanksgiving, just like I said before. I'll expect all five of you and Tucker for Christmas. Keep an eye on Tom, I think he likes Helen, and I'm sure when she gets to know him, they'll make a good couple. Maybe by Christmas she will be ready to look for a new man."

"I understand about not wanting to say goodbye. If you start crying, then I'll start, too. Have a good trip to The Dalles, and I'll see you for Christmas, maybe Thanksgiving." Levi took Anna in his arms, kissed her, and uttered, "I'll miss you and Clarissa." Levi picked up Clarissa and said, "I'll see you at Christmas. Can you give me a kiss on the cheek?"

Clarissa gave Levi a peck on the cheek, a big hug, and said, "Bye papa."

Levi walked slowly over to Bravo and swung into the saddle. "Come on, Tucker, we're heading for the mountains." Levi watched Tucker sitting where the men and women had said their goodbyes. Tucker was turned toward the women, watching them walking away and stood up, took a few steps toward Anna and Clarissa, stopped, reversed his course, and came running after Levi.

"Good boy, Tucker—a little indecision, eh? I don't blame you."

# CHAPTER 22

## INTO THE MOUNTAINS

The gold seekers traveled for about a day and a half before arriving in Idaho City. The gold strike in the Boise Basin that had peaked during the last two years of the war had begun to peter out, and by the middle of 1866, nearly a hundred people were leaving the mining town each month. Disgruntled miners leaving the area told Levi's group to not waste their time looking for gold in the Idaho City area. Levi told them the truth; he and his friends were just passing through. None of the people from the exodus bothered to ask Levi where the five newcomers were headed.

They forded the south fork of the Payette River the next afternoon and had run out of trails to follow. There were dense forests in all directions and the easiest passage was to follow the river on the north bank, which they did for a little more than a day. About noon that day they stopped to rest and have something to eat.

Tom was sitting on a large rock next to the water. He began talking to Levi. "The wheels are taking a beating on the rocks, Levi. I don't think the cart is going to be serviceable much longer. It doesn't look like we'll be able to find a trail through the forest, either."

"I think you're right, Tom. Let's divvy up the food into equal parcels; same with the tools. That way if a horse goes down, we'll still be able to forge ahead. We can come back for whatever we leave. Let's start marking our trail by cutting into the trees with our hatchets. How about a triangle? Anyone have another suggestion?"

Asa answered, "Better make the mark high up, the snow might cover it up if it's too low. Probably should stand on our saddle to make the marks and make them on the east and the north. That way we can tell directions."

James commented, "Damn good idea, Asa."

Ron asked, "What about the oxen—we gonna take them?"

Levi answered, "I guess we'll have to let them loose. Indians will get them...or wolves. What do you think, Tom?"

"I agree with you. I don't want us to herd the oxen through the forest. They're not agile enough to make it up and down steep slopes like horses can. They'd just slow us down or get injured."

Levi said, "Okay. Let's transfer the contents of the cart to our pack horses and get out of here. We've still a ways to go."

Asa took over the distribution of the food from the cart and the others began packing their horses with tools. A half-hour later, they were ready to travel. Asa told the others to go on, he would catch up. He was going to remove the yoke and harness from the oxen and leave the animals where there was plentiful grass. He debated about taking the harness, but decided the extra weight would just hinder his already heavily loaded pack horses. He tossed the harness over a low branch of a dead tree and set off to catch up to his companions. Asa stopped, after leading his pack horses about thirty yards, and looked back at the oxen to see if they were grazing and at peace. They were gone and so was the harness. The yoke had been on the ground, now it was leaning against a tree.

A chill ran down Asa's spine and the hairs stood up on the back of his neck, he was alone and being watched. He scanned the surroundings, but couldn't detect anyone. The only sounds he could hear were his horses' breathing and the stream water passing over rocks creating miniature waterfalls. He motioned his horse forward and in a couple of minutes could see the others. Asa looked behind, to see if they were being followed, but couldn't detect anyone. He was relieved to not have gotten a bullet or an arrow in the back as he left the oxen.

The five men continued riding almost due north for about three hours, occasionally stopping for the horses to drink from mountain streams and to climb down from their saddles for needed breaks. They had made good progress that afternoon, travelling in a fairly wide valley between two more densely forested mountain ranges. As the valley narrowed, Levi signaled the others to stop so he could get a better view of what lay ahead. He told them to wait while he rode to the top of a nearby peak. However, the dense tree growth prevented him from seeing much of anything. A towering pine tree appeared to be jutting above its neighbors, but the lowest branches were going to be difficult to reach. Levi tied a small piece of a broken branch to his rope and tossed the weighted end over the lowest branch. Scaling the tree wasn't the easiest thing he had ever done, but when he reached a point to see above the surrounding tree tops, he observed two mountains to the northeast, which he estimated to be 20 to 30 miles away. He took out his compass and made note of their headings. It took Levi over thirty minutes to get back to Asa and the Jeffers.

"Where the hell did you go, Levi?" Tom quizzed. "We weren't sure you were coming back." They all laughed. "Find any gold nuggets?"

"I had to climb a tall tree to find a likely spot that might yield some gold. I figure somewhere between two big mountains might be a likely place for gold to collect. The streams from both mountain runoffs might come together, doubling our chances of finding the metal. Gold is pretty heavy, right Tom?"

"It's about nineteen times as dense as water, but you can't say it's heavy. For example, a gallon of water is heavier than an ounce of gold. But, if you have a large amount of it, it would be heavy, just like a large amount of anything."

Levi smiled and said, "Thanks Tom. I won't make that mistake again. We'll have to refer to your mining experience more often. Where would *you* look for gold?"

"Your idea about the mountain streams is a good one. We'll do some panning in the streams and if we find some color, we'll look upstream to see if we can find the source. It might not be easy though. Sometimes gold deposits are associated with quartz, so we might find some quartz that contains gold. If so, we'll have to dig out the quartz and break it up to get at the gold. If we find where those miners that your sister mentioned in her letter are working, it might save us a lot of time."

Levi commented, "Well, let's camp here for the night; the light's not good now. In the morning, we'll need good light to see trails that others have made coming and going."

Tom and Levi made a fire while James and Ron secured the horses and unpacked some of their heavy loads. Asa made supper and as they ate, he related what had happened earlier in the day with the oxen.

Ron said, "You sure those animals didn't just wander off?"

"Somebody took 'em, I'm sure about it."

"How come you're so sure?" quizzed James.

"'Cause the harness was gone and the yoke was leaning against that tree. I had put it on the ground. I think we're being watched...trying to figure out what we're doing."

James grinned and said, "I think Asa's scared of the woods, that's all. He's seein' things."

Levi responded, "I know Asa and I believe him. Let's post a guard tonight. Take two-hour stretches. We'll draw straws and use my watch for the time. When your time is up, give the watch to the next man, okay? Anyone not on guard tonight will have to patrol next time. Don't break my watch."

The night passed without incident. Levi had the last session and started the campfire as the sun was coming up. He had spent most of the two hours thinking about Anna, Clarissa, and Helen and wondered how they were faring on the wagon train with George Cabot. Levi had tried to locate Cassiopeia, the constellation that reminded him of Anna, but he couldn't see the big W, the trees blocked most of the stars, except the few directly overhead, and they weren't very bright.

Asa started cooking breakfast as the others began to stir; the odor of hot coffee seemed to make the woods more habitable. Everyone had slept in their clothes; even though it was still summer, the chilly evening in the forest felt more like October in the east than the second week of July. Tucker had gone into the woods apparently to take care of business, about the time Levi started the fire. Levi followed the dog about 50 yards before he lost sight of Tucker. Levi whistled, but Tucker failed to reappear, so Levi returned to the campfire. Everyone was drinking coffee as they waited for Asa's biscuits and bacon when Tucker appeared at the edge of the campsite, sat down, and barked.

Levi quizzed, "Where'd you go, boy?"

Ron suggested, "I think he was checking out a female wolf. Did you hear them last night? Sounded like a whole chorus a ways off to the north."

Levi patted his leg and said, "Here, Tucker."

Tucker turned away, walked about five yards, stopped, and looked back at Levi. "Here, Tucker."

Tucker ignored Levi, and then repeated the same motions, and barked.

Levi picked up a piece of bacon and said, "I guess he wants me to go with him. Okay, Tucker, I'm coming."

Tom stood up and said, "I'll come along. Gotta make sure you come back. No telling who might be out there." Tom picked up his rifle, grabbed a piece of bacon, and joined Levi. "What do ya think the dog wants, Levi?"

"I have no idea, but I guess we'll find out soon enough."

Tom and Levi followed Tucker for about two hundred yards west and came to a small clearing where a stream changed directions. Tucker was waiting for the men at the edge of the clearing and when Levi approached Tucker, he bounded across the grass and downed trees, stopped across the open area next to a tree, and barked. The men had to avoid a large huckleberry shrub to see where Tucker was standing. They picked their way around the shrub and Levi saw what had attracted Tucker, two dead bodies. Not much remained of the two corpses except bones and a small amount of rotting flesh in the boots and the skulls. Animals and bugs had picked most of the bones nearly clean.

Tom knelt beside the bones closest to him and said, "Pretty gruesome, Levi. Look in this one's eye sockets. What is that, gold?"

Levi joined Tom and dropped to his knees to get a closer look. "Damn! I think you're right. This man had his eyes poked out and gold dust poured in. Hope he was already dead when that was done. Let's get a shovel and bury what's left. Whew! They stink something awful!"

Tom added, "I don't see papers or anything to tell us who they were. Maybe we'll meet someone that'll know. Think they were killed here?"

"Don't think so, Tom. The way the bones are...looks like they were dragged here by animals. Yah, I see some claw marks on the ground. It must have been a bear, a big one."

# CHAPTER 23

# MINERS

After burying the remains of the two men, Tom and Levi rode to the northeast to catch up with Ron, James, and Asa, who had broken camp and started toward the two mountains Levi had seen. It was easy for Levi and Tom to track the others; Tucker's nose was very dependable. Late in the afternoon, the five men began to notice horse tracks and excrement. They decided to follow the second set of tracks, which were newer and more prominent than the first set, to see where they led.

They followed the path for about a mile and came to a small stream weaving its way through a gently sloping region of large boulders and many smaller, fist-size, river rocks. The water was less than a foot deep and easy to negotiate, the bottom looked muddy, but the water was clear. After a quarter-mile or so, the boulders were no longer present, just fist-size rocks and pebbles in piles. Tom was the first to comment. "This is a mining area, Levi. These rock piles are manmade. There must be a sluice nearby."

"I thought those piles of stones looked artificial, not nature made."

They rode in the stream for about 50 yards where the water came around a small hill on the right. Levi and Tom saw the miners first, stopped riding, and let Ron, James, and Asa catch up to them. One of the miners yelled when he saw the riders and the miners reached for their weapons. Levi counted six men, three at a sluice box with rifles, two more standing in water with shovels and pistols, and a sixth man, carrying a rifle, running for cover in the trees on the far side of the stream.

One of the bearded men at the sluice called out, "You're trespassing; this is our claim."

Levi replied, "Relax, we're passing through, headed upstream toward those two mountains to the northeast." Levi pointed in the general direction they were headed. Levi fished Helen's letter from his pocket, found the name of her friend and said, "By any chance do you know the name Harriet Blodget?"

The man called out to the miner behind the trees, "Hey Blodg! You know anyone named Harriet?"

"I got a niece named Harriet. She's back east. You got some news about her, mister?"

"No. She knows my sister, Helen Collins Wisdom. She told my sister about you finding some gold in the Idaho area, so we came to check on it. We're the only ones that know."

"Damn! I told her to keep it quiet. I should've never told a woman! They just blab it around. So, who are you men?"

Levi introduced himself and the others to the miners, each giving their name.

The tallest man, balding, named Curly, said, "You mentioned two mountains up yonder. They's Granite Peak and Old Baldy. Nothing up there but hard rock mining. The easy dust's in the waters down here. That's rough country up there, lots of wolves, bears, and Indians. If one of them don't git ya, the winter snow's over twelve-foot. You won't get much done in three months. Then you'll have to git out, or freeze your arses."

The third man, Jed, next to the sluice said, "That's the God's truth. Say, did you gents see two men on their way to Idaho City? They was goin' to be 'bout a week, at most two, but they ain't back yet. Been gone three weeks."

Levi answered, "We found two bodies about fifteen miles back; not much but bones remained. It looked as if a bear had dragged the bodies into a clearing near a lazy little stream. Strange thing though, the skulls still had gray matter, and gold dust had been poured into the eye sockets."

The man replied, "God damn those fools! Harley and Ted Richter was going to Idaho City to get their horns trimmed. They must have stumbled onto some bare-breasted Indian women and took advantage. Shoshone men must have caught 'em and put an end to 'em. The women probly poked out their eyes with sticks and poured their gold dust in the holes. They had two ounces of dust, enough to buy whores and dinner and come back. I guess they couldn't wait."

Tom added, "We buried what was left of them. We can tell you where they're buried."

"No matter. Fools got what was comin'. We got an understandin' with the Shoshone. We leave 'em alone and they leave us be. Too bad about the gold, though. But thanks for the info."

Levi said, "We'll be on our way; don't want to hold up your work any longer. We might see you again on our way down from the valley between those mountains."

Jed said, "Better not stay up there past October. Good luck to ya."

Levi, the Jeffers, and Asa left the stream to avoid the area where the miners were working and moved along the banks until the water came from the west. The men turned back to the northeast and continued riding for the rest of the day toward the two big mountain peaks. They stopped to make camp at the foot of Granite Peak. Old Baldy was estimated to be another five to ten miles, maybe farther, to the east.

While Asa made supper, the others tended to the horses and then grabbed their pans and worked at the stream next to the campsite. Levi had never panned for gold before, so Tom gave him some instructions and watched as Levi practiced.

"That's not bad, Levi; you'll get much better at it with some practice. You're gonna get a lot of that. With experience you'll get more efficient so your arms won't get so tired."

As Levi scooped more dirt and pebbles into his pan, he heard the cry of birds high overhead. Looking up, he could see three large birds, most likely eagles, catching wind currents, soaring toward the high elevations of Granite Peak. Thinking of what the birds could see below, Levi recalled what he had experienced at Fort Laramie when he had too much heat. He wondered what the women were doing and how much further they had to travel to get to George Cabot's farm at The Dalles.

"Come and get it," interrupted Levi's thoughts. Asa's deep voice was easily heard above the ripples made by the cold water passing around the rocks in the stream. Levi dropped his pan on the bank to mark his location and walked back to the campfire, where Ron and James had already started eating. They must have been standing over Asa, mouths drooling, in order to have gotten their food so quickly. Levi smiled thinking the younger men were still growing. *How much would they be eating after a full day of manual labor?*

Levi dried his hands on his trousers and rubbed them together to warm up after having his fingers in cold water for about fifteen minutes. Maybe he would get used to the cold after a day or two of panning. Then again, maybe he and Asa could make a sluice box, which would eliminate some of the contact with cold stream water.

Levi had his mouth full when a question popped into his mind. He swallowed quickly and asked, "When do we call ourselves miners, Tom?" Levi smiled but was somewhat serious. Levi watched Tom, who smiled, but didn't respond immediately. Tom realized Levi's question was not meant to get a laugh. James, Ron, and Asa stopped their conversation and directed their attention to Tom, and listened intently.

"Well, you might consider yourself a miner as soon as you begin the search, but I would require something in addition. When you begin to make more than you have invested and enough additional to put money in the bank, you'd be a miner, at least a successful one. That's the way I see it."

The five men sat in silence thinking of what Tom had said. Howls from the woods broke the relative quiet of the stream water. Tucker got up from lying near the fire and walked around looking toward the darkening area beyond the tall pines in the direction of the howling.

Asa commented, "Wolves. It sounds like a few different voices. Won't be long and they'll know we're here. They'll smell us, the food, and the horses. As soon as we get located, we'd better build a fenced area to protect the horses. It'll keep them from runnin' off if the wolves start nippin' at 'em."

In the morning, the men felt like they had just gone to sleep. Wild animals, Indians, and the low mountain temperatures coupled with unfamiliar surroundings had made everyone a bit nervous.

Tom woke up whenever a wolf howled. He wondered if he would ever get used to the wailing cries. Tom felt like he hadn't slept a wink, was frustrated, and got up at dawn and panned in several locations. He checked along the banks of the stream and on the downstream side of some large rocks, but had only found a few tiny specs of gold. If he hadn't had good vision, he would have missed the tiny particles. He started a fire to warm his hands and Asa joined him to make coffee and biscuits.

As the others collected around the fire for coffee, Tom said, "Let's work this area until noon and move on if we don't find anything significant." Everyone agreed and by one o'clock they had packed their horses and started moving farther east into the valley between the big mountains. As the men picked their way through the trees, they rode through several small creeks, but didn't stop. It was Tom's opinion the small streams lacked the volume of water necessary to wash gold down from higher elevations.

A relatively sudden change in surroundings occurred as they moved up a wide valley at the southeastern foot of Granite Mountain. Levi led the men a hundred yards down a steep decline to a broad, fairly flat landscape with cedar and broadleaf trees in abundance. The rolling hills extended for a half-mile to the north and the east before the tall pines and jagged rocks resumed, hindering easy passage. A stream, a little larger than the one from the previous day, where they had encountered the miners, passed through the higher hills, winding down to their present location.

Ron rode over to take a look at the stream, dismounted and squatted to look more closely through the water at the bed. He reached into the water and scooped up a handful of gray and white sand. Ron didn't make any attempt to look at the grains of sand; he was startled by the warmth of the water. He quickly rinsed his hands free of sand grains, stripped off all his clothes, and splashed into the water, found a pool where the water was about two feet deep, and sat down. Ron hadn't had a warm bath since leaving Fort Laramie. He yelled, "James, bring me some soap!"

Levi had been watching Ron as he rode to the stream, but he was amused when Ron got naked and rushed into the water, sat down, and began splashing himself. Ron was acting like a little boy playing in a public fountain.

Levi laughed when Asa grinned and commented, "Well, now I know for sure why you are white men." Asa yelled back at Ron, "Now I'll have to go upstream to get water for coffee."

Levi watched James ride over to Ron, dismount and search through his saddlebags. Ron and James were talking about something, but they were too distant to be heard. James tossed a bar of soap to Ron, took off his own clothes, waded into the water, and found another deep spot to sit in. Tom, the only brother remaining dry, yelled, "Ain't that water cold? It's coming off the mountain."

Ron yelled back, "No! The water's warm!"

Tom looked at Levi and said, "Let's do some panning. We can take baths later."

Levi and Tom rode about 50 yards upstream and began panning where the stream had broadened and was shallower than the bathing area. Tom dipped his pan into the sand and pebbles and Levi, using his shovel, dug deeper into the stream bed and began panning. In about a minute, Tom said, with disgust, "Nothing!"

Levi, a novice at the procedure, spent several minutes washing the silt from his pan, and repeatedly discarded the less dense material, including pebbles and sand. "Hey Tom, take a look."

Levi was looking at several sparkling gold-colored specks and some tiny, glassy particles with gold colored spots adhering to them.

Tom, his boots half-full of water, trudged over to Levi, expecting to tell Levi to keep trying, a beginner will eventually find something of value, but when he studied the bottom of Levi's pan, he looked up at Levi, smiled, and said, "Damn! Beginner's luck! You've got some colors!" Tom grabbed Levi's right hand, shook it vigorously, patted him on the back and said, "We need to build a sluice box like those miners had, so we can process more material and start accumulating gold dust. We might be able to get an ounce a day, maybe more, from a sluice. Maybe you and Asa can build us one; you did a good job on that cart. Over at the edge of the pine forest, I noticed some downed cedar logs you can split and make into boards. While you are building, me and the boys will work this area. Maybe we'll find where it's coming from."

Asa had set up a temporary camp near a cluster of cedars and huckleberry shrubs while the others were bathing and panning. He had secured the horses to a rope strung between two trees and started a pot of coffee. Levi joined him and showed Asa the gold he had found. Asa looked intently at the assortment of black and white sand, tiny pebbles, and a few sparkling gold specks at the bottom of Levi's pan.

He looked at Levi, frowned, and said, "Those tiny bits are gonna make us rich?"

Levi spoke reassuringly, "We'll get lots more, Asa. Remember that wooden trough those miners had? Tom wants us to build one so we can recover the gold that's at the bottom of the stream. If it works, we can get a month's wages in one day."

"Sure do remember that thing. When you was talking to those men, I was wondering how it worked. I looked at how it was made. I'll get my tools."

Asa and Levi left coffee and biscuits for the Jeffers and made their way to the dried cedar logs. They spent most of the afternoon making a rough plank about eight-feet long, twelve-inches wide, and two-inches thick for the bottom of the sluice. They stopped work to take a warm bath, have supper, and then made sides for the sluice, sealing voids with pine tree pitch. After completing the sluice, Levi used a pack horse to drag the contraption near the camp site. Everyone gathered for coffee before turning in.

Levi asked, "Where do we put the sluice, Tom?"

Tom hesitated, throwing the remainder of his coffee toward the stream, and answered, "There's a spot about a quarter-mile upstream where the water narrows. It should be easy to dam the water there and divert part of the flow through the sluice. We need a height of about two-feet to keep a good amount of water flowing over the riffles. We'll make a dam in the morning."

The bright sunlight vanished quickly in the mountains; the long gray-green shadows lost their green hues, growing darker as the light dimmed. An accompanying drop in temperature caused the men to don their coats. Asa had established camp only a few yards from the warm stream water ripples. The men were all asleep by nine o'clock, having put in an active day, but Tucker sat near the fire next to Levi, alertly listening to the howling wolves' voices coming from the surrounding forests. He tired of the howling, curled up beside Levi, watched uneasily for a few minutes, and closed his eyes.

# CHAPTER 24

# SNOW

Levi was awakened by Tucker's sudden movements and prolonged growl. Levi looked up at a gray sky; the sun was still hidden by the mountains and the forests. Near his feet, ashes from the extinguished campfire had been scattered by a slight breeze during the night. Tucker's second, louder growl caused Levi to look up at his dog, and then toward the stream, where two people were standing next to Asa, who was still asleep. The larger figure stood with his arms crossed, his feet planted firmly in the gray sand, seeming to be waiting for a reply, although no words had been spoken, and the other, smaller figure, a striking young woman, was staring at Asa and smiling, perhaps amused by the large, unaware, soundly sleeping man. Levi started to reach for his pistol, but noted the two Indians were not armed. He relaxed and said loudly, "Asa, I believe you have some visitors."

"What?" Asa rose up on his left elbow, wiped his face with his right hand, looked at Levi, and then at the Indians. Asa tossed his blanket back and sat up cross-legged, eyes scanning the Indians from head to toe. Pulling on his shirt, Asa quickly got to his feet and said something to the man, whose features appeared to be chiseled from granite. The man answered and held his hands, palms up, toward the young woman, and then Asa.

The three Jeffers were awake now, fumbling with their blankets and clothes, looking at Asa and the two Indians. Tom spoke up, "Levi, what's goin' on?"

"I don't know. I can't understand what they're saying, but I think it's something about the woman. We'll have to wait and find out from Asa." Levi watched the woman bend down and rub her fingers together to attract Tucker. Tucker looked at Levi and then at the petite woman and cautiously moved toward her, his tail moving slowly from side to side. When Tucker was close enough for her to touch him, she sank slowly to her knees, carefully reached over and stroked Tucker's head and back with both hands. She said something with a pleasant voice which Levi imagined to be *good dog*. Tucker's tail was wagging as he licked her face, which she turned away, laughing delightfully.

Asa and the Indian had concluded their talking, which to Levi seemed to be bargaining, rather than a neighborly chat. Asa said something to the Indian, who nodded and joined the young woman. Asa was biting his upper lip and was decidedly nervous when he stepped over to talk with Levi and said, "The Indian is a tribal chief called Thunder Eagle, and the woman is his daughter-in-law. He wants me to have her as my wife. Her husband, the chief's son, was killed by a giant grizzly two weeks ago and he doesn't think any of his tribe is worthy of having her. They've been watchin' us and their witch doctor considers me a great warrior, and my dark skin is a good omen because Thunder Eagle's son's name was Black Cloud. Her name is Snow at Dawn. Their present home is a few miles east of Bald Mountain. I told him we don't have any place for a woman, but he said she can sleep on the ground. He has an answer for everything, Levi. What should I do?"

"Did you tell him *no*?"

"I couldn't figure how to do that. He said there are thirty braves in the trees watching us. I believe 'im. He said he would leave the woman for two days and return to see if she is all right. If she isn't all right, they'll kill us. If we get along for two weeks, they will have a wedding ceremony at their camp and we all have to go.

They will protect us from other tribes and we have to promise not to fight against them. What would you do, Levi?"

"Have you looked at her, Asa? She's a beautiful woman, soft spoken, and seems to like animals. Tucker likes her—that's a good thing. I'll bet she can cook, mend clothes, and carry out other womanly duties. What's the risk? If she doesn't like you, she'll leave. Maybe you'll like each other, fall in love and have lots of babies. And your father-in-law is a tribal chief. Sounds like a pretty good arrangement to me. You know any other women around here?"

"No. So you fellas don't mind?"

"Well, it's all right with me. I don't think the Jeffers care as long as you do your share of mining and cook for us. We can help you build a cabin—maybe one for the rest of us, too. We'll start a village with a few houses. Maybe Anna and Clarissa will come to visit next spring. I'll need a house for them, too. But first, I think you should explain the situation to the Jeffers and see what they say."

Asa strode over to the Jeffers, crouched down and began talking. Levi watched as the brothers listened and asked some questions. Less than two minutes later, the Jeffers stood up and shook hands with Asa, who gave Levi the thumbs up and smiled. Asa stepped over to Thunder Eagle and concluded the bargain. The Indian chief gave Snow at Dawn an impassive look, a slight nod, and slowly made his way toward the forest to the east. He didn't look back; he had carried out his obligations as a chief.

Knowing Snow at Dawn undoubtedly felt deserted by her father-in-law, Asa helped her up from the ground and had her sit by the circle of rocks as he started a fire. Her worried eyes darted around the camp, looking briefly at the men, the horses, and Tucker. Unaware of the Shoshone words for nearly everything, Asa started giving her the English names and terms for everything he was doing. In a few minutes, her smile returned and she began to respond, hesitantly beginning to say a few of the English words she had heard from Asa, and telling him the words in her language. As Asa began making breakfast, he offered Snow a taste of bacon, biscuits, and coffee. She approved of the bacon and biscuits, but after making a disapproving grimace, Snow spit out the coffee and wiped her mouth with the back of her hand. Asa offered her a drink of water, but she refused, making some gestures indicating the water from the stream would make her sick.

Following breakfast the Jeffers and Levi began towing the sluice upstream, leaving Asa and Snow to clean up the campsite and continue getting acquainted. Snow watched Asa begin cleaning the metal dishes in the stream, and when Asa scooped up some water for a drink, Snow yelled, and dashed to his side, knocking the metal cup of water from his hand. She picked up the cup and handed it to Asa apologetically, and then made gestures as before, indicating the water would make him sick.

Asa suddenly realized none of them had gotten sick from the water because they had only used it for boiling-hot coffee. Snow took Asa's hand and led him into the forest to a brook, the water cascading from between rocks on the side of a steep rocky hill about two hundred yards from their camp. She cupped her hands, drank the cool water, and then indicated Asa should fill his cup and drink. They went back to camp, and while Snow gathered all the canteens, Asa ran to where Levi and the Jeffers were working and told them not to drink the stream water without boiling it first. When Asa returned to camp, Snow was gone, and so were all the canteens. He returned to the brook to find Snow putting the cap on the last canteen. She had rinsed out all the containers and refilled them with potable water.

Asa thanked Snow in Shoshone and English, slung all but two of the canteen straps over his shoulders, leaving something for Snow to carry. Asa began the walk back to camp, looking back to see Snow smiling as she followed him closely, attempting to place her feet where Asa had tread. They had only gone a few yards when Snow began to laugh; she had to take nearly two strides for one of Asa's, and she was trying to jump to compensate. She gave up and ran ahead of Asa, who couldn't keep up with her and still carry all the full canteens. Asa started chuckling and stopped walking to see what Snow would do. She looked back at Asa, stopped, started laughing, and motioned with her fingers for Asa to hurry up. When he caught up to her, she would run again, stop, start to giggle and run again. Asa began to think Snow behaved more like a little girl than an Indian princess, but he found her actions entertaining.

Asa had been thinking of how Thunder Eagle had said Snow could sleep on the ground. Asa had been taught to provide the best accommodations available for a woman, no matter who she was. It was time to set up the tent he had gotten from Roebling back at Fort Laramie. The men had rarely been in one location for more than one night and putting up a large tent was too much work for just an overnight stay, but a tent would provide some privacy, and shelter for bad weather until more permanent structures were erected.

# CHAPTER 25

# THE LOCKET

After Asa took fresh water to his friends, he returned to his gear piled near the packhorses and removed a hatchet from a small box of tools. He motioned for Snow to come with him and they walked to the site where the sluice box had been constructed. About 20 minutes later, he had two posts, a dozen stakes, and a ridgepole all fashioned from the remains of cedar logs. Asa set up the tent on a small hill, about 40 yards from the campsite on the opposite side of the stream. Snow entered the tent, looked around, smiled at Asa, and said something he didn't understand. He frowned, but when she grabbed his hand and began pulling him toward the camp, he understood what she meant. They had to get his belongings, including his three horses.

As they crossed the stream, Asa noticed the water was very low and the stream was less than half its normal width. Snow had a puzzled expression on her face. She crouched down and indicated the former level of the water was halfway to her knees. She looked questioningly at Asa, who indicated he thought he knew what had happened. He motioned for Snow to follow him and they started upstream, walking through the grass, wildflowers, and small trees, avoiding the bends in the waterway. A quarter-mile was covered quickly, and when Asa and Snow rounded a bend veering to the left, they came upon Levi and the Jeffers, who had dammed the water with large rocks and timbers, diverting most of the stream in two other directions, one path through the sluice and another over the dam, creating a waterfall, into a different channel away from the campsite to the southwest.

Asa asked Levi, "Did you change the direction of the water on purpose?"

"Yes, Asa. We figured the campsite was a good place for a town to be built, but we don't want bad water running through it. We can use the water behind the dam for bathing and for the sluice, about the way we have it now. How are you and your new bride getting along?"

"Bride? Oh, fine. We set up a tent across the creek from camp and are going to move all my belongings over there."

"Tent?"

"Uh-huh. Got it from Mr. Roebling. First chance I had to set it up. Put it on a hill so if it rains, water will drain away. I'll build a cabin where the tent is—good place for a cabin."

"Sounds like a good plan, Asa. Tonight, after supper, I'll make some sketches for streets and locations of our buildings. Start thinking of a name for our little town. I'll get the Jeffers thinking, too, and ask Snow what her people call this place; maybe we'll get some more ideas from her. There's an axe in my gear. Start cutting some timber for your house. You determine the size. We'll help you a little after supper so you'll get a good start."

Five o'clock ended the day at the sluice, and the men returned to camp to discover Asa had begun construction of a cabin around his tent. Once the roof was on the cabin, he would remove the tent. He had been able to interlock two layers of logs by the time he had to make supper for the mining crew. Snow had used a hatchet to remove some of the bark from the interior walls, not wanting to just sit and watch while the men were constantly working.

During supper they discussed names for their town. Warm River was discarded as not suggesting a place to live, but a stream. Asa asked Snow what her people called this area and she replied, "Howling Wolves," in Shoshone. After several more minutes of discussion and a few more amusing suggestions, the men decided on Wolves' Hollow. Snow volunteered to clean the metal pans used as plates for dinner while the men worked for an hour adding another layer of logs to the walls of the cabin. A nearly full moon graced the sky that night, and a slight breeze accentuated the calls of the wolves, suggesting the animals were close to the camp instead of in the woods several hundred yards away.

Asa was the first one up the next morning. He had refused to accept Snow into his bed and wasn't sure how to handle the situation. Levi joined him for coffee before the other men had fully awakened.

"Levi, I need your advice."

"Sure. What's on your mind?"

"It's kind of embarrassing. Last night Snow stripped naked and started to get in bed with me, but I told her no. I believe she thinks there is something wrong with me or maybe she isn't attractive to me, but that's not the problem. She has a locket around her neck, and I was thinking it might be from Anna's father. When I saw the locket, I couldn't get excited, even though she's a beautiful young woman. I'm wondering where she got that locket and if her husband killed Mr. Cabot? What should I do?"

Levi smiled. "You'd better ask her how she got the locket. If she'll let you, look inside the locket to see if there are pictures inside. Maybe the locket belonged to someone else."

"Good idea. I even thought maybe Snow could be a half-sister to Anna and Nathan. Kind of crazy, huh?"

"Jeez, Asa, the chances of that are extremely small, but now you've got me curious, too." Levi had suddenly turned very serious.

"What are you two talking about?" asked Tom as he joined Asa and Levi at the campfire. Ron and James were walking behind Tom carrying their cups ready for their morning coffee.

"Snow has a locket and we're thinking it might be from Anna's father. Asa has to ask Snow how she got the locket. Where is she, Asa?"

He grinned and said, "She had to make a trip to the woods. She'll be here soon."

The five men sat drinking coffee and chewing on two-day-old biscuits as they planned the day's mining activities. Asa began cooking some bacon as Snow arrived and sat with Tucker away from the others. Levi glanced at Snow and noticed she seemed to be a little nervous, perhaps thinking Asa had told everyone what had happened in the tent.

Asa announced, "Bacon's ready, help yourself." He picked up a couple of pieces of bacon and joined Snow, sitting beside her on the ground. He offered Snow a piece of bacon but she shook her head and opened a little leather pouch containing blackberries. She took a few of the berries and gave the remaining berries to Asa, indicating he should share them with the others.

After Asa passed the berries around, he turned to Snow and attempted to ask her where she had gotten the locket.

Snow stood up, faced the men, and said, in very clear English, "My father gave it to me."

Ron had just swallowed some coffee and he choked, and said, "Holy shit! She speaks American!" He looked at Snow and said, "Sorry about my language, but you surprised me."

Snow chuckled and replied, "That's all right, I've heard many bad words from the other miners. They think I don't know what they're saying."

Tom and Levi glanced at Asa and Levi said, "Did you know she speaks English?"

Asa replied, "No! I only taught her a few words. At least I thought I did."

Levi smiled at Snow and said, "You speak English very well. Who taught you? Did you go to school at one of the forts or a mission?"

"Thank you. My father taught me your language."

Levi asked, "Where did your father learn English?"

"He went to an American school in the east."

"That's a bit unusual for an Indian to go to school in the east."

"Oh!" Snow put her right palm on top of her head, raised her eyebrows, started laughing, and said, "My father isn't Shoshone, he's white, just like you."

Levi was trying to digest what Snow had just said and asked, "What's your father's name?"

"Spotted Ear. Oh, you mean his American name. It's..."

Levi didn't wait for Snow to finish before he interrupted her. "It's Leland Cabot."

Snow was shocked. She put her hand to her mouth in disbelief and said, "How do you know this name?"

Levi smiled and said, "We travelled for three months with his daughter and son, Annabel and Nathan Cabot. Their pictures are in the locket."

Snow grasped the locket and opened it. "No pictures. See." She held the locket so Levi could see inside. The locket was empty.

Levi said, "Cabot must have removed the pictures when he gave you the locket. Do you remember any pictures being inside? How long have you had the locket?"

"Father gave it to me long ago, when I was little. Maybe there were pictures, but I don't remember."

"How old are you, Snow?"

"Almost seventeen." She gave a slight smile, tilted her head a little to the side, and said, "Where are my sister and brother?"

"They're on the way to The Dalles."

"The Dalles? Where is that?"

"That's a town where rapids are on the big river to the west, the Columbia. Leland's brother, your uncle, George Cabot, has a farm there. We'll be going there when the weather turns bad. I'm wondering if you and your father would like to come with us. We'll come back here next spring and continue mining."

"My mother might not like to go away from the Shoshone, but I can ask her. I would like to see my brother and sister. I think my father would like to see them."

Asa asked, "Snow, what is your mother's name? Is it as pretty as yours?"

"Her name is Leaves of Water. Her mother saw reflections of tree leaves in puddles of water after it rained. She is very quiet, but always nice to everyone. She is very close to the gods of the earth."

Asa questioned, "Gods of the earth?"

"Yes, the gods that make flowers, grass, trees, and other things grow from the earth. My father said you call those gods Mother Nature."

Asa continued, "What does your father do?"

Snow thought for a few seconds, tilted her head a little to the side, and answered, "Mostly, he makes medicine from the plants and helps the tribe doctor when Shoshone get sick. Sometimes he tells stories about Jesus. He didn't want me to come here, but Chief Thunder Eagle said I should see if you say bad things about Shoshone."

James, a bit disgusted, tossed the remainder of his coffee on the fire and stated, "You're a spy."

Snow replied, "I don't know that word."

Levi said, "Someone who lives with an enemy and gathers information about the enemy is called a spy."

Snow frowned and stated, "But you are not my enemy. You are all good men. I will tell Thunder Eagle you are just here for the shiny yellow rocks and you know of my father and his other children. Thunder Eagle will come tomorrow."

# CHAPTER 26

# RETURN TO FORT BOISE

Snow slept in the tent that night and Asa moved his bedroll to the campfire, joining the other men. Until Asa parleyed with Thunder Eagle and perhaps Leland Cabot, he was unsure of how to react to Snow. Was she putting on an act or were her actions a result of her true feelings? Asa's thoughts were confusing and he hoped his mind would be clearer the next day.

It was early morning, still dark, but Asa, with a blanket over his shoulders, was sitting next to the fire with Tucker. It would be dawn before long, but the clearer mind Asa had hoped for hadn't emerged. He poked at the fire with a freshly cut branch and tossed two more small logs on the fire. He thought the snapping of the fire might awaken the men, but they were sleeping soundly. He was thinking about Snow and how he would miss her if she returned to her tribe and parents with Thunder Eagle. But how could their two days together have formed a lasting relationship?

"Why are you up so early, Asa?" asked Levi as he looked at his watch. It was 5:17 a.m. and the eastern sky was still dark.

"I couldn't sleep. I keep thinking about Snow, Mr. Cabot, Anna, and Nathan. How would I fit into their family? I don't even know whether Snow cares if I live or die."

Levi thought a minute before he replied. "Maybe you're rushing things a bit. Let's see what Thunder Eagle says after he talks with Snow. Maybe they'll ask you to come to their camp. You'll be able to talk to Cabot in English," he grinned. "Should be easier to understand than nods and hand waving."

The men drank coffee and talked for fifteen minutes about mining and construction of several buildings for living and storage before the Jeffers joined them for breakfast. Bacon, beans, and biscuits were enough to fill them up until afternoon when Asa would have fruit and meat for the mining crew. Asa had seen some deer the day before and he had promised venison would be available later in the day. As the eastern sky brightened, the clear blue sky seemed to indicate a nice day was in store for the miners.

Tucker barked, warning the men of three people approaching the camp. There were two men and a woman walking slowly from the east toward the far river bank. Tucker ran through the water to the woman, tail wagging, and followed the three as they approached Levi, Asa, and the Jeffers.

Asa commented, "Huh. I thought Snow stayed in the tent last night. She must have gone back to her village. That other man must be her father. He doesn't look like an Indian except for the long hair and clothing."

As Snow and the two men came closer, Levi could make out the chief, Snow, and an older man with light gray hair pulled back, tied with a piece of rawhide, and decorated with an eagle feather. It had to be Leland Cabot. As they got even closer, Levi could see, in addition to facial resemblances to Nathan, the elder man had a birthmark on his left ear. He was near Levi's height and had missed few meals.

Asa greeted Thunder Eagle and Snow, and the chief introduced the older, bearded man as Leland Cabot. Asa introduced Levi and the Jeffers and invited the visitors to sit at the campfire. Snow sat behind Thunder Eagle and her father. Mr. Cabot spoke in a low, gravelly voice, "Snow told me you are honorable men, and Asa has treated her with great respect, although she was surprised at you, Asa, for not allowing her in your bed. You may not know it, but the Shoshone are a self-sacrificing people. Snow was assigned, at whatever the cost, the task of finding if you held ill feelings toward the Shoshone. She was amused at your attempts to teach her some English, but she genuinely likes you."

Cabot paused for a few seconds as he looked at each of the men, and then continued, "Snow told me you know my children, Annabel and Nathan. I thought I would never see them again. You see, I have no desire to return to the east. Snow said Annabel and Nathan are on their way to The Dalles by wagon train with my brother. I would like to see them again and have them meet Snow and her mother. We will travel with you when the first snow arrives. We must leave quickly then, or we'll be trapped and not be able to escape from the mountains. The first snow will arrive in eight to ten weeks. I think you realize freezing is not a good way to die. We hope to get to know you better before we travel. You must meet my wife, Laurel. She is a kind-hearted, gentle soul."

Asa spoke up saying, "Was Snow married to Thunder Eagle's son, Mr. Cabot?"

"No. She hasn't married yet, but she does have several suitors. She has not made a decision yet; perhaps next spring when the flowers bloom. Flowers are an important part of the wedding ceremony. We want to apologize for making up that story, but it was the only way Thunder Eagle thought we could gain information about you gentlemen. Half of me disliked the thought, but the Indian half thought it was a pretty good idea. We now recognize you are looking for gold and not trouble. I might be able to help you. I can show you a quartz deposit that could be rich in gold, but it will require some blasting. It's not far from here, where the warm water comes from the mountain."

Levi glanced at Tom, who replied, "That's not a problem, we have plenty of gun powder. We bought a barrel of powder at Fort Boise."

Cabot and Thunder Eagle spoke for short period of time, after which Thunder Eagle nodded, turned and walked away toward the trees to the east. Snow and Cabot accompanied the men upstream where James and Ron began working at the sluice. Tom, Levi, Asa,

Tucker, and the Cabots began hiking farther upstream toward higher elevations on Granite Mountain. It took about ten minutes to reach a half-foot thick outcropping of quartz interlaced with rock.

Tom said, "Stand back, I want to knock a chunk off so we can look at it more closely." He swung his pick at the rock-crystal boundary and broke out a fairly large piece of quartz. Everyone watched as Tom carefully studied the fragments.

"What do you think, Tom?" Levi quizzed. "Will it be worthwhile to mine?"

"I believe we have a mine," he smiled. "We can continue with the sluice until we can blast some of this rock out of the way and start a tunnel. Hope this quartz continues into the mountain. Maybe it'll expand as we open it up. We'll make some money on this. Thanks Mr. Cabot. I don't know how long it would have taken us to trace the quartz to this location."

Wolves' Hollow had three cabins, a small barn with an adjacent corral, and a watering trough by the end of September. Asa had done most of the construction, but Levi had designed the structures, and the Jeffers had been able to assist when they weren't working the mine. When the gold recovery from the mine had exceeded the amount from the sluice, all the men had begun working at the mine, ignoring the work at the river. At the end of the first week of October, Tom had estimated the value of the gold they had accumulated was worth over two thousand three hundred dollars. Levi had made markers and mapped the area so they could identify their claim.

The first fall snow arrived late that year in the third week of October. The Indian summer had been longer than its usual ten days, lasting for almost three weeks into early October, followed by gray skies and cold, blustery northeastern winds for nearly a week. The wild animals had sensed the eminent dramatic weather changes the week before the crew at Wolves' Hollow made ready to leave the mountains. Deer, bear, most birds, and the wolves seemed to have left the area by day three of the wind. The morning of the first snow had been very quiet, snowflakes drifting lazily to the ground. The wind had let up and when Asa left his cabin to get some fresh water, the only sounds were his breathing and footsteps in the inch of fresh snow. The usual calls of birds were absent. Asa noted smoke rising from the bunkhouse chimney. One of the other men must be up, probably Levi, making coffee.

The morning was spent putting away tools and gathering possessions for the journey to The Dalles. Snow, Leaves of Water, and Mr. Cabot arrived at the Wolves' Hollow cabins at noon during that first day of light snow. They each carried backpacks heavily loaded for their trip to The Dalles. The Cabots left their belongings in Asa's cabin and put their horses in the corral for the afternoon and assisted the men readying to leave for Idaho City, approximately a day away from Fort Boise. The sun had come out briefly and most of the snow had melted by two o'clock, the ground still warm from the long Indian summer. Cabot reminded the men to remove all food from the structures, and to prevent bears from entering, they nailed boards over the windows. When everything was packed, they had supper and went to bed. They would load the horses and start the trip to Fort Boise in the morning.

By six in the morning, it was light enough to travel, but it took nearly an hour to get all the horses loaded. Fortunately, the digging equipment was stored in the tunnel and didn't have to be packed. They expected to make better time returning to Fort Boise than the week it took to find Wolves' Hollow, especially since Cabot knew of some shortcuts on Indian trails, and without the cart and oxen to slow them down, it took only four days to reach Fort Boise.

Upon arrival at the fort in mid-afternoon, Asa escorted the Cabot family to various stores, a livery, and a hotel where they would stay the night. Levi and the Jeffers went to the government assay office to sell their gold. While Ron and Jim waited for the assay and payment, Levi and Tom went to the post office to check for a letter from Anna. As they walked toward the post office, Tom commented, "Do you think a letter will be here? Thanksgiving is still a month away."

Levi chewed on his lower lip a few seconds and replied, "I don't think so, but Anna might have written early, not knowing for sure when we would arrive back at the fort. If there's no letter, we can start toward The Dalles anyway; someone will know where Cabot's farm is. The Dalles can't be a very big town."

They entered the office, closed the door, and moved to the counter where a clerk was filling out a form. Although it was chilly outside, the office was warm from the heat radiating from a large pot-belly stove in the corner near a writing desk. An American flag was standing in the corner opposite the stove. Levi cleared his throat and the clerk looked up.

"May I help you gentlemen?"

Levi answered, "Might you have a letter addressed to Levi Collins?"

The clerk thought a second or two and reached into a small metal box at the side of his desk and flipped through a stack of envelopes about an inch high. About halfway through the stack, his fingers stopped. He pulled out a small envelope, looked up a Levi, and asked, "Captain Levi Collins?"

"Exactly."

The clerk slid the letter under the metal grill saying, "It's from Hood River."

"Hood River? I don't remember seeing that on the map."

The clerk responded, "It's about 21 miles west of The Dalles towards Portland."

By the time the clerk had said *Portland,* Levi had bit off the corner of the envelope and torn it open. He pulled out a folded sheet of paper with writing on both sides and began to read.

*My Dearest Levi,*

*I hope you, Asa, and the Jeffers are well. We reached the farm without incidence. We are all well and are anticipating your visit. Our plans have changed. Uncle George had been looking for richer soil for the orchard and found a nice plot of land at Hood River. He was able to use his farm at The Dalles as partial payment and we moved the week after arriving in The Dalles. You will love the magnificent location. Uncle George suggested I write you much earlier than we had planned. He said that snow might force you to leave the mountains early. So, come all the way to Hood River. Everyone knows us so we will be easy to find.*

*With all my love, Anna (Clarissa sends you a kiss.)*

Levi flipped the paper over, took a quick glance, and looked at Tom, who was waiting in anticipation for Levi's comment. Levi smiled and handed the paper to Tom saying, "This part is for you."

"Really?"

"Yeh, Helen wrote you a note."

Tom took the paper, stepped next to the window to get better light, and read the message.

*Dear Mr. Jeffers,*

*I hope you, Ron, Jim, and Asa are coming to Hood River with Levi. We are planning a wonderful holiday time. It will be nice to see you again.*

*Sincerely, Helen*

Tom folded the paper, smiled, and handed it to Levi, who stuck it in his pocket.

Tom commented, "I guess we leave for Hood River in the morning."

Levi responded, "Yup. Let's get out of here as soon after sun-up as possible. The Cabots will want to get on the trail, too. Let's find Ron and James and see how much they got for our gold."

# CHAPTER 27

# HOOD RIVER

After paying the assay fees, each of the five men cleared a little more than four hundred dollars. As they traveled toward Hood River along the Columbia with Leland Cabot and his second family, each man was imagining what opportunities the money was going to provide. Ron and James were thinking of starting a business in Portland or Seattle, but they didn't know what type. They had lost interest in farming and mining, desiring jobs that didn't require twelve to fourteen hour workdays. Asa and Snow had grown closer during the trip to Hood River. Asa was beginning to think of becoming a member of the Shoshone tribe, but wasn't sure of Snow's feelings for him. He hoped that would become clearer during the holidays.

On the ninth day of their horseback journey, as they moved along the southern bank of the tremendous Columbia, they arrived at Celilo Falls where they bought some salmon from the Indians. Asa had wanted to catch some salmon himself, but when he saw the structure of Indian nets and the size of the fish, he decided it would be better to buy some fish from the locals. Later that day, the group reached The Dalles and purchased some venison to share with their friends and relatives at Hood River.

They decided to camp on the bank of the Columbia that night and continue on to Hood River in the morning after getting a good night's rest.

Asa, Snow, and Laurel prepared salmon for supper, and as they ate, Levi and Leland discussed how they should approach the meeting of the Cabot children and Leland's reappearance.

"I imagine Anna, Clarissa, and Helen are going to be so excited to see me, and Anna and Nathan won't recognize you, although Anna might. She was about twelve years old when she last saw you. She remembers the mark on your ear."

"I don't think she will know me, Levi, because of my long braided-hair and Indian clothing. I can unbraid my hair so it will cover my ears. Plus, she will be eyeing Laurel and Snow, wondering why they are with you, Asa, and the Jeffers. But, I believe you should introduce me first, and give Anna and Nathan a chance to recover from the shock of seeing me again after all these years, before introducing them to their sister and mother-in-law."

"I suppose you're right. There will be bucketsful of emotions going on. I hope they will be so glad to see you they won't be mad that you didn't contact them years ago."

"When I tell them my story, I think they'll understand. At least I hope so."

Levi replied, "Well, whatever happens, it will be a memorable time for all of us."

It was early afternoon the next day when the group arrived in Hood River. Levi went into a general store and asked for directions to the Cabots' orchard. The storekeeper, a tall skinny man wearing glasses with dark brown hair parted in the middle, was about forty years old, and when he smiled, a wide space between his upper front teeth made him resemble a Halloween pumpkin. When Levi asked directions, the merchant grinned, extended his hand, and replied, "You must be Levi Collins."

"That's right. You must know the Cabots." Levi shook hands vigorously with the merchant.

"I'm Harvey Wilcox, the owner. Glad to meet you. I've prepared a map for you. Annabel asked me to give you directions to the farm. The Cabots are good customers of mine, but their orchard isn't producing yet. I hope to get some of their apples for the store. Here's the map." Wilcox fished a piece of paper from his slightly-soiled white apron, gave it to Levi, and continued, "Annabel and Helen both talk about you in glowing terms. You would be a good addition to our community. We need forward-looking people to develop this area."

"Well, thank you Mr. Wilcox and thank you for the directions. I'm sure we'll meet again. If the Cabots and my sister shop here, you must carry good merchandise." Levi left the store, descended two steps into the street, and looked at the map. Trying to orient the map, he took another step into the street and almost got hit by a passing wagon. The driver yelled and he stepped back, looking up at the wagon to see a young girl in the back sticking out her tongue and shaking her head of red curls side to side. His eyes followed the wagon as it rattled down the street and made a left turn. Levi laughed and walked back to the others who were waiting in front of Burt's Horse and Buggy livery stable.

Levi swung into the saddle and said, "It's not very far. Let's put a family back together! Leland, you better ride with me. Come on Tucker! Let's go see Clarissa." Leland rode next to Levi with Tucker running alongside Bravo. Their leisurely pace disguised the apprehension of both men as they followed the wagon that had nearly struck Levi. They could see the wagon kicking up dust in the distance, as it approached a field of trees and left the road, disappearing into neatly aligned rows of fruit trees. Levi and Leland, riding in front of the other six riders, reminded Levi of leading a squad of soldiers searching for confederate soldiers a few years earlier. His eyes scanned the neatly spaced trees standing at attention like soldiers on a parade ground. These soldiers were present, however, to only bear fruit, not arms.

They rode along a wooden fence for about three-hundred yards and stopped at a large white post at a crossing. The Cabots' farm could be seen across a nearly empty field populated with a few dozen young apple trees close to a two-story house and a large red barn. Tucker must have smelled something or heard a familiar sound, for he started running across the open field in the direction of the house. Levi turned left and followed the road until he came to the entrance to the farm. He made a right turn, and the others followed riding slowly toward the house.

Clarissa was in the yard picking up small pebbles and throwing them at chickens when she heard a dog bark. She looked away from the chickens to see a dog running toward her. At first she was frightened and started to run for the front door on the porch, but she suddenly recognized Tucker. Clarissa counted the riders and after squinting, she recognized Levi.

"Mama! Mama!" she cried out as loud as she could. "They're here!" Clarissa didn't know whether to run in the house or run toward the riders, but Tucker was getting close, so she ran toward the dog. Tucker nearly knocked Clarissa down, raising his front paws to her shoulders and licking her face. She hugged Tucker and started to cry. "I missed you, Tucker. I love you!" Tucker was so excited, he began to run around Clarissa, barking and smelling everything in sight. Anna and Helen, carrying little Frank, came out on the porch and were laughing at Tucker's antics. Anna could clearly see Levi and another rider coming toward the house. She tore off her apron and stepped off the porch into the grassy and pebble strewn front yard. Helen stood on the porch with the youngster in her arms wearing a big smile.

"Anna! It *is* Levi! I wonder who that other man is."

"He looks like an Indian," Anna grinned. "Nathan's going to be surprised." Leland and Levi were only ten yards away now and Anna remarked in a whisper, "No, he's white, just dressed in Indian clothing."

As Levi dismounted he said, "Howdy ladies! It's been awhile."

Anna ran to Levi and they embraced, their lips came together several times before Anna said,

"I missed you *so* much. It's good to have you back." She stepped back and looked at Levi from head to toe and commented, laughing, "No bullets in your butt?" She held his hand tightly, leaned toward him, and whispered, "Who's the man with you?"

"So glad you asked. Look closely at his left ear, Anna."

Anna frowned, glanced into Levi's eyes, and then looked at the heavier set man standing a little behind Levi. She put her hand to her mouth and said, "Oh, my God! Daddy! Is that you?" Leland extended both arms toward Anna. She threw her arms around her father and yelled, "Nathan, come here! It's your father!" Leland was giving Anna a bear hug, his eyes full of tears, and said, "Hello Annie Belle. I didn't think I would ever see you again. Wow, you are a beautiful woman!"

Nathan and Uncle George came through the front door and stepped off the porch toward Leland and Anna. Nathan joined Anna embracing their father and George said, "Well, I'll be damned! Leland, you old fart, where the hell have you been?" George slapped Leland on the back and continued, "You look good, except for the long hair. When did you last see a barber?"

Leland shook hands with his brother and said, "What happened to *your* hair, see a ghost?"

George ran his fingers through his silvery hair, smiled, and replied, "A couple of years ago, my barber told me he was devaluing my golden locks to silver, so this is the consequence."

"That's a good one George, but, enough about our appearances! I have some people for you to meet." Leland motioned to Laurel and Snow, still on their horses, to come closer and dismount. Snow swung off her horse gracefully and walked over to her father. Leland put his arm around Snow's waist and said, "Anna and Nathan, I want you to meet your sister, Snow, and your mother-in-law, Leaves of Water. I call her Laurel." Laurel dismounted more conventionally than Snow had and joined Leland and Snow. Leland introduced Laurel to everyone and said, "After reaching Fort Boise, I decided to do some prospecting since I was nearly out of money, and Susan was gone. I didn't think things out very well. I guess I was still grieving. A couple of men asked me if I wanted to look for gold, so I joined them. The third day out, they took my equipment and what money I had, and left me in the mountains. I got sick and was rescued by Laurel and her sister. They found me near a berry patch and helped me to their camp. About a month later, I was strong enough to travel, and when the tribe moved their camp, I went with them. The Shoshone are nomadic and live from what nature provides, so they don't have permanent settlements."

George interrupted, "Let's all go inside and you can finish your tale while we have some refreshments. We've got tea, coffee, lemonade, and some stronger stuff for you miners." He laughed and continued, "Unless you want some goat's milk."

The women gathered in the kitchen to socialize and provide drinks, cookies, and bread for the men, who sat in chairs or on the floor in the living room. Laurel and Snow felt a bit out of place in this totally foreign environment, but were quickly adapting to metal utensils and ceramic serving plates.

They watched the other women closely, but Snow and Laurel didn't know whether to eat a cookie with a fork or their fingers. Helen noticed their uneasiness and commented, "Use your fingers; we all eat cookies, bread, and such that way."

Snow gained confidence rapidly and was jabbering with Clarissa and Anna, but when she showed interest in little Frank, Helen began to enter the conversations. Laurel was a little shy because her English wasn't very good, but with Snow's translations, she began to smile and laugh at all the doings.

When all the men had drinks and snacks, George asked Leland to continue his story.

Leland began, "Well, it was autumn of 1848 when I felt comfortable with the Shoshone. I began to search for plants I knew about for their drug properties, and the witch doctor and I combined talents. He knew much more about the plant kingdom than I did, so we went on expeditions accompanied by some of the women. Laurel and I hit it off and in a couple of months we were married. The Shoshone make extensive use of flowers and feathers in their ceremony. I got right to work and Snow was born near the end of 1849. I had a new life, but I still had Susan's locket with pictures of Anna and Nathan. In a few years, the pictures deteriorated, but I knew Anna and Nathan were being cared for. I didn't want to leave my new family for fear of not making my way back to a post office to send a message. I knew Anna and Nathan would grow up strong and prepared for life. When Snow was about five years old, I gave her the locket. She was wearing it when she met Levi and the others. I guess Asa suspected the connection with the locket and you know the rest."

Levi and Anna were married Christmas day. Tom stayed on at the orchard until spring when he, Asa, and Levi returned to Wolves' Hollow to continue digging out the quartz vein at Granite Mountain. Asa and Snow were married at a tribal ceremony in southern Idaho in September, before the harsh winter weather came to the mountains. Tom and Helen were married at Christmas 1867, and stayed in Hood River to help run the orchard. Ron and James found work in Portland and Seattle respectively, after leaving the orchard following Levi's and Anna's marriage. They weren't ready to sink their roots at Hood River. Ron worked in management in the logging industry and James made a good living in ship construction.

Levi and Tom were more like brothers than friends and shared the work and rewards at the orchard and the Wolves' Hollow gold mine over the next ten years. They would set out for the mine from Hood River in the spring and return in the autumn for apple harvest. For a few years, they were joined by Asa and his family, and the three men recovered enough gold to make the mining profitable, but they never struck the mother lode. Levi and Tom each fathered a son and daughter. Nathan taught school for many years, as did Anna when she wasn't about to give birth. Nathan met a widow, the mother of one of his young students. They married and lived on the farm with the other Cabots, the Collins, and the Jeffers. His wife, Marcia, gave birth to a girl, who became a nurse but never married. Asa and Snow had two boys, one of whom died of small pox.

There was a series of deaths that changed the nature of the families at the Hood River orchard. Leland expired in 1875 followed by George two years later. They were laid to rest in the family cemetery in the center of the orchard. After the passing of Leland, Laurel moved back to the Shoshone tribe in Idaho. Tucker had always accompanied Levi and Tom to the gold mine until 1873, when he began to have difficulty walking. He remained with Clarissa at the orchard until 1875. One morning not long after Leland passed, Clarissa couldn't find Tucker in his normal place on the back porch. She called for him but with no response. Frustrated, she told Levi and they began searching the farm. After a quarter of an hour searching, Levi and Clarissa walked out to the family cemetery and found Tucker's body not far from Leland's grave. Levi buried Tucker next to Leland, and the next day Levi drove a wagon to Portland and ordered granite headstones for Leland and Tucker.

When Levi's son, William, was 13 in 1881, he began accompanying his father and Tom to Wolves' Hollow and worked in the mine each summer until he was 21. He met a girl from Walla Walla and moved there to manage a cattle ranch near Mill Creek. Asa's family had moved to Montana in 1875 and the families in Hood River lost track of him. Wolves' Hollow was inhabited year-round following the end of the Indian hostilities in 1878. Permanent roads were built and by 1885 the population of the town was 86. Occasionally, prospectors, loggers, and hunters stayed in cabins in the little town.

Early in 1890, Anna began having breathing problems, and after being ill for nearly two years, passed away two days after Christmas, 1891. Anna's and Levi's daughter, Sophie, had a beautiful voice and sang at the graveside. In 1896, Levi decided to make one last trip to the mine in Wolves' Hollow.

The family tried in vain to talk him out of it. Tom told Levi to stay in Hood River and enjoy his time with his grandchildren, but Levi insisted, and at the end of July of that year, he saddled a horse, loaded his things on a mule named Chunk, and set off for the mountains of Idaho. He went alone. He never had another dog after Tucker.

# CHAPTER 28

# FINAL TRIP TO WOLVES' HOLLOW

Levi stopped in Walla Walla to visit with William and his family and stayed overnight. The next morning, he continued toward Boise. Four days later, Levi rode into Wolves' Hollow and rented a small log cabin on North Pebble, the road that had been constructed over the old stream bed where Levi had first discovered gold thirty years earlier. He rode slowly, taking in the landmarks from years before and stopped at the old Collins' Mine entrance. It was still boarded shut as he and Tom had left it three years earlier. It was late afternoon, so he returned to his cabin, took care of his horses, bought some whiskey at the Hollow Mug tavern, made himself supper, and went to bed.

The next morning, Levi dragged himself out of bed, dressed, shaved, and walked across North Pebble to the tavern for breakfast. He recognized the mayor, Jesse Heinz, and they talked for a few minutes while Levi sat at the bar and ate breakfast.

Mayor Heinz grinned and questioned, "What are you doing here, Levi? You're getting too old to be mining, aren't you? How's that beautiful wife of yours?"

Levi paused for a moment and answered, "I'm here to take one last bag of gold out of that old mine. I can still move fast enough to get out the way of the dynamite." He smiled and then gave Jesse a serious look. "Annie passed a few years ago. She was ill for nearly two years. It was tough on all of us."

"I'm sorry to hear that. She was a good woman. Let me know if I can give you a hand. Oh, there have been some no-account drifters around recently. Keep your eyes peeled."

"Thanks Jesse, will do. I hope to be out of here in about three months. See you around."

"Okay. Good luck out at the mine." Jesse pulled out his watch, glanced at it, and commented, "I've got to go. Amy told me to get her some flour and get back home. I shouldn't have come in here for a cigar." The mayor grinned, tipped his hat, and left the tavern. Levi could hear Jesse's footsteps as the mayor took a few strides on the boardwalk and stepped into the street.

Levi went to his cabin for his saddlebags and retrieved his horse and mule from the livery. He kept dynamite in his saddlebags, enough to finish clearing rock from the quartz vein that contained the gold he and Tom had been recovering off and on for thirty years. The entrance to the mine was about two miles from the outskirts of Wolves' Hollow, but Levi and Tom had started a new shaft, perpendicular to the original one, about two hundred yards west of the main entrance, and at a slightly higher elevation. Levi had calculated where the shafts should meet, but Tom and Levi were frustrated when they didn't break through to the old shaft two years earlier.

After tying his horse to the old mine entrance, Levi led the mule to the new shaft and removed the rough boards from the opening. Levi was happy to see that the timbers for shoring up the tunnel were still stacked in piles as they had been left. Apparently, no one had tampered with the mine during the last two years. The picks, shovels, and boring equipment were a little rusty but ready for use. Levi dragged the timbers to the outside of the mine and began boring holes for dynamite. It took all afternoon to get the holes drilled. He took a drink from his canteen, picked up the boring equipment, and walked out of the mine. He took two stick of dynamite from his saddlebags, cut them in half and attached fuses, then went back in the mine to set the charges.

After packing mud around the dynamite, he lit the fuses and headed out of the mine. When he reached the entrance, a young man was standing outside the opening holding the reins to a horse. Levi said, "Better move off to the side, I just lit some dynamite." The kid pulled his horse away from the opening as Levi counted down with his fingers. When Levi's last finger closed to his palm, there was a rumble and a cloud of dust issued from the mine. As Levi waited for the dust to settle, he walked toward the young man and introduced himself.

"Glad to meet you, Mr. Collins. I'm Reed Horner. I'm lookin' for work for what's left of the summer."

"Well, Mr. Horner, how would you like to haul some rock for me? Each time I blast, the rock has to be cleared, but you've got to keep an eye out for the gold. We don't want to lose the gold. Think you can do that?"

"Yes sir. Just show me what to watch for."

Reed was a quick learner, had a stocky build, dark brown nearly black hair, and hardly broke a sweat when hauling a wheelbarrow full of rock 20 yards from inside the mine and piling it outside. He looked over the rock quickly, pulling out suspected gold bearing fragments from the rubble, piling it for Levi to check for worthwhile specimens. Levi had promised Reed three dollars a day and eight ounces of gold, or about $150, when they finished with the mine in October.

One day in late September, when they were taking a break after having punched a hole through the end of the new shaft into the old mine shaft, Reed mentioned he had an older brother, Edwin.

"What's Edwin doing? Is he around here with you? Why hasn't he come by?"

"He's got a job escorting trophy hunters from the east. They come out here to hunt elk, bear, and mountain lions. But they don't want the meat, they just take the heads or antlers and leave the meat to rot."

"That's not right. They should give the meat to the Indians or the people living around here."

"Yah, but I guess they don't want to be bothered. They just kill some animals and go home with their trophies. Ed's pretty busy most all the time. There are lots of easterners that think this is their playground."

Levi and Reed worked the mine until the second week of October. Beginning in early September, Reed had kept a fire burning outside the mine so the two men could warm their hands and feet. Reed kept a pot of coffee on the fire to warm their insides. Levi rarely needed a coat when working inside the mine. The physical activity and the constant temperature of the earth and rock made the air temperature fairly constant at about sixty degrees. On the tenth of October, Levi announced to Reed they would be shutting down the mine for the winter.

"Reed, did you notice the halo around the moon last night?"

"Yes sir. I think it's gunna get pretty cold tonight—maybe some snow by tomorrow."

"That's right. I'm going to close the mine tonight and leave for Boise in the morning. I'll pay you after I clean up the tools and start boarding up the mine. If you want, you can leave now and come back about supper time. I'll have your gold and any pay I still owe you ready then."

"Sounds good to me. See you later, sir." Reed mounted his horse and slowly rode off toward Wolves' Hollow. Levi watched Reed riding off thinking how lucky he had been to have had a hard working young man helping him for almost ten weeks. He would have been awfully tired each night if Reed hadn't been there to help. The passage of time and hard work all his life had taken its toll, even though he didn't want to accept old age was creeping up on him. Levi worked the rest of the day putting things in order, but he took his time. He wasn't sure if he would ever come back to Wolves' Hollow and the gold mine, but Asa, Tom's son, or William might want to investigate the mine at a later date. Levi took a break at mid-day and investigated the side of the mountain near the new shaft.

He had walked about a 50 yards before he decided to turn around. On the way back, he noticed a large tree with a somewhat peculiar root structure not far from the mine entrance. He had a walking stick with him and he prodded the ground around some large exposed roots. The earth fell away revealing a hollowed-out area beneath the large tree trunk. Levi got on his hands and knees and took a look inside. There were small animal bones in abundance as well as a large quantity of spider webs covered with dust. Levi concluded this cavern must have been a wolves' den in the past. He pushed the dirt back, not wanting to disturb part of Mother Nature, and got to his feet. On his way back to the mine, he wondered if wolves had excavated under the tree, or perhaps water had washed the soil away, creating a home for four-legged friends of the forest.

When he arrived at the mine, Levi expected to find Reed waiting, but no one was there. He packed a few items on Chunk and put two sticks of dynamite back in his saddlebags. He checked the cinch on the horse, making sure it was tight, and then moved to Chunk to make sure the mule's load wouldn't fall off. Suddenly, he felt something strike him in the back, at first he thought it was someone swinging an ax or a heavy board, but then he heard a gunshot and knew he had been shot in the back.

He grabbed at Chunk's load and hooked his left hand in a rope. Levi instinctively drew his pistol with his right hand. He was struck again, this time in his left side, and he fell headfirst to the ground on top of his pistol facing toward Chunk. *Damn! Shot in the back twice! I can't move my legs!*

Levi could hear voices. *They're coming in to finish me off. If I play dead, maybe I'll get a chance!*

He could hear footsteps and a voice he knew. *It was Reed. Son-of-a bitch!*

"I've got an idea, Ed. Let's move the body into the mine and blow the mine. It will look like he used too much dynamite and blew himself up, if anyone ever digs up the body."

Ed started looking through Levi's saddlebags, but only found four sticks of dynamite and some fuses.

"*Hey*, Reed, there's no gold in here, just dynamite."

"I told you he keeps the gold in bags hanging from his neck. There's no gold in them saddlebags. Bring the dynamite and the fuses; we'll blow this side of the mountain down on top of him. Come 'ere, I'll show you the gold."

Levi slowed his breathing down so the back-shooters would think he was dead. He could hear the two shooters coming closer.

"Ed, help me flip him over so I can get the gold. There's gotta be a couple of thousand in gold in them bags."

Levi could feel the men putting their cold hands under his shoulder and hip, lifting, exerting pressure as they rolled him over. As he rolled face up, Levi lifted his gun and got off four bullets, two in each man's chest. They crumpled to the ground, sighs escaping from their dying bodies. Levi rose to his elbows and shot one more time into each carcass.

Levi tried to get to his feet, but his legs wouldn't work. "Chunk! Get over here!" The mule looked at him, trying to decide whether to obey or not. The mule finally approached and Levi was able to grab the cinch around Chunk's belly. Levi yelled "Hah!" Chunk started moving slowly, but not in the direction of Wolves' Hollow, just the opposite. At first, Levi wanted to turn the mule around, but he remembered the cavern under that big tree and decided if he could get to it, he could stay the night and get back to town in the morning. It seemed to take forever to get to the tree. Each step of the mule caused pain to rip through Levi's chest.

When Chunk got close to the tree, Levi let go of the cinch and used his elbows to drag his body to the exposed root where there was loose dirt. He used his gun to push the dirt away, making an opening large enough for him to enter the cavern. Levi brushed away the spider webs as he collapsed into the wolves' den. He rolled over so he was halfway sitting up and buttoned his shirt and coat around his neck to keep warm. He could hear a lone wolf crying out in the distance. He sat quietly for a few minutes and said,

"Curl up beside me Tucker. Come on boy, we'll keep each other warm 'til morning."

When sun-up arrived, it was deathly quiet, the wind had stopped, and no birds were singing. The snow was four inches deep.

# PART 2

# PROLOGUE

As the decades passed, Wolves' Hollow grew slowly, from a small camp for miners, to a village, and then to a small town. At the end of World War I, roads were constructed for vehicular traffic from Sunbeam and Challis to Wolves' Hollow. Outdoor enthusiasts began visiting the area to hunt, fish, climb, and ski. A few visitors planted permanent roots. They were primarily artists and authors. By 1940, the population approached 250 hearty souls. During World War II, government mining engineers moved into the area temporarily and dredged the stream beds for gold. North Pebble was filled in and covered with asphalt following the war. When the government was dredging, the engineers constructed a thermal energy facility which provided low cost heating for the town. Even so, remote Wolves' Hollow grew slowly. The winters were always treacherous.

The Collins family, Tom Jeffers, and Asa Adams periodically visited the mine and extracted small amounts of gold to provide capital for investing in ranches and businesses. The old Collins Mine was handed down from generation to generation, and in 1999, Emma and Josh Collins retired to Arizona, leaving the mine to their only child and son, Glen Eugene Collins. The Jeffers boys stayed on the West Coast, never returning to Wolves' Hollow after the 1880s, and Asa Adams became a cattle rancher in Montana. He had much success and his offspring donated land and money to Montana colleges in his name. He had great respect for Annabel Cabot for teaching him how to read. He was deeply saddened when he heard of her death.

As 2013 arrived, few of the residents of Wolves' Hollow knew of the early history of their little town. Twenty-first century economics had encouraged an influx of people wanting to get away from big city life, seeking a simpler time, and a location to enjoy the beauty of the mountains. However, as in any gathering of human beings, there were a few individuals who didn't hold those views. Would the good people of Wolves' Hollow and the mountain spirits be enough to protect their town?

# CHAPTER 29

# WHEELCHAIR

Jill Morran checked out of her University of Idaho dorm room the day after June graduation, 2013, and slid her five-seven slender body into her 2002 blue Aztek. She didn't know it, but her degree in journalism hadn't prepared her very well for her first job, as a reporter, for *The Howling Times,* the newspaper in Wolves' Hollow, Idaho, population 681. The remote small town in the mountains was 122 miles northeast of Boise. But the new graduate had spunk, the gift of imagination, and her fingers moved at blistering speed on a keyboard.

Jill's older sister, Eva, a physical therapist and two-year resident of Wolves' Hollow, had told Jill what to expect: a small town in the mountains lost in time in the 1950s. Well, the inhabitants had the Internet and flat screen TVs, a bowling alley, and two taverns, so it wasn't that bad. She left Moscow in her rear-view mirror at ten in the morning on Saturday and started south on Route 95 toward Lewiston. She passed through or near about fifteen small towns before arriving at New Meadows. Jill stopped for gas, a cheeseburger, fries, and a chocolate shake, and then put her foot on the gas pedal for two more hours, arriving in Boise at five o'clock. Pooped from driving over 300 miles, she checked into a motel room, called Eva, who was still at work, and left a message.

"Hi, Eva. I'm in Boise at Motel 6 on Route 95, room 232. I'll see you tomorrow. I hope I can stay with you for one or two days while I look for a place to rent. Bye." After the call, Jill retrieved her lap-top, her PJs, some clean clothes to wear for the rest of her journey, and locked her Aztek. The burger, fries and shake had contained over 1,200 calories, so she didn't feel hungry. She fell asleep watching TV and woke up during the 11:00 p.m. Channel 8 news broadcast. A slammed car door brought her to the window. She looked between the beige curtains to see a teenage girl and an older man carrying suitcases into the room directly below her on the first floor. The lights and sounds of big trucks, in a hurry to deliver their cargo, came from the nearby highway. Jill heard a female voice from below call out, "Get some ice and some Cokes." The motel door slammed. Jill turned off the news and sat on the bed thinking how lonely it was to be travelling alone. She was startled when her phone rang. It was Eva.

"Hi, Jill. I got home late and just checked my messages a few minutes ago. How's that motel room?

"Just peachy, Eva. Wish you were here to enjoy the luxurious accommodations."

Eva laughed and said, "You can stay with me until you find a place, but you'll have to sleep on the sofa. As you know, my apartment isn't very big. I don't think we should live together; our hours will be very different. Do you want to rent a house or an apartment?"

"I'm not sure. I have to talk with Mr. Novaks at the paper as soon as I get to Wolves' Hollow. For some reason, he doesn't want me running around town."

"That's interesting. I wonder what that's all about. I know Mrs. Novaks. I helped her with therapy after she broke a leg skiing. She's a fun lady."

"Well, Novaks didn't say much in his email; just to see him immediately after arrival. I guess I'll see you after I talk with him. I should get there about noon tomorrow."

"Okay. Make sure you gas up before you get on Route 21; there's lots of up and down driving through the mountains. It's pretty country though."

"All right, sis. See you about noon tomorrow. Thanks for calling me back. Bye."

* * *

Jill drove away from the motel at 8:00 a.m. after washing down a large bagel with some steaming hot coffee and eating an orange. Two and a half hours later, she arrived in Sunbeam. She followed the signs to route 21A, an unpaved road, and in 20 minutes, parked on Main Street in front of *The Howling Times*. The newspaper occupied a modern, two-story, red-brick building in Wolves' Hollow. The entrance was wheel-chair accessible. Jill walked up the ramp to the front door and was surprised when the door swung open automatically.

There were only six names on the directory inside the front door. The building seemed deserted. Few people were working on Sunday. The first name was Nicholas Novaks: Editor. Jill took the stairs to room 205 and knocked on the door.

A male voice said, "Come in."

Jill opened the door and entered the room to find a large man in his 40s sitting in front of a big computer screen. He looked up from a thick book lying open beside his keyboard. Jill walked quickly to the front of the man's desk and extended her right hand.

"I'm Jill Morran, your new reporter." She glanced at the book. It was an unabridged dictionary.

Novaks stood, leaned forward, grinned, and shook hands with Jill. "I'm Nick Novaks, your new boss. How was your trip?

"The first part was tiring, driving from Moscow to Boise. Today was fine. I enjoyed the mountains...very pretty."

"Good. We've got plenty of mountains to go around," he smiled. Novaks' hair was thinning, and he had a comb-over of medium length black hair. He was about six-feet tall, overweight, and his yellow shirt was partially pulled from his khakis, making him look sloppy. Novaks might have just come in from sleeping on a park bench. He wore a pair of cheap reading glasses and, well, looked like a typical newspaper editor, wrapped up in his work.

"I'm glad you came to see me as I asked. I want to give you your first assignment. Have a seat, Jill. Your professor didn't tell me how pretty you are."

Jill smiled and said, "Thank you. Sometimes it's an advantage."

Novaks took off his glasses and leaned back in his chair with his feet on his desk. "I've rented a house for you at 511 North Pebble. That's the next street over, behind this building. However, I don't want you to be seen walking around. You are going to be confined to a wheelchair."

Jill frowned and said, "What?—A *wheelchair*?"

"Yes. I want you to write an article about the difficulties people in wheelchairs encounter in their everyday life. You see, there are a number of people in town confined to wheelchairs because of logging, hunting, skiing, and car accidents. Some of them are permanently disabled and will never walk again. I would like you to investigate their plight.

But, I don't want anyone to know you can walk. You must keep that a secret."

"Can I tell my sister? She's a physical therapist. I don't think I can trick her for long."

"Okay, but she must promise to keep it a secret. We need real reactions from people and if they know you aren't really injured, they won't treat you honestly. I've talked to our custodian and he will follow you to your rental, put you in the chair and get you in the house. You will have to hire someone to build a ramp so your house will be accessible from ground level. I believe there are three steps to the top of the porch."

"What's my rent? Do I have to pay for the ramp?"

"You will pay half the rent; the newspaper will pay the other half, and the paper will pay for the ramp. When you finish the article, you can move or pay all the rent. Rent for cottages in Wolves' Hollow is pretty reasonable; I think you'll be surprised."

Jill smiled and said, "That sounds pretty good to me. Who do I meet to get in the house?"

"Just a moment, I'll buzz him."

Novaks reached over to the phone and pressed a button. A beeping could be heard from the hallway, and a young man, perhaps in his late20s-early 30s appeared at the door. His ethnicity was obviously Native American, and his name tag said Tad Birdsong.

"Come in, Tad. I'd like you to meet Jill Morran. She's new to Wolves' Hollow. She's the one I want you to help get settled over on North Pebble."

Tad shook hands with Jill and noticed Jill was looking at the hunting knife hanging from his belt. He volunteered, "The pig sticker is for protecting my family from the long knives."

Jill cocked her head a little to the side, frowned, and said, "What?"

"That was a joke. The cavalry hasn't attacked us in over 130 years. I use the knife for many things—fixing shingles, opening packages, fighting bears, stuff like that," Tad grinned. "I was in the Army Special Forces and got used to the knife, so I carry it with me all the time. I don't want to rush you but could we get this done? My wife expects me home by two o'clock; I have some things to repair at the motel."

Jill commented, "You own a motel?"

"Yeah, Granite Mountain Lodge, but it's really a motel. Lodge sounds better, though, don't you think?"

"Uh-huh. Where is it? I didn't see it when I drove into town."

"Over on the west side of town, near Warm Creek. We cater to hunters and hikers. Most of our business comes from the Internet."

Novaks was standing, listening to the banter and said, "Tad, why don't you go to the rental and get Jill moved in? I need to get back to work. It was nice meeting you, Jill. We'll be talking."

"It was nice meeting you, Mr. Novaks. Thank you for the help getting located. Talk to you later."

Tad followed Jill in his older model black pickup after telling her where 511 North Pebble was. Five minutes later, Tad lifted a wheelchair out of his pickup and assisted Jill into the chair.

He pushed her up to the porch and set the break. He picked Jill up and she stood by the front door while Tad placed the wheelchair beside her. Tad gave Jill the key to the front door and said, "Let's see you open the door from the wheelchair."

Jill sat in the chair and rolled up to the door, but the chair blocked the screen door, so she repositioned the chair to the side and opened the screen, put the key in the lock, and turned the knob. A rush of hot air greeted her at the front door. She pushed hard and the door swung open wide enough for her to guide the chair inside after bumping over the threshold.

Tad said, "Well, you made it! Congratulations. I'll get the rest of your things from your car and park your Aztek a little bit farther back from the street closer to your garage. I don't think you will be using your garage; the door is hard to lift. It's not automatic."

For the next fifteen minutes, Tad brought in Jill's things as she rolled around the cottage, checking all the nooks and crannies. She turned on the window mounted air-conditioner and a small cloud of debris blew into the room. In a few minutes, the room began to cool, much to Jill's relief. When Tad was finished transferring Jill's possessions from the car, he said good bye and walked toward his pickup. Jill yelled, "Thanks," as Tad climbed in the driver's seat and drove away very slowly. Jill rolled around the house, closing all the blinds and the front door. When she knew she couldn't be seen from outside, she got out of the wheelchair, sat on the sofa and called Eva. It was 12:15 p.m.

"Hi, Eva. Sorry I didn't call you right at noon. I arrived about an hour ago and have rented a house. Can you believe it? I only have to pay half the rent."

"You have a roommate?"

"Nope. My boss, Mr. Novaks, gave me an assignment that requires me to use a wheelchair when I'm out in public. The newspaper is paying half my rent while I'm working on the article. It's going to be a pain in the butt, though. Why don't you come over and help me put away all my things. I'll tell you about my assignment. We can order pizza—there's a pizza place here, isn't there?"

"No, but I'll get a frozen one at the market. Pepsi or Coke?"

"Whatever. Oh! Get a head of lettuce and some blue cheese or thousand island dressing—why not both—the low-fat kind. When can you get here?"

"About five o'clock. I have to work with a couple of patients this afternoon. I'll see you later. You have a stove?"

"Yes, but I'm not sure it works. This place is clean but I think it contains original equipment, circa 1960. We might have to make a bonfire or build a pizza oven," Jill laughed.

"Funny, sis. See you at five. Bye."

# CHAPTER 30

# DINNER WITH EVA

Jill looked around her rental. It was only about five times bigger than her university dorm room had been. She had only invested two hours in the project, and the wheelchair was already ruining her life. Jill couldn't imagine how the remaining 29-plus days were going to develop, but who knew, maybe something interesting would happen, perhaps something to divert her from what she already considered a dull assignment. When she was in school, she had envisioned tracking bears or mountain lions, but now she was thinking she would be chasing skunks.

She opened the laptop and looked at the to-do list she had started when Tad was moving her in. She was supposed to get a contractor to build a ramp for the front porch; the three stairs prevented her from leaving the house. She already felt trapped. Outside the backdoor were four steps down to a sunken flower garden, but there weren't any other steps back up to ground level, only a brick retaining wall about two feet high. Her little yellow house was a desert island and Jill was marooned. She smiled as she considered painting palm trees on the outside walls and getting some sand for the front yard. The June heat was already beginning to get on her nerves. The window air conditioner kept the living room comfortable, but the rest of the house was too warm.

She thought the house might cool off while she and Eva had dinner. The summer heat, extending into September, was going to be nasty, but the mountain elevation might make for some cool mornings and evenings.

The Yellow Pages for Wolves' Hollow gave the names of two builders/contractors in town and several out of town, which Jill ignored. The contractors in Boise were over a hundred miles away. She needed immediate help. Jill thought little brain power would be involved in making a temporary ramp; any carpenter would do. This was Sunday, but Jill ground her teeth together and dialed the first number. She heard four rings but no answer, so she punched in the second number. The phone was answered after the second ring.

A pleasant male voice answered, "Glen's Building and Remodeling, Glen Collins speaking."

"Hi. I'm Jill Morran. I need a wheelchair ramp built so I can get from my porch to the sidewalk. Could you give me an estimate? I live at 511 North Pebble."

"Sure can. I'll be there in about ten minutes. Bye."

Jill said bye, closed her phone and stuck it in her pants pocket. Now she had to get in the wheelchair and act like she knew how to move around the house with some skill. When she was thinking about looking for a rental, she thought 800 square feet would be desirable, easy to clean and an absolutely perfect location. What she ended up with was a little smaller, but she only had two neighbors, whom she had yet to see. There was a small grocery store nearby and a nice park with asphalt pathways, but she desperately needed a ramp. Jill sat down in the chair and began going from window to window, opening the window coverings. Each time she came to a window, Jill had to tell herself to remain sitting, but after finishing her task, she began to feel more comfortable in the wheelchair. The only problem she could imagine was getting a sore neck from looking up at almost everything except her keyboard, monitor, TV, and a few other things. The 46-inch wall-mounted TV was almost too big for her living room, but it was free of charge. Novaks had taken care of the satellite dish.

Jill was startled by loud barking coming from her next-door neighbor's cyclone-fenced front yard. She had heard a vehicle drive up and stop. She hoped it was Glen, the guy she had just called. Jill had opened her file for keeping notes about her experience and had typed about two sentences when the doorbell rang. The ding-dong was fairly loud, so she could easily hear it from anywhere in the house. Jill set the desktop wireless keyboard next to her laptop on the sofa and straightened out the wheelchair so she could roll straight to the door.

She yelled, "I'm coming, just a sec."

The living room rug covered most of the hardwood floor but there was bare wood, about four feet of it, between the door and the heavily padded blue carpet. She used some muscle to get the chair across the rug, and when she hit the wooden floor, the chair rolled rapidly. She banged into the closed door. Jill held back some four-letter words so the caller wouldn't hear her swearing. She made a mental note to be more deliberate with her chair movements on the wood and tile floors next time, controlling her speed with hand pressure on the wheels.

Wrestling with the door was not so easy when the chair was in the way, but she finally got the heavy door open. She almost laughed at her clumsiness. A large man in paint- and tar-stained overalls, a bright yellow T-shirt, and wearing a blue and tan American Airlines baseball cap, was standing on the porch. Jill imagined him to be a plumber rather than a carpenter and pushing forty. He had a good start to a potbelly, probably from burgers, fries, and beer, but otherwise he was nice looking. Jill hoped she wouldn't see a plumber's butt when the man was working. Jill found plumber's butt really gross, especially when it was an overweight butt.

"Hello, I'm Glen. You called about building a ramp?"

"I sure did. Without a ramp, I'm trapped in the house, except for the front porch. I don't know any strong men that would carry me down to the sidewalk," Jill smiled. "Besides, it would be awkward to have to call someone every time I want to go out."

"How'd you get hurt? Glen had a gentle voice and seemed genuinely concerned.

"A kid in a pickup was backing out of a driveway and didn't see me on my bike. He smashed into me and I ran into a parked car. I have a spinal injury and can't use my legs."

"Boy, that's a bummer. Will you get back the use of your legs?"

"I think so. My doctor said it might take as long as a year but I hope it won't be that long. I am doing some physical therapy though. My sister is a PT and will be coming over for dinner tonight. My jaw is going to get plenty of exercise," she smiled.

Jill looked directly into Glen's gray-blue eyes as she told him the lies. She was going to have to remember what she told people so she wouldn't get caught in the middle of a giant heap of BS so deep she couldn't crawl out. She wanted to tell people the truth, but that would change the way they reacted. It was a strange feeling, to be telling lies in order to find the truth.

"Your neighbor's dog doesn't seem to like me."

"I didn't know there was a dog until you drove up. It must have been in the house when I arrived."

Glen grinned and said, "Probably could use a tranquilizer in some fresh meat."

"Maybe it will get used to me and quit barking," Jill commented.

"Maybe. Show me where you'd like the ramp."

Glen held the screen door open for Jill as she rolled over the threshold onto the porch and pointed out what she had envisioned for the ramp. Glen took out a measuring tape, extracted a small spiral bound notebook from his overalls and jotted down some dimensions. Jill watched as Glen completed his notes and looked at the porch.

Glen took off his cap exposing his uncombed brown hair. He scratched his slightly receding hairline and commented, "We can't do it that way; we have to follow the building codes for the width and the slope, and it has to have a railing so you can't fall off. If you went over the edge, you might have even worse injuries. You should also have a railing on the porch."

"Well, Mr.—ah—what is your last name?"

"Collins. A relative founded Wolves' Hollow in 1866. Have you heard of the Collins gold mine? It's out a ways on North Pebble. It's not operating, but I watch over it."

Jill laughed, "A gold mine? So you're a relic of the past."

"Come on! I'm not that old." Glen laughed, "No gray hairs yet, and besides, there is still mining around here. Gold is about $1,400 an ounce now, not $19 as in 1896. I should probably check out the old mine and see if there's any gold left. I might need a gold crown next time I visit the dentist."

As they were talking, Glen sketched the ramp and showed it to Jill. The ramp would be a permanent feature of the small house, adding to the resale value.

"I estimate the cost to be around $500, give or take."

"That includes the porch railing?"

"Yep, that's everything."

"Okay. When can you start?"

"I'll be here at seven in the morning. Can't make noise until after seven; you know—city regulations."

"Well, I should probably get another estimate, but I need a ramp right away. I'll see you in the morning, Mr. Collins, around seven."

Glen tipped his hat, grinned and said, "Just call me Glen. It's a deal, Miss Morran. See you tomorrow. I'll get a permit at the court house. Need help getting back inside?"

"No thanks. My sister should be here soon; she'll assist me if I need help."

Glen climbed in his truck, waved and drove away. Jill waved back. Jill guessed Glen's dark tan, rumpled clothes and oversize stomach made him look ten years older than he really was. Her new estimate of Glen's age was early thirties, about ten years older than herself. He would be a real stud if he lost thirty to forty pounds of table muscle.

Jill rolled around the porch for about five minutes, looking at the shrubs and flowers near the house. Spider webs and dead leaves were everywhere, and gardening would be difficult to accomplish sitting in the wheelchair. The tall pine tree next to the fence that kept the neighbor's dog from attacking had probably been dropping cones during the spring, littering both front yards. Because her house had been vacant for several months, no one had attempted to clean up the front yard; the owner of the property apparently didn't care, nor did her neighbor. A mental note was made to find out how she could best carry out some gardening. Maybe she would have to hire someone to help her, or maybe ask Eva for help. She could always pay Eva with pizza and beer.

Jill worked her way back inside the house and picked up her keyboard, reopened the file for her article and worked steadily for about an hour. When she checked the clock on the computer, it was 4:53. Eva would be joining her shortly. Jill could always rely on Eva's punctuality.

Eva drove up in her little Japanese car at 4:59. As Eva made her way to the front door, she was glad a fence surrounded the neighbor's yard. The barking dog looked mean. Eva knocked on the screen door, but the front door was open, so Eva didn't hesitate. She came into the living room, a bag of groceries in one hand, and a potted plant in the other.

"Come on in, Eva. I've been waiting for you. I didn't even hear your car."

"I'm not late, sister dear." She took a defiant stance and looked at Jill.

"I know...I'm just giving you a hard time, as usual. Close the door so I can get out of this damn chair."

Eva pushed the door shut and it slammed, rattling the windows.

"I'm sorry. That was accidental." Eva shrugged her shoulders.

"Don't worry about it. I think the hinges were oiled when they found out an invalid was going to be living here. I think the landlord sprayed everything that moves with WD40. I could smell it when I moved in. Can you smell it?"

Eva took a deep breath and shook her head side to side. Jill looked around to make sure all the drapes and blinds were closed, got out of the wheelchair, stretched her legs, and gave Eva a hug. Eva was three years older than Jill, but an inch shorter than her sister. Jill touched her toes and did a couple of squats.

"This project is going to be pure torture, Eva. Can you imagine how troublesome it's going to be for an able-bodied person to confine themselves to a wheelchair for a month? I'm going to have to have more patience than ever before. I never encountered anything like this at the university."

Eva said, "I got what you wanted. Here's the salad dressing and the lettuce."

Eva gave Jill two bottles, which Jill put on the table. Jill put the lettuce on the cutting board and got a knife from a box of utensils on the counter.

Eva held out a potted plant, a small cactus.

"Here's something to adorn your new residence. It doesn't need much water, just some sunshine. It might not survive in here. Maybe you can put it out on the porch. I have a name for it—Pokey. I don't have to explain it, do I?" Eva grinned.

Jill smiled and replied, "I get it. Thanks Sis. What have you been up to?"

"You're not going to believe this, but a guy came in the hospital with a dog that had been hit by a car. The poor thing couldn't use its hind legs—spinal injury. We told him to take the dog to the vet. Did you know we have a new vet? The new guy is awesome looking. He came over to the hospital the other day to get some drugs from the pharmacy and all the nurses were wondering who he was. I checked with the pharmacist and got his name. It's Adam Rainen, and you won't believe the name of his practice." Eva laughed and said, "Rainen's Cats and Dogs. Can you believe it?"

"Hey, that's pretty clever! It just occurred to me, if you married him, you would be Adam and Eva," Jill laughed.

"Whoa! Marry him? I don't even know him, but I think I'm going to check him out. I need to get a cat or dog though, so I'll have a good reason to go to the vet. Maybe I should borrow Sarah's Chihuahua, Alex, and pay a visit to the dude. When do we eat? I'm getting hungry."

"I don't think you told me about Sarah"

"Oh, I guess not. Sarah Walker is a nurse at the hospital and a real comedian—says the funniest stuff. Sarah said a couple of years ago an old lady had broken her arm. They treated her while she sat in a wheelchair, and she asked Sarah when she would be able to walk again." Eva and Jill both laughed.

"I'll get the pizza in the oven. You can make the salad. The lettuce is on the cutting board, and carrots, from my dorm room refrig, are in the crisper on the left."

During dinner, Eva asked, "Have you heard from mom and dad?"

"I got an email from them last week, apologizing for not being in Moscow for my graduation. Dad is really busy working on a study of ocean currents off Bermuda. They're staying in the Grape Bay Beach Hotel. Mom said they played golf at Tucker's Point the other day. They seem to be having a good time when dad's not on a ship in the ocean. Mom said to give you a hug for them."

"That's what happens to a woman that marries an oceanographer; lots of travel, shopping, and enjoying the world's beaches. Must be a really tough life."

Jill smiled and replied, "That won't happen if you marry a veterinarian in a little town in Idaho."

"Geez, Jill, it sounds like you want me to go after the new vet."

"Well, if you don't—.

The conversation drifted over various topics and was occasionally disrupted by the neighbor's dog barking. At 10:00 p.m., Eva had to return home to get ready for a meeting in the morning with Sarah and a part-time physical therapist from the hunting lodge, so she said goodnight and went out to her car. Jill got back in her wheelchair and followed Eva to the door. After Eva drove away, the barking ceased. Jill tidied up the kitchen and added some more notes to her story. At 11:00 p.m., Jill couldn't hear any more barking so concluded the dog had been taken into the house or gone to sleep. She thought the earlier barking might have generated some complaints from her other neighbor. Someone lived there; the lights were on.

# CHAPTER 31

# NEIGHBORS

Jill opened her eyes and looked around thinking someone was trying to break into the house, but the noise was from Glen dropping lumber on the porch. Jill got up, brushed her teeth, pulled on some clothes and said hello to Mr. Coffee. She looked at the wheelchair with disgust, sat down in it, and rolled to the front door. The heavy door didn't seem so difficult to open compared with the day before. Jill pushed the screen door open and bumped over the threshold onto the porch.

"Good morning, young lady. How are you today?"

Glen sounded in good spirits. He was wearing the same work clothes as the day before and orange work gloves. He was carrying two large pieces of lumber on his shoulder. His arms looked like they belonged on a weight lifter.

"I'm fine, thanks. Good morning. I heard you unloading your truck."

Jill pointed to a pile of two by fours, two by sixes and about eight sheets of plywood. There were several boxes of nails and screws, some metal brackets and a ball of string in a pile on the porch. Jill recognized a chop saw because her dad had one, but this saw was more elaborate, possessing some dials, and the blade was hidden in a cover of some sort. In addition to the lumber, there were two hammers, a hand saw, and a long level on the porch. Jill wondered how Glen had gotten all this stuff in his pickup.

"You got all these things in your pickup?"

"Nope. I brought a load of wood over last night around eleven o'clock. You must not have heard me. I tried not to make any noise. I put it on the grass by the curb."

Glen asked, "Where's that dog? I thought it would be barking at me by now."

Jill looked toward the neighbor's and said, "That's funny, I haven't heard the dog this morning. I expected barking about the time I got up. That bark would be a good alarm clock."

"Well, maybe your neighbor decided to keep the dog inside when they saw me unloading my truck. They knew the dog would raise the dead. Say, Jill, do you have an exterior outlet where I can plug in my saw? If not, I can plug in an extension cord and run it through the window."

"I think there's one by the porch on the side of the house over there." Jill pointed to the end of her porch closest to the dog neighbor's house. "I was thinking I could use it for Christmas lights."

Glen picked up the chop saw and moved it to the end of the porch, uncoiled the electrical cord, and looked behind the shrub at the corner of the house.

"I found it."

After he plugged in the cord, Glen stepped back from the house, turned to avoid the shrub and glanced at the next-door neighbor's yard, which was littered with pine cones like Jill's yard. Then he noticed something else, behind a bush. It looked like the neighbor's dog was sound asleep.

"Well, Mr. Dog, this saw is going to wake you up when I start cutting posts."

Glen fished a small package of ear plugs from his shirt pocket and inserted the pieces of sponge in his ears, went over to his pickup, slid two more posts from the back of his truck and carried them to the porch. After marking the posts, he began cutting them to size, glancing at the neighbor's yard, watching for the dog to wake up. After preparing four posts of identical length, he stacked them on the porch and returned to his truck.

Bags of cement were not Glen's favorite things to carry, but he wrestled a 90-pound bag close to the porch and went back for a second bag. He hesitated at the truck for a moment, pulled a handkerchief from his pocket, and mopped the sweat from his forehead. He looked up at the sun through his tinted glasses and commented, "Damn, it's going to be a hot one." Breathing a little hard, Glen leaned back against the truck and looked for the neighbor's dog. The dog hadn't run to the fence barking as expected, threatening to bite his leg off.

Glen wadded up his handkerchief and stuffed it back in his pocket. No use folding it, the colorful handkerchief, nearly a rag now, would dry faster if not folded. He couldn't stand wondering about the dog anymore, his curiosity finally taking over. Glen walked to the fence and looked at the dog. It hadn't moved an inch since he had seen it earlier. The dog must be medicated, unconscious, or dead. Glen reached for his cell phone and then remembered leaving it in his pickup. He had broken several phones before, hitting them with tools and dropping boards on them. No matter what the commercials said, portable phones didn't last long at construction sites.

Glen went to Jill's screen door, lifted his sunglasses so he could see in her living room, and said, "Miss Morran, would you call the sheriff? That dog next door might be dead."

Jill looked up from her keyboard and said, "Really? You think it's dead?"

"Yep, that dog hasn't moved a millimeter since I saw it earlier, and it didn't react when I used my saw. Cats and dogs usually run away from the sound of the saw. It hurts their ears."

Jill did a quick computer search for the police and found the number of the sheriff's office when she discovered Wolves' Hollow didn't have a police force. She picked up her phone and punched in the number, held the phone to her ear and looked at Glen, mouthing the number of rings. Three rings and a woman's voice answered.

"Sheriff's office, this is Jeanie. How may I help you?"

"I want to report a dead dog, at least I think it's dead."

"You can move it out of the street and the city sanitation crew will pick it up."

"The dog isn't in the street; it's in my neighbor's yard."

"Can you talk with your neighbor?"

"I don't think he's home and I'm in a wheelchair. I can't get out of my house right now. I'm having a ramp built as we speak. Could you please send someone out to see what's going on?"

"Okay, I'll notify the sheriff. She'll be right there—well, in a few minutes. I have to call her on the radio. She's on her way back from Tumbled Rock. One deputy has the day off and the other one went to Boise. What's your name and address?"

"I'm Jill Morran. I live at 511 North Pebble, next door to where the dog is."

"Thank you Jill. Sheriff Summers should be there in about ten minutes."

"Thank you Jeanie. Bye."

Jill looked at Glen. "The sheriff will be here in about ten minutes, Glen."

"She'll be here in ten minutes then. I know Rif, she's punctual."

"Who's Rif?" asked Jill. "What kind of name is that?"

"It's her nickname. The sheriff's name is Rhonda Summers, but Rhonda doesn't sound like a sheriff, so she goes by Rif. When she was a deputy, running for sheriff, she brought in some kid for breaking a car window and stealing a stereo. The kid was a smart ass. When she told the kid to take the gum out of his mouth, he tore the corner of one of her posters off and wadded it around his gum. Then, the poster said *riff*. Ever since, we've all called her Rif, with only one *f*."

"Do you mind if I watch what you're doing while we wait for the sheriff?"

"Nope. Need a push?"

"No thanks, Glen. I need to do it for myself."

Glen went back to his truck, dragged another bag of cement to the edge of the truck bed where the tailgate was folded down, picked it up and carried it to where he had left the other two bags. After dropping the bag on the ground, Glen stood up straight, stretched his back and said, "Jill, do you by any chance have a wheelbarrow?"

"You know, I'm not sure what's in the garage, but I think the door is unlocked. Go ahead and see if you can find something you can use."

Glen walked to the other end of the porch and went around the corner of the house to the garage. Jill could hear some rummaging around and after about a minute, Glen appeared pushing a wheelbarrow containing a coiled up hose, a small shovel and a hoe.

Glen was smiling and announced, "Found just what I needed."

Jill watched as Glen measured some distances from the porch and marked the positions with pinecones. Just as he started digging some circular holes, a white and dark blue squad car pulled into Jill's driveway and parked behind her car. A tall willowy brunette, deeply tanned, stepped out of the car, slammed the door, and began walking across Jill's weedy lawn kicking at pine cones.

"Hi there, Glen! It's nice to see you. You found a body?"

"Hi Rif. Yep, it's a dog--next-door. But first, I want you to meet someone. This is Jill Morran. I'm building her a ramp so she can get up and down from her porch without help."

Rif walked over to Jill and shook hands. From the wheelchair on the porch, Jill still had to look up to Rif. Rif was close to six feet tall, but she was wearing cowboy boots. Jill figured the sheriff was actually about five nine or five ten, the boots adding another two inches. Even though Rif wore a dark olive-green uniform, there was no way to conceal her curvaceous body, and sun-glasses didn't hide her pretty face. Jill imagined men would enjoy being arrested by this provocative creature.

Rif had on her serious face. "Jeanie said you found a dead dog."

"Yes ma'am. It's next door by the house behind some bushes. Glen noticed it first and told me about it, so I called your office."

"Hey Glen, show me the dog."

Glen and Rif walked over to the chain link fence and Glen pointed to the dead dog.

The sheriff walked along the fence toward the street, hopped over the boxwoods to the sidewalk and made her way to the neighbor's front gate. Jill was impressed with the graceful motion of the sheriff and wondered if the sheriff had taken ballet; she was too tall to have been a competitive gymnast or ice skater. Rif unlatched the gate, swung it open and made her way directly to the dog.

An elderly woman, Jill estimated to be at least eighty, was walking toward Jill's front porch, giving a little wave to Jill. She was a little hunched over, perhaps from years of work at a desk or bench of some sort. When she was about ten feet from Jill, she said, "Hello young lady, I'm your neighbor Fiona Wimsley. Why is the sheriff here? Did that dog bite someone?"

"Hi Mrs. Wimsley, I'm Jill Morran. I work for the newspaper. I moved in yesterday. Glen and I think the dog next door is dead. The sheriff is looking into it."

"You and your husband think the dog is dead?"

"Glen isn't my husband. He's a carpenter building a ramp so I can get down to the sidewalk from the porch. I'm not married."

Fiona smiled. "Oh, I see. I'm not married either."

Jill and Fiona watched from the porch as the sheriff put on a pair of rubber gloves, crouched, and examined the dog's body. She inspected the mouth and rolled the body over, probably looking for bullet holes. Rif spoke loud enough for Jill to hear. "The body is cold and rigor mortise has set in. I'm guessing the dog has been dead for at least eight hours, perhaps longer." She looked at her watch and said, "The dog probably died between 10:00 p.m. and 12:00 midnight. Jill, did you hear any barking after ten o'clock last night?"

"No, Sheriff. My sister left at ten, and there wasn't any barking after that, but I thought my neighbor had taken the dog in the house."

Rif stood, walked to the front door of the neighbor's house and rang the doorbell. No one answered. Rif pressed the button a second time. Still no response, so Rif looked into the house from the front door window and tried the screen door. It was locked.

Rif looked over to Jill and Glen and commented, "I'm going to walk around the house and see if I can get a better view of the interior. Stay where you are, please."

The sheriff stepped off the porch and began looking into the various windows that were accessible from ground level. When she went out of view, Jill asked Fiona, "Have you met the people that own the dog?

"Yes, but I don't remember his name. He's not married, either. He's a philanderist. He sells stamps to collectors. He travels all around the Pacific Northwest buying and selling stamps."

Jill almost laughed when Fiona said philanderist. Fiona had misunderstood the word *philatelist*. Jill smiled at Fiona and said, "Do you have any pets?"

"Yes, I do. I have a female cat called Stripes but she doesn't have any stripes. I thought the name was funny. It's black and white. I'm not sure how she gets on my roof."

# CHAPTER 32

# BODIES

Rif reappeared on the other side of the house where the dog was and walked toward the fence not far from where Glen was working.

"Glen, please come over here—and bring a hammer. I think someone's lying on the floor in there. We could have a second dead body."

Rif spoke into the radio attached near the left collar of her shirt. Jill could make out just two words, *veterinarian* and *Jeanie*. Jill recalled that Jeanie was the name of the woman she had talked with at the sheriff's office, the dispatcher. Maybe Jeanie was to ask a veterinarian to come out and take a look at the dog. Jill thought she might be meeting the new vet, Dr. Rainen, before Eva had the opportunity, and no borrowed animal would be involved.

Glen, with hammer in hand, didn't even attempt to jump the boxwood hedge; he just walked through the plants like a bulldozer. The boxwoods offered little resistance. Glen went through the neighbor's gate and trudged through the long grass and pine cones to the neighbor's porch where Rif waited patiently.

Rif asked Glen to open the screen door. He tried but it was locked.

"Knock the handle off the screen door and break the front door window."

Glen gently pushed Rif out of the way with his left arm and, without hesitation, swung his hammer knocking the handle off the screen door. He swung the metal door open and tried the handle on the front door. Like the screen door, the front door was locked. Glen whacked the window, smashing the glass and started to reach through the opening.

"Stop! Let me do that."

Rif reached in with a gloved hand and unlocked the door. Glen shoved the door open, entered, and pushed the broken glass out of the way with his work boots. He smiled and said, "Please come in, Sheriff."

Rif walked through the living room and stopped next to the front of a large desk covered with stacks of large books and loose stamp album pages, containing mounted United States postage stamps she had never seen before. The materials on the desk had no apparent organization, but she wasn't a collector. She peered over the desk at the floor, then moved behind the desk and knelt beside a body. Rif checked for a pulse but found none and spoke into her radio.

"Jeanie, call the coroner. I'm at 517 North Pebble, next-door to 511, where I was summoned a few minutes ago. I've got a dead body, a Mr. —just a minute."

Standing up, the sheriff rummaged through the middle desk drawer and found some business cards and mail with the name Mr. Simon Wrackler, Philatelist.

"Jeanie, I believe the deceased is Mr. Simon Wrackler. Have Doc Skidmore bring an ambulance. There's no hurry. Oh, and Jeanie, remember to ask Dr. Rainen, the new vet, to come over and take care of the dog. Find out how long Mr. Wrackler has lived here. I don't know him. Thanks Jeanie."

"10-4."

Rif asked, "Did you know Mr. Wrackler, Glen?"

"Nope. Never met the man. How'd he die, heart attack?"

"I can't tell for sure, but there's an obstruction in his left nostril and his mouth is full of blood. I'm sure Dr. Dan will tell us how Mr. Wrackler died."

Rif began checking the windows and as she moved to the kitchen, she said, "Glen, you might as well go back to work on that ramp. Thanks for the help." Rif found that the back door and screen and all the windows were locked from the inside or painted shut. *So, how did the killer get out of the house?*

Jill and Fiona watched as Glen came out of the house and returned to her yard and approached the porch.

"Your neighbor's dead, Jill."

"No kidding? What happened, a heart attack—a stroke?"

"I think he was murdered."

Fiona said, "Oh my! This is getting to be too much for me. I'd better go home and sit down. Bye, Jill. It was nice meeting you."

Jill replied, "It was nice meeting you, Fiona. See you later."

Jill looked at Glen and said, "Murdered? My second day in town and a murder! Any clues?"

"I don't know. You'll have to ask Rif. She's still in there. I'd better get back to work on your ramp. Are you gonna move away from here? If you're gonna move, you won't need the ramp."

Jill wondered why Glen asked if she was going to move. She looked at the hammer Glen had in his right hand and thought the hammer would be a good weapon.

"I'm not planning on moving. Should I be afraid? Why would anyone want to hurt me?"

"I can think of only one reason. You're next-door and you might have seen something. If you're frightened, have your sister or a boyfriend stay with you for a while."

"Thanks for the suggestion, Glen. I'll think about it." She smiled, "I don't have a boyfriend."

Glen laid the hammer on the porch and hooked up the hose to the faucet beside the porch. He put one of the sacks of cement in the wheelbarrow and sliced it open with a utility knife he had pulled from his pocket. Glen added water and mixed the cement with a hoe, added a little more water, and let the wet cement sit for a couple of minutes while he placed the four by four cedar posts in the holes he had dug.

Jill watched with great interest as Glen added cement to each of the four post holes. She noticed Glen doing something she thought was a bit peculiar. He had obtained a handful of shingles from his truck and was tacking shingles to each of the posts. Jill had to know what Glen was doing.

"Why are you tacking shingles to the posts, Glen?"

Glen was a little embarrassed. "You'll think I'm crazy."

"No I won't. I'm just curious."

"I had a terrible nightmare last night. The knots in the wood were eyes staring at me. I couldn't get away from the eyes. It's something that started when I was in the army."

"Sounds scary to me. That would give me the creeps."

"I thought if I covered the knots, the thoughts about the dream would go away quicker, but I can't quit thinking about the eyes when I see a knot in the wood. Maybe I should take a vacation and do something else for a while—maybe see a shrink."

"I can find someone else to make the ramp if you don't want to finish it."

"No, I can do it. If I get a good night's sleep, I'll be all right. Thanks anyway."

"Well, we can paint the ramp the same color as the porch so you won't see the knots. I'll help you. I'll just need a long handled brush so I can reach down to the ramp from my chair."

A noisy old blue jeep drove up to the curb and parked in front of Jill's house. She watched as the driver put his keys in his pocket and pulled a piece of paper from his shirt pocket. It looked to Jill like he was comparing something written on the paper to the numbers on the deceased neighbor's house. Was that Dr. Rainen? He walked to the front of the house and knocked on the door frame.

"Sheriff?"

Rif came to the door and extended her hand.

"Hi Adam. I'm glad you came over. The dog is outside on the ground—toward the back."

Jill watched Adam and Rif shake hands. They held hands for much longer than they would for a regular handshake. Jill wondered how well the vet and sheriff knew each other.

Maybe Adam was just showing his interest in the sheriff, after all, she was gorgeous. Rif came out and they walked to the corner of the house. Rif pointed at the dog and they moved toward it. Adam seized the front paws, pulled the dead dog away from the house and Rif grasped the hind legs. They carried the dead dog awkwardly to the curb and put the carcass in the back of the jeep.

Rif and Adam talked for a minute but Jill couldn't hear what they said. Glen was hammering. Adam put his left hand on Rif's shoulder, looked at Jill and waved. Jill waved back.

The vet got in his jeep and drove off. The engine sounded as if it needed some work. Rif watched Adam drive away, turned, and came over to talk with Jill.

"Miss Morran. Do you own any strychnine?"

"What? You mean rat poison? No way!"

"I had to ask. Dr. Rainen said the dog was probably poisoned with strychnine."

"I've only lived here a couple of days. You can search my house and garage if you want. There isn't much to poke through. Glen is the only one that has been in the garage."

"Why are you in the wheelchair?"

Jill invited Rif into the living room. As soon as the door was closed Jill said, "Well, about the wheelchair. A high school kid backed out of his driveway and I ran into him when I was riding my bike. Neither one of us saw the other. I hurt my back—pinched something so my legs don't function very well. A doctor in Boise told me he thought it was only temporary. After the swelling subsides, I should gradually get back to normal. My sister is helping me with physical therapy."

"That's too bad. Sore backs are a real pain." Rif grinned, "Pun intended. I wish you a speedy recovery."

"Thanks. Would you like something to drink Sheriff? How about some iced tea?"

"No thanks. I'm on duty."

Jill frowned. "It's just tea, no alcohol."

"That was a joke."

"I guess I'm a bit naïve, Sheriff," Jill smiled.

Rif grinned. "You just don't know me. I have to use humor sometimes as armor against some of the rotten things I see."

"You know Dr. Rainen? I saw you talking to him next-door."

# CHAPTER 33

# AMBULANCE FOR JILL

The conversation was interrupted by the arrival of the ambulance. It was an old hearse that had been refitted as an ambulance and painted white. A short chubby man of about 50 got out and approached Jill's porch. The man stopped and talked to Glen and then knocked on Jill's front door.

Jill looked at Rif and shook her head not knowing who was at the door. Rif opened the door.

"Hey, Rif. Where's the deceased?"

"Hi, Doc. Next-door." Rif tilted her head toward Wrackler's house.

"Okay. Want to come with me?"

"No. Ask Glen if he can help you with the body. He's been deputized before." Rif stuck her head out of the door and said, "Glen, you're a deputy for ten minutes."

"Do I get paid?" Glen quizzed and smiled.

"Nope. It's volunteer work—brownie points with the sheriff."

Doctor Skidmore descended from the porch, and Glen followed him to the ambulance. The women watched as the doctor opened the back of the hearse, and Glen helped the doctor pull out a gurney. The wheels dropped to the ground, and the two men pulled the mobile stretcher over the bumpy lawn next-door. Jill rolled over to the living room side window, parted the blinds and watched as the corpse, covered with a white sheet, was transferred to the ambulance. As the old hearse drove off, Rif's cell phone rang. The ring was a dog's bark and a kitten's meow. She fished it out of her pocket. Another bark and meow were heard.

"Hello. Hi, Adam. What did you find out?"

"The poison *was* strychnine, just as I thought. It was in raw hamburger. There was enough to kill a horse. It might have come from a farmer. Farmers use strychnine for killing rats, gophers and other critters."

"Okay. Thanks Adam. Bill the Sheriff's Office. See ya."

Jill commented. "I like your ring tone. Sounds like something a vet would use— better than a siren."

Rif laughed and said, "I almost used a siren, but I thought it would bother some people. I'd have to remember to turn it off when chasing a suspect down an alley, especially at night."

"So you knew Dr. Rainen before he came to Wolves' Hollow?"

"Yeah. Adam and I went to junior college in Boise at the same time. We had a couple of dates. He's very charming, but we were both career minded and never got serious. When Wolves' Hollow's veterinarian left for a job in Portland, I searched for Adam and told him about the opening here. Fortunately, he was moving from Ritzville, a small town in Eastern Washington and decided to move here."

"So he's single?"

Rif smiled. "Uh-huh. Sounds like you're interested, Jill."

"I don't know. I would have some pretty tough competition," Jill smiled. "But it might prove interesting, but you already have a head start and a distinct advantage. You carry a gun."

"Hmm. *You* just might offer some tough competition," Rif laughed.

"Oh! There's another interested party—my sister, and she's not riding a wheelchair."

Rif looked at her watch and started moving toward the front door. "It was fun talking to you, Jill. Good luck with your project. I might warn Adam about you and your sister. On second thought,

I'll keep it a secret. We'll let him figure it out. Hopefully, you won't run across any more dead bodies."

"Nice talking to you, Sheriff. Yeah, I hope not. One dead person is enough for me."

Later that night, Jill had put on her floppy flower-print pajamas and was sitting in her wheelchair working on the newspaper article. The TV was on mute. It was about 8:30. She walked to the kitchen to make some hot chocolate. After removing the hot drink from the microwave, she reached into her big ceramic pig and grabbed an oatmeal-raisin cookie. She was startled by a rapping on her front door. Jill thought for a second and yelled, "I'll be there in a minute!"

Jill picked up her drink and moved quickly toward her wheelchair but was spun around as if she were suddenly grabbed from behind. She tried not to lose her balance and fought to keep from spilling the hot chocolate but bumped into the door jam and fell awkwardly onto the side of the wheelchair right outside the kitchen door. Jill's loose fitting pajamas had snagged on a drawer knob and her sudden movements were uncontrollable. She had completely lost her balance.

Her left foot caught between the right wheel and the chair seat and she tumbled over the back of the wheelchair. She heard a pop and a wave of pain shot through her usually coordinated body. She knew her left leg was broken. There was another loud knock at the door.

A woman's voice asked, "Are you all right?"

It was Fiona Wimsley, her other next-door neighbor.

Jill couldn't get up but began inching herself across the rug toward the front door.

"Just a minute, Miss Wimsley, I fell from my wheelchair."

"Oh dear. Can I help you?"

"Yes, but the door is locked! Just a minute!" Jill's frustration was turning to anger.

Jill was almost at the door. Her pajamas were wet with sweat and hot chocolate, now cold on her skin, and a strange feeling of helplessness was coursing through her mind. She was beginning to feel nauseous but was able to turn the doorknob. She heard the click of the lock and her body slumped away from the door.

Miss Wimsley pushed the door open and saw Jill in a heap on the floor. As the elderly lady entered Jill's house, Jill began to vomit. Fiona, using her cane, walked to the bathroom and brought back a bath towel and a warm, wet washcloth and handed the towel to Jill. Fiona dropped to one knee and washed Jill's face. "Who should I call, dear?"

"Hand me my phone. It's on the sofa." Jill exhaled and threw up again, this time into the towel.

Fiona retrieved the little cell phone and handed to Jill, then went to the kitchen and returned with a glass of water and an empty pan. Jill held the phone until she felt the vomiting had stopped and pressed the dial button to call Eva.

"Hi Jill. What's going on?"

"I broke my damn leg. It's really bad. Have the ambulance come and get me. Maybe you can come and help too. I think I'm going into shock."

"Okay, be right there. Hang in there. Don't worry. Stay warm!"

"Fiona, would you please get me a blanket? Just pull the top one off the bed. My sister said to stay warm and I'm freezing." Jill took a mouthful of water, swished it around and spit it in the pan.

"How did you fall, dear?"

"It's complicated and I don't feel like talking right now. I'm really sick."

Fiona sat beside Jill and wrapped the blanket around the foul-smelling young woman. Fiona turned her head away from Jill to get a breath of fresh air. She gagged.

They could hear the ambulance siren as the reconditioned hearse came speeding up Pebble Street. Fiona stood up, turned the porch light on and looked toward the street. She recognized Doc Skidmore climbing from the driver's seat and moving to the back of the ambulance. The doctor swung the large rear door open and pulled a gurney from the cavernous vehicle. As he moved the stretcher toward Jill's house, a small car screeched to a halt behind the ambulance. A young woman ran past the gurney and came in the door.

"God, Jill! What happened?"

Jill looked at Fiona, then Eva and said, "I fell out of my damned wheelchair."

Eva looked at Fiona and said, "I'm Eva, Jill's sister. I guess you're Miss Wimsley."

"Fiona, dear. I was here when your sister fell. I was outside knocking. I think Jill needs some clean clothes, something to change into at the hospital."

"Okay. I'll get some things from the bedroom."

Doctor Skidmore entered the room and looked on the floor.

"Well young lady, let me look at your legs. Let's get you straightened out lying down so I can check things out."

Jill had seen the doctor earlier and knew he was the coroner. Was she going to ride in that hearse that had carted off Mr. Wrackler's corpse? Jill felt so crappy she decided not to give it a second thought. Doctor Skidmore moved Jill's left leg with care and felt for a pulse in her ankle. He was watching her grimaces as he carefully moved her leg. Skidmore stated, "I think you have more than one fracture. We'll have to get you to the hospital and I'll look at the X-rays. You'll probably have to wear a cast for a number of weeks. I'll talk to you about the situation after we get some pictures."

Jill heard a gentle male voice from outside say, "What can I help you with, Dan?"

"Hi, Adam. We've got to put this young lady on the gurney and transport her to the hospital. It appears her left leg has two fractures. Can't tell for sure until we take some pictures.

Can you help me get her on the gurney outside?"

Jill was mortified. *This was just great! My chance to meet the dreamy new veterinarian and I'm a stinky mess. I look like crap and I feel like I look. Damn!*

Adam dropped to one knee and put his arms under Jill's butt and back and with one effortless motion scooped her off the floor.

He carried her outside to the gurney and carefully placed her on the stretcher. Skidmore helped to stabilize her leg with some rolled up towels and fastened the gurney belts to keep her from moving.

Jill looked up at Adam and said, "Sorry about the smell, it's not my regular perfume. Thank you for helping."

"You're welcome. I've smelled worse from injured animals. Are you comfortable?"

Jill nodded.

Adam held Jill's hand and escorted her to the ambulance. After the gurney was placed in the ambulance, Adam climbed in and fastened the wheel locks to keep the gurney from moving.

"Do you want your sister to come with us?"

"No. I need her to clean up in the house and lock the door. Then she can come over to the hospital. Could you please tell her that?"

"Sure. I'll ride with you. Skidmore's a good driver when he's not transporting a corpse."

Adam smiled, squeezed Jill's hand, and said, "Be right back."

He climbed out of the back of the vehicle and walked toward the house. Adam returned in less than a minute and spoke to Doc Skidmore, "Let's go, Dan. I'm riding in back with Jill."

# CHAPTER 34

## HOSPITAL VISIT

Jill woke up and looked around the beige and white hospital room. There was a chair and small closet in one corner and a medical kit near the door. Behind her bed was a toilet/shower combination, just big enough to squeeze into, in one corner. Tile from the bathroom seemed to be from a 1950's motel, reflected light generating a pink glow. She scanned past a window to a sink and mirror in another corner of the small room. She heard a truck engine, the banging of trash cans, a slammed door, and a truck driving away. She felt a little chilly and thought about trying to pull up the blanket from the foot of her bed, but decided to remain lying down when she saw the IV and the half-filled plastic bag feeding solution into her right forearm. There was a control unit for the bed and some buttons, probably for calling a nurse, but someone would certainly come by soon. She couldn't move her left leg, but it didn't hurt anymore. Jill thanked God for that.

Jill remembered arriving at the hospital and going into a chilly room for x-rays. Adam smiled at her and held her hand as a nurse gave her an injection in the arm. Her last thoughts were about what a nice man Adam was. She couldn't remember whether she had smiled back.

The nearly closed door to her room suddenly swung open and a nurse entered the room. A short blonde, overweight, but smiling, stepped up to Jill's bed.

"I'm Sarah. How are we feeling today?"

Sarah checked Jill's pulse. Her hands were warm and she had a gentle touch.

"Much better than last night, thank you. Can you tell me about my leg?"

"You have a broken tibia—that's your shinbone, and some badly strained ligaments in your knee. Other than that, you're just fine," Sarah smiled. "Dr. Skidmore and two night nurses put your leg in a cast. You'll have to use a wheelchair for a while and then you can switch to crutches after the break has healed some. You don't want to break it again."

"Well, I'm no stranger to a wheelchair."

"Have you been injured before?"

"Well, this is my first broken bone. I've had a lot of firsts lately," Jill uttered. "Sarah. You know my sister Eva, don't you? It just donned on me who you are. Eva told me you have a Chihuahua. Eva likes your sense of humor."

"Oh yes! Eva and I have had a few laughs," Sarah smiled.

Jill looked down at the side of the bed and could see a bag about one third full of yellow liquid. She lifted her blankets and saw that she had a catheter, another first.

Sarah grinned and said, "If you want, you can take that bag home with you."

Jill smiled and responded, "Thanks, I don't think so. I'll leave it with you."

"As soon as you can get up and hobble to the toilet, we'll remove the catheter. It's only temporary until the sedative completely wears off and we can see how you manage with the cast. We'll probably remove the catheter this afternoon or evening, maybe tomorrow. Doc will be in to see you in about an hour. I'll get you some breakfast, here's a menu."

Jill looked at the menu on a small clipboard marked room 19, and read the instructions. She could have one item from each grouping. Jill used a stub of a pencil and checked some things that would approximate her normal breakfast. She returned the menu page to Sarah and the nurse left the room. A familiar voice filtered in from the hallway, Eva was talking to someone and they were approaching Jill's room. Jill leaned back against her pillows and waited, expecting to see Eva and a nurse.

Eva came through the door first, followed by Adam. They were both smiling. Jill wondered if Eva had held hands with Dr. Perfect as she had in the ambulance the night before. *Why was Dr. Rainen at the hospital? Doesn't he have a veterinary practice to run?*

"Hi, sis! How are you today?" Eva moved the chair next to Jill's bed and sat down.

Adam commented, "You look so much better than you did last night. I like your pajamas; they go nicely with your eyes. I'll bet you smell better too."

Jill hadn't paid any attention to her bed clothes until Adam made that comment. Eva must have brought them to the hospital for her. Jill felt completely out of place in the hospital but was enjoying the attention.

"Thanks Eva for bringing my PJs. And thank you, Dr. Rainen, for helping bring me to the hospital. I was really out of it last night. I can't remember feeling that sick—ever! I feel so much better now. The nurse said I broke my tibia and messed up my knee. I have a cast. Would you sign it? Eva, get a Magic Marker."

Eva reached up to her hospital jacket pocket, pulled out a black marker and said sarcastically, "I'm so honored."

Jill started to lower her covers, but suddenly remembered she had a catheter, and jerked the blanket back up. She looked a little embarrassed and said, "Pull my covers up from my feet so we can see the cast. I haven't seen it yet. Does my foot stick out or just my toes?"

Jill watched Adam pull the sheet and blanket away from the mattress and expose Jill's feet. He looked concerned. Jill's toes were exposed. He took a pencil and poked her toes with the eraser. "Can you feel that?"

Jill laughed, "Yes, it tickles."

Adam relaxed and smiled. "Good. I was worried you might have lost feeling in your toes when you asked that question. Wiggle your toes."

"Okay. I thought my toes would be cold if they were sticking out of the cast but they are warm."

"That's a good sign. You're circulation is good."

Jill moved all her toes and Adam signed her cast with *Toes O.K., Adam.*

Adam handed the marker to Eva who wrote *Wait till we start PT. Love, Eva.*

"Well, I've got to take care of some cats and dogs. I'm glad you are doing so much better. If I can get away later, I'll come by again to see how you're doing. Bye." Adam waved and left the room as Sarah arrived with Jill's breakfast.

Jill shouted but not too loudly, "Thanks for coming by!"

Sarah placed the tray on Jill's bed and left the room.

"Thank you Sarah."

Eva looked at Jill, chuckled and commented, "I wish I had thought of breaking my leg so I could get to know Adam. What a dirty trick!"

"That was good planning on my part, wasn't it? I was able to solve two problems with one accident. I got time with Adam even though I had taken a bath in puke and hot chocolate. And now I have to use a wheelchair for real. What a way to start a relationship!"

"But you got to meet him when you were in your pajamas! And today he came to see you in bed. I'm wondering what you will do if you go on a date? Say, if he has a pool, you could go skinny dipping!"

Jill had just eaten a spoonful of oatmeal and she had to put her hand over her mouth to keep from spitting on her sheet when she began laughing. Eva started laughing at Jill's reaction to her comments. Eva reached for a piece of bacon, but Jill swatted Eva's hand.

"No way! Don't you have to go to work today?"

Eva replied, "So now you're running me out, huh? Okay. I can tell when I'm not wanted." Eva pretended to cry and wiped her eyes with her fists like a little kid might do.

Jill laughed. "I'm so sorry Eva. I didn't realize you were so sensitive!"

"Bye, Jill. See ya later."

"Bye, Eva. Thanks for everything, especially the laughs. See ya later."

# CHAPTER 35

# TALK WITH DR. SKIDMORE

Jill finished eating, leaned back against her pillows and sighed. *Not bad for hospital food. But how could anyone screw up break-fast?* She was wondered how long she would be in the hospital, but Jill hadn't tried to stand up yet. She remembered friends telling her how they were nauseous when they tried to get out of bed after being anesthetized and lying flat on their back for a couple of days. She would just have to wait and see how her body reacted. Maybe when she got back home the ramp would be finished. She would be able to roam the neighborhood, visit the park, and go grocery shopping in her wheel chair, or course.

"Well young lady, how are you doing today?"

It was Dr. Skidmore, the coroner. That thought made Jill cringe a little, but Skidmore had driven her to the hospital in the ambulance and taken care of her last night.

"I'm much better, thanks. And thank you for taking care of me. I'm sorry I missed what went on when you put the cast on my leg."

"You wouldn't have been able to stand the pain Jill. We had to knock you out while we straightened your leg and took some more x-rays to verify the correct positioning of the bones. You had a severe break. You'll have to stay here for a couple of days so the bones start to heal without any stress."

"I was hoping to get back home so I could work on my article."

"Your article?"

"Yes. I just started working for the Wolves' Hollow Times. I'm working on a story about obstacles people encounter when they are confined to a wheelchair," Jill explained.

Dr. Skidmore asked, "How did you fall out of your chair?"

Jill had some quick thoughts. Last night's x-rays were probably only of her lower leg. If the x-rays included her back, the doctor might be curious about the absence of a back injury. Maybe x-rays weren't able to show vertebrae injuries clearly. She thought quickly and came up with a plausible explanation.

"I was working on my piece for the paper. I decided to take a break and had an urge to have some hot chocolate. I had just heated the chocolate drink in the microwave but I had to stand up to reach the Graham crackers. The crackers were in the cupboard above the microwave. I stood up and pushed the chair into the living room next to the kitchen door, got the crackers and the doorbell rang. I tried to hurry, keeping my balance by holding onto the counter top, but caught my pajamas on a drawer knob. I was jerked against the door frame, lost my balance and tried to get my butt into the chair. I missed and sat on the side of the chair and went over the back, somehow catching my leg between the wheel and the seat." Jill smiled and said, "Up to that point I hadn't spilled the hot chocolate, but when I went over the back of the chair, it spilled all over me. I heard the bone snap and then I started feeling sick. I crawled to the door, let my neighbor in, and called my sister. You know the rest."

"Well, you were lucky in a way. You could have hurt your back further, too."

"How long do you think I'll have to wear the cast?"

"If you eat right, follow directions, and get a good amount of rest, it will be at least six to eight weeks. After a few weeks, we might have to remove the cast and give you a new one. The muscles in your leg will atrophy and your leg will shrink away from the cast, making it too loose. That will depend on how much atrophy takes place. Your sister can help you with that. I'll give her some directions for you to follow, although she might already know what to do. I'm sure she has worked with broken bones before. She's a pretty smart cookie."

"What about the catheter, Doctor Skidmore?"

"We'll have a couple of nurses here this afternoon, and they will get you out of bed and see how you adjust to standing. We don't want you to pass out and fall. If you are able to move around with crutches, we'll remove the catheter this evening or tomorrow. Okay?"

Jill nodded. "Okay. Doctor, I'm curious. Did you discover how Mr. Wrackler died?"

"Sure did, but I can't discuss my findings with anyone but the sheriff, especially not you Jill. You work for the newspaper. It's your duty to get the news!" Skidmore smiled and added, "I have to be careful what I say around you; it might appear in the paper."

"But I wouldn't say or print anything. Can't you tell me something, please? Just a little nibble?"

"Nope."

"Oh, you're no fun." Jill laughed as Doctor Skidmore said he would see her tomorrow and left the room.

Jill leaned back onto her pillows and wondered why Skidmore hadn't asked why she was using the wheelchair. *Maybe Glen had told him my story. Somebody must have said something. He commented I was lucky to not have hurt my back further. I had better stick to as few lies as possible and not risk complications.*

# CHAPTER 36

## RETURN TO WRACKLER'S

**R**if had finished reviewing email crime notices from the State Police and had talked to her two deputies. Deputy John Funches was about 50, still in reasonable shape, but had a growing belly bulge and was a little lazy. Well, maybe not lazy, but hesitant to start working. He liked his morning donuts and coffee and got down to doing police work by 10:00 a.m. He had a nice wife and two grown children living in Boise. John had one grand-child, a little boy named Jimmy.

Deputy Timothy Cordell had just turned 25 and was a bit of a smart ass. He had an answer for everything. Tim was part-time and had a computer shop about a block from the Sheriff's Office. Rif thought Tim had memorized the encyclopedia Britannica. She had to admit he was pretty smart, but occasionally Tim went overboard on simple cases. Once, he arrested a young boy for riding his bike through a stop sign. He brought the kid into the jail. Rif took over, warned the boy, and let him go. Rif was sure that at least one of Tim's fantasies included her. She could tell by the way he looked at her, but Rif had no interest in Tim whatsoever. Tim was fairly good looking, about six-feet tall, had never been married, and was terrific with computers, adept with hardware and software. Rif told the two men to resume their normal duties and stay safe.

Doc Skidmore had called Rif earlier to inform her about Jill's accident. Rif asked if anyone else had been involved, perhaps Wrackler's killer had caused the "accident." Skidmore told Rif that Jill's broken leg was purely accidental. Then Skidmore informed the sheriff about his investigation of Mr. Wrackler's body.

"I examined the body thoroughly. It appears that Mr. Wrackler was hit in the back of the head and knocked unconscious. I found a round bruise in his hair on the right side of the skull behind his ear. The bruise was about the size of a quarter, but that injury wasn't what killed him. The fatal injury was inflicted by a pair of stamp tongs about six inches long driven through his left nostril and into his brain. That injury caused severe bleeding and death."

Rif asked, "Could Mr. Wrackler have been hit with a hammer?"

Skidmore thought for a moment and responded, "That would have left the bruise and the hammer could have been used to drive the tongs into the brain, although it wouldn't have taken a hammer. Was it a robbery, Rif?"

"I don't know Doc. I'm going to Wrackler's as soon as we hang up. I need to take a closer look at the doors and windows to see if I can determine how the killer got out of the house."

"Well, keep me informed. This is a strange one—perhaps a revenge killing? Bye."

"Bye Doc. Thanks for the info."

Rif drove to Wrackler's and parked in front of the murdered man's house. Glen was still working next door on Jill's ramp. It appeared to Rif that the ramp was nearly finished; Glen was painting it the same color as the porch, gray with a white railing.

Rif walked over to the fence and gave a wolf whistle. Glen was on his hands and knees with his butt toward Wrackler's. He turned his head so he could see Rif and commented, "Same too you, but even louder! You're sure sexier than I am."

"I don't know about that, Glen. I could almost see your cleavage," Rif laughed.

Glen grinned and said, "Sorry about that. What have you heard about Jill?"

"Broken leg. She'll be home in a few days. That ramp will really come in handy."

"Jill doesn't know it but I put a smaller ramp in for the back-door too. I had some extra wood at home in my shop."

"That was nice of you. I'm sure she'll appreciate that. Say Glen, do you have the two hammers you were using the day Mr. Wrackler was killed? I'd like to take a look at them."

"Sure. They're in the back of my pickup. I'll get them for you."

Glen started to get up and Rif said, "Don't bother, I'll get them."

Glen watched Rif walk to her cruiser, open the trunk and retrieve two evidence bags. Then she went to his pickup, looked into the bed and located Glen's hammers. There were three of them.

"Three hammers?" Rif questioned.

Glen smiled. "Yeah, one's a backup."

"Funny, Glen. You can only use one at a time. Are you ambidextrous?"

"Sometimes I need two, one for prying and one for hitting. When I misplace one under a board or forget where I left it, I have a third one as a backup."

"Oh. Okay, but I have to take all three."

Rif put on a rubber glove and placed a hammer in each bag and returned to her car, put the two hammers in the trunk and came back for the third one.

"Hey Rif, how am I supposed to work without hammers?"

"You'll have to borrow one. Besides, I thought you were painting. Do you really need a hammer?"

"I guess not. What's the deal with the hammers?"

"Can't tell you Glen. It's a secret." Rif smiled and said, "Finish your painting, I'm going next door. I'll return the hammers in a couple of days."

Rif put the third hammer with the others and slammed her trunk. As Rif walked toward Wrackler's house she looked over to Jill's house to see what Glen was doing. He was painting the railing and whistling. Apparently he wasn't very concerned about his hammers. Rif stepped on the porch, pulled the crime scene warning tape from the front door and entered the house.

The house smelled a little musty so Rif left the door open but closed the screen. She began checking the windows, noting whether they were locked or painted shut or both. The two living room side windows had curtains, which she pulled back, glanced at the lock and tried to lift the windows. The lock on the first window was closed but Rif tried to lift the window anyway. It didn't budge. After unlocking it, the window slid open easily. The second window wasn't locked but Rif's attempts to lift it failed.

"This one's painted shut," she muttered.

Rif went into the kitchen, the two small bedrooms, and the bathroom. All the windows were locked. When she was in the kitchen, which had a moldy smell, she looked in the garbage and found the source of the odor. Mr. Wrackler probably hadn't taken out the garbage for at least a week. Rif unlocked the back door, picked up a newspaper, the full garbage can, and went out to the alley. After checking through the garbage spread out on the newspaper, she dumped the mess in the garbage can and returned to the house.

As Rif set the plastic garbage container on the floor in the kitchen, she was thinking about the windows. *Why was only one window painted shut? And that one wasn't locked.*

She went back to the suspect window and inspected the sill. The sill had dust near the outside ends but was wiped clean in the middle. Someone could have exited the house through this window.

Rif went to her cruiser, leaned in the window and grabbed her camera from the passenger seat. She tried to get a tape measure from the glove compartment but couldn't quite reach it. She had to open the door and climb in the car. Rif stuck the tape in her pocket and walked to the window in question. The ground beneath the window was fairly soft and three pine cones were partially pressed into the dirt. A fourth cone lay entirely above ground against the foundation.

Rif set the camera at high resolution and took several photos of the area beneath the window. She dropped to her knees and measured the height above ground of the pine cones and recorded the data in her notebook. She spoke into her shoulder microphone.

"Jeanie, please have Tim and John come over to 517 North Pebble, a.s.a.p. I need them to help me with something."

"10-4, Sheriff."

Rif went over to the fence to talk with Glen. He was putting the lid on a paint can and wiping a paint brush on a rag.

"How much do you weigh, Glen?"

"In the buff or clothed?" Glen replied and smiled.

"Clothed. Don't get any ideas Glen."

"About two-thirty, last time I checked."

"How much do *you* weigh, Rif?"

"That's a secret. A man doesn't ask a woman how much she weighs; that could get him in trouble. Don't you know that?"

"Just thought I'd ask. You know—reciprocity."

"You've been reading books again, haven't you?" Rif smiled.

Glen said something but Rif couldn't hear it. Deputy Funches rolled up in his patrol car and got out. Rif watched him straighten his shirt and pull up on his pants. He walked over to Rif.

"What is it, Sheriff? Jeanie said you wanted me and Tim to report to you."

"How much do you weigh John?"

The deputy frowned and said, "About 225, Sheriff. Why?"

"Perfect! Come with me."

Rif marched across the lawn stepping over big pine cones with Deputy Funches following, trying to keep up. Rif stopped in front of the area she had photographed.

"We're going to do a little experiment. Pick up two pine cones from the driveway about the same size as these." Rif pointed to the cones on the ground beneath the window. Rif watched the deputy walk, swaying side to side, to the driveway and drop to one knee to reach the cones. Rif thought, *John needs to lose at least 30 pounds. Maybe I should tell him to lay off the doughnuts.*

John returned with two pine cones. "Here's the cones. What should I do with 'em?"

"Put them in the dirt underneath the window and step on them with one foot--like you were walking." Rif watched as

Funches did as she had instructed. "Okay. Now step away so I can get some pictures and make some measurements."

Rif photographed the positions of the new cones, measured their depths in the ground and wrote the data in her notebook as she had done before.

"Where's Tim?" she asked.

"I dunno." Funches shrugged and looked away from Rif.

"Come on John, where is he? You know."

"Over at the computer shop playing games."

"God damn it! I wish I could fire that little shit!"

Rif spoke into her shoulder mic. "Jeanie, tell Tim to get his ass over here. If he isn't here in ten minutes, I'm going to have Dr. Rainen cut his nuts off!"

About five minutes later, after Rif had explained her experiment to Deputy Funches, Deputy Cordell drove up and walked over to Rif and Funches. He had a sheepish grin on his face.

"Tim, how many times have I told you to stay away from computer games during work hours?"

"I was checking out a report of loud mufflers, Sheriff."

"That's a bunch of bull. If I hear that you are playing games again, I'm going to have the town council dock your pay. I wish we'd never hired you! You aren't worth a shit! How much do you weigh?"

Tim frowned and answered with, "About one sixty-five. Come on Sheriff. I've written plenty of tickets," Tim whined. "Why *did* you hire me?"

"We had two applicants and the other guy had dyslexia, couldn't read fast enough, and didn't know anything about computers. I don't know why he even applied. Come here. Bring a couple of pine cones from the driveway. Put them on the ground under that window and walk across them—just step on each cone with one foot as if you were walking normally. Then I want you to go to Main Street and watch for speeders. See if you can write some legitimate tickets to help support your sorry butt."

"All afternoon?"

"No. After two hours, I want you to patrol the city streets. Can you do that without help?"

"Yes, Sheriff."

Rif watched as Tim followed her directions, walked back to his patrol car and drove off.

"You need me for anything else, Sheriff?"

"No, John. Thank you for coming out here and please try to cut down on the doughnuts.

What are you doing today?"

"I'm catching stray dogs and checking them for licenses. Some of the dogs might have rabies. They've been out in the woods."

"Okay. Get to it."

Rif followed the same routine that the deputies had followed with the pine cones, went to her cruiser and plotted the data on her computer. From the plotted data, she concluded that the person that had stepped on the pine cones beneath the window weighed more than one hundred but less than one hundred forty pounds. The killer was probably a small man or a woman.

# CHAPTER 37

# RIF NEEDS HELP

Rif reentered Wrackler's house and searched his desk, thoroughly this time. She was looking for a motive. Why would someone want to kill a stamp dealer? Rif wasn't even sure what a stamp dealer's activities included. The top drawer of Wrackler's desk was full of pens, pencils, erasers, magic tape, paper clips, etc. Just about everything anyone would need for an office was in that drawer. She didn't find anything of interest to the case.

In the bottom right hand drawer were some half-inch thick folders labeled with the years 1990-2012. Rif opened the folder for 2012. It contained yellow duplicate copies of purchase orders for stamps and supplies for Wrackler's business. The copies had names of stamp companies, auction houses and individuals. The sales slips for individuals had their signatures on them. Rif pulled the entire drawer out of the desk and carried it to her car.

Glen called out, "Need some help, Rif?"

"No thanks. It's pretty heavy, but I can wrestle it into the back seat."

"Okay. Give me a yell if you need some help. Always ready to help a lawman—woman."

After sliding the heavy desk drawer into the back seat, Rif returned to the house, shut the front door and replaced the crime scene warning tape. It took her about 20 minutes to get back to her office. Rif stopped along the way and arrested a diet Pepsi and a cheeseburger for too much sugar and fat, but let the fries go. She had to have something to eat while she sorted through Wrackler's purchase orders.

"Jeanie, after lunch I want you to help me sort through all these papers and see if we recognize any of the names and signatures. If you see Tim or John when you're out having lunch, tell one of them to go over to Ms. Wimsley's and see if she'll let her garage be searched for strychnine, the house too. Fiona Wimsley's address is 507 North Pebble. She's a nice old lady, so tell them to be courteous."

"Okay, Sheriff. I'll be back at one o'clock. Harley and I are going to get Chinese over at the China Station. Their food is really good."

"You mean Harley Richards? How'd you guys get together?"

"We ran into each other last week at the square dance meeting in the high school gym. He's a nice man and about my age. He can't dance a lick but he tries. He's lots of fun. I'd better go, Sheriff. I told Harley to meet me at the China Station at twelve-fifteen, it's after twelve already. See ya later."

Rif thought about Jeanie having lunch with Harley. Harley was in his mid-forties, lived on a ranch, had never been married, and had more money than he knew what to do with. He was about five-eight, balding and a little overweight. Harley had the nicest smile and a wonderful laugh. Lurch, his dog, rode in the back of his pickup. One of Lurch's paws had been damaged when Lurch was hit by a motorcycle. Harley adopted the dog and named him Lurch.

Jeanie was in her late thirties, smart as a whip, wore her hair pulled back from her face formed into a bun toward the top back of her head. Rif smiled when she recalled that her deputies called Jeanie's hair style the doorknob look. Jeanie was part Shoshone, was nice looking and had jet-black hair. She was striking when she dressed up, but was a little shy. However, her demeanor on the radio was all business and fairly aggressive. She was a top-notch employee.

Rif finished with the 1990 file and laid it on the floor. She didn't recognize of any of the names. The addresses were in

Washington: Spokane and Cheney. The next five files were similar to the 1990 file. Jeanie returned from lunch and Rif handed her a stack of five files for the years 2000-2004. Rif continued with the earlier files finding addresses and names from the Tri-Cities: Pasco, Kennewick and Richland. It appeared that Mr. Wrackler had moved from Spokane to Richland in 1996.

Rif took a break from the files and packaged the three hammers for shipment to the Boise Police Crime Lab. Then she called the coroner's office. Skidmore's message said he was at the hospital checking on some patients until 2:00 p.m. Rif left a message asking for a tissue sample from Wrackler suitable for DNA analysis.

"Jeanie, I'm going to the hospital."

"Should I continue with these files?"

"Yes. Put a note on each file indicating the towns or cities on the purchase order receipts. I'll be back in about an hour."

"Okay, Sheriff."

Five minutes later, Rif parked the cruiser and was walking down the east hallway of Wolves' Hollow Memorial. She could see Doc Skidmore at the nurse's station near the main entrance. He was looking at a patient's chart. Skidmore looked up when he heard Rif's boots.

"Hi Rhonda. What can I do for you today?"

"Hi Doc! I need tissue samples from the deceased and Jill Morran. I'm sending some evidence to the crime lab in Boise."

Skidmore thought for a few seconds and replied, "Okay." He turned to Sarah. "Please change the water in Jill's room. Don't touch her straw with your hands. Put it in one of those sterile bio-bags. Give her fresh water and a new straw. Mark the bag and bring the used straw to Sheriff Summers."

"Yes, Doctor."

"Let's go to the morgue, Rif."

Rif smiled. "Gee, Doc. I thought you'd never ask."

Skidmore laughed. "I wish I were 20 years younger. You're feeling pretty good today. Making progress on the murder?"

"I think so. I believe the killer was a small man or a woman but I need more evidence."

"The body's in the cooler. I'll get you a sample. You can wait out here."

"Thanks Doc."

Rif leaned against the wall and looked at her boots. She needed to wipe the dust off and give them a good shine. *I wonder how Jill is doing. She has got to love having a cast on one leg, but she'll be able to get off her porch now. Glen did a good job on that ramp and she'll be surprised to have a ramp in back too.*

The morgue door clicked and swung open. "Here you are Rif."

Rif looked at the bag containing some follicular hair and a small piece of skin. Skidmore had marked the bag with Wrackler, the date and DAS, Skidmore's initials.

"What's the A for, Doc?" Rif asked. She held up the evidence bag pointing at the initials.

"Arnold. He was an uncle, my mother's brother, kind of a turd, in my opinion."

# CHAPTER 38

# NOT A LIE

When Rif returned to her office, Jeanie had finished with the folders and had printed a chronicle of dates and places Wrackler had lived and worked. Jeanie had returned the files to the drawer Rif had brought to the office from Wrackler's. She had added a note after Ontario, OR 2007: signature by G. Collins. Do you think that's *our* Glen Collins?

Rif sat down and said, "Hmm. Jeanie, I want you to see if Glen got a building permit for Jill's ramp from the city office upstairs—he should have. Take the signed purchase order you found and compare the signatures. Get a copy of the signature on the permit and bring it to me please."

Ten minutes later, Jeanie came running down the hall smiling, waving two sheets of paper and nearly yelling to Rif. "They look the same!"

Rif spread the papers on her desk and looked at the signatures. It didn't take a genius to see the writing was made by the same person. Jeanie was correct.

"Good work Jeanie. Glen lied to me. I asked him if he knew Mr. Wrackler and he said he had never met the man. Why did Glen lie? Get Deputy Funches on the radio and tell him to meet me at Jill Morran's house. Glen should still be there. I might need John for back up."

When Rif arrived at Jill's house, Deputy Funches was already there, sitting in his squad car holding half a doughnut and drinking coffee. Rif pulled up behind the deputy and watched as Funches stuffed the remainder of the doughnut in his mouth and washed it down. They exited their cars simultaneously and walked toward Glen, who was cleaning up bits of wood and looking for dropped nails with a magnet on a stick near Jill's front porch.

Rif kicked a pine cone as she and Deputy Funches walked toward Glen who started sweeping off the porch. Rif was thinking about how to ask Glen about his lie.

"Hi, Rif, Deputy. What do you need today, another hammer?" Glen smiled.

"Glen, I think you lied to me about not knowing Mr. Wrackler. Explain why you sold some stamps to Wrackler but never met him."

Glen frowned and said, "I didn't lie, Rif. I was visiting my sister in Ontario. We were getting rid of some things our mom had. Mom had an old stamp collection that was my father's and she kept it around for a long time after he passed away, ten or twelve years I think. When Mom died, Ginny stored all Mom's stuff in her garage. Ginny and I were sorting through it and we found the stamp collection. I took it to Wrackler's shop for appraisal but Wrackler wasn't there. The lady accepted the album and told me I could come back the next day, which I did. Wrackler had gone to Boise but he left a check for $500 for me. The lady, I think her name was Laura, gave me the check. She said if I was satisfied, I should sign the receipt. I signed it and went back to my sister's garage. We split the money."

Rif showed Glen the copy of the receipt and asked, "Is this your signature?"

"Yes ma'am. You can see the initials of the lady that waited on me, LS. I think her name was Laura, but I can't remember the last name. It might have been Schaffer. I know it wasn't Smith," he grinned.

"Okay Glen. You're off the hook. I believe you."

"It's the truth, Rif, so help me God. Do you have a Bible?" Glen smiled.

Rif grinned, handed the receipt to Funches, and asked Glen, "What can you tell me about Miss Morran?"

"Jill? She's very nice and appears to be very smart. She has a good sense of humor. It's too bad she damaged her spine in that traffic accident so she can't move her legs much. And then she broke one of them falling over her wheelchair. I can't figure out how she did that."

"How did she hurt her back?"

"She was hit by a kid in a pickup when she was riding her bike. He didn't see her and backed out into the street and knocked her down."

"Okay. That's what she told me," Rif nodded.

"She said she should get back the use of her legs before the end of the year if everything worked out. Jill's a good lookin' chick, too bad she got hurt."

"Thanks for the info Glen. When we look for a killer, we have to question everything and everybody. Sorry I doubted you. We'll let you get back to work. Looks like you're about finished here."

"Don't worry about it, Rif. It did appear that I had lied, but it was more complicated. Do you think Jill was involved with the murder?"

"Sorry Glen. I can't say anything until we follow all the leads. I have other evidence that you weren't involved. You weren't at the top of my list." Rif was thinking about her experiment with the pine cones. Glen was too heavy to have been the killer.

Glen smiled. "That's good. If I were in jail, who'd build ramps and railings?"

"That's right! We'd have more do-it-yourselfers ending up in the hospital. You're doing a community service." Rif grinned. "Come on John; let's get back to the office."

Glen watched Rif and Deputy Funches walk back to their cars. It occurred to Glen that Rif should stand for "Rhonda is fine." *God, she looked great, and she was smart, just like Jill.* Glen wished he had some money and a nice car, but some things just weren't in the stars. Then he thought *maybe I should get in shape...lose my gut.* Glen finished packing up his tools, filling up Jill's garbage can, and bought a steak at the supermarket.

On his way home Glen thought he would talk to Dr. Rainen about getting a dog, not just a regular dog, but one that needed some TLC. A dog with three legs or only one eye would be okay, and his canine partner could ride in the pickup and be with him at job sites. Glen would have someone to talk to, a real companion with no attitude like his former wife had. He looked forward to a wagging tail rather than criticism for not making more money. After four years, Glen had been glad to get out of that relationship. Eight years ago he thought the divorce had meant he was a terrible failure, but after a month or two, when he came home stinky and sat down with a beer, he reveled in his freedom.

Glen parked his pickup under the carport, grabbed his steak, went in the kitchen and started the meat cooking on low heat. He popped the cap off a cold beer and went in the bathroom and took a relaxing shower. Ten minutes later, dressed in a bathrobe, he finished cooking the steak, turned on his flat screen, swallowed the last drop of his first beer, and grabbed another one. He armed himself with a sharp steak knife, some A-1 sauce, a fork, and started watching a movie. He woke up at 10:17 p.m., put his dirty dish in the kitchen sink, and went to bed. He didn't have anything planned for the next day.

Glen tried to shut off his alarm clock but the button didn't work, the damn thing just kept buzzing. He opened his eyes, blinked a few times and looked at the clock. It was 8:15 a.m. and the noise wasn't from his clock, it was his cell phone. He picked up too late, the caller had hung up. Glen dialed the number of the last incoming call and heard the phone ring twice.

"Hello, Sheriff's Office. How may I help you?"

"This is Glen Collins. Did the sheriff want to talk to me?"

"Hi, Mr. Collins. This is Jeanie. Rif wants you to meet her at Wrackler's at nine o'clock if possible. You need to bring something to pry open a window. It looks like the window is painted shut."

"Okay. Tell her I'll be there. Bye."

"Good bye."

Glen dressed quickly and skipped breakfast. He checked his solvents to make sure he had cans of paint thinner, alcohol, and toluene in his truck, locked the front door and slid into the driver's seat. The engine grunted but didn't start when he turned the key. Glen waited a few seconds and tried again. The engine started, he pulled out onto the street, made a left, and drove toward Wrackler's. Maybe Jill would be home from the hospital today. He could get paid and make sure the ramp worked for her. Adjustments would be free of charge if Jill had any problems getting on or off the sloped surface, but he was confident the ramp would work fine.

The sheriff's cruiser was parked on the street at Wrackler's. Glen left his pickup at the curb behind the cruiser. Rif waved from the porch and motioned for Glen to come to the side windows of the living room. Glen retrieved the solvents from his truck bed and walked toward Rif.

"Hi, Glen. Thanks for coming over here. I hope I didn't interrupt anything."

Glen smiled. "Just my beauty sleep. You look very nice today."

"Thank you, Glen." Rif smiled and commented, "I brought you something to use."

Rif held up a new hammer with a fiberglass handle. Glen hadn't seen it when he first saw Rif. He was watching her face and body, not what she was holding at her side.

"I thought we might need a hammer. Since I took your three hammers yesterday, I didn't know if you had another one. We might need a hammer to pry open this window."

Rif had walked to the window that had the dust removed from the sill, the one that seemed to be painted shut. She pointed at the window with the hammer.

"Let's get that window open. I'd like to see why I can't lift it up."

Glen tried to force it open with his hands but the window wouldn't give. He opened the pint can of methanol and took a large nail from one of his pockets. Glen put the nail on the lip of the alcohol can and tipped the can so a little stream of solvent ran down the nail into the crack between the sash and the window sill. The solvent flowed off the end of the nail into the crack without spilling a drop.

"That's very clever. Where'd you learn that, Glen?" quizzed Rif.

Glen answered, "Chemistry lab. But we used a glass rod instead of a nail."

Rif replied, "I took physical science but we didn't have a lab— that's why I took it. I liked biology though. I'd like to go back and finish my degree sometime—two more years."

Glen set the methanol can on the ground after pressing down the flip-top cap and tried to push open the window. It still wouldn't budge.

Glen frowned and uttered, "Okay, plan B."

Glen picked up the toluene can, pried the lid off and repeated the procedure he had followed with the alcohol. Both Rif and Glen could smell the toluene vapors and Rif backed away.

Glen looked at Rif and commented, "I kind of like that smell. It's not bad if you're in the open air."

"Too strong for me, Glen, but it smells a little like some perfume I put on the other day when I went out to eat with Adam."

"What's the name of the perfume?"

Rif smiled and said, "Capture. When I saw the name, I had to try it. But a little bit goes a long way."

"Did Adam like it?"

Rif laughed. "I think so. It seemed to work."

"I need to get a couple of chisels. Be right back."

Rif watched Glen walk over to his pickup, reach into the bed and pick something up. She noted that Glen walked a little like Deputy Funches—rocking side to side, but not quite as pronounced as John. Glen stuck a chisel under each side of the sash and pressed down on the levers. The window popped open about a half inch and Glen started to put his fingers in the opening to push up but Rif stopped him.

"No fingers Glen, just tools."

"Hammer, please."

Rif quipped, "Yes doctor."

Glen smiled and reached toward Rif. She smelled clean, like slightly scented soap. She handed him the hammer. Glen laid the hammer next to the window and pried up with one of the chisels. When the window was open about three or four inches, Glen used the hammer and pushed the sash up about a foot.

"That's far enough. I'm going inside now. Stay right here."

Glen stepped back onto the dry yellowing grass and waited for Rif to appear in the window.

"Could you please hand me one of your chisels?" Rif was on her knees on the other side of the window. She used the chisel to scrape the inside bottom of the window and caught the falling white particles in a small plastic bag. Rif closed and locked the window and came back outside. When she joined Glen, she handed him the chisel and held the bag so Glen could see the white material.

"What do you think that is, Glen? It doesn't look like paint to me."

Glen examined the fragments visually and worked one of the largest pieces away from the others, folded the bag on the piece he had separated and remarked, "You're right Rif, that stuff isn't paint. If it was paint like on the rest of the window it wouldn't turn to powder, it would bend or break. I think I know what it is though."

# CHAPTER 39

## GLEN MEETS BARNEY

**R**if looked at Glen expecting him to divulge his thoughts about the composition of the white material but Glen didn't volunteer anything. She watched Glen pick up his tools and solvents and start toward his pickup.

Rif was getting frustrated. "Glen! What do you think that stuff is?"

"Oh! I'm sorry, I was thinking about something else. I want a dog."

"Well?"

"I think it's liquid paper. That stuff is soluble in toluene. Pour a little on the sill and shut the window...dries fast. The window is stuck shut and it looks like white paint."

"Hey, that's a good idea, and I can check it out locally. I don't have to send it to Boise for analysis. Thanks, Glen. You can have the hammer."

"Any time, Rif. You know, that's a pretty good hammer; you'd better keep it in your car for the next time. But thanks for the offer. I'm going over to Rainen's to see if I can get a dog. Maybe the vet will know if there's one around here that I can adopt, but I don't want one of those little yippy ones; I'd like one that's XL, maybe ninety pounds or so. But Great Danes and St. Bernards are out; they're *too* big."

"Adam can probably help you, but feeding a big animal will be costly. Thanks for the help. See you later." Rif waved to Glen as he climbed into his pickup and drove off.

Rif thought about Glen mentioning he wanted a dog. Maybe Glen really wasn't a loner as she had thought. In the past she had misjudged the gentle nature of men and women by assuming they were rough and tough because of their behavior or their appearance. Rif still had a lot to learn about people. Being sheriff was providing her with plenty of opportunities. Glen was a nice man, probably about forty, and pretty good looking except for his tummy, but that could be fixed.

Glen headed over to Rainen's with one purpose, to find himself a dog, a big drooling horse of a dog if necessary. When he entered Rainen's, a cat's meow and a bird's chirp announced Glen's presence. *Damned doorbells—what's next?* Glen looked around and saw a teenage girl with reddish-brown hair behind the counter sitting on a bar stool staring at a flat screen monitor. It looked like she was playing a computer game. She had a lot of freckles.

She looked over her glasses at Glen and smiled. "May I help you sir?"

"Maybe. I'm looking for a dog."

The girl pushed her glasses higher on her nose and stepped over to the counter. "I'm sorry you lost your dog. If you have a picture or description, you can post in on the bulletin board over there." She pointed to a large corkboard nearly half covered with notices and pictures of lost pets, a brochure for the ASPCA, and ads for dog food.

"I'm sorry, I didn't say that right. I haven't lost a dog. I came to see if you can get me one. Do you have any animals for adoption?"

"Oh, you'll have to see the doctor about that...or go to the pet shelter. It's over at 1011 River Rock Lane, that ugly faded-green building. They usually have lots of cats and a few dogs for adoption. There's quite a variety over there. Dr. Rainen only has animals that are healing or ones people don't want."

Glen smiled, "Yeah, that's what I'm looking for, a dog that needs some TLC."

Glen noticed the girl had a name tag with Nora written on it. She appeared to be a high school student, learning about animals and earning a few dollars helping Adam, probably only on certain days. Nora turned and walked over to a closed door behind her.

"Just a sec, I'll get Dr. Rainen for you."

Glen looked around the waiting room, walked over to a chart and read about the ages of cats and dogs and their equivalent human years. Glen heard the door behind him open followed by, "Hi Glen. Nora tells me you're thinking about adopting a dog. I've got two little guys for you to look at. Come in the back and you can see them."

Glen turned from the chart and glanced toward Doc Rainen and Nora.

"Okay, Adam, but I want a big dog, not one of those little yippy ones. They piss me off."

Glen noticed Nora smiling, knowing exactly what Glen meant.

Glen grinned and commented, "Sorry for the foul language, young lady."

Nora laughed. "That's all right. I have some friends that cuss all the time. My teacher said they need to improve their vocabularies. The *F* word is unnecessary and sounds bad."

Adam escorted Glen into the back room where he could see several caged animals, some of which had bandaged paws and legs. One little dog had a cone around its neck.

Adam stopped and pointed at an enclosure. The wire bottom of the cage had been removed and the white puppy with black spots was sitting on some papers covering the concrete.

"This is Barney the Dalmatian. The little guy is deaf. Someone took him to the mountains and left him to die, not wanting to care for a handicapped animal. A forest ranger found him in a dilapidated old barn and brought him to me about a month ago. He's healthy and is looking for a good home. Would you consider adopting him? He'll be pretty big when he grows up."

Glen stepped over to the cage and knelt beside it. He reached toward the cage, wiggled his fingers and the puppy came over to Glen's hand and licked his fingers.

"Well Barney, how'd you like to come home with me?"

Glen could see Barney's eyes were focused on him. The puppy wagged his tail, sat down with his eyes focused on Glen, and then stood up again, tail wagging.

"Glen, I think you and Barney have a connection. If you don't like the name Barney you can change it. The puppy doesn't know his name since he can't hear. The only thing I worry about is that you might get frustrated with the dog's inability to hear you. You'll have to figure out a way to communicate. It will require some patience."

"I've got plenty of that, Doc—time too. I'll need a leash and some dog food, enough for a couple of weeks. I'll get some more food and let you know how things are working out by the end of the month."

"I'll send you a note when the next round of shots is due. Let me know if you notice any peculiar behavior, but I think Barney will adjust fine. It will take a couple of days for him to get used to you and your home. Take him out for bathroom breaks fairly often so there won't be any accidents."

"Okay. Say, how was your date with Rif?"

"It was okay. Rhonda is totally immersed in the murder investigation so we just went to dinner and I took her home. Why do you ask?"

"She mentioned it this morning. I was wondering if she told you anything about her investigation. Is Jill involved?"

"Rhonda didn't tell me a thing. I tried to trick her into saying what was going on in that mind of hers but she wouldn't let me in. It has always been that way with her. I guess we're just going to be friends, but that's all right. Whoever marries her will be a lucky man. She's gorgeous, smart, and can be very funny. Do you know if Jill is home from the hospital yet?"

"When I was at Wrackler's with Rif, Jill wasn't home. It might be a day or two more before Skidmore releases her. You like Jill?"

"Yeah. I'd like to get to know her. She's got an older sister, too. Her sister is closer to my age. You think Jill would like to take care of a dog while her leg mends? What were you and Rif doing at Wrackler's?"

"Oh, not much. I helped her open a stuck window, that's all. You should visit with Jill and find out if she wants to care for a pet. It might be something to help pass the time and speed her recovery. It would keep her mind off herself. Thanks for helping me with Barney."

Glen paid for the food and leash and the two men shook hands. Adam carried Barney to Glen's pickup and placed the dog on the front passenger seat. Glen tossed the bag of dog food in the back, climbed in beside his new buddy, waved to Adam, and drove off. Glen watched Barney curl up on the seat and look up at his new master.

"You and me Barney! I'm going to teach you how to communicate!" Glen reached over and scratched the dog's head. Glen was anxious to get home and try out his idea on Barney. As he drove home, he was thinking of a new name for Barney, but he decided to keep the name as Adam had said, since the dog couldn't hear his name anyway. Glen passed by the supermarket and then stopped, made a U-turn in the middle of the block and went back to get some doggie treats. He would need more of a reward than a scratch on the head for positive reinforcement. Glen bought some medium-size Milk-Bone snacks and drove home prepared for doggie school.

Barney was going to stay in the bedroom with Glen the first night away from the kennel.

Glen folded an old blanket to make a bed big enough for Barney and filled his plastic popcorn bowl with water and set it on the floor in the kitchen. When they got up in the morning, Barney would eat breakfast while Glen ate. Glen let Barney roam the house sniffing everything to get accustomed to every odor, even Glen's dirty clothes, piled on the floor at the foot of the bed.

Glen began instructions as soon as Barney had inspected the house and investigated the yard, which was enclosed by a shoulder-high cedar fence. Glen thought Barney could respond to a vibration, so a Barney code was developed, kind of like the Morse code for telegraphy. Glen taught Barney to come by making two short taps on the floor. That evening, Glen sat at the kitchen table and figured out a sequence of taps that Barney could respond to. During the next week, Glen wanted Barney to learn eight different codes. Glen felt that was enough for now, he could always add more at a later time. Glen laughed at himself when he realized he was a rapper of another type. He had never liked rap music, but it allowed people of lesser talent an avenue to be creative, at least in their eyes. Real music was played by an orchestra.

Tomorrow, he wanted to take Barney out to the old Collins gold mine and check the mine entrances to make sure no one had tampered with them. If someone got hurt in that old mine, Glen was liable, and he didn't need any unexpected expenses right now.

# CHAPTER 40

# ANOTHER BODY

As Glen drove away from Wrackler's, after helping with the stuck window, Rif went behind the house to the trash can and tipped it over with a good hard kick from her right boot. She didn't want to touch anything until it was checked for prints. The lid fell off and the most recent trash scattered on the ground. Rif poked through the refuse with the toe of her boot until her eyes saw a small white liquid-paper bottle, probably empty. Rif knelt beside the trash, slipped on a latex glove and dropped the bottle in an evidence bag, which she stuck in her pocket.

After returning the litter to the trash can, Rif picked up a small vacuum cleaner from her cruiser and entered the house. She cursed herself for not vacuuming sooner, the day she discovered Wrackler's body, but this was her first murder case and Rif knew she would probably make some mistakes. Fortunately, since the body was discovered, only three people had been in the house—Glen, Doc Skidmore, and herself. Rif was hoping to recover a hair sample from the killer and carry out a DNA determination if the hair contained a follicle. She had to remember to tell Tim Cordell to check for fingerprints in the area around Wrackler's desk and the window that Glen helped her open.

Then, she would have to have DNA analyses carried out on samples from each person known to have been in the house since finding the corpse, but that could wait until the vacuum contents had been analyzed. On Thursday, Rif was going to have Deputy Cordell take the evidence she had collected to Boise for detailed examination. That would keep Tim out of trouble for at least five hours. Knowing Tim, Rif imagined the deputy would figure a way to take even more time and find a place to play computer games, probably at a mall. She hoped he would eventually realize playing computer games was a big distraction from police work. He could do anything he wanted when not at work.

After stowing the vacuum in her car trunk, Rif went next-door to check out what Glen had constructed. She detected a slight odor of volatile hydrocarbons as she walked up the ramp to the front porch. The paint Glen had applied the day before hadn't completely dried overnight, the cool nighttime mountain air had prolonged the dry time. Rif remembered Glen said he had done some touch-up on the railings. She glanced in the front door window and looked around the living room. The wheelchair was on its side and the rest of the room looked like a tornado had struck. The furniture was turned over and the glass top of the coffee table had been shattered.

"What the hell!" Rif reacted loudly. She jumped to the ground from the porch and hurried behind the house. The broken back-door window was obvious. Someone had broken into Jill's house. Rif drew her sidearm and cautiously entered the hallway between the two bedrooms. The bedrooms had been torn apart, the beds overturned and all Jill's unopened boxes had been emptied. She quickly checked the kitchen and the living room. Clothes, books, and dishes were scattered throughout the house. The toaster had been stomped flat, the stove's electric elements had been pulled out and tossed in the sink, and the TV was broken beyond repair. *Damn! Who would have done this! God, I hope Jill has insurance.*

Rif returned to the cruiser, picked up the mic, and pressed the transmit button. "Tim, pick up the fingerprint kit from Jeanie and come out to 511 North Pebble, asap."

The receiver clicked and Rif heard, "10-4."

Rhonda stood by the car thinking, then turned and walked over to the front door of Miss Wimsley's light blue cottage. She pressed the doorbell, heard the bell ring, and saw Stripes jump onto the front window sill and look at her. There was no response, so she rang the bell again. Rif wanted to ask Fiona if she had heard any noises coming from Jill's during the night. Rif waited about 30 seconds, enough time for the elderly lady to come to the door from anywhere in her home. Impatient, Rif reached over and tapped on the front window. Still no response, so Rif peered into the living room, but couldn't see anything out of the ordinary. Fiona's cane was leaning against her favorite chair. Fiona always took that cane with her when she left the house. She must be home. Maybe she had fallen. Maybe she was in the kitchen running a mixer and couldn't hear the bell.

Rif walked to the back door and knocked several times. A cat's meow was all Rif heard.

She tried the door. It was unlocked, so Rif cracked the door and called out, "Miss Wimsley? It's the Sheriff. Are you in the house?" There was no answer. Rif pushed the door wide open and Stripes ran out, surprising her. Rif stepped into the mudroom, looked into the kitchen, and saw Fiona on the floor. She knelt beside the body and checked for a pulse. Miss Wimsley was dead, her body cold. Rif's mind was cluttered with thoughts. Wrackler's murder, the ransacking of Jill's house, and now Fiona Wimsley's death had Rif baffled. Three adjacent houses on the west side of the street had been sites of death and destruction. Rif stepped back from the corpse noting its awkward position. Fiona's right arm, elbow bent, was under her body, her head bent sideways touching her shoulder. This was another murder.

"Jeanie, have Doc Skidmore come out to Fiona Wimsley's house. We've got another body."

"Fiona's *dead*? Oh, my gosh! She was such a nice old lady. What happened?"

"I'm not sure, but I think she was murdered. Tell Skidmore to bring the ambulance, no siren."

"10-4."

Rif checked out the remainder of Fiona's home but found nothing suspicious. Rif put on latex gloves and looked at Fiona's fingernails. She didn't see anything that might have come from an attacker. Fiona was too frail to have offered much resistance, and she was probably too afraid to have even thought of fighting back. Rif went out the backdoor, walked around to the front porch, and sat on the steps. Maybe Fiona heard the commotion next-door and saw something. The killer must have seen Fiona, come to her house, barged in, and strangled her. But Fiona might have had a weak heart and died of fright—Skidmore would know about that. Miss Wimsley, nearly disabled, was a defenseless old lady.

Deputy Cordell drove up, parked, and got out of his car carrying a blue-plastic case the size of a small tool box. Tim was in civvies, having been at his computer shop. He knew if he had taken time to change, Rif would have been on his case.

Cordell yelled from the street, "I heard Miss Wimsley was murdered. Want me to print her house, too?"

"Geez, Tim. You don't need to announce it to the entire neighborhood!"

"Come on, Rif. These three houses are the only ones within 50 yards. Nobody heard anything."

"Well, tone it down a little. Check Jill's house first. You can do Miss Wimsley's after Skidmore removes the body. Go back to Wrackler's house and check around his desk and around the window where we did the pine cone experiment."

"Okay, but I might run out of tape."

Rif didn't comment. She spoke into her shoulder-mic to Jeanie, "Have John come out to Wimsley's and bring another roll of print tape. Also, call Eva Morran at the hospital and tell her Jill's place was broken into and everything's a mess. Thanks Jeanie."

"10-4, Sheriff."

The ambulance rolled up in front of Wimsley's and Skidmore walked slowly over to Rif.

Rif stood up, and motioned to the side of the house.

"We'll have to go to the back to get Miss Wimsley. She's on the floor in the kitchen. I didn't see any wounds."

Doc Skidmore replied, "Well, Fiona had a weak ticker. I'm not surprised she passed away. Jeanie said you thought Fiona was murdered."

"That's right. See what you think after you look at the body."

Skidmore was puffing a little when he arrived at the body. He looked at Fiona from several angles before he knelt and examined her neck. He scratched his head, grabbed the edge of the counter and stood. He looked at Rif and commented, "You're right, Rif, her neck's broken. It looks like she might have fallen against the counter top and hit her head. Might have a snapped spinal column, probably died instantaneously. I'll get the gurney."

"Sheriff?" Deputy Fuentes was outside the back door. "Where's Tim? I've got a roll of tape for him."

"Hi, John. Take the tape next-door to Tim and bring the gurney from the ambulance. We need to move Miss Wimsley to the morgue."

Skidmore leaned against a cabinet and said, "Possibly two murders in the same neighborhood. What are you thinking, Rif?"

"I don't know, Doc. Jill's house was ransacked last night. It's a real mess. It might be the murders are unrelated; maybe some drunks broke into Jill's. Fiona might have seen something and she was killed to silence her. I don't know why anyone would have torn up the inside of Jill's place though. Of course, drunks do stupid things. I was just thinking that maybe Wrackler's killer thought Jill had seen him, so he came to kill Jill, but she wasn't home and Fiona saw him. Of course, the killer might be a woman. Tim's checking for prints at Jill's. He'll check for prints here and at Wrackler's. Maybe we'll get lucky."

John Fuentes returned with the gurney and helped Skidmore lift Fiona off the floor and transport the body to the ambulance. Rif heard the ambulance drive off and a minute later, Fuentes returned to the kitchen.

"What's next, Sheriff?" John seemed eager to get working on Miss Wimsley's murder.

"What would *you* do now, John?"

"I'd go down the street to Slayer's house and ask them if they saw or heard anything last night."

"Good idea, John. You do that. I'm going to put up some tape and lock up here. I'll see you back at the office."

Thirty minutes later, Deputy Fuentes walked up to Rif's office and tapped on the frame around the open door. Rif looked up from the list of towns where Wrackler had purchased stamp collections.

"Come in, John. What did you find out?"

The deputy entered Rif's office and sagged into a chair by the door.

"I talked to Darcy Slayer's mother-in-law and she remembered seeing a black pickup with some kind of equipment on the back around eleven-thirty. She had gone outside for a smoke. Darcy won't let White Deer smoke in the house because of the kids."

"What kind of equipment?"

"White Deer said they had wheels and handlebars, but not motorcycles, they were bigger. I think she saw some four-wheelers but she wasn't sure—just got a glimpse. It was too dark."

"Which direction was the truck going?"

"North on Pebble. That's all I found out."

"Good job, John. Go check for more rabid dogs."

"Thanks, Sheriff. Okay. I'm quitting at five today."

"All right. See you tomorrow."

"Why in hell did you kill that old lady? That's two people you idiots have murdered this week. What the hell are you doing? You were hired to scare people, not kill them."

The driver answered, "We didn't have anything to do with that Wrackler dude. Someone did us a favor. The old lady saw us in the reporter's house and was goin' to call the cops. We broke in her house to scare her. I grabbed her arm when she reached for the phone. She tripped over my foot and fell against the kitchen counter. I think she broke her neck. I couldn't feel any heartbeat. If she had been alive, Brad would have called 911. Ain't that right, Brad?"

"Uh-huh. I would've called 911, Harv. She didn't see our faces, we had masks on. Ain't that right, Harv?"

"That's right. So what do else do ya want us to do now, Cutter?"

"Has anything else happened?"

"Oh yeah. We killed an old man that saw us in the mine getting our four-wheelers. That old fart stopped and asked us why we were opening the mine. Wanted to know if Collins had sent us there. While I was talking to the old man, Brad snuck behind him and hit him with a rock. We found some plastic bags in his truck and wrapped him up. We drove the truck into the mine and put a rag over the plate so no one could see it."

"So where's the body?"

"It's in the back of the truck, Cutter."

"Shit! You guys got to get it out of there. It'll start stinking up the place. Drive that truck out to the ravine, put the old fart in the truck, and drive it off the road. It'll probably start on fire when it hits the rocks at the bottom of that steep incline. If it doesn't burn, go down there and start it on fire. Use the battery to light the gas. Don't use matches or a lighter. You got that? Oh, make sure you take the plastic bags off the body."

"Anything else, boss?"

"Yah. Take me back to the motel."

The black pickup went another mile, made a right turn, and followed a forest service road back to Wolves' Hollow. It was dark when the truck pulled into the motel parking lot.

# CHAPTER 41

# THE OLD MINE

Glen didn't have anything planned for Thursday, except he wanted to check the old Collins gold mine to make sure both entrances were still secure. After feeding Barney and having a heaping bowl of raisin bran with a little too much sugar, some hot black coffee, and watching the morning news, Glen tapped on the floor and Barney followed him to the pickup. As soon as Glen opened the cab, Barney took his place on the seat and pawed at the side window. With the window down, Barney stuck his nose out as soon as Glen started driving. In a couple of minutes they were on North Pebble headed toward the base of Granite Mountain. At the edge of town, the road abruptly turned to gravel and wound its way between some large pines, and over a small hill, gradually veering to the left.

The pickup moved another hundred yards as if it were a wolf sneaking up on a rabbit. Glen was inspecting the mine's exterior as he moved closer to the sealed entrance where a *No Trespassing* sign was mounted above the mine entrance on a nearly vertical rock wall about 20 feet high. Glen stopped a few yards from the entrance and let Barney out of the cab, leaving the door open. Barney began searching, sniffing the area around the old mine. Glen inspected the warning sign but found little deterioration of the white paint on the green plywood sign. Glen's phone number and a warning were prominently displayed.

Barney was sitting beside the pickup watching Glen for a signal that he understood. When Glen turned away from the rocks, Barney stood up, tail wagging. Glen motioned with his hand and Barney climbed into the cab. As Glen drove to the second entrance, he inspected the area closely, looking for anything out of the ordinary. When the truck was within 20 yards of the second sealed opening, he noticed tire tracks deviating from the dirt road toward the mine. He stopped and got out of the truck to get a closer look. The tracks were too close together to be from a car or truck. A four-wheeler had made the tracks. Closer inspection revealed the tracks had been made by two different sets of tires. The tracks appeared to continue past the sealed off mine entrance.

Glen returned to the truck and retrieved a flashlight from under his seat. With the aid of the light shining through spaces between boards, Glen could see the back end of a light-green pickup. A rag covered the license plate. *I'd better let Rif know about this. I can see where someone has tampered with the entrance planking.* Glen climbed back in the truck and, in ten minutes, arrived at the Sheriff's Office.

Barney followed Glen into the building staying on Glen's heels. The outer part of the Sheriff's Office was on the right side of the Court House and always open to the public. Jeanie sat at a desk sandwiched between two rows of black metal cabinets. A keyboard and monitor occupied about a third of her desk top. A small closet behind Jeanie contained a couple of coats, a printer/copier/FAX machine, and a stack of about ten reams of paper.

"Hi, Glen! Who's that with you today?"

"Hi, Jeanie. I'd like you to meet Barney. Don't call him, he's deaf. Tap on the floor twice with your heel."

Jeanie tapped and Barney went to Jeanie, waiting for her to pet him. He sat when Jeanie stroked his head. Glen tapped three times and Barney raised his right paw to shake hands.

Jeanie shook hands with Barney and exclaimed, "What a nice dog, Glen. What can I help you with today?"

"I need to talk with Rif."

Glen heard Rif's voice. "Come on in, Glen. I want to meet Barney."

Glen went into Rif's office with Barney close behind. Rif got up from her desk and knelt in front of Barney. Glen tapped twice, paused and tapped once more. Barney went to Rif and began licking her face.

Glen laughed, "I told him to give you a kiss."

Rif laughed and said, "I'm glad it was the dog." Rif wiped her face with her shirt sleeve and asked, "What did you need to see me about, Glen?"

"Somebody broke into the mine. There's a light-green pickup parked in there. The license is covered with a rag. But I didn't try to go in the mine. It's still nailed shut." Glen grinned, "I didn't have a hammer."

Rif replied, "You poor thing, a carpenter without a hammer. How will you survive?"

Rif laughed and continued, "I tried to give you a new hammer and you refused, remember?"

"Okay, I could have used a crowbar, but I didn't want to disturb any evidence."

Jeanie raised her voice from the outer office, "Sheriff, we just got a call from Mrs. Turner. She says her husband is missing. He's been gone a whole day and should have been back from Sunbeam yesterday afternoon. He's driving a light-green pickup. What should I tell her?"

"Tell her we think we know where the pickup is. We'll see if we can find her husband."

Rif looked at Glen as if to ask him if he wanted to go with her to the mine.

Glen said, "I'll ride along and we can open the mine without a search warrant. Besides, I've got a crowbar. Your hammer wouldn't be stout enough to remove the planks from the opening. Get your hammer, we might need it, and I'll meet you out in front at my truck."

"Okay. I've got to make a pit stop before I leave the office. Be right out."

Glen tapped on the floor and Barney followed him out of the building and jumped into the cab as soon as Glen opened the driver's door. They waited for Rif for about two minutes. She came running out of the building carrying her new hammer, climbed into the passenger seat and attached her seatbelt. Glen had already started the engine and pulled away from the curb as soon as he heard the click of Rif's seatbelt.

Glen smiled at Rif and said, "I've never given a sheriff a ride before, it's another first for me." Glen turned onto North Pebble and accelerated, moving passed Jill's house at about 35 miles per hour.

Glen grinned and said, "Oops, I've exceeded the speed limit. Will you arrest me?"

Rif had a strangle hold on the hammer, her knuckles were white. "No. Let's consider this an emergency. Mr. Turner might be in trouble. Do you have a gun, Glen?"

"Sure do; a rifle. It's behind the seat in the cab. Think we'll need more than your sidearm?"

"Never can tell. I just want to be sure of where any guns are if we need them. By the way, you're deputized for the rest of the day. I sent Tim Cordell to Boise with evidence boxes. He won't be back until late this afternoon—I think."

Glen grinned. "Do I get a badge?"

Rif didn't answer. They were approaching the main entrance to the mine and she was looking around to see if she could spot any activity. Glen didn't slow down and drove past the boarded up opening to the mine. Rif frowned and Glen said, "I saw the truck at the other entrance. We're almost there.

Rif said, "Stop the truck, Glen. I want to get out here."

Glen slammed on the breaks and the pickup skidded to a stop on the dirt and gravel road. Dust swirled around the truck for a few seconds and as the breeze blew the cloud off the road, Rif climbed out, followed by Barney. It was too late for Glen to signal Barney to come back, so he let the dog go with Rif.

"Go slow, Glen. I'll walk behind you." Rif pulled out her gun and crouched down, using the truck bed for cover. Barney ran ahead to the mine entrance and sat down, waiting for Glen and Rif. Glen parked the truck in front of the entrance, grabbed his flashlight, and joined Rif at the boarded up entrance. Glen gave Rif the flashlight and said, "Look between the boards, you'll see the truck."

Rif peered between the boards and then stepped back, putting her gun back in its holster. "Was this all a joke, Glen?"

"What? Can't you see the truck?"

"There's no truck, Glen. There's nothing in the mine." Rif gave Glen the flashlight and he looked between the boards.

"Well I'll be damned! The truck is gone."

"Step over by your truck Glen."

"You're going to arrest me?"

"No, I want to look at these tracks." Rif pointed at the ground. There were tracks that went under Glen's pickup and out to the road.

"Sheriff?" Rif's radio came alive. Both Glen and Rif were taken by surprise and flinched.

"Yes, Jeanie. What is it?"

"I just got a call from Don Sloan. Don and his son, Corey, were out cutting dead trees for firewood and they saw some black smoke rising from Deep Rock Ravine. They said there is a truck on fire at the bottom—looks like it's completely destroyed. They couldn't tell if there was anyone in it."

"Thanks Jeanie. Glen and I will check it out. That's about five miles from here."

"10-4."

Rif looked at Glen. He nodded and said, "Let's check it out." Glen opened the passenger door for Rif, but Barney jumped in front of her, almost causing her to stumble. Rif swung into the seat and fastened her belt. Glen got in and they headed up the road toward the ravine.

"I wonder if the burning truck is the one I saw in the mine."

"If it's the one reported, there might not be any paint left to tell what color it was. We'll have to get the VIN and see what it's supposed to be. Anyway, we'll find out who it belongs to."

"So, Rif, do you believe that I saw a truck in the mine?"

Rif grinned, "Sure. I believed you from the very start, and I wanted to ride in your pickup."

Glen laughed, "That's a good one, a beautiful woman wanting to ride in a pickup with a deaf dog and a carpenter without a hammer."

"Thanks Glen. I guess I know how to pick 'em."

They approached the ravine with care since the road was only a car width wide, with a drop off of seventy feet to the rock-strewn river bed below.

"Let me out here and you can find a wide-spot to park. Okay?"

"Yeah. There's a wide spot about a quarter-mile ahead. I'll park and walk back. Be careful along the edge, there are loose spots where you might slip."

Rif climbed down from the cab and moved to the edge of the road, looking into the ravine as she walked. Glen stepped on the gas, driving ahead to a spot where another vehicle could pass. Glen got out and tapped on the cab telling Barney to come with him. Barney jumped out to the ground and moved to the side of the road away from the steep drop off into the ravine. Glen walked along the edge about three feet from the precipitous drop, looking down to see if he could identify wreckage of a pickup. He walked over a hundred yards before he saw the charred wreckage of a truck with wisps of black smoke rising from the remains of tires. The pickup was upside down and almost completely black. The shiny metal bumpers stood out from the blackened body of the truck.

Rif was still about 50 yards away, but she had seen the wreckage and was walking as rapidly as possible up the slight grade. She was out of breath when she arrived and said, smiling, "I got out a little too soon, didn't I?"

"Well, we're not going to be able to get down there. We need a winch with a hundred feet of cable. What about your jeep, Rif?"

"Yeah. That would work. I'll have John drive out here. He can bring us something to eat, too." Rif talked with Jeanie and gave her instructions to relay to Funches. John drove up to the site of the wreckage about 25 minutes later. While Glen and Rif waited, they inspected the edge of the ravine where they discovered tracks leading over the edge.

Rif said, "If Mr. Turner is in the wreckage, this has got to be a murder. Take a look at the tracks, Glen. The tires made impressions over the top edge as if the truck was pushed and the bottom of the truck skidded in the dirt. If the truck had been driven over the edge, the ground wouldn't be torn up this badly."

"I think you're right, Rif. You might have another murder to worry about."

# CHAPTER 42

## MR. TURNER?

John pulled up in Rif's jeep and locked the brakes. He left the engine running so they could use the winch. Rif walked over to John and he handed her a paper bag.

"What did you bring us, John?"

"Chinese, but it wasn't my choice. Jeanie told me to get it, and she had me get some dog food, too."

Rif opened the bag, looked in, and said, "Just what I asked for." Jeanie had made sure there were three bottles of water. Rif laid the bag of food in Glen's truck bed and said, "Do you want to go down there, Glen? I'll go with you if you're scared. John can run the winch."

Glen smiled, "I'll go. I've always wanted to jump off a cliff with a woman."

"Okay. Got gloves?"

Glen walked over to the cab of his pickup and pulled a pair of gloves from under the seat. He motioned for Barney to come to him. He put Barney in the cab and closed the door, but left the window half-open.

Funches had to pay out about 20 feet of cable, enough so Rif and Glen could begin rappelling down the steep slope. Glen grabbed the end of the cable and said, "Want me to go first, Rif?"

Rif thought about a second, grinned, and said, "I think we should go down side-by-side. That way, I can help you if you have any problems." They grabbed the cable and backed over the edge, walking backwards down the steep slope. When one of them slipped, the other held the cable up to steady the descent. After reaching the bottom, Rif and Glen had to climb over several large boulders to get to the wreckage.

Rif was first to notice the charred remains of a body. There wasn't much left after the intense heat had converted most of the tissue to carbon dioxide and water vapor. The skull and big bones were still intact, as were the ribs. The feet were blackened, but not completely burned, having been spared complete combustion by the presence of work boots. Rif found the metal plate on the dashboard and copied down the VIN.

Glen walked around the metal frame of the truck looking for a spot of paint that had not been burned off, but was unsuccessful. When he got close to the remnants of the driver's body, he stepped back several yards to get away from the odor of burned flesh and truck tires.

"Have you got all you need, Rif?"

"Yeah. Let's have John pull us back up. I'll call Jeanie and have her check the VIN."

Glen yelled up to John, who was watching from above. "Okay, Deputy, you can pull us up now."

As soon as Glen and Rif reached the road and dusted off, Rif called Jeanie and gave her the ID off the truck. As Glen and Rif sat on the bed of the pickup eating lunch, John asked, "How can you eat after seeing that burned body?"

Glen replied, "There was no bloody mess, everything was black. The person was undoubtedly knocked out or dead when the truck hit the bottom of the ravine, so whoever it was felt no pain. After going down there and coming back, I'm hungry." He looked at Rif.

Rif responded, "That's good enough for me. I've got to feed the inner woman."

Rif's shoulder phone crackled, "Sheriff?"

"Yes, Jeanie."

"That VIN belongs to a pickup registered to Vince Turner."

"Thanks Jeanie. I'll drive out to see Mrs. Turner and tell her we think her husband was killed in an accident. We'll have Doc identify the remains. Oh, Jeanie, what is Mrs. Turner's first name?"

"Gloria."

"Thanks Jeanie."

"10-4."

Glen volunteered, "I'll take John back into town. You can drive the jeep out to Turner's place."

"Thanks, Glen. I shouldn't be gone for more than an hour. Thanks for lunch!" Rif grinned as she climbed into the jeep, adjusted the seat belt, waved, and drove farther north on Pebble.

"I'll get my pickup, Deputy. It'll just take a few minutes." Glen motioned to Barney and he ran ahead of Glen.

"Hey, Mr. Collins, I'll walk with you. There's nothing to do here."

As the two men walked the slight uphill grade, John asked, "What's in that old mine, Mr. Collins?"

"Call me Glen, Deputy. There's nothing much in the mine, a stack of old timbers and some old rusty tools that have been there for years. Nobody has taken gold out of there in a long time. I plan on trying my luck before long, now that the price of gold is so high."

John replied, "I saw on the morning news that gold is $1320 an ounce today. If you need any help, I'd be glad to give you a hand for, say, ten percent. I have a brother in Boise that has done some hard rock mining. We might get some tips from him."

"Thanks for the offer. I'll have to think about when I want to investigate the mine. I need to get some geology and mineral books so I know what to look for. I'm sure the easy gold was removed long ago by my ancestors. But who knows?"

As they approached the mine, Glen commented, "That big old stump needs to be removed one of these days. It will probably take some dynamite to get it out of there. I'd like to widen this road so cars and trucks can pass, but that amount of money isn't available."

John quizzed, "Have you been playing the lottery?"

"No, but if I won the lottery, I wouldn't have any need for gold."

"I guess you're right. You can drop me off at the library. I need to check my voice and email to see if I have any messages from my kids."

Glen stopped in the street in front of the library and let him out, then went to the hospital to check on Jill and tell her the ramp was finished. As Glen entered the hospital, he was greeted by Doctor Skidmore.

"Hi, Glen. Flu shots aren't available yet. You'll have to wait a couple of months."

Glen laughed and said, "I just wanted to tell Jill I finished her ramp. Have you heard from Rif?"

"No. Was she going to contact me about something?"

"Yeah. We found another body—out in the ravine—burned beyond recognition. You'll have to ID what's left of the corpse. We think it was another murder, maybe Mr. Turner. The burned out pickup belonged to him. Rif is out at Turner's talking to the wife." Glen looked at his watch. "She'll be back in about 50 minutes. If you need help recovering the remains, let me know."

"Thank you, Glen. I don't think I will be going down in the ravine any time soon. We might have to hire a wrecker and pull the whole mess up to the road. I'll talk to Rif and we'll develop a plan. Oh, Jill's in room 19."

"Thanks, Doc."

As Glen was walking into room 19, Rif was comforting Gloria Turner. She had just told Gloria that Mr. Turner's truck had been burned with a body inside the cab. The body was thought to be Vince Turner. However, there was a small chance it could be someone else, but Dr. Skidmore would have to ID the remains. It might be a couple of days. Rif advised Gloria to stay with a friend or relative for a few days. Rif told Gloria the Sheriff's Office would notify her as soon as Rif found out for sure who was in the truck.

It had been 40 minutes since Rif had left the burned out wreck when she started back toward Wolves' Hollow. Previously, she had estimated it would have taken her about an hour. Rif was right on schedule. She was 20 minutes from her office. As she neared the upper entrance to the Collins mine, Rif decided to take another look at the tire tracks and foot prints in the dirt next to the closed entrance. She stopped about five yards away from the mine and got out of the jeep. Her eyes were glued to the area below the boards. It looked like there were three sets of footprints.

She bent down to examine the prints and then noticed the boards had shiny nails where they had been reattached to the timbers. She ran her fingers over the new nails noting her hammer would never have enough leverage to pull the boards off the mine opening. She would have to get Glen's crowbar. That would give her a good reason to ask Glen for assistance. She grinned, thinking it was funny how she suddenly found Glen interesting. She turned toward the jeep and suddenly her left shoulder exploded with pain and she spun around, knocked off her feet, falling on her back. She couldn't have been more surprised at being shot.

Her face was bleeding. She could feel blood running down her neck soaking into her shirt. Rif knew she would probably get shot someday, but she had no idea where this bullet had come from. She grabbed her left collar bone with her right hand. Her fingers were covered in blood. A handkerchief from her back pocket wasn't big enough to cover both entrance and exit wounds. The exit hole seemed larger, so she stuffed the handkerchief under her shirt trying to cover the hole to stem the bleeding.

Whoever had shot her must be across the valley at about the same elevation as the mine. The shooter hadn't followed up with a second shot. Rif realized she had fallen behind the jeep, concealing her from a second shot. *I've got to call Jeanie. I need help.* She reached for the button on her mic, but the mic was gone. The bullet had smashed through the radio on her shoulder. She felt her face and realized there were pieces of plastic stuck in her skin. When the radio was struck, it exploded in her face, but she could see from both eyes, so her vision was all right. *I've got to get some shelter.*

Rif looked around and the only thing she could get behind, beside the jeep, was that big stump about 15 yards away. She had to get away from the jeep; the gas tank was nearly full. She didn't want to get burned alive. Rif rolled to her hands and knees, pulled her gun from its holster and got ready to run. She estimated it would take her two to three seconds to get to the stump. She couldn't afford to fall. That might give the shooter a second shot. *Okay, here goes!* She crouched down, moving as quickly as she could, and got behind the massive stump. When she stood up, her left boot sunk into the soft ground. Rif grabbed for the tree, but the ground opened up, both feet were sinking into the ground. She began to slide under the stump.

Rif's instincts were to fight the sliding motion, but when her butt hit the ground, her feet struck the bottom of the hole and she stopped sliding. She pushed aside the loose soil around her hips and looked into the cavity. Everything was in shadows, but she could make out a few bones protruding from several inches of loose dirt. *This must be an old wolves' den.* Rif could see there was enough room for her to get in the below-ground cavity, so she wiggled the rest of the way beneath the old dead tree stump. She felt a little safer; she had cover from whoever the bastard was that shot her.

As her eyes adjusted to the shadows, Rif realized the bones were not what she had originally thought. They were human bones! What she thought was a large rock pressing against her back was a human skull. *For God's sake, who is buried beneath this old stump? Damn, another murder!*

Rif had temporarily forgotten about her wound, but the pain brought her back to the immediate situation. *I have to take off my shirt and tie up my shoulder to put pressure on the wounds.* She squirmed out of her shirt and wound it around her neck and upper arm in a figure eight to cover the wounds and try to suppress the bleeding. She leaned back and attempted to relax, but how long was it going to be before they missed her at the office?

Rif could hear motors approaching, but they were from four-wheelers, not regular vehicles. She decided to listen rather than call out to the riders. They might be the ones that shot her.

Rif picked up her gun, ready to shoot anyone that looked into her hiding place. The little vehicles stopped and it became quiet. Rif could hear two voices.

"I thought you knocked her down with that shot, Brad. Where's the body? There's no blood on the ground, either."

"Geez, Harv, I'm sure I hit her in the head. I've made a shot at 250 yards before. I saw an explosion through my scope when the slug hit her. It knocked her off her feet. There should be a headless body here by the jeep."

"We'd better not hang around. Someone will see the jeep and wonder where the sheriff is. It's better if no one sees us."

Harv looked around for tracks but couldn't see any. "Shit! Sodwim is gunna be pissed."

"Oh, screw Sodwim. He hired us to come out here from New York to cause trouble and we're sure as hell doin' it. Maybe we should've told him to do the job himself. Course, he paid us plenty to come out to this hick town. Look on the bright side, another week and we'll be gone."

"Come on, let's get out of here."

# CHAPTER 43

# BONES

After visiting with Jill, Glen had walked from the hospital to the Sheriff's office with Barney. He expected to find Rif in her office doing paper work about the wreck in the Ravine.

"Hi, Jeanie. Is the sheriff back yet?"

"I haven't heard from her, Glen."

"Doesn't she check in with you periodically when she's out of the office?"

Glen looked at his watch. It had been almost an hour and a half since Rif had gone to see Gloria Turner. "Can you call her, Jeanie?"

"Sure." Jeanie reached for a switch and spoke into her mic, "Sheriff, Glen is here to see you."

There was no answer, just silence. Jeanie frowned and said, "Usually, I hear something—static or road noise. I don't hear anything now. That's strange. I wonder where she went."

"Well, I'll wait for a few minutes and you can try again. Okay?"

"10-4. Oh, I'm sorry. Okay."

"That's all right Jeanie. I know what 10-4 means." Glen smiled and said, "I've been a deputy before." Glen sat down and scratched Barney, picked up a magazine, looked at it nervously, and tossed it back on the pile of periodicals near the door. He stood up and said,

"I'm driving out to the mine. Maybe I'll see Rif coming back from Turner's. If she gets back in the next 20 minutes or so, tell her I'm sorry we missed her."

"10-4." Jeanie laughed.

★　★　★

Glen and Barney walked back to the hospital, got in Glen's pickup, and started toward the mine.

Five minutes later, Glen stopped at the old mine entrance and looked around. He stepped on the gas and started toward the second entrance. In a minute, he saw Rif's jeep parked next to the other mine opening. He gave the truck more gas and skidded to a stop next to the jeep.

Glen and Barney got out of the truck and moved to the jeep, but saw no sign of Rif. Glen made a motion to Barney and he jumped into the jeep and sniffed the area around the steering wheel. Glen tapped on the jeep and Barney jumped down and began sniffing the ground. It took him about five seconds to locate Rif's scent and he started up the road. Barney stopped at the over-sized stump and pawed at the ground.

"Glen? Is that you?"

"Rif? I hear your voice, but I can't tell where you are."

"Glen! I'm under the big stump. I've been shot."

Glen walked over to the stump and looked at the base. There was an opening at the roots, but Glen couldn't imagine how Rif could have gotten through it. He got down on his hands and knees and looked through the hole. He could see Rif's hair and that her shirt was wadded over her left shoulder. "Son of a bitch! Who would shoot you?"

"Can you get me out of here? I've lost quite a bit of blood. I'm feeling a little light-headed."

"I'll call Doc Skidmore, just a second. I'll start digging you out."

Glen punched in 911. Jeanie answered.

"911. What is the nat...?"

Glen yelled into his phone. "This is Glen. Send the ambulance out to my mine! Rif's been shot! Tell Skidmore to hurry and send a deputy or Dr. Rainen." Glen stuck the phone in his pocket, ran to the bed of his pickup, and grabbed a shovel and a piece of rope about ten feet long. He started digging about three feet back from the hole and worked feverishly throwing dirt and rocks down the slope.

"Hurry, Glen. I might pass out."

"Hang in there, babes. It looks like you were shot in the shoulder. I don't want to pull on your arms. I'm going to tie a loop in a rope. Do you think you can get it around your waist?"

"There's not much room in here to move around, Glen. Maybe you can pull me out if I grab the rope with my right hand."

"Okay, let's try that. Here's the loop. I'll pull very slowly. Tell me if it's hurting you."

Glen pulled the slack out of the rope and Rif slowly emerged from under the gnarled roots of the old tree stump. She was able to push with her legs so Glen didn't have to pull very hard. When Rif was out from under the stump, Glen pulled an old blanket from behind the truck seat and laid it in the truck bed. He went back to Rif and helped her sit up; then, he knelt down, and picked her up. Her skin was ashen. Glen carried her to the truck bed and laid her down. The top of her vest was spattered with blood. Glen could hear the ambulance siren in the distance—Skidmore was on the way.

He went to the cab and grabbed a plastic bottle of water and had Rif drink as much as she could. The ambulance siren was growing louder. Skidmore was almost there. When the ambulance quit skidding and stopped, Skidmore moved from the driver's seat like a man possessed. Glen had never seen Doc run before. The passenger side door opened and Adam jumped out and went to the back of the old hearse, opened the door, and pulled out the gurney. The wheels dropped and Adam attached a post so Skidmore could hang pouches of fluids for intravenous injection.

Skidmore inserted a line in Rif's arm and started plasma flowing. He had gotten Rif's blood type from the hospital records.

He began removing Rif's blood-soaked shirt from her shoulder, washing her skin with antiseptic.

"Let's get her back to the hospital. I need to sew her up and remove the bits of plastic from her face. I'll have to inspect the wound to see what damage has been done. Can you gentlemen move the vehicles so I can turn the ambulance around?"

Rif's natural skin tone was returning as they loaded her into the ambulance. As Adam and Glen put the gurney in the back of the big vehicle, Rif said, "Thank you Glen. You are such a sweet man. There's a skeleton underneath that old stump—I'm not delirious. See if you can get all the bones so it can be reconstructed. I'd like to know whose bones those are."

Glen joked, "Okay. I'll dig up the bones and give them to Skidmore. He can probably tell us if it's one of our relatives." Glen smiled and added, "I don't think it's one of my ancestors."

Rif replied, "I could hear the men that shot me talking. Their names are Brad and Harv. They're from the East coast—work for a man named Sodwim. See if Jeanie can dig up something on them. They might be wanted on the East coast. They were driving four-wheelers."

"Okay. You take care. I'll see you at the hospital. Maybe you and Jill will be roomies."

Adam held Rif's hand for a second and then shut the door of the ambulance. He tapped on the outside to let Doc know Rif was ready for transport. Ten minutes later, Rif was being wheeled into the operating room.

Adam drove the jeep back to the sheriff's office, parked and took the keys in to Jeanie.

Glen was concerned about Rif being shot, but there was nothing he could do. If he went to the hospital, he wouldn't be able to talk with Rif until she came out of the anesthesia, which would mean several hours. In the meantime, he would start removing the skeleton from under that ancient stump. Glen drove to his house, loaded a chainsaw and gasoline into the truck, and tossed in a pick, just in case he had to do some aggressive digging. He was just about to leave for the mine when he thought to toss in a length of heavy chain in case he had to pull the stump away from the edge of the road.

He went in the house, grabbed three bottles of water from the fridge, and signaled Barney to get in the pickup. While Glen was preparing to cut down the stump, he was trying to understand why two men named Brad and Harv had shot Rif. Since he was going out to the mine alone, he had better have his rifle. Glen put a handful of cartridges in his pocket, went out to the pickup and checked behind the seat. The gun was on the floor. "Okay, Barney, we're ready. Let's go." As they drove toward the mine, Glen looked at Barney, wondering if anyone was doing research on implants for deaf dogs.

Ten minutes later, Glen parked his pickup next to the tree stump to give him a little cover if someone took a shot at him. He leaned his rifle against the front fender a few feet from the stump, then got down on his hands and knees and looked at the root structure. He decided to cut the roots after removing some of the dirt from the base of the stump. As he dug nearer the edge of the depression below the stump, he could see some of the bones Rif had mentioned. It appeared that whoever had died there had been sitting, almost reclining, beneath the tree.

Glen started his saw and cut through two massive eight-inch diameter roots. He dug around the roots about two feet from the trunk and cut them off. He tossed them aside, giving him a clear view of the skeleton. *Hmm, this person was fairly tall.* Glen had easy access to the leg bones, so he pulled them from the dirt and leaf accumulation, and poked them into a large black-plastic trash bag. Glen considered using a rake to pull the bones from under the tree stump, but decided against it. The rake might break some of the bones and erode the bone surfaces, making it more difficult for Skidmore to determine the cause of death.

Using the chainsaw, Glen cut through two more roots, but when he cut through the second root, the tree trunk shifted. Glen scrambled to get out of the depression so he wouldn't get crushed under the weight of the massive stump. That's when Glen decided to use his pickup to push the stump over, hoping it would tumble down the slope away from the road. He moved his tools and gun away from the area around the stump and backed his pickup against the now unstable tree trunk remnant. He gave the pickup a little gas. He could hear the wood in the remaining roots starting to splinter and crack. He set the brake and got out of the truck to see the location of his wheels. Glen didn't want to back off the road and have to ride his truck backward down the hill attached to a massive stump that outweighed his pickup.

Glen got back in the truck and pulled ahead a few feet. The stump remained leaning over the edge of the road, so Glen used the chainsaw and cut the remaining roots. The stump started shifting, the last few portions of roots snapped, and the stump tipped over, sliding and tumbling down the hill away from the road. Glen put the saw down, picked up the trash bag, and stepped into the crater to continue the retrieval. As Glen freed the bones from refuse, and added them to the bag, his knuckles struck something hard, but it didn't feel like rock or bone. With the dirt and leaves removed, Glen could see a weathered leather bag. He was surprised when he lifted it. The small bag weighed several pounds. He thought it was full of lead bullets from long ago. Glen sat it aside and continued picking up bones, a few of them broken. After he put the skull in the bag, he ran his fingers through the dirt, discovering another heavy bag and several small bones, apparently from fingers and toes.

Glen looked at his watch. It had been over two hours since he had started removing the stump. It was time to get back to the hospital to check on Rif and deliver the bones he had recovered to Doc Skidmore. As he drove back to the hospital, Glen planned a return trip to the site to sift the dirt to recover small bones and anything else that might provide clues to ID the skeleton.

# CHAPTER 44

# THE MORGUE

Skidmore was checking on Rif when Glen and Barney arrived at the hospital. Glen was lugging the trash-bag full of bones when he saw Skidmore coming down the hall toward the admissions desk.

"Hi, Doc. How's Rif? Can I see her?"

"You can see her, Glen, but she's sedated. It will be a few hours before she can talk. Have you got a present for me?"

"Yeah. These are the bones from under the stump where Rif was hiding. Where do you want them?"

"You can put them in the morgue. The door is unlocked. The burned body from the truck in the ravine is being transported. It should be here in the next hour. You can assemble the bones on the table against the wall, unless you want me to do it."

Glen frowned, "Okay. I'll try it. You can correct my mistakes." He grinned.

Glen had never been in a morgue before. He didn't feel surrounded by death, but he could understand the creepy feeling most people experienced. It was cold, sterile, and the scary movies had made nearly everyone aware that a zombie might appear. A person would have to fight for his or her life. Glen looked around first, making sure no zombies were present, and dumped the bones on a large stainless steel table where the skeleton could be assembled and examined. Glen remembered a skeleton from high school biology that hung in the corner of Mrs. Danka's biology lab. He felt the bones in his body for reference. Glen felt foolish thinking about zombies; he knew they didn't exist. He grinned as he thought about it. The ribs and backbone offered some problems, but when Skidmore looked at Glen's assemblage, he said Glen would earn a grade of A-. He had only made a few small mistakes.

"Glen, we're missing some small bones from the hands and feet, but you've got about 98 percent of the skeleton here. Good job."

"Thanks, Doc. I'm going out there and sift the dirt tomorrow. I'll probably find some of the missing pieces. What type of bullet hit Rif? Have any idea?"

"It had to have been a rifle bullet, but it struck her portable radio first. That helped deflect the slug up through the neck muscle above her collarbone. Speaking of bullets, it looks like your man on the table here was shot in the back, twice. He's got two broken ribs, one on each side. Those wounds in the back were fatal. When you sift the ground out there, you might find two rifle slugs. We should be able to ID the caliber."

"Can I see Rif now?"

"Sure. She's in room 17, next to Jill. I don't think Rif will respond yet, but you can sit with her if you like. Maybe you can go next door and visit with Jill."

"Oh! I almost forgot. Take a look at this bag. I was going to open it out by that stump, but I forgot about it. I wanted to see how Rif is doing." Glen had to work the bag out of his pocket. He handed the bag to Skidmore.

"Whoa. What's in here—lead?"

"I figured it was full of lead bullets from over a hundred years ago. I've got another bag like this out in my truck."

Skidmore moved to the autopsy table and used a scalpel to cut the bag open. He poured it out and whistled. "Damn, Glen. This is gold! You must have five pounds here. Do you know what that's worth?"

"Gold? Really? Deputy Funches told me gold was selling for over $1,300 an ounce."

Skidmore thought a few seconds and said, "This bag has about a $100,000 worth of gold in it. You're a rich man, Glen. And you have another bag like this?"

"Yes, sir. It's about the same size."

"Don't call me *sir*, Glen. *I* should call you *sir*." Skidmore grinned, "Say, when is the last time you had a checkup?"

Glen laughed. "Are you after my gold, Doc? Geez, I'd better keep this a secret from the women. Course, it might change my luck."

"I don't think you have to worry. Rif and Jill are not that type of woman. They know you're a good man."

"Thanks, Doc. I'm going to see Rif now. Put the gold in another bag, please. I'll get it later." Glen smiled and whispered, "Don't tell anyone."

★　★　★

Glen walked down the hall to the reception desk, turned down the corridor to the right and entered room 17. Sarah was sitting next to Rif talking.

Sarah looked at Glen and said, "You have a visitor, Rif. Glen has come to see you."

Rif tried to lift her head but couldn't, and her head went back into the pillow. The left side of her face was bandaged where the plastic parts of her radio had been removed from her skin.

Glen gave a concerned look to Sarah.

Sarah said, "Don't worry, Glen, the facial cuts are superficial. She might have a couple of tiny scars, but they can be covered with makeup. Her shoulder is pretty torn up. She'll have some rehab to go through. Jill's sister, Eva, will be able to help with that. Except for some scars, she'll be good as new."

"Boy, that's a relief. Can she talk yet?"

"Not yet, but I think Rif understands what we're saying. She just can't think straight yet. Maybe another hour and she'll be hard to shut up. It will be like a dam broke."

"Okay. I'll sit with her for a while. I have something to tell her."

"All right, you go right ahead. I have some pulses to check, and a couple of blood sugars to measure. I'll be back in about thirty minutes."

Glen slid the chair closer to Rif's bed and sat down. Rif raised her hand and reached toward Glen, but she couldn't hold her hand up, and it dropped back against the blanket. Glen reached over and took Rif's hand in his and said, "I recovered nearly all the bones you found under that stump, and I found something else. There were two bags of gold with the skeleton.

Skidmore said each bag was worth about $100,000 dollars. Can you believe it? Since you found the bones, one of the bags of gold is yours. I'm going back out there and sift through the dirt to see if I can find the bullets that killed the man, and some small bones that I missed."

Rif squeezed Glen's hand and smiled. She had understood what Glen had told her. She opened her mouth to speak, but her eyes closed, and she went to sleep. Glen held Rif's hand and watched her for about five minutes, all the time wishing he could castrate the shitheads that shot her. He heard noises down the hall, apparently from the nurse's station/admissions counter, and decided to investigate while Rif slept.

When Glen arrived at admissions, Skidmore was directing three men carrying a stretcher occupied by a body covered with a blanket. The men wore uniforms with shoulder patches identifying them as State Forest Service workers. Glen followed the men to the morgue and watched from the hallway as a severely burned charcoal-looking body was transferred to the main examination table in the center of the room. It was from the burned out pickup in the ravine. Glen didn't relish working on this corpse, meat was still attached to the bones. This one was going to be messy. Doc Skidmore thanked the Forest Service men and shook their hands. They walked back past the admissions counter and out the door.

Skidmore turned out the lights and came into the hallway. When he saw Glen, he sighed and said, "This is going to be a long evening. Want to help me?"

"Are you serious, Doc?"

"Not really. I doubt whether you would be able to hold down your dinner. I've got some office work to do first and then I'll get started on the body. If you want to observe, come back about six-thirty this evening."

"Thanks, Doc. I'll think about it."

Glen went out to his pickup and to check on Barney, who was in the truck bed sleeping on a blanket. Glen had used a piece of rope to restrain Barney to the pickup, not sure that Barney would stay in the pickup while his master was out of sight. A puppy might run off exploring if not tied up. Satisfied that Barney was all right and secure, Glen went back to see if Rif had awakened.

As Glen approached room 17, he recognized the voices of two women, Jill and Rif. Glen tapped on the door frame and stood in the doorway. Rif was in bed leaning against several pillows, almost sitting up. Jill was in a wheelchair next to Rif's bed.

"Hello, ladies."

The women spoke in unison, "Hi, Glen."

Jill rolled back from the bed so Glen could sit beside Rif in a chair.

Jill commented, "You look tired, Glen. Sit down."

"Thanks. I was in the morgue reassembling the skeleton that Rif found under the stump. It's kind of like a jigsaw puzzle. Maybe I look tired because I have been worried about Rif." Glen looked at Rif and she reached over, grabbed his hand, and said, "How nice to have you worry about me. We were talking earlier. You said something about a bag of gold. Did I dream that, or was it real?"

Glen looked at Jill and hesitated.

"I'll let you guys have some privacy so you can talk."

"No, that's all right. You might as well hear about it. Secrets don't last long in Wolves' Hollow. When I was digging the bones out from under that big old stump, I found two bags of gold."

Rif smiled and said, "Was there a rainbow?"

Jill laughed, but Glen grinned and continued, "I showed one to Doc. I thought the bag was full of lead bullets from long ago, something a pioneer might have had. Doc cut the bag open and poured out gold flakes and nuggets. He estimated the bag weighed five pounds, so the gold is worth about a hundred thousand dollars. But, get this, there are two bags. One bag for Rif and one for me, since we both had a hand in finding the bags."

Rif raised her hand to her mouth and said, "Oh, my gosh! But the gold is on your property, Glen. It's yours."

"Okay. If it's mine, I can share it. Right?"

"Well, yeah. That is very generous of you. Thank you. There is something I want to share with you, too."

Glen had no clue what she was going to say. He looked at Rif's bandaged face questioningly.

"I want you to be the acting sheriff while my wounds heal. I have the power to appoint a temporary sheriff, as long as the town council is agreeable."

Glen smiled, "Geez, Rif, do I get a badge *and a gun?*"

"Glen! It is *not* funny! Can you be serious?"

"What about your deputies? Won't they be pissed?"

"Neither of them is capable of taking over for me. Tim is still a juvenile and John is over the hill—eating doughnuts," Rif grinned. "They do okay when following orders though."

Jill was listening intently and began to laugh. "You guys are so funny!"

"Well, Glen, will you do it?"

"All right, you've twisted my arm. I know the town council has to agree. Let me know when it's official and the mayor can swear me in, or do you do it?"

"Okay, thank you. It should happen tomorrow. Let's see, tomorrow is Friday, right? The mayor will give you the oath. It'll be more official that way. I've got another handgun locked in my office desk, but the belt might be too small." Rif grinned.

"I've already started slimming down. My table muscle should be gone by the end of the summer." Glen smiled and patted his stomach.

# CHAPTER 45

## THE NEW SHERIFF

About the time Skidmore was starting the autopsy, Cutter was sitting in the motel reading a magazine when he heard his wife say, "Tad, you have an email." Connie, Tad's wife, had been working on reservations for the rest of the month when she noticed Tad had received a message.

Tad said, "Thanks, hon. I'll read it from my laptop in the bedroom. I need to put on a different pair of shoes." As soon as his lap-top came on line, Tad opened his only message. It was from Sodwim. It said, "Cutter: Take care of the two rats—permanently. Those rats are going to ruin things. Dispose of the critters in Collins's mine. You will be rewarded." Tad deleted the email and turned off his computer. *So Sodwim wants me to get rid of Brad and Harv. No problem. I don't like them anyway. They're both idiots. I'll take care of them tomorrow. They're supposed to pick me up here at 4:00 p.m. I'll give them their final instructions.* Tad patted his hunting knife on his belt. He exchanged his shoes for slippers and went out in the lobby to watch the news on the big screen.

★ ★ ★

Glen had gone home with Barney and had dinner. He worked with Barney for about a half-hour and then went back to the hospital to talk with Rif and Jill. When Glen arrived at room 17, Rif wasn't there, but he could hear voices as before. The ladies were next door in Jill's room.

Rif said, "Hi Glen. Jill and I are going to live together in my house until Jill's house is renovated. Novaks came by and told Jill the owner, Connie Womack, had renter's insurance and everything will be replaced. We're going shopping with Mrs. Womack tomorrow."

Jill was sitting in the hospital wheelchair next to her bed. The catheter had been removed and she had free run of the hospital now. She had been practicing walking with crutches, but it wore her out quickly. Jill decided to spill the beans about the wheelchair. She didn't want to put on an act any longer, especially lying to her friends.

"I have a confession to make."

Rif frowned and replied, "A confession? What did you do?"

"I lied to everyone. I didn't have an accident when I was riding my bike. No one backed into me like I said. Mr. Novaks wanted me to do a piece on people in wheelchairs about the problems they face in everyday life. But then I accidently broke my leg, and I really have been in a wheelchair. Now that I can get around with crutches, I don't have to use a wheelchair, unless, of course, I need to relax."

Glen said, "Is *that* what you're confessing? For a moment, I thought you had killed your neighbor and his dog, but I didn't think I had misjudged you."

Rif said, "Jill, this is very serious. You lied to a sheriff. You could go to jail." Rif looked at Jill and watched her squirm. Jill looked back and forth at Rif and Glen."

Glen and Rif started laughing. Rif said, "We got you!"

Jill had nearly started to cry, but said, "You guys are terrible! I'll remember this." She grinned and continued, "I'll get you when you least expect it!"

"Okay, no more kidding around. I would like you to help me with some computer work at my house. I'm going to have Deputy

Cordell install some new computers so we can search rapidly. It just might help solve some of these crimes. What do you think?"

"Oh, I'd like to help, but what about my newspaper job?"

"I'm sure you can handle both. You type about four times faster than I do, so a couple of hours a day would be all you'd need. I'll have to pay you from our backup funds, so it won't be a permanent job, just long enough to solve some of these crimes. I'm afraid if I don't figure these out soon, the city council will call in someone from the state capital. I don't want people barging in to Wolves' Hollow."

Jill's enthusiasm was almost boiling over. "When do we start?"

"We'll go to my place in the morning, and then do some shopping in the afternoon. I'll get Tim to install computers in my house so we can work from there. Glen, come into my office at 10:00 a.m. The mayor will be there."

"Okay. Good night ladies. See you tomorrow."

Glen's alarm started beeping at 7:00 a.m., but was immediately silenced. Barney had gotten up and was drinking from his water bowl in the bathroom. Glen popped a cinnamon roll in the microwave and pulled on pair of pants over his day-old underwear. Barney ate half a can of dog food and went back to the water. Glen grabbed a shirt from his dirty clothes pile and put his wallet in his pocket. Keys in hand, he tapped on the floor and Barney ran to the door. In another minute they were on the way to the crater where the old stump had been.

As Glen sifted through the debris from under the stump, Barney sat beside the pickup in the shade, watching. After 15 minutes, Glen had recovered half a dozen small bones and two bullets. He had sifted the top two inches of earth before deciding the recovery job was complete.

"Well, Barney, that's all. We're all done." Glen talked to Barney, even though Barney couldn't hear the words. Barney saw Glen's sign and stood up, ready to climb into the cab. Glen slid the piece of screen behind the seat and dropped the bones and bullets into his pocket. In ten minutes, he was home and in the shower. Barney was lying on the porch soaking up the morning sun.

Glen donned clean underwear and a pair of gray slacks, a white shirt, and a tie that still had a knot in it. He couldn't remember when that knot had been tied. His electric razor made short work of his stubble. He reached under his shirt and applied a liberal amount of deodorant. He could have shined his shoes, but they only had a couple of scuffs. Glen combed his hair and drove to the Court House. He walked in the door at 9:30, and went to Rif's office.

Jeanie looked up from her flat screen and said, "May I help you, sir?"

Glen started laughing. He suddenly realized Jeanie didn't recognize him. "Is Rif here yet?"

Jeanie was embarrassed. "Oh! I'm so sorry, Glen. I didn't recognize you! I've never seen you cleaned up. You look so nice!"

"Thanks, Jeanie. I thought I'd better clean up for a meeting with the mayor. Did the council vote me in?"

"Rif's at the meeting as we speak. We'll know as soon as she gets back from the library—that's where they're meeting. Take a seat. It should only be a few minutes."

"Thanks, Jeanie. I'll stand. I'm a little nervous." Glen looked down at his armpits to check if the sweat was showing. He had used a liberal amount of antiperspirant, knowing how nervous he got when involved with civic duties. So far, he was okay.

He was leaning against the doorjamb, scratching his backbone, when he heard voices and movement in the hallway. Rif was first, leading the Mayor, Bob Buckley, and Doc Skidmore.

Rif's face was still bandaged and her arm was in a sling. Buckley and Skidmore had khakis and plaid shirts on. They hadn't dressed up. Glen relaxed; this wasn't going to be a big deal. *Maybe they had decided against having me as the temporary sheriff.*

Rif stopped in front of Glen and said, "You look handsome this morning. Getting married?"

Glen laughed. Rif must have figured he was nervous and she wanted him to relax.

The mayor spoke up, "Let's get this over with. I've got to mow the lawn. Raise your right hand and repeat after me—."

A minute later, they all shook hands, and Rif handed Glen her sheriff's badge.

The mayor said, "I hope you're up to this. The murders are getting us all a bit on edge. We'll give you two weeks to make some progress. After that, we'll have to call in some help. I've got to go—got a date with my lawn mower. Keep me informed."

They said good-bye to the mayor and he left the building.

Skidmore said, "Glen, I want you to keep an eye on Rif. She shouldn't even be here today. It's going to take a while for that wound to heal. If she messes it up, she might have more problems in the future."

"Okay, Doc. I think she'll be riding a desk for the next few days. I'll be doing the leg work. Say, what about the burned body?"

"It's Vince Turner, all right. He had a fractured skull. Looks like someone hit him in the back of the head. That injury probably killed him. There was nothing in his pickup that could have done that. It was another murder. I went out and talked with Mrs. Turner last night after I finished the autopsy. Her sister is coming to live with her until they can sell the property. She's a strong woman, she'll be all right."

Glen remembered the things recovered the day before. "Here are the bones and bullets from under that stump, Doc." Glen emptied his pocket and gave the palm full of little bones and two lead slugs to Skidmore. "That's all I could find."

Skidmore looked at the lead and commented, "Looks like .38 caliber, but I'll have to check. The bones should complete the skeleton. Good work, Glen."

"Thanks Doc."

"Well, I've got to run by the hospital. I'll see you later."

Rif said, "Bye, Doc. Thanks for your help."

Skidmore walked away, raised his left hand, and waved, never looking back.

# CHAPTER 46

# COMPUTERS AND DEATH

Rif invited Glen into her office and said, "I can tell you about the Wrackler case now. I had Tim take the evidence into Boise to the crime lab. We should get the results Tuesday. The killer was probably a small man or a woman. This is how I know...." Rif brought Glen up to date on all she knew about the killings, the ransacking of Jill's house, and what she heard when she was shot. She unlocked a drawer of her desk and gave Glen a pistol and holster. He would have to get his own belt; hers was too small.

"That's about it Glen. Jill and I are going to meet with Mrs. Womack this afternoon at the furniture and appliance store so Jill can replace the items damaged in her house. Mrs. Womack had insurance that covers all the losses. Jill is staying with me for a few days. You are welcome to come by. My address is 209 West Acorn. If you have any questions, call me. Here's my number." Rif pointed at a list of phone numbers on a pull out near the top of her desk. "My desk is yours—unless I come to visit." Rif grinned and then grimaced. A pain had just shot through her left arm. "Doc said that might happen. Oh, here are the keys to the jeep." Rif tossed a key ring to Glen. "Keys for the cruiser are on that ring, too. There's a credit card in the glove box. I've got to get home. Tim is installing two computers so we can work on the cases from home. I need to make sure Tim is not doing anything weird. Jill's there alone with him. Bye."

"Okay. I'll call you this evening and tell you about my first day on the job. Bye." Glen watched Rif walk down the hall. She moved more like a man, although gracefully, than a woman that could be a model. Glen wondered about her ancestry. His thoughts were interrupted by Jeanie.

"Sheriff, Mrs. Wiley called about a bear in her backyard. It's breaking into her garage. They have frozen fish in a freezer. Her husband wants to shoot the bear. He's got a shotgun."

"Tell him to take the shot out of the shells and refill them with rock salt. Then, shoot the bear in the ass. I'll be right there for backup. What's their address?"

"Eight-one-one Granite Drive. I'll tell them what you said."

"Okay, see you in about 30 minutes."

The entire day went like it started. A bear in the backyard, two deer in the garden, a porcupine in the shed, and a skunk under a car kept Glen busy until 3:30 p.m. He had grabbed a burger between the deer and the porcupine calls, so he wasn't hungry. He drove the jeep back to the office and parked it on the street. He had one more trip before calling it a day.

"How's everything, Jeanie? Any problems at the school?"

"Everything is fine. School's out for the summer, Glen. Last day was last Friday. You wouldn't have known that, no kids and all."

"Thanks for the info. That's why you're makin' the big bucks." Glen smiled and said, "I'm going out to the mine to check if anyone has been in there fooling around. I should be back in about an hour. Is John still working?"

"Yeah. John's on 'til 6:00 p.m."

"Send him out to the mine if I'm not back by 5:15."

Jeanie grinned, "10-4, Sheriff."

★  ★  ★

Harv and Brad drove into the lodge parking lot at 3:45. When Harv beeped the horn, Tad came out of unit 6, and climbed into the cab with the two men.

"Let's go out to the mine. I want to show you something. What have you been doing the last couple of days after shooting the sheriff?"

Harv started towards the Collins mine, driving slowly, so he wouldn't get a ticket.

Brad asked, "Is she dead? I knew I hit her."

"Nope—bullet went through her shoulder. She was in the hospital for a couple of days. The doc sewed her up."

"Shit! I never shot a sheriff before. I thought I killed her."

Tad quizzed, "You guys keepin' score?"

Harv answered, "Kind of. I've got one more than Brad, but he's probly a better shot. It just wasn't his day." Harv spit in a beer can and placed the can between his legs. "We was in Boise. Got our horns clipped. That's a nice town, but too small. We like the cities where we can get lost in the crowds—and there's a lot more business for us. We like to keep busy. It's more excitin' that way."

As they approached the mine, Tad said, "Go to where you shot the sheriff. It's in there."

"What's in there?" asked Brad.

"What I want to show you. I'll bet you've never seen it before."

Harv stopped in front of the side entrance to the mine and all three men got out. Tad walked over to the boarded up entrance and said, "Got a crowbar?"

Brad reached into the back of the pickup and tossed a crow- bar on the ground next to Tad. "There ya go."

Tad pried two planks loose and let the sag to the ground. He bent down and stepped through the opening. "Come on in. It'll just take a minute."

Brad and Harv came through the opening and stood beside Tad looking into the darkness of the mine.

Harv said, "I don't see nothin'."

"Can't see it from here. Come on, follow me." Tad started into the darkness, pulled a small flashlight from his pocket and illuminated the floor of the mine. He walked about 20 feet and switched the light to dim, and walked another few yards. He switched the light off and stopped. "Damn, my batteries are dead. I should have checked them. Harv, have you got a flashlight in the truck?"

Harv answered, "Yeah. Want me to get it?"

"Yeah. We'll wait right here. You can see the entrance. Go get your light."

"Okay. Be right back."

Tad could see Harv step through the opening and he made his move. He pulled his pig-sticker from his belt and stepped behind Brad, put his hand over Brad's mouth, and slit his throat. Brad struggled for a moment and then sagged to the ground. He was unconscious in ten seconds. Tad leaned against the wall of the mine and waited to see the illumination from Harv's flashlight. Tad stepped between the body and the oncoming light and waited.

As Harv approached, he could see Brad on the floor of the mine. "What happened to Brad?"

"He tripped and hit his head—knocked himself out. He'll come to in a minute. Why don't you give him a shake and see if he'll come out of it."

Harv laid the flashlight on the ground and bent down to help Brad. Tad was too quick. He stepped behind Harv and slashed open the other killer's neck. Harv grabbed at Tad's legs, then his own throat, and fell beside his dead partner. He tried to say something, but the sound was just a gurgle. Tad picked up the flashlight, found the truck keys in Harv's pocket, and walked toward the opening.

Glen hadn't driven a jeep much since he was in the service. He had been an M.P. for three years of his four-year stint. The passenger seat was empty. To be more comfortable, he took the gun out of his belt, and laid it on the seat. He pulled away from the curb and started toward the mine. No traffic was present on North Pebble and Glen pushed the jeep past the speed limit, arriving at the mine in less than five minutes. He smiled when he thought he should arrest himself for speeding, doing 50 in a 35 zone. He hardly looked at the first mine entrance, and as he approached the second entrance, he saw a black pickup sitting at the boarded up mine opening. He could see two boards had been pulled loose and were sagging down toward the ground.

Glen quickly shut off the engine and set the break, picked up the 9 mm handgun, walked 20 yards to the pickup, and waited. Ten seconds later, a leg was extended through the opening to the mine. He watched as Tad Birdsong appeared from the mine. Tad reached for the crowbar to use it as a hammer to reattach the loose boards. Glen didn't give him a chance and said, "Hands up, Tad."

Tad turned quickly and saw Glen. "Boy, you scared me; I didn't know anyone was here. What's the gun for?"

"You're under arrest for trespassing. Can't you read? Whose truck is this?"

"It belongs to one of our guests at the motel. He said I could borrow it. How can you arrest me? You're a carpenter."

"I'm the temporary sheriff. Why did you break into the mine?"

"I've always wondered what it looked like on the inside, so I thought I'd check it out."

Glen spotted the knife in Tad's belt and said, "Take the knife out and drop it on the ground."

"What if I don't want to?"

"How would you like me to shoot off both your kneecaps? If you don't think I can, let me give you a demo." Glen elevated the barrel of the gun a squeezed off a round. The bullet went through the center of the letter O in the no trespassing sign and ricocheted off the rocks.

"Now drop the knife and back toward me, *slowly*, with your hands up."

Glen pulled a pair of handcuffs from his back pocket and cuffed Tad to the roll bar of the jeep. A search of Tad's pockets revealed a small flashlight. Glen checked the light. It worked, so he took a Nylon wire-tie and secured Tad's feet to the seat support beneath the passenger seat cushion. Glen entered the mine and flipped on the flashlight. He found the two bodies, saw the still wet blood that had gushed from their necks, and realized what Tad had done. Glen decided to take Tad to the jail, and send Doc Skidmore and John Funches out to retrieve the bodies. Glen placed Tad's hunting knife in an evidence bag to preserve fingerprints and traces of blood. As Glen was getting in the jeep, he remembered the crowbar. After putting it in a large evidence bag, he drove his prisoner back to the jail.

Deputy Funches was getting into his cruiser when he saw Glen pulling up to the Court House. He walked over to the jeep and looked at Tad wearing handcuffs.

"What's going on, Sheriff?"

"Put Tad in a cell. He's under arrest for two murders. There are two dead men out in the mine—throats cut. I'm sure Tad did it. Who does the finger printing?"

"Tim usually does it, he's the computer expert. Doesn't take long for a match. He's got a knack for it."

"Is he still at Rif's?"

"I think so. I haven't seen him all day. He's probably having the time of his life with Jill and Rif—showing them tricks with the computers."

"I'll go over there and talk with Rif. Put Tad in a cell and *be careful*; he's an expert with a knife. Don't take the cuffs off until he's locked in a cell. You got that?"

"10-4, Sheriff."

Glen drove over to Acorn Street, but he wasn't sure of the address. *Was it 209? Yeah, that was it.* But he didn't have any trouble finding Rif's house, a small yellow ranch style. There were two cruisers parked outside. He tapped on the front door and heard Rif yell, "Just a second!" The door opened and Rif said, "Hi, Glen, come on in. Tim's almost finished giving us instructions." Rif leaned toward Glen and whispered, "I think Tim and Jill like each other," and raised her eyebrows.

Glen grinned and walked into the living room. Modern beige and gray furniture with clean lines and a modest flat-screen TV made the room look comfortable. A vase of blue and white wild flowers sat on a coffee table in front of the sofa. The wild flowers added a touch of cleanliness and contrast to the earthy colored sofa and La-Z-Boy recliner. Blue and white flowers were Glen's mother's favorites. She said they reminded her of clear winter sky and snow on the ground. Winter was her favorite season.

The dining room had been converted into a computer center. Jill waved and Tim gave a half-assed salute, and then went back to pointing at Jill's monitor. Tim's face was pretty close to Jill's. Glen thought, *I hope Jill ate some garlic for lunch.*

"I came over to tell you about two more murders. I think the dead men were the ones that shot you."

"What happened?"

Glen told Rif, Tim, and Jill of watching Tad exiting the mine, and how he forced Tad to drop his knife. He related how the knife and crowbar were taken for evidence and how he transported Tad to jail. John was to lock Tad up and call Skidmore about the bodies.

Rif was thinking way ahead. "Tim, I want you to print the crowbar and knife, and do blood typing for the bodies and the knife. Jill, I want you to search police records in New York, Philadelphia, and Pittsburgh for Harv and Brad, just as a start. Maybe you'll have some luck. We might have to broaden the search later. Glen, you and I will question Tad Birdsong, and see if he talks before lawyering up. Okay, let's do it."

Glen said, "I couldn't have said that better myself," and grinned.

# CHAPTER 47

# LAWYER AND SEARCHES

**W**hen Glen and Rif reached the holding cell, Birdsong's lawyer was already present. Glory Ames, about 50, had been an advocate for Native Americans for a number of years. Her office was in Challis, only a 30 minute drive from Wolves' Hollow. She was well fed, about five-six, and, in Glen's opinion, must have been an ugly baby. However, she was very smart, and took advantage of all the loopholes in the law. If there were a way to evade a law, she would find it. Glory had little regard for the government and she let people know it.

Rif had heard of Ms. Ames, but until now, had never met her. Glen had no knowledge of the woman whatsoever. Rif was perplexed. *How did Glory Ames know about Tad Birdsong? Tad had been in jail for less than an hour.*

After introductions, they moved to the sheriff's office. Ms. Ames said, "What are the charges against Mr. Birdsong?"

Without hesitation, Rif answered, "Two counts of first degree murder and trespassing."

Ms. Ames replied, "What is the bail?"

Rif said, "We can't set bail. A judge will determine bail on Monday, but due to the severity of the crime, and flight risk, I'm guessing bail will be denied."

Ames tried to smile, but without much effort, and said, "Well, I'll see you in court." She turned and stomped out of the office, apparently trying to make as much noise as possible. Ames had certainly studied psychology.

Glen replied, "Nice meeting...," but caught himself and didn't finish the comment.

Rif looked at Glen and said, "I have the same feeling, Glen."

"So, Rif. Who is leaking information? John, Tim, Jill, Jeanie, you, and I are the only ones that knew about Tad."

Rif thought for a moment. "It's got to be Tim. I'm sure none of the others would even know how to contact Ms. Ames. I'll check his lab computer tonight when he's gone. He must have contacted someone. All messages in and out are logged, same with the telephone. But, he might have used his cell phone. If that's the case, I'll have to put in a request to the phone company for his calls for the last few days. I think I'll do that anyway. Oh, we forgot someone! Doc Skidmore would have known about Tad and the dead men."

Glen asked, "Do you really think Doc is involved?"

"No, but we have to put him on the list. Have to cover all the bases, right?"

"Yep. You're the sheriff," Glen smiled.

Rif laughed, "No, you're the sheriff, and I don't want to argue. Let's check with Jill to see what she has found out."

Jill was working at one of the computers when Rif and Glen arrived. It was a few minutes after six and Glen's stomach was growling, loudly enough for Rif to hear it.

"What do you guys want for dinner, Chinese or pizza?"

Glen deferred to Jill who said, "Chinese, it's less fattening."

Glen patted his stomach and said, "*You* have nothing to worry about."

Rif called in an order to the China Station and joined Glen and Jill at the computer table.

Glen said, "Jill found Bradley and Harvey Markesan in the police records in Pittsburgh. They both have numerous arrests, once each for murder, but they got off. A witness changed her story. I'm thinking because of intimidation."

"Did you download mug shots?"

"I did, Rif. Here they are in all their glory. What handsome young men," Jill replied sarcastically.

Rif showed the pictures to Glen, who said, "Yep. Those are the dead men, but they're even uglier now. I wonder why they came to Idaho. Is there someone here that knew them in Pittsburgh?"

Jill added, "I'll bet they didn't graduate at the head of their class. They probably advertised as assassins on Craigslist."

Rif grinned and said, "Jill, you shouldn't think less of a person that didn't go to college."

Jill laughed, "I'm sorry. I take it back. They probably didn't finish middle school."

Glenn grinned and said, "Boy, now you're getting downright mean."

The doorbell rang; Glen pulled out his wallet, and went to the door. Glen could see a young woman holding several containers with red and gold China Station lettering. He opened the door and the girl turned around.

"Oh! Hi, Mr. Collins. How is Barney doing?"

Glen frowned and then recognized the young lady from Rainen's Cats and Dogs. It was Nora. "Barney is doing great. I've been communicating with him. We developed a sign language and a code of vibrations he responds to."

"That's wonderful! Here is your order from the China Station. It's $23.50."

Glen gave Nora $25 and said, "Keep the change, Nora. That should pay for about five minutes of college."

"Thanks, Mr. Collins. See ya."

"Bye Nora."

"Rif, do you have a card table?"

"Yes, in the hall closet." Rif pointed it out for Glen.

Glen unfolded the legs, set up the table in the living room, and said, "Come on, ladies, the food is getting cold." He wanted to dig in, but waited for Rif and Jill to open the containers. When he smelled the food, his stomach began turning into knots. He felt like there was a little person in his stomach that would reach out from his mouth, grab a handful of rice and vegetables, extend the other hand, and spear a dumpling with a chopstick. Glen had to remember to avoid eating like a slob. He had manners, he just had little occasion to use them. However, he made it through dinner without any embarrassment.

Rif quizzed, "How much do we owe you for dinner, Glen?"

"Nothing. Your company was enough. I've never had dinner with two pretty women before. It was a first for me," Glen smiled. "I've got to get home and take care of Barney. He's been alone all day. He's probably lonesome and hungry."

"Okay. Thank you for dinner. I'll be going to the office tonight at 8. to check Tim's computer in the lab. He shouldn't be there. He'll probably be at his store downloading porn or more computer games."

"You're welcome. Maybe someday we can go to a nice restaurant and have dinner—not that I didn't enjoy eating here. You know what I mean?"

"I know. That would be nice—maybe after we solve the murders and I get the bandages removed."

Jill yelled from the dining room, "Bye, Glen. Thanks for dinner!"

"No problem. Take care of that leg. See you ladies later."

The office was quiet when Rif arrived a few minutes after 8:00 p.m. It was still light outside, the sun had dropped below the mountains, but no one had turned on their lights yet. When nine o'clock arrived, the Wolves' Hollow street and house lights would be coming on, and children would be going inside to avoid mosquitoes.

Rif unlocked the door, went in, and relocked the door. She went directly to the lab, two doors down from her office, and flipped on the lights. The lab computer was in sleep mode, so Rif moved the mouse to activate the menu. She entered the administrator's password and brought up the day's log. There were two emails; the remaining entries were fingerprint library searches. The email sent was to rsodwim@hotmail.com. Rif clicked on *READ* and began scanning the two line message. It said: *Tad Birdsong was arrested for killing two men.* and *What should I do?* The return email said *Nothing.*

Rif closed the message and put the computer back in sleep mode.

"What are you looking for, Sheriff?"

Rif hadn't heard Tim come into the building, being engrossed in reading Tim's email.

Even though she was startled, Rif tried not to show it. She looked at Tim and answered, "I was trying to find out if you had identified the fingerprints from the knife and the crowbar."

"You're lying, Rif. I saw the screen refection in the window. You were reading my email."

"Well, Tim, how did you get involved in the murders?"

Glen had fed Barney and let him in the house. He put Barney through his tapping routines and sat down on the sofa, but he felt uneasy about Rif being in the office alone. *What if Tim showed up?* Glen stood, grabbed his gun and keys, and went out to his truck, leaving the house lights on for Barney. Three minutes later, he coasted up to the Court House.

When a block away, Glen had seen two cruisers, one behind the other, parked at the curb. Either John or Tim must be in the building with Rif. It must be Tim; John had no reason to return to the office in the evening. Glen cut his engine and slowly rolled up to the building. He left the pickup door ajar and entered the building, barely making a sound. He could hear Tim's voice coming from the lab.

"Those two idiots went into the old lady's house to scare her, but she tripped and hit her head on the counter—broke her neck. It was an accident. But your death will be due to stupidity, getting too close to a prisoner in a jail cell. Let's go down and visit with Tad, another murder won't make any difference to him. Sorry to see you go like this, you're a good lookin' woman. Come on, lead the way. Remember, I've got my gun on you."

Glen was right outside the door to the lab and he heard every word Tim said. He pulled his gun from his belt and waited. Rif came through the door first, but didn't see Glen. Tim followed her about a yard behind. Tim's gun appeared first. Glen grabbed Tim's wrist, pushed down, and stuck the muzzle of his .45 under Tim's jaw.

"Drop it, or I'll scramble the shit you have for brains!" Glen's vise-like grip prevented Tim from doing anything but giving up, so he dropped his gun on the floor.

"Oh, my God! Am I glad to see you, Glen. I had no idea you were here. Why did you come back to the office?"

"I thought if butt-head showed up, you might need some help. I guessed right. Let's throw this piece of crap in a cell next to Tad. They can talk over what their plans are while they're in prison. You know what prisoners do to former police officers, don't you?"

"Sure do. They usually last for less than a month before they have a fatal accident."

Tim's eyes opened wide and he protested, "Wait a minute, I haven't killed anyone. I just told Sodwim what was going on."

"Yeah, you're just an innocent bystander. Come on, Rif, let's lock him up."

Rif slapped a pair of cuffs on Tim, arms behind his back, and they started toward the jail cells, Rif on one side and Glen on the other. Just before they opened the door to the cells, Tim made an offer, "Don't put me beside Tad. He's a killer. Keep an empty cell between us."

Rif said, "And why should we do anything for you?"

"I'll tell you about the Markesan brothers if you put me in cell 3. Tad's in cell 1, right?"

Glen quizzed, "What have you to tell us?"

"Well, the Markesans messed up the reporter's house and killed that old rancher. Then they were told to burn the pickup in the ravine with the body in the truck. But, when they shot you, Sodwim said to get rid of them, and leave the bodies in the mine to incriminate Collins. He wants the mine and the whole neighborhood where the reporter was living."

Rif asked, "So who killed Mr. Wrackler?"

"Don't know. It wasn't anyone I know."

"Okay. We'll put you in cell 3."

# CHAPTER 48

## WRACKLER AND SODWIM

The weekend was spent recuperating, mentally and physically. Glen put in a half-day at the sheriff's office doing paperwork, keeping up with reports of the previous two days. Saturday afternoon, he took Barney and drove to Lake Ofalloc, about 20 miles northwest of Wolves' Hollow, and spent the rest of the day fishing. Barney chased birds, squirrels, and pine cones thrown by Glen, and then went swimming, although briefly, because the water was still quite cold from the melting snow and ice at higher elevations. By mid-July, the water would warm up, and campers could swim without suffering hypothermia.

Rif and Jill spent Saturday sleeping, talking, and searching for R. Sodwim, without any success. Rif dictated and Jill typed reports on the computer as Glen had done at the office. In the afternoon, Rif went to the office and checked with John, who was taking care of the prisoners. While Rif was there, Connie Birdsong came to see her husband. She was accompanied by Glory Ames. They talked privately in a small interrogation room for nearly an hour.

Sunday was uneventful, except for one thing. Glen took Jill over to the newspaper office where she prepared a job opening notice for Rif. Wolves' Hollow needed a new deputy. The notice would appear in the Tuesday paper. Interviews were scheduled to commence the following Monday at 10:00 a.m. After completion of the listing, Rif, Jill, and Glen went to Jill's house, opened boxes of items Rif and Jill had purchased, installed some new appliances, and made sure Jill could use the ramps.

Monday was anything but normal, although the day started off pretty much like any other sunny June morning. Jeanie arrived at the office at 8:30, as usual. She checked the phone for messages and started coffee. John walked in at 8:50 with his customary dozen glazed doughnuts and talked about Deputy Cordell being arrested. Rif and Glen showed up about five minutes apart, Glen at 9:05.

Glen asked, "Did you notice that car parked across the street with two men in it?"

"They're in suits," added Rif.

Jeanie and John hadn't noticed the car or the occupants. Jeanie stood up and went to the window. "There's no one in that car now." Jeanie turned around and looked at Rif.

"What is it, Jeanie?"

Jeanie wasn't actually looking at Rif, she was looking past Rif. Jeanie pointed toward the door. There were two suits standing in the office doorway, not two men, but a man and a woman, the woman looked a little older than the man. She was about five-seven, had short black hair, and was above average looking. She wore a Navy blue jacket, a gray skirt, and black flats. The man was about six feet tall, blond hair, and glasses. He wore a nicely tailored light- brown suit, in better taste than would be expected. He was tanned and looked like he was enjoying his work.

The woman spoke, a little raspy quality in her voice, "Sheriff Summers?"

Rif replied, "Yes, what can I do for you?"

"I'm agent Sandra Burger, and this is my colleague, agent Dan Ochs. We're from the FBI office in Boise." They flashed their IDs.

"FBI? Who called you in, our mayor?"

Agent Ochs answered, "We weren't called in. We're here about a Mr. Simon Wrackler. You sent some tissue in for DNA analysis. Can you direct us to his residence? We need to talk with him."

Rif smiled, "He is currently in the hospital—actually, in the morgue. He was killed a week ago. Why did you want to speak with him?" Rif noticed neither agent wore a ring.

Miss Burger asked, "We weren't told he was deceased. How was he killed? Do you know who did it?"

Rif replied, "You need to talk to Doctor Skidmore about that. We have no idea who did it. We've been working on several other murders. His death is apparently unrelated. Why are you so interested in Mr. Wrackler?"

Agent Burger replied, "We've been after him for over five years. His DNA matches samples from at least six rapes in the Pacific Northwest. The rapes took place in Portland, Seattle, Spokane, Pasco, Ontario, and Boise. There might be more, perhaps some unreported ones also. Wrackler was a serial rapist. Someone has done the government a big favor and saved future victims."

Rif said, "He lived next door to a friend of ours, Jill Morran. God, Jill could have been another victim. Well, I'm glad he was murdered. I'm not going to put much effort into finding his killer. Solving that crime won't be very high on my list."

Agent Ochs commented, "Can't blame you for that. Let the scum sink to the bottom. However, we need to see the corpse to take a sample for DNA comparison—just to confirm the death and close the rape cases. Could someone show us the body?"

Glen spoke up, "Sure. I'm driving a jeep, just follow me. I need to see the coroner about something anyway. I might as well do it now and get it out of the way." Glen wanted to get his gold from Skidmore and ask about the killings of the Markesan brothers.

The agents drove their burgundy Grand Cherokee to the hospital, parked, and met Glen at the reception desk. Agent Burger was carrying a small blue-plastic container about the size of a child's lunchbox. Glen asked for Dr. Skidmore and the receptionist paged the doctor. They waited about two minutes before

Skidmore appeared, walking down the hall from the morgue. He was holding a plastic container in his left hand against his body.

Skidmore waved at Glen and held up the container. Glen smiled and said, "How'd you know I was coming to get my gold?"

"I knew you wouldn't leave it with me very long, so I got it ready—repackaged it for you." Skidmore looked at the FBI agents and then Glen and said, "Who are your friends?"

"FBI agents from Boise. They came to see you."

Skidmore replied, "FBI?" He paused and then cleared his throat. "What can I do for you?"

Agent Burger said, "We'd like to get a sample from the deceased, a Mr. Wrackler, for DNA testing. We need to verify the samples you sent to the crime lab last week were from the deceased. It should only take a few minutes. Could we please see the body?"

As they walked down to the morgue, agent Ochs asked Glen, "That container is full of gold? How much does it weigh?"

Glen handed the container to Ochs, who seemed a little surprised at the weight of the small receptacle. He raised and lowered the container a few times and said, "That must weigh about five pounds. Let's see...damn, Mr. Collins, that's nearly a hundred thousand dollars! Where did you get it?"

"It was under a tree."

The agents began laughing and Ochs said, "I know, at the end of a rainbow." He smiled and continued, "I can't blame you for wanting to keep it a secret."

"I'm not kidding. The gold was in some bags with a skeleton in an old wolves' den under a tree. I'll show you the bones; they're here in the morgue."

Skidmore unlocked the morgue, flipped on the lights, swung open the bottom cabinet door, and rolled the body out of the refrigeration unit. He folded back a cover and said, "Agents, this is Mr. Wrackler."

Agent Burger removed a small camera from her container, photographed the body, and then took several samples for DNA analysis. She turned toward Glen and said, "Show me the bones you found under a tree."

Glen pointed at the table across the room and said, "It's possible the skeleton might be from one of my ancestors. I've been checking our family records and the bones might be those of my great-great-great grandfather, Levi Collins. The last time he came to Wolves' Hollow, in 1896, he was never heard from again. I believe he was born in Pittsburgh in 1836. Is there any way to check DNA from the bones for comparison to my DNA?"

Agent Burger commented, "I've been working on my family tree, so I know what you are looking for. I've been interested in genealogy for the last five years or so. Let me inspect the bones. If they aren't too weathered, it might be possible to get a sample from inside the bone. Then you can compare your DNA with that from the bones. If it is your ancestor, there should be a very close match, especially if the Collins males form an unbroken chain. Of course, there is no guarantee, but that's where a family bible or other recorded family history can help."

The agent picked up the right femur, inspecting it closely. After about ten seconds she said, "Doctor, do you have a drill? I can take a sample and run the test for you, Mr. Collins. I'll need some DNA from you also. Let me swab the inside of your cheek."

Glen asked, "Is the test expensive?"

"That bag of gold should cover it," agent Burger laughed. "Actually, it won't cost you a cent. I'll include the test with the one for Mr. Wrackler. The government will pay for it."

"Thank you. Next time I'm in Boise, I'll buy you and agent Ochs dinner."

"That sounds like a deal. Thank you."

The federal agents thanked Doc Skidmore for helping with the DNA sample. Agent Burger told Glen she would contact him about his DNA and that from the bone. Glen watched the agents leave the hospital, get in their car, and drive off toward the highway for their two-hour trip back to Boise.

"What have you found out about the two dead men, Glen?"

"I really shouldn't say, Doc, but since you are the coroner, I guess I can tell you. They were sent here from Pittsburgh to cause trouble. They were brothers and killers. They killed Mr. Turner and shot Rif. If I had caught them, I'd have shot them in the nuts, but I wouldn't have killed them. I'd just make sure they couldn't have any children. Were they killed the same way?"

Skidmore smiled, "Yes. The killer knew what he was doing. I was a little surprised that it was Tad Birdsong. He must have had good reason. Well, I've got work to do. See you later."

"Bye Doc."

Glen climbed in the jeep and went back to the courthouse. Rif was talking on the phone when he walked into the sheriff's office. He waited outside the door until she finished the call.

"Glen. That was Jill. She's been searching for the name Sodwim and can't find anything. She said maybe Sodwim is an anagram. What do you think?"

"Hmm, I hadn't thought of that." Glen smiled, "I knew Jill might come up with some new ideas."

"Sure you did. Who was it that asked Jill to help?" Rif grinned.

"I don't remember. Could it have been Sheriff Summers? Hand me a piece of paper, please. I want to see what other words can be made from *sodwim*. There are 720 different combinations of those letters."

Rif frowned, but gave Glen a piece of paper and a pencil as he had requested. "How do you know there are 720?"

Glen smiled and said, "Have you forgotten? I'm a carpenter."

"Oh, forget I asked." Rif grinned. "You'll tell me—someday."

Glen wrote for about five minutes and then looked up at Rif. She had been watching Glen, amused at his regular progression through the six letters. Glen asked, "Want to help?"

"No." Rif grinned. "Just kidding. Tell me what to do. Maybe it will save some time."

They spent a half-hour writing combinations of the letters contained in *sodwim*. Glen looked at Rif and said, "I think we have enough to work with. What do you think is your most promising six letter combination?"

Rif had circled one name that seemed to make more sense than any other. Glen had done the same. It was wisdom. When Rif said "wisdom," Glen smiled and said, "Same here, and you know what? My sister has been researching our family history. She sent me a copy of the results. Levi Collins's sister's first husband was named Wisdom, Frank Wisdom. He had tried to smother their baby and she divorced him in 1867. Let's see if Jill can find someone with the name R. Wisdom. But doesn't it seem strange that a person with the name Wisdom would be involved with something going on here in Wolves' Hollow after all these years?"

Rif did a quick calculation and said, "Yes, it's been 146 years. It must be just coincidental, or maybe we don't have the right name, but I'll ask Jill to check into it."

# CHAPTER 49

# WISDOM

While Glen was at the morgue, Rif had begun interviewing the first candidate for the new deputy position. Ron Sieberns, a former marine, had made the ninety-minute drive from Salmon, Idaho, with his wife, Jan, and five-year-old son, Michael. As Glen came into the Court House, the boy pretended to shoot Glen with his finger-gun. Glen grabbed his leg and started limping toward the office.

"I'm sorry, sir. Mikey is hoping his dad will be a deputy. He's kind of excited."

Glen sat down beside the pleasant looking, nicely made-up young woman on the hallway bench outside the office.

"That's all right. I'm the temporary sheriff, Glen Collins. I'm helping out while the regular sheriff mends from a gunshot. I'm only doing this for a few weeks. Where are you folks from?"

"I'm Jan Sieberns and my husband is Ron. We're from Salmon."

Glen could hear Rif's voice, "Thank you for applying. I'll let you know next Monday. You have a very good chance to get the job, especially since you are computer savvy. That's something we need here."

The marine appeared in the office doorway smiling at his wife. He gave her the thumbs up and said, "It looks like we might be moving, hon." Ron Sieberns stood about five-ten and had the build of a football player. He would make a deputy with whom few people would argue. He was ruggedly handsome and had short brown hair. He looked like a marine.

Glen stood and extended his right hand. "I'm Glen Collins, temporary sheriff. Sounds like you had a good interview. We could use some computer help on a case we're working on."

"I guess you met my wife. I'm Ron Sieberns. I got back from Afghanistan about six months ago. This job would come in very handy right now. We're running low on savings."

"I hope it works out for you. If you want to tour the town, it should take about five minutes." Glen smiled and continued, "Most of the people are real friendly, the ones that aren't are in jail."

"It was nice meeting you, Mr. Collins. I hope to see you again—next week." Ron and his wife walked toward the door, herding Mikey ahead of them. Jan waved bye as they left the building, and Mikey shot at Glen with his finger-gun as Jan grabbed his shirt and pulled him away from the open door.

Glen walked into Rif's office laughing. "Is that our new deputy? He's got a nice family. The little boy is a real character."

"I wondered what you were laughing about. Do you like kids?"

Glen smiled, "Sure, as long as they're someone else's."

"So that's why you're single—not interested in kids?"

"I'm single for several reasons. I had a difficult time getting over my divorce, and I don't want to go through that again. I'd like to have a better-paying job, too. I don't want to raise a family living in poverty. It's not fair to the marriage and the children."

"But Glen, you have a hundred thousand dollars now."

"Yeah, that's a start, but Wolves' Hollow doesn't have a lot to choose from. Most of the ladies here are either too young or too old. Say, has Jill found anything about Wisdom yet?"

"I don't know. Why don't you come over for lunch and we can see what she has found out."

Glen smiled, "Hmm, I don't know about that. What's for lunch?"

Rif grinned and said, "I was thinking chicken-noodle soup, cheese and crackers, and apples or bananas. Interested?"

"Sure. Most of that fits into my diet. I just have to stay away from too much salt."

Rif looked concerned. "Are you serious? I can never tell whether you're pulling my leg or telling the truth."

"I'm kind of serious. I'm trying to lose weight and get in better shape. Then, I'll have a better chance with the women. You know, except for the short hair, I used to look like a marine." Glen turned away so Rif couldn't see his smile. "Let's take the jeep. I'll drive. You can rest your arm."

Rif laughed and said, "Which one? Jeanie, we're going to lunch at my place so we can talk to Jill. We'll be back at twelve-thirty and you can go to lunch, okay?"

"10-4, Sheriff. I'll tell Harley to meet me at twelve-thirty."

★　★　★

When Rif and Glen arrived at Rif's house, Jill was sitting in her wheelchair on the porch with her laptop. She looked up and waved when the jeep stopped. Jill looked at her watch, noting it was eleven-thirty.

Jill smiled and said, "Early lunch? Hi Glen!"

"Rif twisted my arm and suggested I have lunch with you guys. I thought I'd better cooperate; she still has a gun."

"You big rat! You know that's not true." Rif punched Glen's shoulder and grinned. "We came here for lunch so we could talk with you about the name R. Wisdom. Have you found out anything yet?"

"The only R. Wisdom I could find is Richard Henry Wisdom, M.D. He lived in Pittsburgh until ten years ago, when he lost his medical license and disappeared. Apparently, he was involved in a plan to sell unapproved foreign drugs to old-age care facilities. He lost his license, but didn't go to prison."

Rif was quiet for about ten seconds and then said, "You know, that's about the time Doc Skidmore came to Wolves' Hollow."

Jill said, "I know. I thought about that and checked on him. The only Dr. Skidmore I could find any records of is Daniel Arnold Skidmore, M.D."

Rif acknowledged, "That's the name of our Dr. Skidmore, Jill."

"I know, but guess what? Daniel Arnold Skidmore, M.D. died eleven years ago. He was 78 years old."

Glen had been listening intently to Rif and Jill. He was having a hard time believing Doc Skidmore was really Dr. R. Wisdom, but he realized there was one way to prove it. They had to trace the email from R. Sodwim. If it came from one of the hospital's computers, or Skidmore's home computer, they had caught the person behind the killings. He had been issuing orders from here in Wolves' Hollow while everyone involved thought he was in the East. Glen told Rif and Jill what he was thinking.

Rif said, "How old would Wisdom be now, Jill?"

"He was in his early forties when he lost his medical license, so he would be in his early to mid-fifties now."

Glen replied, "That's about Skidmore's age, don't you think?"

Rif, expressionless, added, "I think that's about right."

While they ate lunch, the idea that Skidmore was really Wisdom was a possibility as foreign to the women as it had been to Glen. Doc Skidmore had taken care of Jill when she broke her leg, and he had done a top-notch job of caring for Rif. They were indebted to him. How could they believe he had orchestrated several killings? However, the circumstantial evidence was starting to make sense. But how could they track the email? Following information on the Internet led Jill to a website that could tell them the state, county, and city, but not the street address.

"Nuts! I have to pay a fee for the service."

Glen tossed Jill a credit card and said, "Here you go, put it on this card, I hardly ever use it. If I don't use it pretty soon, they'll close my account." Glen watched Jill's fingers move in a blur, and then she read, "Wolves' Hollow, Idaho" from the monitor. She looked at Rif excitedly and said, "The emails from R. Sodwim came from here! But who sent them? It says a street location can't be determined. Do you think they came from Skidmore? I wonder what he's been planning."

"It's beginning to look that way. The only thing of value around here is Glen's old gold mine. I'd better talk to Judge Miller and get a warrant to impound Skidmore's computers—and the computers that Tim was using at his store. But right now, we'd better get back to the office and relieve Jeanie." Rif smiled and said, "We don't want Jeanie to miss her date with Harley. He'd get an upset stomach."

Glen said, "Good work, Jill. We'll see you later, or at least Rif will. I've got to spend some time with Barney. He needs some TLC. This job as sheriff is taking all my time, although I like working with two good lookin' ladies. Barney's going to be jealous."

When Rif and Glen arrived at the Court House, Jeanie rushed out of the door yelling at Glen before he had shut off the engine. "There's a note on my keyboard for you. See you in an hour." Jeanie rushed across the street, jumped into Harley's truck, and waved as they drove toward the city park, four blocks away.

Rif observed, "I think they're having a picnic, but when I talk with Judge Miller, it's not going to be a picnic. He has great respect for Skidmore. I might have to visit the county judge in Challis to get the warrants."

Rif and Glen entered the office and Glen found the note Jeanie had left. Lillian Bauman had called and said she wanted someone arrested for shooting one of her ducks with an arrow. Glen knew where the Baumans lived, so he took the note and told Rif where he was going.

Rif replied, "Okay. I've decided to go to Challis to talk with the judge and the county attorney. I'm also going to hire Ron Sieberns temporarily to help us with impounding Skidmore's and Cordell's computers. It will be easier on everyone if a deputy Skidmore doesn't know does the dirty work. Also, Sieberns will be able to help us recover evidence from the computers. I don't think Jill should be doing that. I don't think she would do anything bad, but she's still a reporter. Oh, you'd better get John to help here until Jeanie comes back. He should be watching the prisoners and eating doughnuts."

Glen grinned. "Are you able to drive all right with one hand?"

"Sure, as long as I don't have to shoot out the window, but I'll keep my eyes on the road. I should be back in time for dinner. Jill and I are going to eat at her house tonight—you're invited." Rif laughed and said, "Maybe Mrs. Bauman will donate that duck."

"All right, just be careful. See you later at Jill's—about 7:00?"

"That's about right. Later."

# CHAPTER 50

## WHILE THE BOSS IS AWAY

Glen hadn't talked with Lillian Bauman before, but he had seen ducks in the pond near her house more than once. She lived in a log cabin with a steeply-pitched, green, steel roof. Glen had assumed the ducks were wild, he didn't think they belonged to anybody, but the ducks were lucky to be under Lillian's influence. She was known for her kindness to animals. One time she ran a bear away from her garbage cans using a big broom and some loud whistles. She had a shotgun, loaded with rock salt, just in case, but had never used it.

Glen knocked on the door and heard, "Just a minute." He waited for about ten seconds and the door swung open. Lillian was carrying a kitten, a tiny black one with white paws, and a small white spot on its nose. She was wiping its face with a washcloth. Lillian was wearing a white sweat shirt, a thin gray jacket, light-blue Capri pants, and flip-flops. Her medium-length black hair was pulled behind her head and held with a rubber band. After wiping the kitten's face, she looked at Glen and smiled. The dimples were still a prominent part of her forty-year-old, pleasant looking, oval face.

"May I help you?"

"I'm Glen Collins, temporary sheriff. You reported someone had shot a duck with an arrow. Can you direct me to the bird?"

"Oh, sure. Let me show you."

Lillian, who was nearly as tall as Glen, bent down and gently put the kitten on the linoleum floor. The little cat was a bit wobbly, but wandered away from the door. Lillian came out on the porch and pointed, "It's over there, in the water."

Glen looked where she was pointing—out in the middle of the pond. Sure enough, there was a duck with an arrow sticking out of it. The bird seemed happy enough, but looked a little odd with the arrow apparently stuck under its left wing. It might not be able to fly with the added appendage. Glen commented, "I had assumed the duck was dead, but it certainly isn't. Have you got a net, or can you call the duck out of the pond? Could you entice it to come to us with some food?"

Lillian made some strange guttural noises and pulled a handful of breadcrumbs from her jacket pocket. She tossed some of the crumbs on the water and made a little pile of them near the water on a large, flat, rectangular rock. Amazingly, the duck swam over to the crumbs, picked a few from the water, and then approached the pile. Lillian edged slowly between the water and the duck, made the strange noise again, stooped over, and picked up the duck.

Glen stood beside Lillian and smoothed the bird's feathers near the arrow. Lillian made that unusual noise again, which seemed to soothe the duck, almost like it were hypnotized.

"Okay, Sheriff Collins, you can look under the wing to see where the arrow is."

Glen slowly raised the wing and could see where the arrow had gone. It was just stuck amongst the feathers, but hadn't entered the bird's body. There wasn't a bit of blood. Glen gently withdrew the shaft, carefully avoiding damage to the bird. He looked at the arrow and said, "This isn't a hunting arrow. It's a kid's arrow. The suction cup has been taken off the tip, but it isn't a hunting arrow. I think you have some neighbor's kid shooting at your ducks."

Lillian replied, "Oh! I think I know who shot the arrow. I'll have a talk with him." Lillian put the duck down and made another noise. The bird suddenly quacked and ran into the water, swimming out to the middle of the pond where it had been before, just as if the entire incident had never occurred.

Glen looked at the arrow, and then at Lillian, and grinned. "That was amazing, Lillian. How did you learn to do that?"

"I'm not sure how it happened, but I have a connection with animals. When I was a young girl, I began to experiment with sounds around birds and squirrels. I guess I speak their language, kind of like some humans say they communicate with God, but in tongues, not English. Those people aren't crazy, you know."

"Well, if you find out who shot the arrow, tell them to cut it out, or I will come see them. We're lucky to have the ducks around during the summer. The birds add to the beauty of Wolves' Hollow. Thank you for sharing your gift with me."

"Well, thank you for coming out so quickly. I wanted you to see what someone had done. I'm glad it wasn't a hunting arrow. Have a nice day."

"Thank you, Lillian. I'll tell the new veterinarian about your ability. He might need your assistance someday. Bye."

As Glen drove back to the office he thought how interesting this temporary job had become. When he had read the note on Jeanie's keyboard, he had envisioned extracting an arrow from a dead duck. What he had experienced was something quite extraordinary. Maybe he should start going to church—nah, that would be too radical; he would save attending church for something more important than a duck, maybe a wedding. But then, should a duck be any less important than any other animals created by God? Glen had to give up those thoughts; theology and philosophy didn't occupy a significant amount of his mind. He felt more comfortable with real objects such as wood that could be assembled into useful objects.

He stopped in front of the courthouse momentarily, and then decided to visit former deputy Cordell's computer shop to see if it was secure. His computers had to be checked for email relating to R. Sodwim. The computer shop was only three blocks away, so Glen turned off the engine and went in the office.

Jeanie and Deputy Funches were talking about food when Glen entered the office.

Glen smiled, "Talking about doughnuts?"

John answered, "Nope, Chinese. I've decided to quit buying doughnuts in the morning."

"That's a good idea, John." Glen grinned and said, "You've decided to have the doughnuts later in the day?"

Jeanie started laughing and said, "Sheriff, you're funny."

John grinned and said, "Nope. Sheriff Summers told me to cut down on the doughnuts. I guess I've gotten a little chubby in the last year. If I had to chase someone, I wouldn't be able to catch 'em. I'd have to shoot 'em. Then I'd have to do a lot of paperwork."

"Well, John, come with me. I'm walking over to the computer store to see if it's secure. I'll bring you up to date about solving the murders. We'll both get some exercise."

As they walked to the computer shop, Glen explained the latest suspicions about Dr. Skidmore, and the reasons Rif had gone to Challis.

"So the new deputy was a marine?"

"That's what Rif said. He sure looks like a marine. He's supposed to be good with computers, too. I hope he can help us find all the R. Sodwim messages from and to Tim Cordell and Tad Birdsong; they're supposed to be stored out there in computer memory somewhere."

"I'm afraid I can't help with computers. I'm always worried I will delete something important and screw up the program."

Glen replied, "I know what you mean. I trying to get past that stage, but my mind wants me to use my calculator, and I'm not interested in those social networks. Besides, I'm too busy with carpentry and working with Barney. I'm going to miss this temporary job, though. I'm getting used to working with Rif, Jeanie and you."

"You kind of like her, don't you?"

"You mean Rif? Sure do. Here we are. Let's check the front and back doors—make sure they're locked." Glen tried the front door and it was locked. "You want to check the back?"

"Okay."

Glen watched John walk slowly down the sidewalk and disappear around the corner. About a minute later, the front door of the shop opened, and John stuck his head out.

"The back door was open, should I lock it?"

"Did you check for intruders?"

"No. You think somebody might be in here?"

"John, you need to be more cautious. What if somebody knifed or shot you when you were walking through the store? I'd sure hate to have to tell your wife you were in the hospital or killed in the line of duty. While we're talking here, someone could have sneaked out the back."

"I guess you're right. Most of the time Wolves' Hollow is so quiet, except for recent times. I guess I've gotten lazy."

"Now that you're in there, let's take a look around and see if any of the computers are on."

The two men found everything was turned off. Glen checked the back door to make sure it was locked, and returned to the front door. After Glen stepped onto the sidewalk, John relocked the front door, backed onto the concrete, and pulled the door shut. Just as they started back to the office, Doc Skidmore walked up to the computer store.

"Was there a problem in the store, Sheriff?"

"Nope. We were just checking to make sure the doors were locked. Did you come to pick up something?"

"Well, yes. Tim ordered a new disk drive for my home computer. I wanted to see if it had come in."

"You know Tim's in jail, don't you?"

"That's what I heard, but sometimes he leaves the back door unlocked. I thought I'd go in and check to see if there's a package for me."

John said, "I locked the backdoor. You'll have to talk with Tim about the disk drive, maybe he'll loan you his key. You'll have to ask Rif about that."

"All right, gentlemen. I'd better get back to the hospital; it's getting close to four o'clock.

I've got to do a circumcision before dinner."

Glen replied, "Nice seeing you, Doc. Bye."

Glen and John watched Skidmore as he walked to the end of the block, crossed the street, and started back toward the hospital. As John and Glen ambled to the courthouse, John observed, "That made me nervous."

"Talking to Skidmore?"

"Yeah. I was afraid I might say something wrong. If he's guilty, I don't want to help him in any way."

"You did fine, John. You just have to remember not to reveal anything about the case. Don't even talk about it with your wife until it's all over."

"When do you think that'll be?"

"I really don't know. I'll check with Rif this evening, when she gets back from Challis. Say, is that Jill?"

John stopped and looked around. "Where?"

"On the ramp over at the library—in the wheel chair. Let's see what she's up to."

There was no traffic. They crossed the street and Glen called out, "Hey, Jill, where are you going?" Jill turned the chair and her head so she could see who had yelled at her. She waved and waited for the two men to catch up to her.

"Hi, guys. I'm going back to Rif's. I thought if I went to the courthouse, someone could give me a ride. I don't think I can make the trip uphill without help."

"Good idea, Jill. I can take you back to Rif's. John is going to do something for me."

John looked at Glen, but didn't say anything. Glen grabbed the wheelchair handles and started pushing Jill toward the courthouse.

"John, when we get back to the office, I want you to ask Tim if he had ordered a disk drive for Dr. Skidmore."

John nodded and said, "10-4."

Jill quizzed, "Guess what I found in the library, Glen."

Glen looked at John, grinned, and said, "Books?"

Jill replied, "Something in the books."

"You've got me. What did you find in the books?"

"I found the background of North Pebble. It was once the stream bed for a warm spring.

Your great-great-great grandfather, Levi Collins, discovered gold there in 1867. He started your mine, too. Levi came here from Hood River, Oregon in 1897 and disappeared. Do you think those bones you found are his?"

"Might be. The FBI is running a DNA test to find if I'm related. I'll know in another week or so."

"Guess who Rif is related to."

"I don't know, who?"

"One of the other founders of Wolves' Hollow, Asa Adams. Asa married a Shoshone Indian girl named Snow and they moved to Montana. There's not much information about them. I don't think they ever returned here after about 1880 or so. Maybe Rif's family tree would show something about her great-great-great grandfather, Asa Adams. I'm going to ask her tonight. It's kind of exciting to find that both your male ancestors were friends."

# CHAPTER 51

# BACK FROM CHALLIS

**R**if returned from Challis at 6:34 p.m. After checking in at the office to see if there were any messages, she drove home. The jeep was parked in her driveway, so Rif assumed Glen was in the house talking to Jill. Rif entered the house and received greetings from Glen and Jill. She put a handful of papers on the little table next to the front door, collapsed on the sofa, and put her feet up.

"What a day!"

Glen stood up from the computer table and offered, "Want your boots off?"

"Oh, yes. My feet are killing me. They're so hot!"

Glen started backing up to the sofa and Rif laughed, "They're not that hard to pull off, Glen."

"That might be, but what about the smell? I want my nose to be as far away as possible."

Jill laughed and said, "You'd better be careful, Glen, she hasn't taken off her gun yet."

Glen pulled off Rif's boots and tickled her feet. Rif threw one of the couch pillows at Glen and said, "You're lucky I have only one arm or I'd take you down, and make you smell my boots."

"Sure, maybe you and Jill together!"

Glen changed the subject. "Rif, you took the bandages off your face. You look fine. I can only see a couple of red marks."

"Yeah, I took off the bandages before I talked to the judge. I got search warrants for the computer shop, the motel, the hospital, and Skidmore's house. Also, Ron Sieberns will be here in the morning to help with the warrants. He's eager to get started, even if the job is only temporary. He said he can probably trace all the emails. He did some of that type of investigating when he was in the Marines."

Jill asked, "How are you going to pay him? Will the mayor give you some more money?"

"I already thought of that. We've got a pickup and two four-wheelers to sell. We can use the money for salaries."

Glen asked, "What about a uniform for the new deputy?"

"I told him to wear a marine uniform, but take all the insignias off. That should work, don't you think?"

"Sure, he'll look more official than I do."

"You look fine, Glen. The white shirt and khakis are fine, especially with the badge on your pocket. I was going to ask John to loan you one of his shirts, but I didn't think you would wear it, grease stains and all. Those doughnuts leave traces." Rif couldn't help but laugh. Jill and Glen joined in.

Glen added, "John said he wasn't going to bring in any more doughnuts in the morning."

Rif commented, "Yeah, he'll probably get them in the afternoon."

Glen grinned and said, "That's what I said to John and Jeanie in the office."

Jill thought for a moment and said, "You sheriffs seem to think alike. I wonder if it's contagious."

Rif smiled and sighed, "What's for dinner?"

"Hamburgers. I took the meat out of the freezing compartment at noon. It should be ready to cook. Glen, light the charcoal; Rif, stay on the couch. We'll tell you about our day's activities."

During dinner, Rif asked Glen what John had found out about Skidmore's claim to have ordered a disk drive from Tim.

"I don't know. After I brought Jill back from the library, I went home and took care of Barney. I forgot to call John."

Rif pulled out her cell phone and called John. She talked for a minute and hung up.

"John said Skidmore didn't order a disk drive. Doc lied to you and John. He probably wanted to go in the shop and delete everything from the computers. Tim doesn't know we suspect Skidmore is actually R. Sodwim."

★ ★ ★

That evening, after dark, Glen left the ladies, and went home to get Barney. He took his truck, leaving the jeep at home, and drove with Barney down to the computer shop. He parked on the street in front of the shop, poured a cup of coffee from his Thermos, and leaned back in his seat. At eleven o'clock, he wished he had a doughnut, but thought about John, and decided to quit eating junk food. Glen wondered how long it would be before he would notice his waistline was shrinking. He planned to start weighing himself each morning, keeping track of the numbers on a calendar.

Knocking on the driver's side window startled Glen awake. He blinked and looked out to see John standing in the street looking into the truck. Glen lowered the window and said, "I guess I fell asleep. Last I remember it was 2:30 a.m. Good morning. What time is it?" Glen looked at the digital clock in the dash, but John spoke before Glen's eyes could focus.

"Hi, Sheriff. It's seven thirty. You know there's a law about sleeping in a parked vehicle on the street." John smiled and continued, "I guess I won't arrest you. You're on duty guarding the computer shop. You'd better let the dog out or you'll have a wet interior. You'll be driving with the windows down until next spring."

Glen reached over Barney and opened the door. Barney jumped out and found the nearest maple tree between the sidewalk and the curb. Glen reached into the glove compartment and pulled out a plastic bag, but didn't need it. Barney returned to the truck and jumped in beside Glen.

Glen said, "Good boy, Barney," forgetting Barney couldn't hear him. Glen gave Barney several pats and scratched under Barney's chin and around his ears.

"I'll see you later at the office, John. Thanks for waking me up."

"10-4." John grinned, walked back to the patrol car, waved, and drove off.

Glen went home, took a shower, and shaved. After a quick breakfast of Cheerios and coffee, he climbed in the jeep and went to the office. It was 8:30 a.m.

Ron Sieberns was in Rif's office getting instructions about serving the warrants for the computers. When Glen came in the office, Ron turned and the two men shook hands.

"Glad to have you with us, Ron."

"Thanks, Sheriff."

Rif grinned and greeted Glen, "Good morning sleepyhead. I heard you were homeless last night."

"John tattled on me, huh? I'll have to have a talk with him."

"John told me he was just checking to see if you had any illegal doughnuts."

Glen patted his stomach and replied, "I've lost three pounds, about 30 more to go. So John, the snitch, told you I stayed in my truck next to the computer shop."

"Yep. I've got eyes everywhere. You'd better be alert. But thanks for doing that, I was so tired, it didn't cross my mind that we should monitor the shop. However, after today, we won't have to worry about it anymore. Ron's going to check out Tim's computers this morning, but first we need to pick up Skidmore's machines from the hospital and his home. The hospital said he doesn't come in until 10:00 a.m., so let's go to his house first. We'll start his day by giving him something to think about. John will go to the hospital with Jeanie and get the computers from Doc's office and the morgue. Any questions?"

Glen said, "I've got one. Where are we going to put all this stuff?"

Rif answered confidently, "Jail cell 2. Everything should be secure in there."

Glen grinned and responded, "Why didn't I think of that?"

"You haven't been a sheriff for as long as I have, you're just a little rusty. Oh, shoot! I forgot about the motel. Glen, please go to the motel and get Tad Birdsong's computer. Then join us at Skidmore's. Here are the warrants each of you need." Rif checked the warrants and handed the documents out. "Make sure you label each item you confiscate. Jeanie will give you the labels you need. Put down the location, time, and initial each label. Let's go!"

✦   ✦   ✦

John and Jeanie found one desktop computer in Skidmore's hospital office, but John remembered to search the morgue. John borrowed the key from the receptionist and unlocked the morgue. At first Jeanie didn't want to go in, but John said, "I've got a gun. Don't worry about zombies."

"That's not funny, John. I feel Indian spirits in there. We'd better not disturb anything."

"Okay. Come on in. We'll be careful—we're just looking."

Jeanie stuck her hands in her pockets and walked around the room. When she saw the skeleton, she avoided that side of the room.

"I don't see anything like a computer in here. Let's go. Oh! Where are the bodies?"

"They're in that big cabinet over there." John pointed at the refrigeration unit and said, "I don't think we need to look in there."

"Are you sure, John? Maybe Skidmore figured no one would look in there. Come on, let's check. We want to tell Sheriff Summers that we looked everywhere. Besides, I'm getting my confidence back. I've never seen a real dead body from a murder. This place isn't as creepy as I thought it would be." Jeanie still had her hands in her pockets and grinned.

John pulled out one of the refrigerated drawers, but it was empty. However, the next drawer held the charred remains of Mr. Turner. John flipped the covering sheet back and quickly re-covered the remains before Jeanie could see them. "You don't want to see that, Jeanie. Let's try another one." John pulled out another cabinet drawer, flipped back the body cover and looked around the body. "Nothing here."

Jeanie stepped closer, took a look, and turned away. "I wondered if his eyes were open. Didn't they used to put silver dollars over their eyes?"

John laughed. "Yeah, but I think they used pennies—they were bigger then. That was to keep vampires from entering the body."

"John! Stop it!"

John shoved the drawer shut and pulled out the last occupied one. With the body exposed, Jeanie stepped closer and said, "What's that under the head, John?"

"Looks like a gray pillow, doesn't it? *That* is a laptop computer, Jeanie. I'll lift the head and you pull it out from under."

"Boy! This thing is cold. We'll have to warm it up before it'll work. Let's go back to the office, I'm getting cold."

It took Rif's crew about ninety minutes to take possession of the various computers. Ron was the last to return to the office. He had gone to Skidmore's with Rif, then to Tim's computer shop, and brought back three computers, a printer, and some blank DVDs. Ron was able to jimmy the back door to get into the shop without having to break the lock or door. Glen and Rif were the first back in the office with Skidmore's two home computers; a desktop and a laptop.

"I wasn't there when you asked Skidmore for his computers. How did he react?"

"He was surprised and not very happy, Glen. He warned us about looking at patient records. I told him those were safe. We were looking for something else. Doc slammed the door when we left his house. He was a little pissed."

Glen said, "He must know we're on to him; he's not stupid. I've got Tad's laptop. His wife swore he never answered his email with the motel computer. I believed her. She can't accept that Tad killed the Markesan brothers, but he's been under a lot of stress lately. They owe quite a bit on their mortgage. She's afraid they might lose the motel. Tad told her he would be getting some money soon for some work he had been doing for a man on the East Coast. She thought it had to do with a hunting trip."

# CHAPTER 52

## EVIDENCE

Everyone working with Rif, including Jill and Jeanie, gathered after lunch in the courthouse conference room. Rif conducted the meeting like a seminar, presenting all she knew about the murders, suspects, and theory of the involvement of Doctor Skidmore. Both Jeanie and Ron took notes and everyone asked questions.

About the time the coffee maker had run dry, Rif said, "Thank you for your help. I think Ron now knows what we are looking for on the computers. I didn't bring doughnuts—two of our group can't eat them anymore due to waistline problems." Rif looked at John and Glen and smiled. "Do you have any questions, Ron?"

"Only one. There isn't any electricity in jail cell 2. Do you have an extension cord about 30 feet long?"

Glen volunteered, "I've got a heavy duty cord in my truck. I'll get it for you. We'll tape it to the floor so no one trips over it."

John commented, "Keep it away from cells 1 and 3, we don't want any hangings."

Rif complimented, "Good point, John. We don't know what's in the minds of our prisoners."

★ ★ ✶

Ron numbered the computers one to eight, and worked all afternoon searching files, copying, and printing information relative to the case. By 5:15, he had thoroughly investigated Tim's three computers and Tad's laptop. After locking the jail cell, Ron put the keys to cell 2 in his pocket, and made the half-hour drive to Challis. He got home at six o'clock, just in time for dinner.

Jill wanted to move back to her rental. She felt she was imposing on Rif, and there would be little danger, the bad guys were either dead or in jail. Rif invited Adam and Jill's sister, Eva, to join Glen, Jill, and herself for dinner. Jeanie had a prior commitment with Harley, and John's daughter and her children were visiting the Funches. After dinner, the group went to Jill's place and checked out her remodeled rental. Rif noted Adam was paying a good deal of attention to Eva, but Rif wasn't jealous. Rif had her eyes on Glen.

At ten o'clock, the men left, but the girls talked for another thirty minutes before Jill began to yawn. Lugging the cast around tired her out. During the gab fest, Eva had Rif attempt some flexibility movements with her left arm, but Rif experienced a great deal of pain. Eva told Rif to come to the hospital in a couple of days to start a rehabilitation program.

At 11:05 a.m. the next morning, Bob Buckley, mayor of Wolves' Hollow, came into the sheriff's office. He had a look of concern on his face. He asked Jeanie where the sheriff was.

Jeanie looked at the wall clock and answered, "She had to take her cruiser over to have a flat fixed. She should be back any minute. Have some coffee while you wait. If it's an emergency, I can call her on the radio."

"Well, it's not really an emergency. Thanks, I'll wait."

About five minutes later, Jeanie could hear Rif's boots on the hallway floor. "Mayor, the sheriff is back."

As Rif entered the office, Jeanie mouthed *mayor* to her, and pointed into Rif's office.

Rif nodded and said, "Thanks, Jeanie." Rif greeted the mayor as she went behind her desk and sat down. "What can I do for you, Mr. Mayor?"

"The hospital called me about thirty minutes ago. Dr. Skidmore has left town. We have no doctor now. I'm going to see if Dr. Timmons in Challis can come here at least one day a week until we can find someone to take Skidmore's place."

"Damn it! I was afraid he might take off. When we seized the computers, he must have decided to run. I've got a deputy working on Skidmore's computers now. We're looking for evidence of Doc's involvement in the murders. I think he's responsible. We should have what we need to arrest him this afternoon. I guess we'll have to chase after him. I'll have to call the State Police for help. Jeanie, where are John and Glen?"

"John's in the jail with Ron. They had to rearrange the computers to have more work space. Glen drove out to check on some stop signs. Someone sprayed them with black paint so they can't be seen at night. Glen was going to remove the spray paint. He thought he'd be back by noon."

"Thanks Jeanie."

"No problem. Do you want me to contact the State Patrol?"

"Not yet. I need to talk with Ron to see what he's recovered from the computers." Rif rose from her chair and walked to the jail cells without any expression on her face. She wanted to get to Skidmore before he had an opportunity to leave the country, but she had to follow the correct legal procedures.

Ron was just finishing his notes and copying files when Rif arrived at cell 2.

"What have you got, Ron? Can I call the county attorney and tell him we've got proof of Skidmore's involvement."

"Yes, Sheriff. His goose is cooked. We have all the evidence needed to arrest Doctor Skidmore. Actually, his name is Dr. Richard Henry Wisdom. He used to live in Pittsburgh. He was involved in a scam to use drugs, prescribed for nursing home patients, for sale on the street. The elderly never got the drugs, and in many cases weren't needed, but Medicare paid for them. Pennsylvania took his medical license. He somehow assumed the identity of Daniel Arnold Skidmore, a deceased physician, and took the job here in Wolves' Hollow about ten years ago." Ron continued, "Skidmore hired the Markesan boys, but realized they were out of control when they killed Mr. Turner and shot you. Skidmore told Tad Birdsong to kill them, and put their bodies in the Collins mine."

"Good work, Ron. I'll call the county prosecutor in Challis. He'll have the state police arrest Skidmore."

★ ★ ★

Dr. Wisdom was picked up trying to cross the border into Canada. He was jailed in Challis during the trial and sent to the state prison for 25 years. Tad Birdsong was convicted of murdering the Markesan brothers and was given a life sentence. Tim Cordell was sent to prison for two years. The trial ended on July 10.

Wisdom had been planning to buy all the property on the five-hundred block of North Pebble, dig up the roadway, and recover the gold from the bottom of the old stream. He was unaware that the gold had been removed years ago. He just hadn't done his homework. He also was planning to take over the old Collins mine after framing Glen for the murders of the Markesan brothers. When he heard the history of North Pebble during the trial, he turned pale, put his head in his hands, and sank into his chair.

Following the trial, Glen returned to remodeling and general carpentry work. During the trial, Agent Burger of the FBI contacted Glen and told him the sample of DNA from the bones was too degraded to provide evidence of any relationship. Glen however, was confident that the bones were those of Levi Collins. Glen arranged to have the bones returned to the Collins family cemetery in Hood River. Levi's remains were buried next to the grave of Annabel Collins. He purchased a matching headstone. Glen thought it was an appropriate use of a small fraction of the money received from the gold recovered from under the old stump near the Collins mine.

Glen and Rif travelled to Boise, sold the gold, and met with Agents Ochs and Burger for dinner. They didn't just talk about police work. Sandra Burger needed some remodeling done and after discussing the project with Glen, she hired him. Rif accompanied Glen to Burger's during the remodel, and helped with drywall and painting. After that involvement, she began thinking of how she wanted her own house to look. The funds were available from selling the gold, and Glen gave Rif rock-bottom prices, not even charging her for his time. They began dating regularly. Glen had stuck to his diet, losing another ten pounds by the third week in July.

While in Boise, Glen took Rif to dinner at the Chandelier Restaurant one evening after working on the remodeling project. The lighting fixtures in the dining area were all antique chandeliers from the early 1900s. As they ate dinner, they enjoyed the live jazz music coming from the bar.

Rif commented, "I can't believe how Wisdom could perpetuate a grudge with the Collins for nearly a 150 years."

"I don't understand it either. After Helen Collins divorced Frank Wisdom, he remarried and had several children. But that marriage fell apart, too. Frank eventually took his own life, but the Wisdom family blamed the suicide on Helen Collins, his first wife. Very strange."

Ref replied, "It makes me wonder if Frank's instability was in his DNA, and the twisted logic, after all those generations, ended up in Richard Wisdom. He had to come to Wolves' Hollow and try to implicate you in the Markesan killings. What a twisted mind! Even though he harbored those weird feelings, he was a pretty good doctor. Another Jekyll and Hyde story."

★ ★ ★

Rif had resumed her job as sheriff during the trial. Physical therapy was an absolute necessity for Rif to recover full use of her left arm. The muscles of her shoulder had to be strengthened. She began visiting the hospital with some regularity to see Eva for help with therapy. Rif had never done much weight training before, but after a hard workout, Eva would massage Rif's back and shoulder. Their friendship began to develop during the therapy sessions.

Eva was working on Rif's shoulder one evening when she asked Rif, "Why is it you've never gotten married?"

"Well, I know you won't repeat this, but I was raped when I started college. It was a jock, and nothing was ever done about it. Jocks were protected back then, and it was my word against his. So now, I'm very careful about the men I date. I went into law enforcement because of what happened to me. I wanted to make a difference."

"But you really like Glen, don't you?"

"Oh yeah. He's easy to talk to, smart, and funny, although sometimes his humor is a bit dry. He's also lost quite a bit of weight." Rif turned her head to look at Eva and smiled. "He's on his way to becoming a hunk. Also—he's a good kisser."

Eva laughed, "So is Adam. You knew we were dating, didn't you?"

Rif smiled, "I've heard some gossip to that effect. I think Jill mentioned it to me. I think you and Adam make a nice couple. Oh! Adam and Eva!"

"You *have* been talking to my sister."

"No, she didn't tell me that. It just came to me." Rif grinned. "I guess you are doomed if you stay together."

"I've been hesitant to get into a close relationship, too, but Adam is caring, patient, and we enjoy each other's company. You and I have something in common. I too, was raped. I hate to even talk about it. I used to have bad dreams, but not anymore. I haven't decided to tell Adam what happened."

"Well, I've known Adam for several years. It won't make any difference. You just need to be honest with him."

Eva stopped massaging and said, "Have you figured out who killed Wrackler?"

"No, and I'm not going to pursue that case. All the evidence I collected turned out to be negative. Glen's hammers were clean. Whoever hit him might not have used a hammer. The county attorney said not to spend any time on it. That man got what he deserved. He messed up too many lives."

"But if you knew who did it, would you make an arrest?"

"No. Whoever did it was probably one of his victims."

"You're right about that."

Rif looked at Eva questioningly. "Eva, you know who did it?"

"I sure do. I did it."

"*What? I don't believe you!* You wouldn't hurt a soul." Rif sat up and looked into Eva's eyes. "Tell me what happened." Rif reached out and held Eva's hands.

"I was doing a class project for psychology at the University of Idaho. It was near the end of the spring semester. I was walking home from entertaining kids at the hospital. I was dressed in a clown's costume with lots of makeup. This guy stopped and asked me if I wanted a ride. I said no, but he insisted. I should have run but I froze. He got out of his car with a knife and forced me into the back seat. I was afraid he would stab me. When he was on me, I saw a book under the seat. Afterwards, he shoved me out of his car onto the ground and drove off, but I remembered the book."

"The book?"

"It was a stamp catalog; it lists the values of stamps. So, I knew the guy was either a collector or a dealer. I watched the newspapers for announcements of stamp shows and went to a few to see who was there. I think it was the third one I went to, and there he was, a stamp dealer. I talked with him, recognized his voice, and remembered his face. He didn't have a clue that I was the clown he had attacked. I got his business card and wondered how I was going to turn him in."

"So you didn't think of killing him?"

"*Oh, no!* I wanted to catch him and turn him in to the authorities. But then, I got the job here and things were getting better. One day about four months ago, Wrackler came to the hospital to have some blood work done. I couldn't believe he was living in Wolves' Hollow. But when Jill came here, and ended up living next door to that shit, I had to do something to protect her. When I left Jill's that first night, I drove about a block and parked the car, went back to Wrackler's and tossed some poisoned meat in the yard. After about thirty minutes, I went to his back door. He was surprised; a young woman was at his door. I asked him if he could identify some old United States stamps for me, and he invited me in. He walked in front of me to his desk, and I hit him in the head with a small hammer. He fell to the floor. I took a pair of six-inch stamp tongs and pounded them up his nose. Then, I went out the window, sealing it with liquid paper that had been in a little bottle on his desk."

"Wow! What a story, Eva. Don't worry. I'll keep your secret."

CPSIA information can be obtained
at www.ICGtesting.com
Printed in the USA
BVHW070124261021
619844BV00016B/929

9 781956 517484